JOCKBLOCKED

A Gridiron Novel

Jen Frederick

To the two Lees in my life.
I love you both.

AUTHOR'S NOTE

❖

NATIONAL SIGNING DAY IS GENERALLY the first Wednesday of February, but for the sake of the story, I pushed it back a few weeks. I also took a lot of liberties with how the mock trial tournament in college is run to make the final scene more exciting. I hope those familiar with both will forgive me these literary licenses.

ACKNOWLEDGEMENT

❖

IF YOU CAN'T TELL FROM the book, I love football. The idea of this book grew out of the story of Braxton Miller from Ohio State University. Miller was a heralded and much feted quarterback for 2011, 2012, and 2013. He missed the 2014 season due to injury and when he returned, he had to compete with two other players for the QB position. In June of 2015, he announced he would move to wide receiver.

He handled it was such grace and aplomb that I couldn't help but admire him. Plus, he made a kick-ass wide receiver. I hope I get to see him play in the NFL.

This book would not have been written without my family's support and that of a few amazing friends. Thank you to Elle, Kristen, Daphne, Jess, Meljean, Michelle, Mel, Nina, Nicole (an amazing assistant), Lea (wands up!), Lisa, and Robin.

Special thanks goes out to Nicole McCurdy and Joy Ann Jumaud who tirelessly recommend my book to others. Thank you so much, ladies!

And finally, a shout out to the ladies of the Locker Room, The Chroniclers, and all the amazing bloggers who share their love of books with others. The romance community would be lost without you. I know I would be.

And to all the readers who love books, I salute you!

ABOUT THE AUTHOR

JEN FREDERICK IS THE *USA Today* bestselling author of *Unspoken*, part of the Woodlands series, and *Sacked,* part of the Gridiron series. She is also the author of the *Charlotte Chronicles* and has had several books on the Kindle Top 100 list. She lives in the Midwest with a husband who keeps track of life's details while she's writing, a daughter who understands when Mom disappears into her office for hours at a time, and a rambunctious dog who does neither.

jensfrederick@gmail.com

1

LUCY

I FLIP MY PEN AROUND my thumb again as I contemplate my mock trial dilemma. Should we include the expert in ice formation or the co-worker? *Flip.* Randall wants to go with the expert because they always score well with the judges, but we all know ice is slippery. *Flip.* A co-worker who testifies about what a hard worker our client is would go a long way toward us winning. *Flip.*

Not to mention that a lay witness versus an expert witness would be far easier for our new teammate Heather to pull off. *Flip.*

Ugh. Heather. Practice earlier was a friggin' disaster. This is my freshman nightmare all over again. Newcomer blows the judges' socks off with a prepared closing she'd practiced all summer and then new-comer ends up ruining the team because she can't perform under pressure.

That newcomer was me once. I hate that my team is suffering through this again, and I'm going to do everything I can to prevent that, even if I have to write every question of every examination and every word of every argument.

I check the score sheet again, but the numbers don't change. I exhale heavily. Randall's right. Historically, an expert witness scores at least two points better than an ordinary witness does. *Flip.*

I flip the pen again, frustrated that I can't seem to come to a solution. I'm a solution girl. This is my thing. I assess situations, measure risks, and advise the best course. But the best course in this case isn't clear to me. I run my hand through my hair and study the mock trial case once again. It doesn't matter that it's a mock trial—to me it's as serious as it gets.

As I turn the exemplar tabulation over, a packet of aspirin lands next to my hand.

I drop my pen and pick up the packet of medicine. Looking up, I check to see if it's raining aspirin or if someone was playing table hockey and flicked the goal across the room accidentally, but I only see the lights of the ceiling and the bent heads of the few people in the room.

"I'm worried that if you sigh again, a tornado may form. Those are some heavy puffs," a deep voice from behind me says.

I twist to see a guy the size of a small car dwarfing the upholstered chair next to the fireplace. For most people, that chair is oversized. He fills every inch. Even beneath his long-sleeved gray T-shirt, I can see the definition in his arms and chest. I allow myself a few seconds of covert gawking. Have to get my thrills in where I can.

"Maybe I have asthma."

"Then you'll be out of luck because I don't have an inhaler on me. Just the aspirin."

"Sad. Not much of a traveling pharmacist, are you?"

He smiles, and I grip the side of my seat to make sure I don't fall out of my chair at the brilliance of it. Some people, like my roommate

Sutton, are blessed with an unreal amount of beauty. This guy is one of those people. Even his black plastic glasses make him look like the studious model in an Abercrombie ad.

Crinkles form by eyes so blue I find myself scanning them for a telltale lens, but they appear to be real.

The only real downside to this guy is that he has the look of a gym rat. Big arms, broad shoulders, V-shaped torso all scream of a guy who spends a lot of time watching himself in the mirror. Those guys just don't interest me. They're pretty to look at, but a huge headache to deal with.

"You'll have to blame my mom. She's a pediatrician and has a weird propensity for sticking those things in all of my pockets."

"Thanks, but my headache is induced by my homework. I don't think a couple of aspirin are going to help." I offer him the packet back, but he waves me off.

"It's the second week of the semester. Isn't it too early for homework to be causing anyone stress?" He glances around the room. "In fact, I'm surprised by the number of people here. Is everyone here studying? Isn't it Wednesday? People study on Wednesdays?"

I think the last question is a joke, but I'm not entirely sure. "First time at the Brew House?"

He gestures for me to come close, as if he's going to tell me a secret. "Don't tell anyone, but I'm not a fan of coffee," he stage whispers behind a screen formed by a hand big enough to make a Great Dane look like a toy poodle.

"So why are you here?" I find myself whispering back against my better judgment, caught up in his flirtation.

"Didn't want to go to a bar. Didn't want to be in the library. Didn't want to be at home. I wandered around and found this place." He waves his hand around the room. "But now I'm worried because I feel like I should be doing something serious instead of doing this."

He raises his tablet to show me the game he's playing.

"I would guess at least half the room is playing that game. It was sold for a billion dollars a couple of weeks ago."

"I'd much rather learn how you do that trick." He tips his head toward my hand.

I catch my pen reflexively, not even realizing I was flipping it. "It's a bad habit."

"Nah, it's cool." He gets up and is at my table in two steps. "Matthew."

He holds out his hand. When I clasp it, I'm surprised by the roughness of it, as if he does something more with his hands other than typing on a keyboard or holding a pen. "Lucy."

"Nice to meet you, Lucy. So what's the trick to this?" He bounces one of my highlighters in his hand.

"No real trick. I tap the long end of the pen with my middle finger and let the momentum carry it around my thumb. Like this." And I repeat the action, neatly catching it between my thumb and forefinger.

Matthew tries it, but the highlighter goes flying out of his fingers and skitters across the table. "Shit."

I cover my laugh as he scoots over to pick up the marker. He tries again and the highlighter zips two tables over.

"Maybe not as much force next time. You aren't launching a rocket into space," I advise.

"I think you've made a deal with the devil," he says after trying again.

"If I were to make a deal with the devil, do you really think this is the gift I'd ask for?" I spin the pen. "There are at least a million better things than a pen-spinning trick."

"Good point. What would you ask for?" He lifts my mug and takes a sniff, making a face when the coffee scent hits his nose. He doesn't even like the smell of coffee? I guess he has to have some flaws.

"Is this a straight trade, so I get eternal life in hell in exchange for something great on earth?"

"I suppose so. Are there other trades the devil will make?" He reaches back to grab his Gatorade off the floor next to the chair he's no longer sitting in. His arms are so long he doesn't even have to rise from his seat. His shirt pulls out of his jeans, and I catch a glimpse of well-defined abs.

I avert my eyes when he swings around so he doesn't find me staring at his body like a creepster. One look is okay, two and I've definitely crossed over into bad behavior. "I don't have any direct experience with the devil, but I'd try to make a bargain that does not include eternal hell. I'm not made for that kind of punishment."

His lips quirk up. "Yeah, you do seem...sweet."

"The devil doesn't like sweet things?" The words pop out before my brain catches up with my mouth.

Matthew's lips go from half-mast to full-out grin. "He might. But I think if he had the choice, he'd pick hot over sweet." Sultry blue eyes rake over me. "Don't worry, you've got the hot part covered, too."

This time it's *my* pen that flies across the table. Chuckling, Matthew snatches it out of the air.

"Nice reflexes," I mutter. My cheeks feel like they're flaming. I haven't engaged in this kind of flirting since…well, I can't remember the last time. And with this guy? It's totally out of character.

"I'm good for something." He winks and hands me the pen.

Our eyes meet, and the connection between us pings and arcs, warming me as surely as the flame of the fire five feet away. The register rings behind me, reminding me why I haven't had sex in so long. Keith, my co-worker at the Brew House, was the last person I had sex with. It was uninspired sex—so boring that I think we both fell asleep before the deed was even done. I couldn't really blame it on him either.

We were both distracted—him by some serious bio project and me by the mock trial case. Keith made out better than I did. He got an "A" on his bio project whereas my team didn't make it out of regionals for the second year in a row. That time it wasn't entirely my fault. We were just uninspiring, which is why Heather Bell is now part of the Western State team. She nearly brought everyone in the room to tears with her prepared closing statement during tryouts. The problem is that she doesn't know a thing about how an actual trial works despite being the daughter of a superstar trial attorney.

As gorgeous as this Matthew guy is and as flattering as it is to have his attention, my priority is making it out of semi-finals this year. Two years of being beat down at something I'm supposed to be good at is wearing at my confidence. Giving up would be something my mom would do. Giving up and trotting off with the cute guy is her go-to plan. She's done it my entire life.

Winning at mock trial doesn't guarantee that I'm not going to end up like my mom, living from one boyfriend to the next, cutting out when there's the least bit of tribulation on the horizon, but success would prove to myself that I'm her polar opposite.

I take my comforts where I can find them. And besides, I really enjoy mock trial. Not every aspect. Who loves everything about anything? But for the most part, I get off on crafting the questions, the courtroom atmosphere—all of it.

With school, work, and mock trial, I don't have a lot of time for outside activities. Besides, I'm not sure how I'd even handle a guy like him. The sexual energy he radiates is thrilling, but I can't deny it's also a tad terrifying. I don't have a type, exactly, but if I had to lump the guys I've dated in the past into one category, I guess I'd say…safe? Serious? Definitely not in-your-face sexual, that's for sure. More like…well, Keith. Not too tall, not too short. Not too attractive, not unattractive. I fit with those guys. I'm comfortable with them. Nothing about this delicious male makes me comfortable.

"You're sighing again," Matthew cuts in.

"I'm not." If I was, I didn't mean to.

"Okay, you're breathing heavily." He cocks an eyebrow. "Or your asthma is acting up."

"Fortunately, asthma is one ailment I don't have. But sighing is clearly a problem. Does your mom do house calls?"

"Nope. But I can prescribe you the perfect thing for stress."

I raise my palm. "Don't say sex."

He snickers. "I was going to say exercise, but sex is good, too." Those blue eyes conduct another sweep of my face, then linger briefly on my chest. I'm wearing a plain black, long-sleeved, crew neck sweater, but the way his gaze smolders, you'd think I was topless.

There's something familiar about him—as if I've seen him before. Maybe he models, though he's a little broad-shouldered for that. But still... "Have we met before?" I ask warily.

A flash of something—irritation, possibly—skips across his face... Maybe he gets this question a lot. "You probably saw me on campus and said to yourself, who is that fine-ass guy and how do I get his number? But we were like sliding doors, a missed connection. I read Craigslist. You should've reached out."

Yeah, he's tired of that question. "Nice story. You sound like a Lit major."

"Sociology, actually. You?"

"Poli-Sci."

"What do you plan to do with that? Learn how to take over the world?"

"If I had the responsibility of the world on my shoulders, can you imagine the sighs that kind of stress would generate? They'd be like gale force winds."

"Good point."

Matthew stretches his long legs on either side of my own chair. If I fell forward, I'd land in his lap.

And that's a bad thing because...?

I shove the naughty thought aside. If I want some lap time, there are other, less magnetic guys I could turn to—

Less magnetic? You need help, girl.

The exasperated voice has a point. It might as well have come from my roommate, the one who is constantly teasing me about my play-it-safe attitude toward men. But careful suits me.

"You seem less tense now," he observes. He studies my face again, the weight of his gaze almost a tangible thing. "Maybe you should keep me around."

"Where would I do that? My lease only allows for three people, and I'm not sure I earn enough here at the Brew House to feed you on a regular basis," I say lightly. This guy is entirely too smooth for me. I have a feeling *flirt* is his default setting. Which is fine. Nothing wrong with that, but it means I can't—and shouldn't—take him seriously.

"I'm pretty quiet. I don't think you'd notice me."

I raise a disbelieving eyebrow. "That's not even within the vicinity of truthfulness."

"I can be quiet." He raises two fingers. "Scout's honor." We both look at his fingers. "I was a Scout but dropped out at the age of fifteen."

"What happened at fifteen?" I ask, almost against my will. I want to quit the conversation, but I keep allowing myself to be dragged back in. See? This is some practiced shit.

"I grew. I was a scrawny kid with questionable health, but somewhere between fourteen and fifteen my body said 'to hell with that, we're going to be big and strong.'"

"And the Scouts got left behind? Poor fellas."

"I was a shitty Scout. I was way behind on my badge acquisition. It was really a boon to the troop when I left. I think they might have thrown a party."

I can't stop the laugh from bubbling out. "Your Scout troop was giddy with relief that you left, but you still think I should keep you?"

"I know how to cook and have, at some points in my life, operated an iron." He ticks off each skill on a finger. "I always bring the good booze when I'm invited to a party, and I make my bed in the morning."

"You had me at *know how to cook*." Truthfully, all those things sound like the characteristics of a fairly responsible person. Safe even. But a guy this good looking who knows how to cook is single *and* hitting on me in a coffee shop before booty call hour? It's all too strange. And I don't have the time or energy to puzzle this out.

"Awesome. So when should I move in?" His eyes twinkle playfully.

I pretend to consider it again. "I think I have to say never. But I wish you luck on your roommate quest."

He looks unfazed. I get the feeling nothing fazes him. "How about you just invite me over, then? I promise to bring the good booze." When I hesitate, he swiftly changes gears. "Or we'll go out instead. Grab some dinner."

"Oh. Thanks for the offer, but I really don't have the time." I stretch my arm and drop the medicine on the top of his backpack. I won't lie and say I didn't enjoy this flirting session, but a date? That doesn't fit into my plan. This year I'm winning the mock trial championship, and I'm not going to be distracted. I spent my entire winter break plotting out this semester's game plan. Nowhere on that schedule of events includes taking a chance on a guy like Matthew.

Something about him makes me nervous. Not in a he's-going-to-turn-you-into-a-skinsuit nervous, but more that I don't like the way his vivid eyes and easy smiles make my heart pound. I feel the need to pull out my glucose measuring tool to make sure an unexpected hormone release isn't wreaking havoc with my body.

He tilts his head. Then rubs his chin. Then sweeps his hair back away from his face. "This is new," he mutters to himself. He gives me a tight smile. "Can I borrow your pen?"

I hand it to him warily, hoping he's not going to spend the rest of the night trying to spin the pen while simultaneously trying to convince me to change my mind, but he doesn't. Instead he pulls the rules book toward him and writes down seven digits. "This is my number. If you find some extra time, give me a call."

2

IT'S BEEN A LONG TIME since I've been rejected. I hadn't come to the Brew House with the intention of picking up a girl. I was going stir crazy at home, and none of my roommates was around for me to talk to, so I decided to take a walk. This place was on the far end of campus and I'd never stepped foot inside it before, which meant that it was as safe a spot as any.

Then she strolled in, her long blonde hair streaming down her back like shiny ribbons. She sat down and started flipping her pen and sighing so hard I thought she might blow herself off the chair.

It would've been a crime to not offer her an ear. And when she looked at me with her big brown eyes, I couldn't tear myself away. The invitation came out of my mouth because…well, that's what guys do with pretty girls. They ask them out. And I guess they get turned down, too.

I'm not a slouch in the academic department. I get good grades and have been an Academic All-American every year since I've been eligible, but no one I know starts studying until a week before midterms.

Studying as a reason for rejection lies somewhere midpoint between *I can't because my mom died* and *I can't because I'm clipping my toenails.* At least she looked regretful turning me down, as if she wished she could take me out for a ride but couldn't quite bring herself to throw her leg over the saddle.

Any other night, maybe I would have pursued her harder. Or just brushed off the rejection, snapped my fingers, and waited for a willing babe to magically appear and soothe away the sting. Which isn't exactly a stretch—when you play football for Western, there's no shortage of willing babes at your disposal. But I'm not in the mood tonight.

I'm not sure why. It's not because I popped into my friend Masters's place this afternoon and he was reading a book while Ellie was on her computer. They looked domestic and boring. The little pang in my chest was probably heartburn from the three burrito bowls I had at lunch. It wasn't…envy

Halfway home, my phone buzzes in my pocket. Pulling it out, I see a text from Stella Lowe, one of the team managers.

Stella: *Coach wants to see you.*

I wonder if I'm the only one who thinks it's weird Stella calls her dad Coach. The digital clock reads 8:05 p.m. It's been a week since the National Championship game. You'd think he'd be enjoying some R&R. Guy certainly deserves it.

I've taken full advantage of the post-championship high. There's not a bar in town that doesn't have a bottomless tap for a Warrior player. Not a girl on campus—or off it—who isn't chomping at the bit to do a little chomping on *my* bits.

Okay, maybe there is one girl who isn't interested, but for the most part, I'm sitting on top of the mountain of life. Other people are struggling. Other people are sighing their asses off in the coffee place. Me? Anything I want is mine for the asking. I could walk into any bar in the city and people would be trampling each other to buy me a drink. At the Gas Station, there are coeds who would suck me off under the table while I watch *SportsCenter* highlights.

Life is good. So good that I don't even care I just got shot down. So what if some uptight girl—who's spending a Wednesday two weeks into the semester studying so hard that it makes her head ache—turned me down for a date? Just gives me more time to enjoy my off-season, what little of it that I'm allotted. Spring ball will be here soon enough, and I'll have to fend off hungry freshmen and sophomores who think they should be ahead of me on the depth chart.

Until then, I'm planning on coasting through classes during the day, napping long into afternoon, and enjoying late, wonderful nights.

Well, and apparently random evening summons from Coach.

On it. I type back.

* * *

"You wanted to see me, Coach?" I stick my head around the corner into Coach Lowe's office. He is on the phone but gestures for me to enter. I suppose he's recruiting. The official signing day starts in about four weeks.

No one likes coming into the coach's office. Meetings on the field, inside the locker room, during film—you know what those are all about. When you're summoned to his office, you're literally being called on the carpet.

I step inside gingerly and make my way across the thick pile—dyed

Western State Warrior blue—and over the helmeted head of our mascot woven in rich gold, black, and white, to stand by one of the heavy leather chairs situated in front of a massive dark wood desk.

"Sit down, Matthew." He gestures to a chair in front of him. Coach Lowe doesn't look like a football coach. He's small, under six feet, and wiry. He never even played college ball, but it hasn't hurt him. He's got two national championships under his belt in less than ten years. That's enough for the whispers of "dynasty" to start.

Coach Lowe steeples his fingers together and leans forward, his wrists resting on some cut sheets. Reading his own good press? I'd do that, too, if I were him.

I position my hands the same way and wait patiently. Mirroring is a good technique to set someone at ease per the sociology class I'm taking on human interaction this semester.

Coach Lowe examines something on his desk before turning his attention to me. "You enjoying your off-season, son?"

Not the question I was expecting.

"It's going okay." *It's been pretty fricking awesome, thank you.*

"I'd like to win another National Championship next year. How about you?"

"Yessir. I want that, too." My interest perks up. I've been wanting to discuss draft placements, combine invitations, and scouting visits, but figured that wouldn't take place until spring ball or the summer camps. This is probably what I've been antsy about today, why I didn't want to go to the Gas Station to get laid, why the rejection from Lucy at the coffee shop hung with me longer than it should have, why the sight of my friend Masters and his wife, Ellie, made me feel like I was missing out.

What I really want to hear is that the scouts are drooling over me and that Coach Lowe is telling them I need to go high in the draft.

"You still hungry to win? Because some kids win once and they take their foot off the pedal. They stop training as hard. They let the outside world become a distraction. They lose focus and then they lose games." He glances down at the photos under his wrists.

My good mood evaporates. From what little I can see, those pictures contain nothing good. If I'm here to talk to Coach about those, I better brace myself for a tongue lashing—and not the sexy kind I got a couple of days ago from a cute red-headed Delta Gamma in the bathroom at the Gas Station.

"I want to win," I repeat slowly. "Nothing's going to be more important come fall than making sure the BCS trophy stays here at Western State."

"Hhmmph," Coach grunts.

Err. Not the answer he was looking for?

"This is my worry. Without Masters pushing you every second, is the defensive squad going to be as sharp or tough? Physically and mentally, are you going to be a National Championship team?" He reaches for the photos and tosses them toward me.

I look at the colored papers and inwardly cringe. After the championship game, it's safe to say we went a little crazy. People treated us like gods and there was a never-ending funnel of booze that night. And the women. Holy shit. They were everywhere, and they came in pairs and more. They were all tens. Maybe elevens.

I couldn't count much that night. I don't have to look at the pictures to know what they contain. They'd been on the Internet within hours of the game's last whistle. Hammer and I and the D-line were getting drunk, doing whipped cream body shots off of various coeds.

There's a worse photograph that I don't see in the pile. That's the one where I'm lying on a bar top with one girl's head between my legs while Hammer is pretending to spank her in the ass. Another girl is leaning over my mouth feeding me a shot. My mom raked me over the coals for that one. My "I had my pants on, Ma," excuse didn't fly with her, and I suspect it would go over equally poorly with Coach.

"This was after the season was over," I point out.

He taps a finger on the top photo. "Where's your captain in these photos?"

Knox Masters was fucking his new wife, the girl you had banned from having any contact with the team, is what I want to answer, but I know that'd go over like a lead balloon. Besides, I'm not throwing my teammate under the bus, even one who's no longer technically a Western State Warrior.

"At his hotel."

"Right." He gives one final tap and shoves backward. The motion sends the photos flying off the desk onto the floor, and I see the last one in the pile is indeed the foursome picture. Fan-fucking-tastic. "Your captain was at the hotel, avoiding the press and ensuring the Western State Warriors' reputation was untouched while you and the rest of your crew were out there making us look like a bunch of high school kids who'd never seen a set of tits before. Do you know how hard it is to assure a worried mama that we're going to take good care of her son and won't let him sin his way through college when these pictures are everywhere?"

"No, sir." *The mom may not like it, but the son sure as shit does.* I keep that nugget to myself.

He pins me with a hard stare. "You're a superb talent, Mr. Iverson. You will undoubtedly be drafted, but how high you go depends a lot upon the off-the-field qualities you show. Your scouting reports say that your leadership potential is unknown. Being captain of the defense could go a long way to shoring up your intangibles."

Captain? That's not something I've ever gunned for. I love playing the game because that shit is fun, and all the other hard work I put in, from eating the right foods to working out hours a day to studying game film, helps me do what I love at a high level. But captaincy? Leadership? That sounds like a lot of BS that I don't really care to shoulder, but I can't really say so to Coach.

If he's asking, the appropriate answer is always "yes" because if you say no, you're getting volun*told* to do it anyway. Might as well make yourself agreeable. Path of least resistance and all that.

"If that's what the team wants from me, that's what I want to give the team."

Coach Lowe gives no indication my lack of enthusiasm bothers him. "With Masters gone, someone needs to keep the defense in check. I don't want to see more of this." He gestures toward the pictures I have awkwardly collected in my lap.

"Not a problem."

"If it does become a problem…" His threat hangs unspoken in the air. I didn't even sniff the field my first year behind a first team All-American linebacker who was drafted in the third round by the Niners. He's not in the league anymore, but when I walked onto campus, he was one of the big men and I was his understudy.

Since my sophomore year, I've held that inside linebacker position against all challengers and I'm not giving it up now no matter how many blue chip recruits and backups are chomping at the bit to take my place.

"It won't."

"Good." He leans back into his chair and swivels so he's looking out the window onto the practice field. "I think you would be a good captain, Matthew. Your teammates like you and more importantly they listen to you." The dry note in his voice says that right now they're listening to all the wrong things. "But taking your direction in this"—he brushes a palm across the clippings—"is an easy path. You need to prove to me you can lead them in something else."

"Absolutely." I straighten in my chair. I've always gotten good grades, and I have no problem cutting down on the booze and chicks. The guys on the defense don't mind having someone else in charge. Between Hammer and me, we'll have it covered. "What do you need?"

"No more pictures with girls. No more excessive partying." He ticks a finger with each order. "And convince Anderson that he'd be better off at safety."

I nod. No chicks. No booze. Get Ace—

"What?" My screech is high enough to be mistaken for a teenage girl, and I think my hearing short-circuited. JR "Ace" Anderson is our quarterback. The one we won the National Championship with. Coach knows all of this, so I must have misheard him. The only thing I can think of to say is, "I'm on defense."

Coach Lowe doesn't even spare me a glance. "I've got a commitment from Remington Barr out of Texas. He'll come if he can start. That kid won four straight Texas State High School Championships. I want him. He's going to be the key to my future here. Ace is athletic, but we both know he's not good enough to play at the next level. So you convince Ace to move to safety and the C is yours." He shoves a patch toward me.

The circular patch in gold and blue, with a big old "C" in the middle, is sewn onto a captain's jersey. It's an honor to wear the patch, but in order to own this letter I've got to tell my quarterback, the one who just helped us win us a national title, that his time at the vaunted QB position is over?

I swallow hard. Not only do I play on the opposite side of the ball as Ace, but my time spent with him generally consists of running by him during practice since he's considered off-limits even when we're wearing pads. We aren't best buds even though we do play on the same team.

"I...I'm on defense." I sound like a broken record. "I mean that I don't have any classes with Ace. We don't hang out. I've never had a meaningful conversation with the guy beyond encouraging him to play well. I think my influence over Ace is about the same as I'd have over a herd of cats."

There. That sounds reasoned and sane unlike Coach's bizarre request.

"I haven't asked you to ride herd over cats. Besides, you don't have to convince Ace directly. You're free to talk to the rest of the team. If he doesn't have the support of the team, he'll move on his own."

Is there any way to tell your coach that he sounds like he's taken one too many drags off the pipe? That he's talking out his ass? Because this shit seems off to me. Shouldn't he be talking to Ace and addressing the team? Why me? I try another tack. "I have no problem playing monk for the rest of my tenure here—"

"Son?" Coach Lowe interrupts, tone mild as if he hasn't just released napalm in his office.

"Yeah, Coach?"

"You're dismissed."

Okay then. I heave myself out of the chair and walk toward the door. Maybe if I turn around and come back in, the conversation will be completely different.

"Mr. Iverson," he calls. I turn back just in time to see the patch sailing across the room. I catch it reflexively. "You forgot something."

3

LUCY

WHEN I GET HOME, I find my two roommates installed in front of the television eating ice cream and watching *Say Yes to the Dress*. While none of us is even dating, we seem curiously addicted to the show. I think it's because we have shitty relationships with our moms and this show is all about the momma and daughter drama.

"Tell me there's a half gallon left of that." I don't wait for an answer but throw my backpack on the chair and start rummaging in the freezer. If there was ever a night for real cream, sugar, butter and eggs, tonight was it. I need some relief after talking with Matt Iverson. His number has implanted itself in my head followed by the words *call me*.

But I can't eat sugar unless I want to risk sending myself into a diabetic coma, so I resign myself to the sugar-free, fat-free frozen yogurt, which I tell myself is just as good. Just like turning Matt down was the right choice. I stare at my frozen yogurt container with a frown.

"I was going to ask how your mock trial practice went, but since you're shoving yogurt into your face like tomorrow is the last day on earth, I'm guessing it was shitty?" Sutton rests her pointed chin on the edge of the sofa. Her streaked violet hair clashes against the rich red velvet of the cushion.

"Shitty is too nice of a word to describe how poorly it went." I throw myself into one of the two Papasan chairs that Sutton contributed to the décor and dig into the yogurt. The icy tartness hits my tongue, and some of my agitation melts away. "But it's early. We still have a lot of time." Regionals are right before Spring Break so there are nearly two whole months for us to get our act together.

"Don't get too comfortable," Charity, my other roommate, informs me.

I pause, my spoon halfway to my mouth, and narrow my eyes. "Why not?"

"Remember 1C complaining about cockroaches?"

"What now?" 1C is an apartment inhabited by two Stepford Wives in the making—both blondes with stick straight hair, identically styled. Every time I've seen them, they're wearing headbands. Who above the age of eleven still wears headbands? Even if their matching hairstyles didn't remind me of the plastic women from the infamous novel, the robotic looks on their faces and the fake smiles they wear creep nearly everyone out.

But the number one reason we don't like 1C is because they complain all of the time, and they regularly canvas the apartment complex to get others to sign on to their complaints. They've complained about everything from noise (it's a goddamned college apartment complex) to garbage (too many pizza boxes stuffed down the trash chute) to non-resident visitors after ten (again, we're goddamned college students).

"They got enough people to sign their maintenance petition, so an exterminator crew is coming next Tuesday. You can keep your stuff here, but you'll have to find a place to stay."

I do a quick calculation in my head. Five days. I'm not even convinced that they saw a cockroach. I don't like changes in my routine. I can already feel my anxiety ratcheting up. Change is not my favorite thing in the world. I live by my routine. Hell, my health depends on it. "That's bullshit."

"I know," Charity says glumly. "I'm staying at the house. I asked if you could come, but they're so strict. We're still in pledge mode, so only full sisters can stay." Charity belongs to the Alpha Phi sorority whereas Sutton and I are those Goddamned Independents or GDIs as Charity calls us affectionately. I'd have pledged a house if it didn't cost an arm and a leg. I have to save those limbs to pay for graduate school.

"Where are you staying?" I ask Sutton.

"I've decided that Luke is worth a second night," she admits. "Basically I'm sexing him up so I have a place to stay. Let's hope he doesn't expect a third time around because if tomorrow is anything like Saturday night, I'm going to have to diddle myself to have an orgasm once he falls asleep."

"I think I'd rather stay here and be exterminated." I grimace. "I suppose I can stay with JR. He'll be back by then and there's so many bedrooms in his house that at least one will be free."

"Speaking of our vaunted Western State Warriors, guess who finally showed up in my Public Safety class." Charity waggles her eyebrows.

Apparently someone hot and sexy. "Dunno. Coach Lowe?" I tease.

"No! Matt Iverson."

"Who's that?" Sutton doesn't know a thing about football. She fell asleep during the one game we watched together here in our apartment. And the live games? Forget about it. She left after the first quarter. Charity sometimes attends with her sorority sisters if it's part of some fraternity exchange party but otherwise, they have zero interest in the game. The players, on the other hand? They are interesting but JR—or "Ace," as everyone here at Western calls him—and I made a pact. No pissing in the other's pool. I don't date football players and he doesn't mess with my roommates.

"He's on the defense," I explain. "Linebacker. Will be a pro after his senior year." I look at my spoon and then down into the half-empty carton of frozen yogurt. I should probably stop.

"He's this huge mountain of sweet male meat," Charity shares with Sutton. "He's got this longish black hair that stops around here." She waves her hands under her chin. "And the bluest eyes. I swear they're fake. Are they?" The question is directed at me.

I drag my attention away from the icy treat and to my two roommates who are looking at me with intense interest. "I have no idea. I've never talked to him. Ace hangs out with the offense, mostly Ahmed and Jack Campbell, more recently." Ahmed's the running back, and Jack Campbell is a new guy—a tight end with magic hands that never seem to drop a pass and with sticky feet that somehow always manage to stay inbounds. "I think Iverson is best friends with Hammer Wright and Knox Masters. According to Ace, anyway. I don't hang out with his teammates."

Well, I did once. Operative word being *once*. The one time I went to the Gas Station, the preferred hangout place for the football team, Ace was swallowed up by well-wishers. He forgot I was there, and I had little interest in being shoved around by the mass of people trying to slap his back.

He'd apologized the next day, but I didn't go out with him again. When we do hang out, it's usually here although I've been over to his house a few times. I try to avoid that because nine times out of ten, someone is having sex in the living room or the kitchen. JR—I mean Ace—says it's because sex is an athletic activity, no different than lifting or running.

"Ohhhhh," Sutton breathes out. "I had Intro to Communications with Hammer Wright first semester sophomore year."

"Sutton, are you blushing?" Charity exclaims. Sutton is not a blusher. She can rip off the bawdiest statement as if she's standing in church reciting the Lord's Prayer, so this slight reddening of her cheeks is highly unusual. "You are! What did you and Hammer get up to?"

"Nothing." Sutton grins ruefully. "Unfortunately. I threw myself at him several times, but he never noticed."

"He's a dog. You are better off," I offer comfortingly. I don't know the defense well, but most of the single guys, Ace included, freely partake of what their elevated social status provides—a never-ending line of college girls wanting to know what it's like to sleep with a star. It's one reason I'd never date a football player. They don't know how to hit the "off" button once they're not on the field anymore. Life's a big fat game to them, and girls are just objects they move around on the board.

"A hot one," Sutton admits.

"And his hot dog has probably been licked so many times he's on the WHO list of dangerous diseases," I retort.

Charity waves her hands, the multitude of bangles clanging cheerfully against each other. Charity would never be able to sneak up on anyone. She wears too much jewelry. "Who cares? I can't stop staring at this Matt guy. He's always wearing short-sleeved shirts, no matter how cold it is outside, and when he takes notes, his biceps muscle flexes. I swear the room gets ten degrees warmer when he walks in. I'd love to give him a little ride."

"It'd only be for one night," I caution.

Charity shrugs. "Again, who cares?"

Sutton disagrees. "Here's my theory. I think guys do one-night stands because their egos can't take the blows that a more sober second hookup would deliver. They don't want to hear they are bad in bed, so they do one-time-only events."

"What's our excuse for our lack of regular companionship?" I joke.

None of us has had a decent relationship since we came to college. I broke up with my high school boyfriend a month into my freshman year. Sutton has tried to date guys on and off, but when none of those relationships panned out, she's settled for random hookups with guys like Luke. Charity was madly in love with one of the Western basketball players, but he graduated in December and hasn't called her since, thus confirming my anti-athlete bias.

"We're looking for the unicorn," Charity says. "The guy who's a good lay and decent out of bed."

"I had a good lay once," Sutton informs us. "Two years ago. Spring Break. Greece." She fires out details like they're bullets shooting from a gun. "That guy from the Philippines had a tongue like a snake."

"That's a terrible visual." I shudder.

Sutton is undeterred. "It felt amazing. He licked places I didn't even know had nerve endings."

"Two years ago was your last good sexual experience?" Charity asks with genuine concern.

Sutton nods. "With a partner. I can get myself off fine, but that's about two minutes and then what?"

I nod. She speaks the truth. I miss having sex with a guy I have feelings for. I think that's why my relationships here at Western have failed. I can't summon up the requisite...passion for any guy. I keep trying. Keith is the fourth guy I've *tried* with, but the sex is so bland I'm better off masturbating. Alone.

Charity shrugs. "I've had good sex with partners. You have to be more vocal and take charge though. Most of these guys think just jabbing you is going to get it done. Not to mention the opposite end of the spectrum, where they think they're awesome and want to show off their amazing moves."

"No, the worst is whiskey dick where they keep going and going and you're willing to do anything for them to either come or get the fuck off," Sutton interjects.

"Jesus, we're jaded." Maybe I should start looking at sex like exercise. Lord knows, with the increased stress in my life from mock trial, my glucose levels are going to be completely out of whack. I'm going to need to do something besides eating right to manage my blood sugars. And gobbling a tubful of frozen yogurt isn't the way to go about it. I get up and shove the nearly empty container back into the freezer.

"It's all part of growing up. Welcome to adulthood," Sutton jokes.

Sadly, though, I think she's not too far off the mark, which is yet another reason why turning down the gorgeous guy at the Brew House was a good idea regardless of how sultry his lips looked forming my name or how his rough hands scraped against my softer, more tender skin. I have a sinking feeling he's good in bed. He's got a way with his body—graceful despite the size—that said he was comfortable in his own skin.

"What're you thinking about now?" Sutton asks.

I give myself a little shake. I really need to stop dwelling on this guy no matter how blue— *Oh, god.* I turn back to my roommates.

"Some guy hit on me at the Brew House," I say slowly as the puzzle pieces click together. Blue eyes. Jet black hair. Muscles so nice they'd get a nun excited.

"Jon Cryer or Charlie Sheen?" Sutton is a film major.

I make a face. "How about neither?"

"Okay, pick your own look-a-like actor."

"How about, instead of an actor, I pick Western State football player. I didn't recognize him last night without the eye black and helmet. Plus, he was wearing glasses."

Sutton hoots. "He Clark Kented you!"

Jingle. Jingle. Charity waves her hand at Sutton to get her to stop laughing. "Seriously, Matt Iverson hit on you last night? What'd you say? Are you going out with him?"

Sutton jumps in. "I know exactly what she said. He's not my type." She turns to me. "Am I right?"

I shrug. "So I have a type. Sue me. I don't think liking a certain flavor of unsweetened yogurt is a bad thing."

"Sure, if you're eating *yogurt*," Charity cries in dismay. "But this is prime, Grade A manflesh."

"We need to hold an intervention." Sutton sighs. "What was the excuse you gave?"

I make a face at Sutton who, in turn, sticks out her tongue at me. Fine, I did give him an excuse. "I was working on my mock trial stuff. Plus, he seems like he'd take a lot of effort. Doesn't matter now. Ace and I have the pact. No football players for me."

"There are eighty guys on that team. Who cares what Ace thinks?" Charity's long hoop earrings swing as she bobs her head in indignation.

"Agreed. Besides, Ace just made that stupid pact up so he can keep you to himself."

I reach into the cupboard so Sutton doesn't see me roll my eyes. I've heard her theory before about Ace's crush on me. Sounds like she's still clinging to it despite the number of times Ace has been in this very apartment talking about the girls he's been banging.

Charity is beside herself with disappointment. "Other than your extracurricular activities, sixteen hours of school, and twenty hours of work, surely you could make time for someone who looks like that. I'd bang him so hard."

"Then you call him. Here's his number." I stomp over to my bag, pull out the paper he scrawled his digits on and shove it toward her.

"He gave you his number?" Sutton says in disbelief.

"Yup."

"I give up on you." She turns around and folds her arms across her chest in disgust.

"You're the one who said good-looking guys are probably bad in bed," I remind her, ignoring that inner crone voice yelling, *Liar!* "Besides, most of the single football players go through women like tissues. Look at Ace." I'm gratified when both of my roommates give reluctant nods of understanding. "Matt just gives off this vibe of someone whose default toward women is always 'on.' He'd probably flirt with a tree if he knew it was female."

"You know this how?" Sutton challenges.

"He hit on *me*. At the *Brew House*."

"You say that like the Brew House is a nun's sanctuary. I know for a fact that you and Keith hooked up there."

"First, we did not hook up there. We work there. And because we work together and spent so much time together, it was natural that we would sleep together. But do I have to remind you how boring it was? How I nearly fell asleep one time when we were having sex? If that's not a reason to stay away from men turned on by the smell of coffee, I don't know what is."

Charity makes a face. "I suppose. Still, I think Matt Iverson would be worth at least one roll in the hay. You could do it for me. For womankind. You could test out the theory whether really good-looking guys actually know how to satisfy a woman. Report back as to whether he's a dud or a stud."

Stud. Matt Iverson's hot body looks like he could take some abuse. I keep that thought to myself lest Charity launch herself at me in frustration.

"Oh sure, let me go and sacrifice my night for you." She sticks out her tongue at me. "How about this," I say placatingly. "I'll fantasize about him. I'll probably have a better orgasm by myself, objectifying him, than *with* him."

"True," Charity says glumly. "If he really was good in bed, he'd be the unicorn, and then we'd wonder why he was single. Like, what is so wrong with him that he's out trolling coffee houses for companionship? He should be able to go to the Gas Station and clap his hands and have a dozen babes at his feet."

"Thank you. My point exactly." But being right doesn't make me feel better.

4

MATTY

I FIND MYSELF AT THE Brew House the next night. When Josie Weeks announced she was forming a study group for our Criminal Practice and Procedure class, I wasn't interested. When she said they'd meet at the Brew House at seven, I couldn't get my name on her list fast enough.

I tell myself it's because I need to study, but the moment I walk in and set eyes on Lucy's long blond hair, I admit it's because I want to see her again. Despite her rejection, I'm still hot for her in a way I can't remember feeling toward another girl.

Plus, focusing on Lucy, even if she did turn me down, is a thousand times better than dwelling on the ridiculous task Coach wants me to undertake. He's the coach. If he wants a player moved, he moves the player. He doesn't come to a linebacker with that request. I'm ignoring it for now. Ignoring it and, instead, applying my energies in a different and better direction: convincing sweet Lucy to go out with me.

At Josie's table, there are two chairs and she's sitting in one of them. Either everyone else is late or it's just going to be the two of us. I ignore the way she's patting the chair next to her and drag one around so I can sit facing the counter. This is a definite two birds, one stone moment.

"Did I scare everyone away or are we it?" I ask, pulling out my glasses and opening up the textbook. Lucy is mostly blocked by the machines, registers, and glass cases displaying sugary carbs, but I know she saw me when I walked in. I gave her a little wave and she frowned. She recognizes me. I'm taking that as a sign of encouragement.

"No, it's just us. Isn't that nice?" Josie's words break up my inspection.

Whoops. Forgot why I was here for a minute. I quickly process Josie's response.

"I definitely need a study group," I answer diplomatically.

Her smile dims a watt or two but doesn't completely disappear. "I'm glad I can be there for you."

Spring semester is always a little harder for me to stay focused. I only have a few weeks of spring ball, but the rest of the time, my schedule is wide open. Most of the trouble we players get into is when we don't have a coach breathing down our necks and 7 a.m. full pads practice.

From my limited study of Josie, I don't know if she's interested in sleeping with me or merely bagging, tagging, and hanging me trophy-like in her sorority house. In prior years, I'd have tapped that ass in a heartbeat. Nowadays, I've learned to be pickier. If we were at the Gas Station or a post-game party, the rules are pretty clear. Here? She might be angling for something more than I'm interested in giving.

Jersey chasers are a dime a dozen, always willing to take a ride on the football side, but you've got to be careful with the overly eager ones, the ones who aren't just trying to make a trophy outta you, but a fuckin' Lifetime Achievement award. As in, poking holes in condoms and look at that, you're a baby daddy. I don't know if Josie falls into that latter category, but she's a little too eager for my taste.

Too eager? Since when do I complain about eagerness?

A husky laugh draws my eyes to the counter again. Oh right. Since the hot blonde turned me down. *She* makes my dick move. I lean forward, wanting to be part of whatever is making her smile. Josie follows my gaze. Her eyes narrow with laser-like focus.

"Do you know Lucy Washington?"

"Nah, I'm not much of a coffee drinker." I don't go into my theory about sweat-infused water. My main drink of choice is Gatorade followed by Gatorade and vodka chased with a beer, which is why I've set foot inside the Brew House maybe a half-dozen times since I started attending Western.

"I'm not sure what her major is. Communications. Political Science? Something like that. She's very strange."

I swivel back to Josie, surprised at her bitchy comment. Usually when girls run down other girls in front of me, they have more finesse. It's more along the lines of "she'd look so much better in a different dress" and not so much with the "she's an ugly bitch, stay away" because even self-absorbed people realize at some point that those kinds of comments are off-putting. "In what way?"

"Why do you want to know?" She frowns.

I've spent enough time around women to recognize danger when I see it. Josie's intuitive enough to sense she has competition. Actually the competition is all in her head, but that's still a problem. I intentionally draw her attention away from Lucy by tapping my book. "Why don't we start with the fruit of the poisonous tree doctrine?"

This seems to work as Josie's attention is diverted. Lucy's saved and she doesn't even know it. Josie and I buckle down to work for all of ten minutes before Josie hops on her phone.

"What do you think of this picture?" She flips her phone toward me. The display is filled with her and three friends wearing tiny bathing suits. "That was last year in St. Thomas. We were thinking of going back there this year."

"Looks good," I say dutifully. I'm a big fan of Instagram. And Twitter. And Snapchat. All of these things have made it exceedingly easy to find like-minded women—women who want one good night and that's it. But I want to study now, and it's a struggle to keep the irritation out of my voice.

My non-effusive compliment doesn't deter Josie. Instead she pages through more photos and turns the phone around again. This time she's wearing a shiny sparkly dress standing next to another girl in a sparkly dress. I can barely tell them apart. Idly I wonder whether they'd serve as a disco ball if we strung them up on the ceiling. Maybe we'd just need the dress.

"This was at the fall formal last year. I think I look heavy in this dress. What do you think?"

I squint. She looks as if she ate a diet of carrots and celery for two years. "I think you look nice."

This time, she frowns. "Nice?"

"Yes. Nice. Pretty. Great." I keep tacking on adjectives in hopes I hit on the right one, but I don't inject enough enthusiasm in my voice. And my half-hearted efforts to compliment her kill her desire to study, if she ever had any in the first place. She buries her nose in the phone and after about five minutes of silence, I decide I'm thirsty.

As I wait in line, I stare at the board wondering what the best tasting coffee is for someone who doesn't like coffee. Dark roast seems out. Maybe the light roast? Is that like a steak? The coffee beans are only slightly roasted and so still taste like whatever an uncooked coffee bean tastes like.

"Can I help you?" Lucy cocks her head to the side. Her long blond hair is caught up in a ponytail, the ones that I like wrapping around my fist while—

I cut off my train of thought when she clears her throat and delivers a well-mixed look of disdain and contempt as if she knows what I was thinking about just now and figures I'm not much good for anything else. Were her eyes this big last night? Were they this…soft? They look like a puppy dog's eyes. Brown, warm, and endearing. If the puppy thought I was an idiot, that is.

"I'm trying to decide which is the best coffee for me."

"I thought you didn't drink coffee."

"I don't." I shrug. Can I be more obvious? I don't think so. Unfortunately, Lucy isn't taking the bait. Another girl would be leaning against the counter, maybe twirling her hair around her finger. Lucy looks bored. That should bother me more, but instead I feel kind of energized by her dismissiveness. It's sure as hell different. "You didn't use my number."

"I was studying. We have eight different kinds of tea."

"I have the same problem with tea as I do coffee. Anything else?"

She opens her mouth to ask me what my problem is, then snaps it closed almost immediately. Hmm. Maybe I'm cracking her barrier a tiny bit.

"How about a spiced mulled cider?"

I perk up. "You can make that?" It's January and as cold as a penguin's ass, so spiced cider sounds great.

"Yup." She scribbles something on the cup. I'm guessing it's not her phone number because the vague smile she directs my way is the same one she gave the two students before me and undoubtedly the next one who will come behind me.

I shouldn't feel a twinge of disappointment, but I do.

"Anything else?" she asks tentatively.

Because, like a dumbass, I'm still staring at her. I shift over to the glass case. "I could use an apple streusel."

I'll have to do an extra ten minutes on the sleds tomorrow to pay for that, but what the hell. We just won the championship. I have three weeks until spring ball starts. If I want to eat a piece of cake, this is the time.

"We make it fresh every day." She recites the line with enough boredom to convey she's tired of saying it. As she reaches inside the glass case with a pair of tongs and picks out the biggest slice, she asks, "Would you like it warmed up?"

"I don't know, will I?" The words slide out, husky and provocative, and totally unintended.

Her eyes widen. "Ah, most people do." She shoots me an irritated look and ducks around to heat up my cake while I feel like a total idiot. Not since sixth grade have I been so unpolished with a girl.

My phone buzzes.

Hammer: *Where are u? The chicks at the Gas Station are so hot to-*

night. It's like winter doesn't exist for them. God bless band-aid dresses.

Me: *Bandage.*

Hammer: *Same thing. Where are u?! Do you think the Christmas break makes these Western girls hotter? I don't remember them being so fine last semester.*

Me: *How much have u had to drink? It's only 8.*

Hammer: *Where are u?*

I sigh. If I don't answer him, he'll probably run out of the Gas Station and start yelling my name like the guy who keeps yelling "Stella!" from that movie my mom loves so much. Huh. I wonder if that's why Coach named his daughter that. I give myself a mental head slap for falling down that particular rabbit hole and punch in a response to Hammer.

Me: *Brew place. Striking out.*

Hammer: *Noooooo.*

Hopefully, Hammer's drinking with a friend tonight.

My phone vibrates again but this time the screen displays the number fifty-five. It's Masters. Damn, I'm going to miss that bastard when he leaves school at the end of this year.

Masters: *Hammer texted me. Sounds like you need help.*

I roll my eyes. *What'd Hammer say?*

Masters: *Screenshotted the convo he could fit on one screen.*

Me: *Hammer's shocked to find out that there are women outside the Gas Station. Worse, they have the word* no *in their vocabulary.*

Masters: *Situation appears dire. Look around. Do you see any adults?*

I look up at Lucy, who's talking to her co-worker and actively avoiding me. I think that's a good sign.

Me: *My ball size indicates I'm the adultest thing here.*

The microwave dings, and she slides the streusel out. That's not a good sign. I no longer have an excuse to loiter here at the counter. I point to the first thing I see. "I'll take one of those, too."

"It's *coffee* cake. This version is made with actual coffee." I don't even have to look at her to know her expression is hovering between *this guy is an idiot* and *when is he going to take his shit and go back to his table*.

"Yeah, give me a big piece."

She clearly thinks I'm short-changed in the big head. No clue what she thinks of me otherwise.

Me: *I haven't been rejected this hard since I tried to block the punt in that game against OSU last semester.*

Masters: *My wife says rejection is good for you. Makes you mentally tough.*

Me: *You love saying that phrase "my wife."*

Masters: *You bet your fat ass I do.*

Me: *You don't think it's completely strange that you're 21 and acting like a Taylor Swift song?*

Masters: *Bro, sorry you feel left out. Stop by later and I'll give you a hug.*

Me: *Fuck off.*

Masters: *I have MY WIFE to do that for me. Thanks, though. Hug still stands. I'll even let you smell me. MY WIFE says I smell delicious.*

Me: *I've smelled you before, which is why I'm not sure how you convinced Ellie to marry you. She must have defective olfactory senses.*

Masters: *Me and MY defective WIFE will be getting it on tonight. While u have only Rosie Palm.*

Me: *Don't worry. I get plenty of variety. Left-hand Laura sometimes steps in.*

Masters: *Heard you were out with Josie Weeks. Be careful. She eats little linebackers like you for breakfast.*

And the fact that I don't even want to make a sexually charged comeback tells me exactly how I feel about Josie. Hope she doesn't mind being just study partners.

"Here's your apple streusel *and* your coffee cake."

I tuck my phone back into my pocket. Lucy's cheeks are back to a normal color, and her smile is one that says any future flirtations from me are about as welcome as a nighttime visit from a spider.

"You ever going to use that phone number?"

"I already did." She tips her head down toward the end of the counter. "You can pick up your cider down there."

I open my mouth to say something extremely witty when her male co-worker starts shouting out my phone number. So that's what she wrote on the cup. The entire coffee house looks up at the skinny, hipster dude with his hair gelled so immaculately he might actually be a Ken doll come to life. Lucy spares me a glance under her eyelashes, and I can't help but laugh.

I lean forward. "I like that you have it memorized."

She pinkens, and I walk back to Josie's table, laden with goodies and the sweet knowledge I actually won a tiny round against the formidable Lucy Washington.

"You know she's a druggie, right?" Josie huffs when I sit down and start eating.

"Who?" I shovel the last of the streusel into my mouth and dig into the coffee cake, hoping there's enough butter and sugar in it to overcome any actual coffee taste. After the first swallow, I realize I *am* an idiot because the cake is gross. I take another big bite and wash the entire mess down with a chaser of Gatorade.

"Lucy Washington!"

I rear back. "Lucy? The coffee shop girl?"

"Yes. One of my sisters lived in the same dorm as her and saw her shooting up her freshman year. Right before she sat down to eat!"

I can't help but be impressed. "That's hardcore. You really think she'd be injecting drugs in the middle of the college cafeteria?"

"Why? Do you want some of your own?" Josie says in disgust.

Obviously my lack of dismay over Lucy's supposed drug addiction is a sign of moral depravity. I'm okay with that. I finish the coffee cake off before answering.

"No. I get random drug tests and wouldn't be able to play if I test positive, so no." There are guys who smoke weed to help with the pain. We have lots of guys on Adderall, too. Painkillers are handed out like candy by the team doctors, but I'm trying to avoid those aids as long as I can. Once you go down that path, I think it's hard not to lean on them too much. "But anyone who is so addicted to drugs that she'd shoot up in a public place can't function like she does."

"So you know her?"

God, what's with the fricking inquisition? "Yeah, we're seeing each other," I lie. I figure Josie's not going over to confront her about this, so my lie is about the safest one I've ever uttered.

Josie's mouth drops open. "Why'd you even come tonight, if you're already dating someone?"

Now it's my turn to be offended. "You said it was a study group."

"And you believed me?"

"Why wouldn't I?" Hell, maybe I shouldn't venture outside the Gas Station. It's too complex out here. "This is college, and study groups do exist. A lot. College is to study groups as libraries are to books. They go together."

"But you're a football player. A starter, right?"

"So?"

"So you don't need to study."

"Maybe not, but that's because I'm smart, not because I get a pass for being a football player."

"I thought…" She trails off and looks down at her papers in frustration.

I help her out. "You thought I was a dumb jock and would be grateful for your attention?"

She purses her lips. That's exactly what she thought. "I can share my sorority sister's outline with you." She shoves a set of papers toward me.

"Thanks, but I don't really need it. All of us dumb jocks get free tutoring."

Josie picks up her phone and presses something on the screen. She turns it around to face me. With a plastic smile, she says, "How do you like this?"

It's a Snapchat picture of me looking at Lucy like she's the tastiest treat in the entire place. The text overlay reads *Matty Iverson can win at football, but he loses at life.*

"Thanks for taking the picture from the right." It's apparent I should be offended, but Josie's game is too obvious. Anyone will read that and know *she's* the one who got turned down. "It's my best side."

She releases one of those silent screams, the kind where she swallows most of the sound but you still know she's screaming at the top of her lungs. Her bag is packed in seconds, and she takes off in such a rush her hair slaps me across the face.

"You forgot your cider," Lucy calls over. "You look like you could use a beer, though. We sell that, too."

"We were just studying."

Lucy turns to look in Josie's general direction. "That's an unhappy study partner you have there."

"We had a misunderstanding. She thought this was a date and I thought it was a study group."

"So you're not losing at life?"

Apparently the Snapchat is spreading faster than an STD in a frat house.

"When it comes to you, apparently I am."

She rubs a knuckle under her chin. "I get off in fifteen minutes and I need to eat something. You can join me if you want."

I brighten. "Really?"

My obvious enthusiasm earns me a slight frown. "Don't get any ideas. It's not an invitation for anything but sitting across the table from me while I eat."

This is a date even if she won't admit it. "Do I get to eat, too, or do I just sit and watch?"

Her eyebrows squeeze together in a rather adorable way. "You had coffee cake and apple streusel."

"I'm a bottomless pit, or so my mom tells me." My hand falls to my stomach, and her eyes follow in a gratifying way. Maybe I'm not strik-ing out because the way her gaze is eating me up right now tells me she'd like a side of Matty with her meal.

"Great. Meet me out front in fifteen." Then she spins around and goes back to bustling behind the counter. As if I'm not even here.

Or hell, maybe she's inviting me to dinner to tell me exactly how much she doesn't want to see me again. That would actually be a little on the crazy side, which means I should walk away, but she's hooked me good. So good that, at this point, I'd pretty much follow her pretty ass anywhere.

5

LUCY

"OKAY IF WE GO TO Crowerly's?" I ask when I meet Matt outside the Brew House. To his credit, he doesn't make a face when I suggest the vegan restaurant. Or he has no clue what they serve.

"Lady's choice." He sweeps out a hand, indicating I should lead the way.

"It's vegan," I tell him.

"All the better. We both know I've had enough sugar and carbs to-night to send a small kid into convulsions. Are you sure you didn't give me two pieces of the coffee cake?" he accuses.

"We are closing in an hour," I admit. "It would've been tossed out if it didn't sell. Besides, I didn't expect you to eat it all."

"Look at me." He holds his arms out wide. "Do I look like a guy who turns down cake?"

I can't stop myself from looking at him. He's got the classic V-shape with the broad shoulders and trim waist. Nothing about him says "cof-fee cake eater." More like bland chicken and a boatload of vegetables. Of course, he works out two hours or more a day, so maybe he can eat all the cake he wants.

And why do I even care? "I guess not."

Crowerly's is only two blocks down, and neither of us says another word until we're seated across from each other in the booth.

"Did you come to the Brew House tonight because of me?" My tone comes out sharper than I intended, but he doesn't seem insulted. If anything, he looks amused.

"Nope. I told you, I thought I was coming to a study group."

His expression is a bit too innocent for my liking. And damn it, he's too gorgeous for my comfort. Somehow in the span of twenty-four hours I managed to forget how frickin' hot this guy is. I can see now why Charity was all but drooling when she brought up his name.

"Right. Your study group." I show him with my eyes just how much I believe him. Which is not at all. "And I guess knowing I work there had nothing to do with your thought process."

"You give yourself too much credit, Luce. My studies happen to be my number one priority." He smiles sweetly.

"First off, *Luce?*"

"Yup. We're on a nickname basis now. You're Luce, and I'm Matty." His lips curve ever so slightly. "Unless you want to pick a different nickname for me. Something like…hmmmm…Gorgeous? I'd answer to that."

I choke down a laugh and snatch the menu. I give it a quick scan just as the waitress appears to take our orders. I ask for a bowl of the butternut squash soup and a coffee, and when Matt winces, I look at the waitress and add, "If you could bring the whole coffee pot and just leave it here, that would be super. My friend *loves* the smell of fresh-brewed coffee."

He glares at me.

The waitress just looks confused. "Oh, I'm sorry. We can't do that. But I can bring you the jumbo mugs." She glances, mystified, at Matt. "Is that all right?"

Matt sighs.

Once she's gone, he turns to me in exasperation. "Really? Now you're punishing me? For daring to ask you out?"

I can't help but grin. "No, that was just too fun to resist." I go serious again. "As for the 'asking me out' part, I already told you, I'm not interested."

His blue eyes are smug. "Then why are we having dinner together?"

"We're not."

"You're ordering food. I'm going to order something when she gets back after we talk about this menu—"

"Get the tofu fries and yogurt dip," I interrupt. "They're delicious. Actually, get two orders and I'll eat whatever you don't."

His lips quirk up again, as if he's not at all irritated that I cut him off. "Okay, two orders of tofu fries and then we'll be eating. Together. You do know what together means, right? Close to or in the proximity of another person."

"Very nice, Mr. Dictionary."

He folds his arms on the table and leans across. He's so tall, and the tables at Crowerly's are so small, he's virtually touching me.

"I'm your man if you need some SAT words for your papers." A naughty grin spreads across his face. "I'm a verbal guy. I like saying things almost as much as I like doing them."

He doesn't explicitly define what "things" are, but I'd have to be a total newb not to get his gist. He's talking about sex things. Dirty things. Hot things. The image of this guy bent over me whispering exactly how he's going to touch me, feel me, be with me? I'm going to need a pitcher of water not a mug of coffee. The whole idea of Matty—geez, am I really calling him Matty now? He's in my head, and I need to push him out.

"How is that even true?" I say skeptically. There's no way he enjoys talking as much as he enjoys screwing some girl.

"Never enjoyed a little dirty talk during your fun time?" He looks disappointed.

"Not that it's any of your business, but I think talking is overrated. Maybe you should practice one aspect—such as the physical—before adding in another component," I say in my most clinical and repressive tones, but even as I utter those words, I know what he's going to say in return. The problem here is that Matt could probably turn anything into a sexual innuendo.

"I'm a big believer in "practice makes perfect," and I don't get my feelings hurt in the face of criticism, which is why you should test out both my physical and verbal skills. Say, tomorrow night?"

I'm saved from answering when the waitress appears with our two big mugs of coffee. Matt shoves his aside and places his order for fries and dip—Crowerly's version of it, at least—and a glass of water. The water appears moments later, as if the waitress can't stand being away from him for even a second.

"I'm busy tomorrow night. I have mock trial practice."

"Nice. I like that. A real excuse. It helps soothe the sting." He rubs his chest in mock pain, and I have to force myself not to stare at how well defined his muscles appear even under his T-shirt.

You don't like muscles, I remind myself.

"Let's go back to this no-dirty-talking experience. What kind of guys are you dating?"

"Nice ones."

"I'm a nice guy, and I love a little dirty talk. If you sat on my lap right now, I might say something like 'I've been waiting all day to have your ass in my hands,' and you could reply with 'Matty, you're so big.'" His falsetto brings a reluctant smile to my face. "I like *big, hot, strong* as adjectives. Just an FYI. And then I'd pull you closer so I could nuzzle your neck and say—"

The bell tinkles as the restaurant door opens and four girls walk in. I grab Matty's water and gulp it down. His little tame sampler of dirty talk made me uncomfortably warm. This is exactly why I don't date guys like him. I'd have to take an extra glucose shot every day just to keep up.

The girls must have spotted Matt because they bypass three open tables to walk by ours. As they pass, there's a contest of who can flip her hair over her shoulder the hardest. I swear the last two eyefuck him so hard, it's a wonder they make it to their own table upright.

To his credit, he's more interested in the yogurt and tofu the wait-ress delivered.

"This is tofu?" he asks enthusiastically between giant bites. It only takes two for the entire thing to disappear into his mouth. He wipes off his mouth before telling me, "Tom Brady eats a lot of vegan dishes during the season. Says it keeps him healthy. I should try more of this stuff. I didn't realize it tasted so good."

I'm partly relieved the food has distracted him from his discourse on dirty talking but also partly disappointed. He's...well, dammit, fun to talk to. Ugh. Why? Why can't I smoosh Keith and Matt together? Matty's personality with Keith's safe and quiet attractiveness?

I eat my soup, which somehow tastes better than it ever has before, and I know it's not because there's a new chef. It's because I'm enjoying myself so much.

He eats all but two of the fries and pushes the plate toward my side of the table. "Let's trade. I want to see if I like squash soup because it sounds disgusting and looks a little like the pureed carrot shit I had to eat as a baby."

We exchange dishes, but I don't eat anything. Instead I watch as he uses my spoon to taste the soup. He pulls the spoon from his mouth with a pop, and I swear my entire body starts tingling. "Mmm. Good. A little spice and a little sweet. Don't know how much of that is you and how much is the soup, though."

This is like foreplay. I'm going to have to douse myself in a glass of water. Under the table, I squeeze my thighs together, but that movement only serves to remind me how little action I've seen downstairs. Between him licking the spoon and telling me he wants to *taste* me, I'm more turned on than I can ever remember being. Which really, really sucks. "Why are you flirting with me?"

He gives me a look that says I can't be that dumb, but apparently I am. I blame it on him. "Because you're smoking hot and I'd like a taste of you directly from the tap." He sets my spoon down. "The better question is, why won't you go out with me? I'm not bragging because there's something between us."

"Where do I start?"

He laughs. He actually laughs at that. "Geez, you have that many. Hold up for a sec. Need to put my big boy pants on."

I roll my eyes. "How about you answer a question of mine?"

"Sure. Shoot."

"Why are you trying so hard?"

"Honestly? Because it's fun."

I raise a brow in pretend confusion, but I know exactly what he means. "Fun?"

Cheerfully, he eats more soup, still using my spoon, before answering. "Haven't had to try this hard in ages. Again, not bragging. It's just the truth. I don't need to work for it anymore. Girls come to me."

"Right, you're *so* not bragging."

"I'm not." He shrugs. That's just how it is." He pauses. "I play football."

"I know." His eyes light up, and I know what he's thinking. I hold up my hand. "I didn't ask around about you. I recognized you after you left last night. Why didn't you tell me you played football?

"It didn't seem important."

"Bullshit. Being a Western State Warrior is a big deal on campus. Girls fall all over themselves to be with you."

"Sure, but is that what kind of guy you think I am? Or maybe the better question is whether you're the type of girl who's impressed by that? Because I don't see it." He arches an eyebrow.

He's got me there. "I'm not impressed by that stuff. It's the other way around, actually."

For the first time tonight, he frowns. "That's why you won't go out with me?"

"You could talk anyone you want into dating you. You could probably sell ice to a polar bear."

"If that's true, why are you still resisting?"

I think about my deal with JR, which was pretty much a non-issue until this moment. Promising to stay away from football players wasn't exactly a sacrifice on my part—I have nothing in common with Ace's teammates, and their lifestyles don't mesh with mine. I'm not a prude or anything, even though Ace has accused me of being one from time to time. Having sex in public isn't my thing. Nor is getting so drunk I can't remember who I slept with the night before. I'm not a party girl. And I'm not interested in party boys.

Matthew Iverson, as attractive and as tempting as he is, definitely falls into party boy category. Or at least I think he does. I mean, he plays for Western—he has to be a party dude, right?

He's also waiting for an answer. I settle on, "You're not my type."

By the way his brows shoot upward, I can see I've surprised him. "You're anti-football or anti-athlete?"

"I've never dated either, so I can't tell you."

"It's not fair that you're anti-football player. It's discriminatory. I'm going to need to speak to the Honors Council about this," he jokes. "Who is your type?"

I toy with the last tofu fry. "I dated Keith, my co-worker at the Brew House."

"Keith?" Matt's forehead furrows as he tries to remember the rather unremarkable Keith. "He looks like a Ken doll. His hair is all—" Matt rubs his hand over his own perfectly mussed black locks.

"He uses a lot of product," I admit.

"So you like metrosexuals?"

"No." It never occurred to me that Keith is a metrosexual, but he did have more products in the bathroom than I do. "I guess I thought he was…" I don't have a better word, so I just say it. "Safe."

I'm kind of embarrassed at how weak my reasoning is. It doesn't sound good stated out loud. I feel my cheeks starting to burn. Scrambling, I try to articulate a few better excuses. "You're funny and attractive and any other girl would be thrilled to be sitting where I am right now." I tip my head toward the table of four girls who still can't tear their eyes away from Matty. "But I'm busy, you look like a lot of effort, and I don't think you're a good risk.

He bobs his head as he considers my defense. "Those are all good reasons, but they don't really apply to me. The busy thing I can buy— hell, I've used that myself. But I look like a lot of effort? And I'm not a good risk? What the hell does that mean?"

I sigh. "You're like a really expensive designer purse. I want it but know a) I can't afford it and b) even if I could I'd be so obsessive about checking the condition that I wouldn't even enjoy it. Plus, everyone else would want to touch it, hold it. Someone might even want to steal it, and that'd be a certain kind of stress I wouldn't want to deal with."

"You're overthinking this, Luce."

"I don't doubt that I am. I look at things from all angles. Every. Single. Angle. Maybe that's weird, but that's what I do." What I have to do. My whole life is about risk assessment. Can I eat this new food or that new food? Can I have one drink or two tonight? Did I get enough rest? Enough walking in today? Will tonight be the night my glucose levels go haywire and my roommates have to call 911 because I'm in a coma? I don't want to explain this to Matt, so I choose a different story. "I'm this way about all of my life decisions, even the small ones. I was breaking out last year because of my shampoo, so I needed to switch. I spent a week researching dozens of different brands. After culling the list to ten, I made up a matrix listing all the ingredients, their function, and the comedogenic rating before settling on one I could still buy at the drugstore but wasn't going to break me out. The process took three weeks."

Matt looks a little winded by my example, so I hit him with another one.

"Remember how hot it was last fall?" He nods. I'm sure he does. Ace cursed about it every day, saying he'd rather play for a cold climate team than a hot one. "My roommates and I went to Lake Wanachakee. There's a little private watering hole on the north side. My roommates, Sutton and Charity, decide to strip down and go skinny-dipping despite the big white sign that says 'No skinny-dipping, punishable by a fine of up to $500.' They yelled for me to get in while I considered all the scenarios of getting arrested, of being dragged down the beach without any clothes on, of how many snakes were in the water. I'd read an article about a woman getting leeches up her girl parts." Matt blanches at this as any sane person would. "And since it wasn't chlorinated, how many people had peed in it? But I was so hot, and the water looked so good."

"Did you do it in the end?" he asks, but he probably knows the answer.

I shake my head. "By the time I decided to take my clothes off, Sutton and Charity were cold and got out."

He sighs. "Sounds like your risk assessments keep you from having fun as opposed to keeping you safe."

"I don't look at it that way. The odds are in my favor. Risky behavior is labeled risky because there's a chance someone is going to get hurt. There's nothing negative with wanting to avoiding being hurt or injuring someone you care about." I find myself explaining my reasoning in elaborate detail. Is it because he looks interested? I wish I could shut up.

"You don't regret not swimming with your friends? Because it kind of sounds like you do. That was a wistful note when you said the water looked so good." He leans toward me again. "How about this. I'll take all the risks and you just come along for the ride."

"Matt, dating isn't the risk. *You're* the risk." I lay down a few bills for my meal. "I'm not unhappy with how I live now. There's nothing wrong with making measured decisions and weighing the risks versus the benefits."

He watches me while I pull on my coat. "You're right that there's nothing wrong with how you're living. I'm not judging that. I'm just saying maybe your life could be happ*ier*. And that sometimes taking a risk gives you big rewards."

"And you're that big reward?"

He smiles wide. "You won't know unless you give me a try."

6

MATTY

"WHAT CRAWLED UP YOUR SHORTS and died?" Hammer bursts into my room the next morning. Hammer isn't happy I've skipped going out with him.

I swivel in my desk chair, hoping my head blocks the computer monitor behind me. "Are you missing me when you go out to the bars? Is it difficult to pick up chicks when I'm not around? I told you that you got to stop using the line about being an advice columnist. That shit isn't attractive."

"Are you studying?" he asks incredulously, ignoring my insults. It's three in the afternoon, and I can smell the booze on him even though he's ten feet away. Granted, it's Friday, and off-season Fridays are meant to be days spent drunk and lazy. "Is this because of the girl that turned you down?"

"Nope. Just trying to keep my head down," I lie. Geez. I'm lying to randoms and to my best friends. The only person I'm being completely honest with is Lucy, and she doesn't want to have anything to do with me.

But I did take away something other than rejection from dinner last night. Lucy's approach to risk-taking is crazy as all get out—who makes an extensive pros and cons list about *shampoo*?—but one thing she'd said had stuck in my mind.

I look at it from all angles. Every. Single. Angle.

Me, I'm a one angle kind of guy. As in, the easiest option available to me. The path of least resistance.

This particular issue needs more finesse. Coach wants me to persuade Ace to give up the *quarterback* position, for fuck's sake. And to persuade the guys—including the offense, who are rabidly loyal to their QB—to support this course of action. They say you can't make an omelet without breaking a few eggs, but in this case, I'm smashing the entire frickin' carton. There's no way to do this without pissing off some, if not all, of my teammates.

And seriously, when did I become the omelet chef in this scenario? I'm not sure I even *want* to be captain, dammit. Responsibility makes the back of my neck itch. I'd much rather be one of the happy, oblivious sheep than the stressed-out shepherd who has to guide them.

Except…the thing is, I can't say no, not when it comes to football. This sport is in my blood. I live and breathe it. I'm good at it. And, corny as it sounds, I think I was *meant* for it.

I wasn't ever supposed to play football. I'd been born prematurely, with a weak heart, having been nourished for the last twenty or so weeks in the womb by only a tiny bit of placenta. The rest had detached from the uterine wall. I was lucky to be alive.

My mom coddled me, and my dad watched me with worried eyes. I didn't look like I could run a mile, let alone deliver a hard hit, until I was fifteen.

Somewhere along the line, I shot up like an unchecked weed. Filled out. Starting lifting and took to football as if I were weaned on Gatorade and leather.

One reason I'm so good on the football field is my uncanny instinct to know exactly which weakness I can exploit in the easiest, most economical way, ensuring that my hits at the end of the game are as hard as the ones at the beginning. Part of it comes from hours of film study, which helps me to immediately recognize what play is going to be run based on the position of the offensive players. The other part is God-given talent.

I operate the same way off the field. I don't have to analyze or over-think the dilemma but just pick the solution that makes the problem go away the fastest. There's no film study for life. Or if there is, I haven't found it.

This is why, for the last four hours, I've been watching videos of Mr. Texas. The captain's patch is currently burning a hole in my desk drawer, but I don't want the captaincy bad enough to dick over my quarterback. I might not always love what Ace does on the field. There've been a few games when the offense couldn't generate more than thirteen points and made the load on the defense fucking hard. And even though we won those games, a few of us grumbled under our breath. But thinking you'd like to kick your quarterback in the ass is one thing; doing it is entirely different.

Hammer studies me and comes to some inebriated conclusion that requires him to drag my reading chair from by the window over to the desk.

He folds his hands and gives me a serious look. "Do you have a fucking test or something? You can't be failing any classes yet. The semester just started two weeks ago."

"I'm not failing anything. You smell like you took a bath in a tub of vodka, Hammer." I wave a hand in front of my nose. "Where were you?"

He lifts his shirt and sniffs. "Fuck, I can't smell anything. Do I really stink, because I got a girl coming over in"—he checks his phone—"ninety minutes."

"Then you best go take a shower." Anything to get him out of here.

"Nah, I mean, if you got a problem, brother, then I can meet up with this chick later." He types something into his phone and looks up at me with bleary eyes.

Damn, he's a good friend, and frankly, I need someone to share this shit with. As soon as this recruit signs his intent papers, it's going to be all over the news anyway. But…I'd rather talk to a sober Hammer. It's hard to tell with him. His capacity for alcohol is kind of shocking.

"How much of your stink is from your drinking and how much is just from you rolling around on the floor of the Tau Omega house?"

He throws up his size fifteens onto the desk, and I push them off. "I had four shots."

Four shots is sober for Hammer. I wheel away from desk and turn around. "Come here."

He leans over, one hand braced against the desk. "Please tell me we're watching porn."

"With you hovering over me like a mother on her first recruiting visit? I'm not even going to watch a cooking video with you this close."

"Mmm. You know I love me some Giada De Laurentiis. That chick is a fucking goddess."

"Swear to God, you touch your dick right now and I'm going to punch you in the nuts." I click through my list of previously played videos and pick the one where Mr. Texas played the worst. He only passed for 240 yards that game, and his team only won by twenty-two points. Only.

Hammer makes a grunt of annoyance when the video starts playing. "Shit, son, are you so bored during the off-season that you've resorted to watching highlights of North Arlington High? This is what you're blowing me off for? Jerking off to some high school player in Texas—" He stops talking when the quarterback slides out of the defender's grip, steps up into the pocket and releases an arrow thirty yards downfield off his back foot. "Wait, what did I just see?"

I reach back and try to massage some of the tension out of my neck. The tightness appeared midway through Coach Lowe's lecture and hasn't left me since. "We're not scouts, Hammer. We play the game someone else has invented. We take the playbook, study our opponents, and then try to make them cry on Saturdays. That's the full extent of what we're supposed to do, right?"

"I guess?" he says cautiously. "I mean, we study film, so in a way we're scouting the opponent." He peers over my shoulder again to stare at the screen. The smell of souring vodka is too much, so I push away from the desk and start pacing.

Hammer begins cycling through the videos. After five minutes of total silence, he jerks to his feet. "Let's get Darryl and Masters in here."

"Masters isn't on the team anymore," I point out. Masters's early declaration for the draft makes him ineligible to play another down, so the lucky bastard doesn't have to deal with this. Instead, he's training like a demon so that he kills it at the combine in April.

"Yeah, but like you said, we aren't talent scouts. Let's get some other eyes on this."

There's no point in protesting because Hammer's out the door by his last word, yelling for Masters and Darryl, our nose tackle, to come up.

Masters appears first. His new wife must be busy because usually they're in Masters's upstairs apartment trying to break some kind of record for most sex in a twenty-four-hour period. Masters was a virgin before he and Ellie hooked up, and now he's trying to make up for all those lost years. It's a miracle Ellie can walk.

Masters claps his hands together. "Heard you were holed up in your bedroom for two nights running, so either your pipes are getting backed up or you have some girl stashed under the bed. And I have to tell you that the type of girl willing to live under your bed for days at a time is the type that will kill you in your sleep."

"Is this from personal experience? If so, I want to be the first to tell you that it was nice knowing you and I hope you're okay with me comforting Ellie after your unfortunate passing."

Masters gives me a death glare. "I'm going to kill you right now, asshole. Right now."

"Hold up," Hammer says from the doorway. "No killing until after we watch these videos."

"What's up? We playing a game?" Darryl appears, eyes bloodshot and feet unsteady.

Yeah, it's called *Rip the heart out of your starting quarterback.*

Masters points to each of us. "Seems to me if I lay waste to all of you, I can avoid watching game film and go upstairs to—"

"My wife," we all chorus in unison.

He's addicted to calling Ellie his wife. It's mildly irritating, but Masters couldn't give a fuck. He's always marched to the beat of his own drum.

"What're we watching?"

"This." I start playing the videos. The guys crowd around the monitor while I watch them. Their expressions turn from *slight boredom* to *interest* to *this guy is the greatest thing since Joe Montana drank his chicken noodle soup at halftime and went out and scored three touchdowns*. Video after video plays, each showcasing Mr. Texas's perfect passes, his pocket sense, his rocket arm, and his ability to elude the defense.

"Was that an eighty-yard pass?" Hammer asks.

"Did he just get by five tacklers?" Masters wonders. "I know this is high school ball, but that Houdini act of his is ridiculous."

"That run got me hard," Darryl groans.

"Me too," Hammer agrees.

"Dick's in hand," Masters confirms.

Finally, Hammer pushes away. "Someone shut that porn off. I can only get so erect."

He collapses on the bed and looks at the ceiling. Darryl looks confused, but Masters catches on right away.

"Is Coach recruiting this kid?" He jerks a thumb at the computer screen.

"Has recruited. Has a commitment. Wants me to smooth his path."

"What about Ace?" asks Darryl. He's not the brightest crayon in the box, but he is one of the best run busters in the country.

Masters strokes his chin. "Recruit has a better arm than Ace. Makes decent decisions on the field. Ace's primary skill is not making mistakes, keeping a cool head, and seeing the short option down the field."

Last year, the few explosive, big-time passes came courtesy of our running back, Ahmed Strong, who averaged eleven yards after the catch—meaning he caught short passes and muscled his way down the field for a ton of extra yards.

"We wouldn't have won the National title without Ace." I feel the need to defend him. He is our quarterback, after all. "He's smart and had only a few fumbles and a handful of interceptions."

"But the strength of the Warrior team is in this room," Masters points out. "And you lost two starting offensive linemen who are being replaced by sophomores and juniors."

We all fall silent. Last year's team had seven first team All-Americans, six of whom were on the defense. Ahmed was the only decorated offensive player. The new offensive line might be even worse than it was this year.

But we won last year because our defense didn't allow people to score. We were big and mean and tough up front, so Ace didn't need to be a superstar. We needed him to hold on to the ball, not turn it over too often, and make a few first downs. He did all that.

Introducing a high octane offense might change our dynamic, change the whole makeup of our team. I'm not convinced it's the right move.

"What's this got to do with you?" Darryl asks.

I exchange a grim look with Masters. He gives me a sympathetic glance but remains silent, his eyes telling me this is my show now.

The defensive unit operates near flawlessly because we're so tuned into each other. When one person is out of sync, like the time that Masters and Ellie were fighting and he played like utter shit, we struggle. If we want to repeat as National Championship winners next year, we need to work as one unit.

That means everyone has to support the choice of quarterback.

I give my neck one last squeeze and then drop my hands to my sides. "Coach is going to make this change regardless of whether we're on board, but he wants us to be supportive. I think if the team stood behind Ace, Coach wouldn't start this guy. He'd let Ace play until we lost. And when we lose, the loss will be on our shoulders and not his." Masters nods in agreement. I continue for Darryl and Hammer, in case they haven't fully grasped what a shit show our team could turn into. "Coach wants me to persuade Ace to move so that the switch from him to the new guy is bloodless. No unhappy, anonymous leaks; no sock puppet forum posts; no rumors of locker room dissension."

"Why not move Ace to backup?" Hammer asks.

I sigh because I don't know for sure. "Coach didn't share his reasoning with me, but if I had to guess, this is a way to make nice for Ace. He still plays, plus he positions himself better for the draft. No one is drafting Ace at the QB position."

Everyone falls silent because while we all know it's true, it's not the kind of thing we like saying out loud.

"The minute Mr. Texas announces, all those sports guys are going to be talking about what this means for our future anyway," Darryl points out, finally catching on.

"Not if Ace is willing to move to safety. No controversy, just a celebration." Which is what Coach wants. Even though the screen has gone dark, the plays the high school quarterback made keep running through my mind. I make one last-ditch effort at convincing my friends that Mr. Texas is not the golden child. "We watched an admittedly great high school player, but so what? Every starter on Western was the best high school player in their division. Good high school stats mean squat in college."

The guys all exchange looks and then Hammer speaks first. "You got to do it, man. An arm like that, even on a true freshman, could be the difference between a perfect season and a one-loss season. With our defense and an awesome quarterback, we would be unbeatable."

Darryl nods slowly. The idea of having a little less pressure on the defense is appealing. "We should at least give him a chance. Have them fight it out during the summer."

"A quarterback controversy?" Hammer balks. "Who are you—Rex Ryan?"

"The noise level would be insane. Press would be contacting all of you guys nonstop about which quarterback you supported. Emails. DMs. You don't want that kind of distraction," Masters says. He turns to me. "You're the signal caller for the defense now. You gotta call this one."

"Coach hasn't said that'll be my responsibility," I object. I haven't even decided it should be my responsibility regardless of what Masters is trying to silently project.

The videos have started replaying, but I've watched about as much

Mr. Texas as I can stomach. I reach over and flick the computer off.

"I gotta go shit and shower," Hammer announces and rolls his rank carcass off my bed. "I'm a worker bee. Tell me which target to destroy and it's gone. But I'm for Mr. Texas. Ace will come around." At the door, he pauses, "Either way, I've got your back."

"Same," Darryl declares and disappears with Hammer. Only Masters remains.

"You know you gotta do this," he tells me.

"No, I don't know anything." I find my wallet and stick it into my back pocket. The room is stifling. I need to get out of here.

"Matty, you gotta be the leader here."

"Why?"

Masters gives me a perturbed look. "Sophomore year we played Penn. We were set for a blitzing play, but I ended up intercepting the ball. Why?"

"When we got to the line, the offensive was set up for a dig route across the middle by the slot receiver. Blitzing would have put our guys out of position."

"Right. You came over to me and we changed it up. Had four men rush the quarterback. I dropped back, and the ball landed in my hands.

"

"You ran it back for a touchdown." I grin. That was a good play.

"Because you recognized the offensive play. I didn't. I have great natural talent, but you memorize the game. We sit in film and you see it once and it's imprinted in your head. That's why the defense is going to follow you."

"I don't want that. I don't want that kind of responsibility."

"Too bad," he says unsympathetically.

"This isn't even leadership," I scowl. "It's mutiny."

Masters tries a different tack. "You once told me your favorite character from your favorite series was the bad guy who'd done a heinous deed because it helped save the world."

I pause with one arm shoved into my winter coat and glare at my friend. "That's fucking low, Masters. Real fucking low. I was drunk off my ass when I told you that story."

"I know," he says unrepentantly. "Don't change the facts, though."

7

LUCY

"YOU GRABBED THE STEERING WHEEL as the ice resurfacer took off?" Heather Bell asks, her voice heavy with disbelief.

In the chair we designated as the witness seat, Emily Hartwig nods with pretend wariness and probably very real confusion since Heather is not supposed to be cross-examining her.

"Is that a yes?" I mutter under my breath. Heather misses her cue, though, and stands, forgetting that all non-verbal responses have to be verbalized or it's not part of the appealable record. It's something we're specifically scored on in competitions. I hold my breath. Please tell me she's not going to approach without—

"Let me show you what you said in your deposition," Heather says and swishes her way across the fake courtroom floor.

Beside me, Randall groans. Heather whips around with a glare hot enough to make the papers in front of us burst into flames.

"What did I do wrong this time, Mr. Perfect?"

Randall rests his fists against the surface of the table, looking ready to spring out of his chair and launch himself at Heather. "How long do we have because that entire line of questioning is completely insane.

Emily is our client. We don't cross-examine our own client."

"Randall, she's new," I remind him. The last thing we need is for Heather to blow her top, too. In the four practices we've had since the semester started, these two have been at each other's throats, rendering the whole team tense and unhappy. Regionals are in the middle of March, right before Spring Break, and none of us is going to make it to the tournament at this rate. We'll have clawed each other to death well before then. It'll be our own version of the Valentine's Day Massacre.

"Are you sure you're Paul Bell's daughter? Surely he would have taught you something," Randall remarks snidely. I kick him under the table, and that earns me an unhappy look.

On the makeshift witness stand, Emily's once perky brown hair lies limply around her face. She's wearing the same expression we're all sporting—tired and defeated. She's been up there for the last thirty minutes, while Heather has tried to work her way through a direct examination—something she'll be required to complete error-free in under eight minutes at competition.

The rest of our mock trial team shifts impatiently behind us. It's time to call it a night even though we achieved nothing productive.

I get to my feet. "We've been at this for two hours. Why don't we adjourn for tonight and we'll take it up again in two days?"

"Hopefully Miss Bell will practice in those two days. Maybe read a few of our materials on how to conduct an examination?" Randall sneers.

Heather's response is predictably tart in return. "At least I actually bring some emotion to this dead room. Your opening was so monotone that five minutes felt like five years. Plus, do you have any clothes that don't scream tacky? Hand to God, I've seen mannequins at the Salvation Army tricked out in better clothes than you have on."

Beneath his dark skin, Randall blanches and turns ashy pale. Heather's good at dishing out insults like this. And Randall, a scholarship student like me, readily takes the bait. "If only you'd inherited some actual skill from your dad instead of just his wallet."

When Heather opens her mouth to deliver another cutting remark, I jump in. "All right. We don't need to snap at each other. I think we're tired, hungry, and just need a break. Heather, if you could, there's a set of sample questions in the original packet that show the difference between cross and direct. I can resend them to you via email if you want." Hell, I'd write the entire examination if she'd agree to memorize and read it, but any time I've hinted at offering help, she shuts me down. "Randall, Heather's new to this. We've got ten weeks, and I'm sure we're all going to make mistakes between now and the Regionals, so let's give each other room to make them. Patience." I give them both a smile.

Randall's a stellar attorney-in-training. He's sharp witted, quick on his feet, and can deliver a rousing argument. We need him. But we need Heather, too, because despite her inexperience, her tryout was the best we've seen since...well, our freshman year. Once Randall's blood stops roaring in his ears, he'll remember why we chose Heather in the first place.

I made out an extensive risk assessment spreadsheet—even factoring in that Heather was inexperienced—and Randall had agreed with every item on the list. I guess I weighted her father's influence too heavily, though.

"Pack it up," I tell the rest of the crew, who gratefully shove their materials into their backpacks and scoot out of the borrowed class-room.

"Thanks," Emily murmurs as she passes by the desks Randall and I pushed together to form our attorney table. "I was dying up there."

"No problem. You did well. You looked vulnerable and victimized. The judges will love you."

Our mock trial matches are judged by a panel of three individuals, usually attorneys in the community where the competition takes place. They score us on everything from correct courtroom procedure to wit-ness demeanor and believability. After two straight years of losing in Regionals to Central, Randall and I were determined to field a winning team.

We recruited students from the theatre department to play our wit-nesses, and we were going to ask Riley Hart, a Poli-Sci pre-law major to be our third attorney, but then Heather tried out and the closing argu-ment she delivered in the tryouts nearly moved Coach Jensen to tears.

After Heather explained she had a lot of experience with the law and that her father was the famous Paul Bell, there was no question who was going to fill the third attorney spot.

Bell's a criminal defense lawyer hired by athletes, politicians, and actors whenever they get accused of doing something wrong. He actu-ally got an athlete out of a robbery charge by claiming the football team had coerced him and he was under undue duress. I may have been a little star struck when Heather was talking to me. Yeah, I definitely put too much weight on the whole "daughter of Paul Bell" thing.

I pause while putting my things away. Is it possible my risk assess-ment toward Matty—I mean *Matt*, because we are not on nickname terms—also includes incorrectly weighted items? Not all football players are horndogs. Ahmed, one of Ace's closest friends on the team, is seriously devoted to his girlfriend. And didn't one of the Warriors actually get married last month? That's serious grown-up stuff.

"You forget something?" Randall asks as he wrestles one of the desks back into position.

I look up in mild surprise. I'd forgotten where I was for a moment. "Nope. Let me help you with that." I have to get Matt Iverson out of my head.

We finish tidying up the room, putting all the desks and chairs back into their uniform rows while Heather inspects her nails by the door. I try not to let that irritate me. Randall, on the other hand? He huffs and puffs and sighs the entire time, which is annoying in its own way.

Once we're done and I've worked up an unfortunate sweat under my button-down, Heather saunters over to run a finger along a desk.

"I think this isn't quite straight." She shoves it lightly with her hip.

Randall releases a growl from the back of his throat while I bite back a snarky retort. Taking a deep breath, I try again to play peacemaker.

"Did you need something, Heather?" I'm not sure why she's hanging around.

She shrugs, a delicate movement. Heather is very pretty. In fact, if she wasn't so intent on being an attorney, she'd have done a great job as our jaywalking victim who got struck by a car. "Not particularly. I was wondering, though, how it was decided that you'd be in charge, Lucinda?"

I school my features into an impassive expression, not wanting her to know that I hate being called by my full name. I've told her at least twice that I prefer to be called Lucy, but since she continues to call me Lucinda, my guess is she's trying to get every last dig in wherever she can. "I'm not in charge. Coach Jensen is." Coach Jensen is a local trial attorney who volunteers her time to train us.

"But you put the team together. You were the contact person on the sign-up sheet for this elective." She rubs her finger along the side of the desk, looking sweet and innocent, but I've spent two weeks with this girl and it's been long enough to realize that sweet and innocent is an act Heather adopts when she wants something.

"Randall lost his cellphone so it made sense for me to put mine on there while he was getting it replaced," I explain.

"That's convenient for you, isn't it?"

I glance over at Randall because I have no idea where she's going with this. Randall's expression is one of confusion, too.

"I don't know if I'd say it was convenient. I had to field a hundred calls and about a quarter of them were crank ones that asked me if the try out was for my ass."

Heather smirks. "You're still in charge. The others in the group listen to you."

"None of us is in charge. We're all working together toward the same goal. You told me last fall when you tried out that you wanted to join to help us defeat Central and hopefully go on and win Nationals," I remind her.

"See, that's why I'm worried."

"About what?" I shoulder my backpack, wishing I had escaped with the rest of the team, but that would mean leaving Randall and Heather alone, and I was afraid if that happened, only one would be alive for our next practice.

"I'm wondering whether we've assembled the right pieces for the team. You're good as an administrative point person. You know, signing us up, getting us the schedule, passing out the materials, but you really don't have the killer instinct a lawyer needs." Ouch. But her ability to accurately hit at all of our insecurities after just a short time means she'll be really good in competition, I remind myself. Heather keeps going, "I'm going to ask my father to come and evaluate the talent. He can coordinate with Ms. Jensen. They belong to the same club."

"We've already set the roster. Why would we change it now?"

"So that we can win." She states the words as if the answer is obvious.

I grit my teeth, but Randall's had enough. "Lucy is the best attorney on our team."

She arches a perfectly shaped eyebrow. "If Lucinda is so amazing, why isn't she doing either the opening or closing? Why am I, someone you say has no experience and no skill, delivering the closing? Isn't that the most important role of the whole team? We can hide the weak link between the two of us." She drags her eyes down Randall's perfectly fine outfit once again. "But if you don't dress better, no one is taking us seriously."

With that last arrow, she spins on her heel and walks away.

"I can buy a suit, but you can't buy class," Randall yells after her.

"Might want to brush up on your insults," Heather calls casually over her shoulder. "That one's older than your shoes."

"I got these shoes last year."

"From Goodwill?"

I step in front of Randall as he lunges toward the doorway Heather just exited.

"It's not worth it," I tell him.

"We can't have her on the team. She's a cancer," Randall rages, pulling away from me and straightening his sweater in a huff. "Don't you care that she basically called you incompetent?"

I shift uncomfortably because, while Heather's words stung, I don't know if she was entirely wrong. I mean, I'm not incompetent, but isn't part of competence knowing your limits? "I thought you were sitting right beside me when I crashed and burned our freshman year?"

Randall clicks his tongue in sympathy. "It was a mistake. You froze. We've all had a similar experience once in our lives. When I was in eighth grade speech class, I couldn't get more than two words out in rebuttal."

"Randall?"

"Yeah?" He smiles brightly.

"You're not helping." I squeeze his shoulder. "I don't like the way she says it, but we both know where my skill set lies and it isn't with on-the-fly exposition needed for a good closing argument. And you hate doing rebuttals, so we needed a closer. We all agreed she was the best of everyone who tried out."

He makes a face. "You could do it if you wanted to."

"Then I guess my answer is I don't want to." I'd rather suffer a hundred insults than have to stand up and speak for ten minutes straight while everyone sitting in the audience picks apart every single word I've said wrong. Been there, done that, failed epically.

"You need to keep that bitch in check," Randall says. He pulls on his winter coat in sharp, exaggerated movements. He doesn't want me to miss that he's pissed off. As if it wasn't obvious. But, I suppose his dramatics are partly why he's so engaging.

"It'll be fine," I soothe. "Once she gets the hang of things, you'll be thrilled."

"She better," he says ominously.

"Or what?" I ask, losing my patience. "You'll quit?"

"Maybe." He sticks his nose in the air, looking every inch like Heather as he waltzes out the door. I should videotape him next time so he sees exactly how similar the two are. I want to throw a pencil at his head.

Between the stress of mock trial and the conundrum of Matt Iverson, I'm going to worry myself into an early grave. Could one thing go my way? Just one?

* * *

I'm still worrying about both topics when I show up to my shift at the Brew House the next day. At least with mock trial, we have weeks of practice to work out the kinks. With Matt, I fear the only way to exorcise him is to move across the country and enter a nunnery. He's popping up in my dirty fantasies far too often. This morning I got up early because I feared if I stayed one more minute in bed, I'd call him and beg him to come over to help me work off some of my tension.

Which is why I'm thirty minutes early for work. I quickly discover this is a good thing, because a familiar figure is waiting for me when I walk in.

JR "Ace" Anderson rises from his table and greets me with his trademark ladies' man grin.

"Hey, Lucy."

I bustle over and give him a big hug. "When did you get back?"

"Just this morning."

Ace doesn't get the holidays off, so after the Championship game, he flew to his dad's place in Massachusetts for a week. His parents have been divorced since he was ten. I still remember when he found out. He showed up at my front door after school and wouldn't leave until my dad let him in. I'd been at band practice. When I got home, Ace was lying on my bed and his face was wet from crying.

I didn't say a word, just picked up my bike helmet. He followed me out and we biked for two hours around the city. I've never seen him cry again.

Ace and I, we're tied together by our family history. It's not pretty and, for a time there, the only people we had to lean on were each other. Besides my dad, Ace is the one steady thing in my life, so even though I find him exasperating and a little too arrogant nowadays, I still care for the big lug.

"How's your dad?"

"Same old." The two have a rocky relationship but at least they talk, unlike my mom and me. Ace claims the only reason his dad wants to connect now is because he thinks Ace is going to be a rich NFL player. I don't think Ace is entirely wrong. "Had some interviews with the local Boston stations. Kind of a 'hometown boy done good' sort of thing."

"You didn't grow up in Boston," I point out.

"Who cares? It was fun."

He is really loving the post-win attention. "I got to give my NFL Super Bowl picks. We talked about the draft."

"Was your dad there?"

"Yup. He was like a kid at Christmas."

I bet. "Everything else going well? No one gave you any shit for missing a week of classes?"

"Lucy," Ace chides. "I just won the National Championship. No one is giving me shit over anything."

"Good. Because I need to take advantage of your good mood."

"Sure. What do you need?"

"I'm getting kicked out of my apartment on Tuesday. Mind if I stay at your place? I can sleep on the sofa."

"No problem." His eyes warm up as he pulls out a small, wrapped gift. "Happy belated Christmas."

"You already gave me a present," I object. We exchanged gifts on Christmas Eve at my dad's house. Dad and I went in together to get Ace a nice pair of sunglasses. He'd been complaining all fall that the ones he had were low rent and janky. The school supplies him with endless athletic gear, all the shoes he wants, and he got some sweet gifts for going to the bowl game the previous year, but not one pair of sunglasses.

Ace gave me a pair of gold hoop earrings. I think his mom picked them out, but they were nice. I wish I had worn them today.

"I didn't pay for it, so it doesn't really count." Ace's job is football, so he doesn't have a lot of extra cash around, which makes me really curious about the gift. I slide a fingernail under the tape and pop it open, careful not to tear the paper.

"Come on, Lucy. It's just newspaper," he scolds.

"I can't help it." It's some old newspaper but it's still wrapping. As I lift off the paper, I gasp in surprise. It's a pair of cordless headphones—a very expensive pair. I know this because it was a selection in a catalog of items that one of the bowl sponsors was allowed to gift the players as a thank you for playing in the bowl. "Ace, what is this?"

He grins. "I know you were saying how you hated wearing your headphones because the cords get tangled in your hair."

"You should have picked something for yourself." The generosity of this gift makes me uneasy. The echo of Sutton's teasing voice tickles at the back of my brain. *Besides, Ace made that stupid pact up so he can keep you to himself.* I'd scoffed at her then, but I don't feel so sure now.

"I did. I picked the same pair. The voucher was enough to get two pair."

"I thought you were getting a television." We actually discussed this. He showed me the brochure, pointed to the 42" flat screen, and said it would look great in his room. I agreed.

"There are plenty of guys with televisions in the house." He shrugs. "It's non-returnable, so don't make a big deal out of it, yeah?"

I can see he's uncomfortable, too, so I tuck the headphones away in my bag and lean over to kiss him on the cheek. Halfway there, I think better of it and reach over and squeeze his arm instead. "Thank you."

Ace gives me a crooked grin as if he knows I changed my mind midflight, but thankfully he doesn't ask me about it. He's probably relieved. "So how's mock trial going?"

I take the change of subject and run with it. "It's not. We're sucking right now. That new girl, Heather, is killing us. I thought for sure that she'd have picked up on some trial procedures from her dad, but it's like she doesn't even know he is a lawyer. I feel like I've made a bargain with the devil. I can't handle her, and Randall is livid at nearly everything that comes out of her mouth."

"That bad, huh?"

"You have no idea."

"Send her over to the field house. We'll whip her into shape. Although…" Ace trails off, looking momentarily troubled.

"Although what?" I prompt.

"Coach is acting kind of weird. I went in there to do a few sets before class and ran into him. He kind of mumbled hello into his hand and took off."

I make a sympathetic noise. Ace has always complained that his relationship with Coach wasn't what he wished it could be. I told him that maybe he shouldn't sleep with Stella Lowe, the coach's daughter. Ace brushed me off, saying that no one knew.

Given how many times *I* saw them together, and I don't even hang out at the Gas Station or where Ace lives, I figured he was wrong, but Ace is so darned hard-headed. You can't get him to change his mind once he's convinced he's right about something. Even if you shove all the facts in the world into his face, he'll still believe what he wants to believe.

"Coach probably doesn't know what to do with himself now that he can't yell at you guys to do push-ups."

"Is that what you think we do at practice?" he teases. "Endless amounts of push-ups?"

"Who knows? I ask you what you're doing during the season and the answer is always 'working out' or 'lifting.'"

"Fair enough," he grins. "What's been going on with you besides hating mock trial? You know, you are allowed to quit things you don't enjoy."

"You hate football sometimes, and I don't see you quitting."

Ace raises an eyebrow. "I've never hated football."

"Yeah, well I don't hate mock trial either. I love it." I love putting the pieces of the puzzle together and drafting up the arguments and questions and answers. It's the extemporaneous speaking part I struggle with. "Even if I didn't love it, my scholarship depends on me being part of the team. And if I'm going to be part of the team, we're going to be good."

Ace nods. One thing we both enjoy is winning, which is why the last couple of years have been kind of a downer for me. Maybe that's why I'm so interested in Matt Iverson.

He's fun to be around and when I'm with him, I don't dwell on how crappy my mock trial is going or how I have to shoot myself up with insulin twice a day because my body doesn't make it or how I was forced to spend Christmas with my mother and her current boyfriend. He was the third guy she'd dated this year. I didn't realize how many over-forty single men there are out there. Although, my mother doesn't limit herself to single men. That'd be too silly.

So it isn't a great surprise that I find myself asking Ace about Matt even though I know the topic will bring out a great deal of scowls and lectures. But his phone number is burning a hole in my head, and I'm afraid if I don't use it, I might suffer some permanent head trauma. "I ran into one of your teammates the other day. He was in here. You spreading the word about our great coffee?"

"Hell no. I keep this place a secret." Ace looks almost serious, almost…pissed off that one of the Warrior football players has dared step foot into the Brew House. "Which one?"

As nonchalantly as possible, I say, "Matt Iverson."

Saying his name out loud conjures up all the shivery feelings he roused in me. He was so much fun to talk with, and his offer to show me risks, to take all the risks so I could just go along for the ride…God, I want to test out his verbal skills. I hope I'm not blushing.

"That hound? I hope he didn't say anything to you. Ives can't walk by a vagina without wanting to test it out," Ace says crudely. It takes me a second to realize he calls Matt by the nickname of Ives. These boys and their constant nicknames. What's wrong with their given names?

"He did ask me out," I admit.

"And you turned him down, of course." He smiles. "I shouldn't worry. I know you can take care of yourself."

I ignore the compliment and latch on to the *of course*. "Of course? Why, of course?"

First Sutton and Charity and now Ace? Am I that predictable? Actually, yes, I am that predictable. And that used to be okay. Why does it bother me now?

"Because there are rules, Lucy. There's a locker room rule of no dating girlfriends or sisters."

"But I'm not either your girlfriend or your sister," I object.

"Close enough." He waves his hand as if semantics aren't important here, and I suppose Ace and I have been friends for so long we are as close as brother and sister. "Besides, even if there wasn't a locker room rule, which there is, we made a deal."

"Would it really be a big deal if I broke it?" I don't know why I ask because I have no intention of using Matt's number, no matter how many times I've punched it into the keypad only to erase it. "Not that I want to," I say, not sure if my words are meant to reassure Ace or myself. "I'm just asking out of curiosity."

"Absolutely," he says firmly with a frown on his face. "Because if you dated one of them, I'd have to kill them.

"Why? You always say you'd take a bullet for your teammates."

"Yeah, I would. But if one of them broke my best friend's heart? I'd be the one pulling the trigger." He leans forward. "How many times have I told you? The guys on the team are no good."

"They can't be all bad."

My lack of agreement only makes Ace frown harder. "You're a nice girl. You don't hang out at the Gas Station and you're not a jersey chaser. You're not built for the one-night stands that these girls are looking for."

"There's nothing wrong with one-night stands. Nice girls do plenty of one-night stands," I object. "I've had them and they aren't any better or worse than sex in a long-term relationship."

Ace winces. "Can we not talk about your sex life?"

If possible, his frown lines become even more prominent, which makes me laugh. "I love how you suddenly turn prudish when the subject is me having sex. I'm not a virgin."

"If you say so." He glowers, making me chuckle even more. "Look, Lucy, just because the guys are good teammates doesn't make them good boyfriends. These guys get offered so much pussy that they don't know how to treat a girl right. They don't have to. They just need to whip their dick out and the girls are fighting to be the one to jump on it."

Now I'm wincing because that's an ugly picture of both the guys and the girls involved. But somehow I get the sense that Ace is speaking from actual experience, so I feel even grodier. The thing is, Matt didn't come off that way. As he pointed out, he didn't play the football card when he so easily could have, when it had such good results in the past.

"Iverson didn't seem like a dog. He was kind of nice."

Ace snorts. "Yeah, he's real nice. Here, let me show you how nice he is to girls."

My heart lurches, because I don't like the disgust in Ace's eyes. And I'm worried when he pulls out his phone. He scrolls through a #WarriorsWin hashtag, and while there are pictures of the players celebrating a touchdown, there are also plenty of pictures showing Matt Iverson kissing many, many, many girls. So many different ones I start to get dizzy. #WarriorsWin clearly has more than one meaning to the Warrior faithful.

"He's fully clothed," I point out, but it's a weak attempt to make what I'm seeing less...sleazy, I guess. But damn it, I didn't get a sleazy vibe from him at all. He didn't look at other girls in the restaurant even once. The waitress practically tried to rub her tits into his nose, but his attention was focused solely on me.

The picture of Matt constructed from my interaction with him is entirely different than the one that Ace has painted, but truthfully, didn't I really believe, deep down, that Matt's interest in me was shallow and would last no longer than one night, maybe two? That's why he's got so many checkmarks in the risk column. I add another one there, just to be on the safe side.

Ace tugs on a hank of my hair. "Stay away from Iverson, Lucy. Promise me that. I don't want to spend the off-season worrying about you."

"I will." The words sound unconvincing to me, but Ace looks pacified.

Inwardly, I worry that I'll be breaking promises all over the place. To Ace, and most importantly, to myself.

8

MATTY

THE WEEKEND IS SHOT TO shit. I have no interest in smoking weed, drinking myself into a coma, or getting laid, and end up taking long walks around campus. I find myself outside the Brew House several times and looking up at different apartment complexes wondering if Lucy's inside.

For some reason, I failed to get her number. For some reason, I still want it. I've never pursued a girl in my life, and I don't even know if this is the time to start, particularly with all the team shit going down.

What do I even know of this girl, other than that she eats tofu, works at a coffee shop, and has puppy dog eyes I keep seeing when I close mine. And she's risk averse.

I need some of her analyzation skills right now. We could make a pro/con assessment of Ace moving or me sticking my nose into the whole mess as Coach ordered me to. And then, after I've worked it out on paper, we could release some tension between the sheets.

I've got a lot of built-up tension. Coach and me exchanged terse words about my conditioning on Saturday, which is complete and utter bullshit because I work harder in the weight room than anyone on defense. I'm there every day of the week, even during the off-season, for frickin' sake. Coach Benson, the linebacker coach, had to come over and drag me away before I said anything stupid.

Coach's words had zero to do with my lifting and everything to do with the fact that I haven't persuaded Ace to move to safety. Shit, it's been less than a week. I know that National Signing Day, the day that all the top recruits announce their college choices, is only a few weeks away, but give a guy a moment to breathe.

I went to the Gas Station with Hammer on Friday and Saturday nights, just to settle him down and so I can report back to Coach that I at least carried out part one of his directives. Arms folded, I stood in the middle of the bar and glared at all my teammates.

Hammer told me to pick a girl and leave because I was bringing everyone down. But being the heavy hand was the point.

And no one did anything stupid under my watch that night. No bathroom sex. No under-the-table hand action. No shot-drinking challenges. The team ended up going home early, taking the party—and the women—with them.

I went, too, but alone, because there wasn't one girl in the place who made my dick move. Apparently my dick likes rejection because it gets hard when I think about Lucy, when I stand outside of the Brew House, but not when hot babes wearing down-to-fuck dresses are batting their eyelashes at me.

I swear to God, the scent of coffee Hammer was brewing this morning had me mooning about her. Jacking off to a girl I exchanged a few words with at a coffee shop is a new one for me.

The only thing to do is talk to her again. I can admit when I'm hung up on something. After all, I have no problem admitting I love football, and I really don't have a problem with being drawn to one particular girl. The only issue is that she views me as a bad risk.

So how am I overcoming that?

My sour mood follows me all the way to the weight room and then plummets into my feet when I spot Ace working out.

There are only a few people even up this early on a Sunday. Some are at church, but most of them are hung over or even still drunk from last night's revelries. I like that we're keeping it close to home, so it didn't bother me to wade through a mess of bodies, beer cans, and pizza boxes. No cop is going to bust us for drinking in our own place, and there are going to be a lot fewer guys who think they'll prove their manhood by picking a fight with a Western player. We made the girls drop their phones in a bucket on their way in, solving the whole picture problem.

In all, keeping the guys in line was one task that wasn't particularly onerous. It's the Ace issue that gnaws at my belly like a dog with a bone.

I grunt a hello to Ace and Jack Campbell, the junior college transfer with hands like glue and a bad academic problem. Hopefully he gets that sorted this year. We'll need him to be at the top of his game. He's one of the guys who Ace throws to on a consistent basis, and from what I saw last year, they're developing good chemistry.

I pause just inside the door and watch the two heckle each other. A new quarterback may not have the same relationship with the O-line or the receivers, so no matter how good he is on film, it could be a huge mistake to stick him into the starting lineup. I don't get why Coach doesn't let Mr. Texas watch the game for a year. That's what I did, and it paid off big time.

Over by the mats at the end of the room, Masters is doing army crawls. He's the argument for the flip side. A physical freak of nature, Masters walked onto the field as an eighteen-year-old and dominated men who were three and sometimes four years older than him. He's declared early for the draft and is now training for the combine—a workout session at the end of February where the pro teams assemble 335 college players and run them through different tests, like how fast can you run the forty-yard dash, how high is your vertical leap, how much can you bench press. Dude wants to break records when he tries out for the pro teams, and I have no doubt he will.

I head for a free weight bench. Nice thing about being one of the early birds is that the place doesn't stink of sour sweat and unshaved pits. Someone else will be breathing my stink today.

I get fifteen minutes into my routine and I'm working up a good fucking sweat. Ordinarily I'd be riding that endorphin wave, but any good feeling is negated by Ace's presence in the room. I run a scratchy towel over my face as Ace goes through yet another shoulder exercise.

There are a total of four guys in here working their tails off on a day that doesn't count, and one of them is Ace. I can't do this to him. I can't go behind his back and foment some kind of insurrection against him. The defense would follow my lead. I know they would, but what kind of teammate would that make me?

I slam my towel on the bench and get up. Masters just happens to be taking a break, and I jerk my head toward Campbell. He needs to go. Masters nods.

"Hey, Jack, I was thinking about buying Ellie this jacket. Would you mind taking a look at it?"

Jack is Masters's brother-in-law.

"Sure, what've you got?" Jack rises from the leg press and walks over to Masters.

"It's out in my bag."

I wait until the door closes behind Masters and Campbell before turning to Ace. "Got a minute?"

He lifts his chin in acknowledgment, and I wait as he finishes his set.

"What's up, Ives?" he asks, dropping his weights to the ground.

I rub my chin. "There's no easy way to say this but Mr. Texas is signing with the Warriors."

Ace looks unimpressed. "So? I figured he would. I was part of the recruiting team, and I know that kid didn't have a better time at any other campus than this one."

Recruiting trips are legend at Western. Coach Lowe picks up every kid personally from the airport. They get a police escort to school. Once you arrive on campus, the cheer squad is there to greet you and your parental units. The adults are squired around. They get a first-class dinner on campus and a tour of the athletic facility, which is plusher than some pro teams' with its mahogany lockers, carpeted floors, individual showers, training rooms, saunas, hot tubs, and a weight room reserved for just the football team.

After dinner, the potential player is introduced to a select few teammates, usually those who play the same position, which is weird if you think about it. The existing players are there to persuade the potential player to come to Western. But if that trip is successful, the same kid you showed the time of his life to might take your position.

And that's exactly what happened here. Ace and our other quarterbacks and probably Ahmed took this kid out, got him lit and laid. Mr. Texas decided that between the first-rate education, the top-notch athletic facility, the number of times we're on national television, and the smoking hot babes who willingly and eagerly service every whim, Western was the school for him.

"Maybe you showed him too good of a time," I reply. "Thing is that Coach Lowe has it in his head that Mr. Texas is going to start."

Ace laughs at this. Just flat out opens his mouth and guffaws, long and loud until he realizes I'm not smiling at all. "What the fuck, Ives?"

"He'd like you to move to safety."

"You're serious?" Ace stares at me with wide-eyed incredulity.

"I would never joke about shit like this."

The look on Ace's face? I don't ever want to see that kind of devastation again. He stumbles, and we both pretend I don't see that. Steadying himself with one hand on a nearby weight rack, Ace manages to choke out, "How do you know this? Is it out yet?"

Meaning does anyone outside of our organization know about it. Are the blogs on it? Is it on Twitter? Is he going to start getting phone calls and emails asking him how he feels about being replaced? My throat tightens up in sympathy.

"Coach Lowe told me, and no, it's not out." The news cycle is focused on the playoffs for the pros. Super Bowl talk is heating up, and our college championship is yesterday's news. Right now, that's a really good thing. We do not need to be in the spotlight while we're working through this issue.

"How far away is Signing Day?" Ace finally asks.

"Four weeks or so." Four weeks until all the high school seniors have to declare what school they're attending.

Ace straightens. "So I have around thirty days to convince Coach Lowe that I deserve to start next year. He wants four years out of this freshman, then he can redshirt him." He slaps his wet, sweaty towel in my chest and storms out. I take the towel to the laundry return chute and resume my routine. Hopefully Coach realizes that this thing needs to be worked out with Ace before the rest of the team gets involved.

I don't get more than two reps of my deadlifts in when Hammer bursts through the door.

"Look at this!" He waves his phone excitedly.

"I can't see a damn thing unless you stop swinging your arm," I growl and reach up to rip the phone from his hand, but Hammer's my size and weighs about ten pounds more than me. Plus, I'm sitting, so I have no leverage. He holds the phone out of my reach.

"I see you woke up on the asshole side of your bed."

No. I woke up on the good side of my bed with the taste of a dream Lucy still in my mouth. I woke up pretty damn happy with a sizeable morning chub that I rubbed out in the shower before I came here. None of which I tell Hammer. "Just give me the damn phone," I growl.

"You're going to have to buy me dinner tonight to make up for your bad attitude." He hands me the phone.

I ignore him and try to zoom in on the image, which appears to be a tall, brown-haired guy standing next to a girl with blond hair. For a second, I wonder if that's Lucy, followed quickly by the desire to rip the guy's arm away, or even off his body if he doesn't step aside. I give myself a mental head slap for that kind of stupidity and zoom in, but I can't make out a thing. "Did you take this picture with your phone or a potato?"

"Ah, shit." He takes the phone back. "It's dark in there, and I could hear people coming."

"And 'there' is…" I gesture for him to fill in the blank.

He shoves the phone into his pocket. "Ace has two photos in his locker. One is with his parents, but the other is Ace and this girl."

"Ace has a girl?" Ace isn't known for taking up every available jersey chaser's offer, but he doesn't spend many nights alone. Although during last year's season, it was a pretty open secret that he was banging Stella Lowe.

"He must, right? Because you don't hang a picture of a slam piece in your locker. That's serious girlfriend and wives shit."

"Okay, but what does Ace having a girlfriend have to do with anything? Given that you didn't recognize her, she's his girlfriend from high school or goes to some other college. Is she coming here and going bunny-killing crazy when she finds out that Ace is being…" I pause to choose some other word that means demoted. "…moved to safety."

Hammer waves his finger in my face. "I never said I didn't recognize her. This girl goes to Western. I've seen her. I think she works at a restaurant. Or a bakery or something like that. I remember her and coffee, which is why you wouldn't know her, what with your dislike of the nectar of the gods."

"You're essentially drinking the sweat of coffee beans, so no thanks." Why can't people get their caffeine fix from Red Bull and/or pop?

The pieces finally add up for me. Well, not all of the pieces, but

Hammer must think we should cozy up to this girl and enlist her help in convincing Ace that quarterback isn't his natural position.

"I'm telling you for the thousandth time, it's not sweat," Hammer insists.

"The beans are ground up, soaked in heated water, and then you drink the bean-flavored moisture. That's sweat of the bean, dude."

Hammer looks frustrated. "The way you talk about coffee is not natural. You know what else is not natural?" I bend over to pick up the weighted barbell and resume my deadlifts, but Hammer continues anyway. "Going two weeks without sex. You're going to forget what pussy feels like, and that would be a fucking tragedy."

"The tragedy is that you're both keeping track of my sex life and writing for that women's magazine. Yet here you are, two articles in and the world still hasn't stopped spinning." Last year Hammer got it into his head that he should be an advice columnist, offering his shady advice about males to women. He submitted a couple of articles and they were published online. Now he thinks he's Emily fucking Post or some similar shit.

"I was doing research for my next article. It's on Tantric sex. You heard of that?" He also has the attention span of a gnat.

"No. Regular sex is good for me."

Hammer continues as if I haven't said a word. "According to these Tantric sex gurus, you can make a girl come just by breathing on her."

I raise a skeptical eyebrow. "Breathing? I don't think any woman is having an orgasm even if I gusted tornado winds into her pussy."

"Not with that attitude you won't."

I can't tell if he's joking or not. Ever since he's started writing for

Monologue, he's reached new levels of strangeness. I blame it on the so-called research he's doing for these articles.

"Look, Tantric sex is all about being in tune with your partner. First you clear away all the distractions. Turn off your phones, computers, televisions. Then you sit her on your lap, legs around your waist." Hammer demonstrates the leg position in the mirror. I huff through two more lifts as he continues. "You stare at each other and every time she breathes, she's supposed to rock against you. Pretty soon, you're matching your breathing to hers." My mind begins to match Hammer's words with images of Lucy and me in my bedroom. Her long, sexy legs draped on either side of my hips, rocking her wet pussy against—

I drop the barbell with a clatter. "Will you shut up? I can't lift 500 pounds with a hard-on."

Hammer smirks. "Can't have an orgasm by just breathing, huh?" I give him a one-fingered salute. "See, this is proof you need to have sex. That's why you're in college, dude. That's why we play football. For the Grade-A pussy."

I sigh. "Can we get back to the chick in Ace's locker? Do you know her?"

Hammer is relieved to get away from the terror of dating and immediately answers. "She's blond and hot. Do I need to know anything more about her?'"

"That's all you got?"

"Her name is Lucy."

I spin toward him, my mouth falling open. "What?"

It can't be. I toss my towel into the bin and sprint out of the weight room. There's a small group in the locker room but not enough to deter me. I arrow my way to Ace's locker and shove his jersey aside. Sure enough, taped onto the back of his locker is a picture of Lucy, her arm thrown around Ace's waist, looking into the camera and smiling as if she's just had a good laugh. And Ace is gazing down at her like she just told him he's going to play in the NFL.

Oh, this is so fucked up on so many levels I can't even begin to count them.

9

MATTY

WORD OF ACE'S SITUATION SPREADS throughout the team like a nasty virus. Ace didn't keep his voice down when he confronted Coach Lowe, and by noon, everyone knew the general gist of the problem because locker room gossip moves fast. The assistant coaches were dispatched to make sure each player understood that if one word leaked from this locker room about the quarterback situation, that player's scholarship would be immediately pulled—no football, no college education, just a boot in the ass kicking you as far away from the Warriors as possible.

No assistant came to me. No, I received a special ass kicking from Coach Lowe for not handling my part of the deal with any kind of finesse.

"This is a surgical procedure, not a goddamned hatchet job," he bellowed as he stood over me. Coach Lowe made sure that I was sitting so when his saliva-covered words rained out of his mouth, my head was in a good position to catch it all. He spent a good thirty minutes ranting on how inept I was and how I'd get the captaincy as soon as his ass turned green.

I bit back some stupid comeback about how his diet wouldn't affect my play on the field, and just bent over and took whatever he had to give me. He's my coach, after all. His word is law, and his verbal beat downs are the kind where you just lie down in an awkward position and hope he maybe feels weird as he fucks you.

After he wound down, he sent me out to reinforce the message from the assistant coaches—alone. No Hammer, Masters, Darryl. By myself, I tracked down and talked to every defensive player, all thirty-eight of them, even the walk-ons. It takes me five hours.

By the time I arrive home, I'm exhausted and pissed off and not in any kind of mood for Hammer to be sitting in my room. It used to be that I could go to Masters's apartment—he has a single at the top of the house—but now that he's married, Ellie's up there and the door is always locked because they're fucking.

There's no damn privacy in this house.

"What's up?" I ask curtly, throwing myself into my desk chair.

"You need a beer." He tosses me one.

I don't break down at the sight of the cold booze, but it's a close call. I twist open the cap and drain half the bottle. "Shit, that tastes good."

"Where were you? We've been looking all over for you."

I give him a "you're shitting me" look. "Coach had me go to every defensive player to remind them to keep their yaps shut over this. Remember?" I spoke to Hammer first because he was loitering in the locker room waiting for me.

"You just got back?"

I nod and take another long draught. "Caught one dumbshit posting to a message board pretending to be an anonymous booster."

"Ah hell. What did you do?"

"I told him that even when he isn't on the field, he's still a Warrior and a member of the team. We wouldn't be on the opposing team sidelines telling them all our secrets during the game and we don't after, either."

Hammer pauses with his beer at his lips. "Shit, man, that's good."

"I also told him that if he screwed up again, we'd make him run suicides nude in the quad until he puked."

"An appeal to his emotional connection to the team followed up with a threat of public humiliation. I like it." Hammer tips his bottle toward mine. "While you were out doing Coach's dirty work, Darryl, Masters and I compiled this."

He hands me a folder. "More stuff on Mr. Texas?" I ask. I set down my bottle and flip open the folder. It contains a class schedule, a work schedule, and a couple notebook sheets with meticulously printed information. The handwritten notes had to come from Darryl, our engineering major.

"It's everything you need to know about Lucy Washington. She works at the Brew House, takes sixteen hours, is a junior Public Policy major who enjoys spending her free time doing something called mock trial. She lives with two other girls—both babes—and weirdly has had no serious boyfriends since she's been at Western." Hammer reels off Lucy's autobiography like he's a narrator on the History Channel. "Ahmed said she broke up with her high school boyfriend before parents' week her freshman year and that she's had a series of hookups, mostly with a few fraternity guys her roommate Charity introduced her to, along with some classmates. There's a list in there." He nods his head toward the folder.

The last piece of paper is a sticky with seven lines on it, which must be names, but I can't really decipher Ahmed's handwriting. I carefully shut the folder so I don't give in to the urge to rip the yellow sticky into tiny pieces.

"How does Ahmed know her?" I try to school my voice into being as disinterested as possible.

Hammer spreads his hands in disbelief, the beer bottle dangling precariously between his index and middle finger. "He says Ace and her are friends. Childhood buddies. Couldn't believe it because she's hot and there's no way you can be friends with someone that hot, even if you're Ace, right?"

I nod because Hammer's speaking the truth. There's no way I could only be friends with Lucy.

"So he just barfed up this information to you?"

"Not exactly. His girlfriend was there when I asked about the picture in Ace's locker. She kind of told me everything. Ahmed just wrote it down."

I toss the folder onto the desk, feeling guilty and a little dirty for knowing this stuff about Lucy. I don't even ask where they got the other information. There's always someone around who's willing to bend the rules when a Warrior's in the equation.

10

LUCY

BY TUESDAY, I'M A JITTERY mess and I can't even blame it on my diabetes. The sad fact is that I can't get Matt Iverson out of my head. He's dominating my thoughts when I should be focusing on mock trial and figuring out just how I'm going to fix our terrible team dynamic.

Over the weekend, I created a few instructional sheets for Heather—a list of courtroom procedures along with a detailed list of the objections she could make. She only needs to make a couple for the judges to give her a good score. Tonight I'm going to work on crafting a tight direct examination.

She may not want them, but I'm doing this stuff anyway.

But mock trial doesn't hold my interest long enough, and Matt creeps in again. I know I'm right about him—he's bad news for me. He might be the sweetest guy in the world for the right girl, but I'm not her. My mom might be easily turned by a pretty head, but I'm not, no matter how powerful Matt's sex appeal. He's like an Exxon Mobile disaster, spilling his pheromones all over the ocean of female good intentions.

Good sex is not a reason to date anyone. To have a hookup? Yes. To date? No.

So just have a hookup, an inner voice suggests.

Because good sex leads to wanting more, and the one vibe I don't get from Matt is that he's a second- and third-round sort of guy. There are too many checks in the risk column and too few in the reward column.

As I'm putting on my coat, the worst thought occurs to me. What if he spots me going to Ace's house and thinks I'm stalking him? Hurriedly I grab Sutton's wool pea coat and tug a black cap over my head, hoping that it's enough to render me unrecognizable.

In the few times I've been to Ace's, I've never seen Matt, but today would be the day for that, wouldn't it? I can just see him saying, "Hey, Luce"—and of course it would be 'Luce' because my two syllable nickname is one too many for Matt—"Hey, Luce, I didn't realize you wanted my address instead of my phone number. But come on inside, my dick's ready for you."

Actually, my sex-deprived brain added that tidbit. He probably wouldn't say that to me—emphasis on the *probably*.

All my worry is for nothing because by the time I get to the Playground, there's no sign of him. The front door to Ace's house is open, so I just walk in. Fortunately, only Ahmed and Jack are sitting in the living room.

Jack flashes a worried look in Ahmed's direction but Ahmed waves his hand. "It's just Lucy. She doesn't care, do you, Lucy?"

"Nope."

Apparently Ace has a girl in his room. I check my watch. It's three in the afternoon. I swear to God that Ace can't go one twelve-hour period without having sex. Because the guys all watch each other's back religiously, if I was dating Ace I wouldn't be allowed upstairs until he was done with his current fling, Stella.

Only it's not Stella standing in the doorway of Ace's bedroom. It's a thin, busty blonde wearing the traditional gear of all winter Midwestern sorority girls: tight yoga pants, Ugg boots, and a pretty coat with an infinity scarf. Maybe the two were practicing yoga poses in there, although that wouldn't explain why his tongue is currently exploring the back of her throat for what I presume to be tonsillitis.

"Ahem," I clear my throat. Ace's head rises lazily to look in my direction while his companion makes a throaty sound of disappointment. "Should I wait downstairs?"

I wonder if they had sex on the couch and whether I can find a clean pair of sheets in this place. One of the perks of living in the Playground, a set of eight houses bought by a booster to house the starters, is the laundry and cleaning services. It's a good thing, because otherwise this place would smell like balls and sperm.

The first time I came here some guy was casually fondling himself on the couch. There are more women in and out of the bedrooms, bathrooms, and game rooms than go through the MAC counter at Macy's on Black Friday. Less than half the guys on the team have girlfriends, and even the ones who are in relationships have a loose idea of fidelity.

If I wasn't friends with Ace for so long, if he wasn't like a brother to me, I'd probably have a hard time hanging out with them. As it is, I shut one eye to their indiscretions and remind myself that as long as I'm not the one putting my heart on the line, the team is full of good guys.

When I arrived on campus as a freshman, Ace and his buddies—already moved in from summer camp—were there to carry everything from my dad's truck up three flights to my dorm room. Three weeks later when my high school boyfriend of four years decided we'd never make a long-distance thing work, they took me out, filled me full of vodka and orange juice (and made sure I didn't end up in a coma), and proceeded to tell me how pretty I was and how worthless the shithead was. Ace and his merry band of linemen, wide receivers, and running backs are sweethearts as long as you don't fall in love with any of them.

Ace is giving me a high-def example of why Matt is a bad risk. I take him on and I'll be just one girl out of a long line of girls who have crushed over a Warrior only to have her feelings hurt.

Plus, the guy hasn't shown his face at the Brew House since last Thursday. He knows I work there and showed up two days in a row, but after Crowerly's it's been radio silence. If he thought me being a vegan was bad, which I'm not, just wait until he gets a load of my diabetes. It's a hassle and some guys get really impatient with my strict dietary habits. Again, the pretty boys are flight risks. They, like my mother, don't stick around when the going gets tough.

It just goes to show that football players will say anything to get laid. All that stuff about how much fun it was for him to have to try so hard with a girl, making me think he was actually serious about putting in the work to win me over? Ha! Maybe Matt did his own risk assessment and decided I wasn't a big enough reward.

Not that I care. I *want* him to quit pursuing me. Makes it a whole lot easier to put him out of my mind.

You've spent all day thinking about him, dummy. He is on your mind!

Fine, that's true. But starting right now, I am not allowed to think about him anymore.

I lean against the wall and watch Ace stroke the blonde's hair, no doubt telling her that he'll see her later even though if he did, he'd probably avoid her. She giggles and lifts her face for another kiss. Ace plants one on her forehead, which isn't what she wanted, then he turns her toward the stairs and gives her a friendly pat on the ass.

She frowns when she sees me, so before she incorrectly assumes I'm here for sloppy seconds, I lie. "I'm his sister."

The girl's face brightens immediately but falls when Ace interjects. "More like kissing cousins, really."

"Ace was dropped on his head as a baby, so most of the time whatever comes out of his mouth doesn't make sense," I reassure his friend.

She flicks her gaze from Ace to me, and from the way the lines around her mouth relax, I can see that she's categorized me as nonthreatening. It could be because my hair is lying limply against my sweaty face. Damn, Sutton's coat is hot. It could also be because I'm wearing ratty old jeans and a pair of boots that look like I'm headed for a construction site, but it's Ace. I don't have to dress to impress him.

She gives me a patronizing smile and turns back to Ace. ""I'll see you tonight at the Gas Station then?"

He raises a hand. "I'll be there."

I barely refrain from rolling my eyes at his noncommittal way of seeing her off. It's enough for the girl because she blows him a kiss and trips lightly down the stairs.

"Not even going to walk her to the door?" I ask as I brush by him into the room.

"That implies I invited her here, which I didn't. She showed up, took her clothes off, and told me she felt like celebrating with a winner today because she'd gotten some good news. I had some time to kill before we went out tonight."

Okay then.

It smells like sex, but his bed is perfectly made. I remind myself to put a blanket on the sofa if I decide to sit on it. I stride over to the windows and throw one open. Ace chuckles but lights a stick of incense.

"Thanks for letting me crash here tonight." I set my backpack next to the bed and gingerly climb onto the side.

"It's no problem. So your place is getting exterminated?" Ace throws himself into the corner of the sofa.

"The girls down in 1C convinced management that we had a bug infestation and that they'd sue if something wasn't done. Then they went around and got a bunch of the residents to sign some anti-bug petition."

Ace squints. "1C. Those the Stepford twins?"

I nod. I'm sure I've complained about them before to Ace.

He gets a faraway look in his eyes. "I think I slept with them last semester."

"Ace," I groan. "Why?"

"They offered to do me together. Who turns that down?"

Normal people. "You know I can't stand them."

He shrugs. "I'm not dating them. I just slept with them."

I throw a pillow at his face. "You're terrible."

He throws it back. "They weren't that good actually. I thought they'd be all over each other, but one watched while I did the other. It was actually kind of weird. Hey, I bought diet pop for you and picked up a bag full of Splenda if you want to bake tonight."

This is Ace in a nutshell. A horndog who manages to wrest his attention away from his own dick long enough to be a thoughtful friend.

"You like this star quarterback business." Even in high school, Ace's stint as quarterback was overshadowed by a star running back. He came here without much hope of ever starting, but injuries opened up a space for him last year. He made the most of it, and I'm thrilled for him.

"It's the bomb, Lucy girl. All the chicks I want. Everyone bends over backward to give me a pass. Even my professors give me a high five and the TAs suggest that I can take it easy. It's nothing like high school, that's for sure." He stretches his legs out and folds his arms behind his head. His smug look reminds me again of what he was doing before I arrived. Or should I say as I was arriving?

Which reminds me, "Am I going to need a set of sheets for the sofa?"

"Take the bed. Marissa and I didn't make it to the bed." His words hold about as much emotion as a stone. Poor Marissa. As if to emphasize his disinterest in the topic of Marissa and their hookup, he flicks on *Family Feud*. Steve Harvey asks what the top five answers are for the question "something people do when they are tired."

"Drink caffeine," I guess.

"Take a nap," is Ace's answer, then he asks off-handedly, "Want to come to the Gas Station with us tonight?"

"No." I kick my backpack. "I'm working on some things for the mock trial team."

"I can go and beat her up," he suggests.

"You really can't because I'm sure that would be grounds for suspension. I can see the headlines now. 'National Championship quarterback arrested for assault and battery.'" But I'm touched by his instant defense.

Ace tips his head back and drains his bottle. He has the next one open and poured down his throat before he responds. "Better than 'former National Championship player demoted in favor of true freshman recruit,'" he says bitterly.

I blink in surprise at his quick change in mood. A moment ago, he was complacent and self-satisfied and now he's pissed off? What'd I miss? "What are you talking about?"

Ace's face darkens. He finishes the second bottle and opens a third. "Nothing. It's nothing."

Every once in a while, he gets in these *I hate everyone so I guess I'll go eat worms* moods. Privately I refer to it as male PMS, but I shouldn't be surprised because Ace's bad moods usually occur in the off-season.

During the season, he's focused and determined and he rarely sulks. These small snippets of time when he can generally ignore school and focus on drinking and screwing girls all day is when he becomes maudlin and unbearable.

You'd think he'd be the most upset during the season. I read the sports blogs, sometimes. I can't spend too much time on there because I get angry on Ace's behalf, but no one talks about him being an NFL quarterback. In fact, no one really talks about him playing beyond college. When they talk about him, it's almost as if he's a liability to the team—one that the vaunted defense manages to overcome game after game after game.

But no, it's the downtime that gets to him. Ironically, that's when I get to spend the most time with him because he isn't up at the crack of dawn for practice and going to bed early because of curfew. And in this mood, he's not going to share anything unless he's ready, so I try changing the subject, but he beats me to it.

"You see Matt Iverson again?" Ace's tone is nonchalant, but I don't miss the slight edge to it.

"No. Why?"

He shrugs, not taking his eyes off the game show. "Just wondering if he's still bothering you."

"He was never bothering me to begin with. I told you, he was nice." This new topic is just as bad as the old one.

"And I told you, he's a dog. You're not in the locker room, Lucy. They're *all* dogs. Or maybe they wish they were, because if they could lick their own balls like a dog, they'd never leave their rooms."

Matt Iverson is a foot taller than me, ripped like a stone statue, and big enough to break me in half. I nearly swallow my tongue at the image of the big guy bent over, sucking his own dick because that is kind of hot. Wisely, I don't share this thought with Ace.

"Guys like Ives spend hours on Instagram before away games, looking up sorority pictures or local 'talent,' as they call it. Then they private message these girls and set up hookup dates. On every single away game," he stresses.

Okay, that is skeevy and gross when Ace puts it that way, but something impels me to pony up yet another defense of Matt. "They're young and single, right? And as long as they aren't hurting anyone, then it's none of my business."

"Hammer, Ives's best friend, nearly sat a game last year because he'd been injured by his girlfriend. He went to an away game, hooked up with a local. His girlfriend drove up to surprise him."

I grimace. "I can guess what happens next."

"Not really. He convinces his side piece to hide in his gym bag. Girlfriend comes in, starts making out with Hammer, his dick still wet from his previous go around." I hate it when Ace gets like this, but I started it, so I have to sit back and let whatever is bugging him eat its way out of his system. "But it's hot in the gym bag, so the side piece pops out and tries to leave. Almost makes it out before the girlfriend sees something move out of the periphery of her eye. The two get into a big fight. Hammer gets bashed on the forehead with a lamp. That's Ives's best friend."

I don't point out that the story is about the best friend and not Matt but I get Ace's point. Matt is exactly that expensive purse. I give up on offering up excuses for him and instead, pat myself on the back for relegating him to the *bad for me* column along with carbs and too much liquor.

"Speaking of girlfriends, what's going on with you and Stella? I'd think she wouldn't be thrilled about the blonde in your bedroom."

"Eh." He shrugs carelessly. "Stella's always unhappy about something. Why do you think she's sleeping with me?"

"I don't know. Because you like each other?"

He looks at me in disbelief.

"What?" I throw up my hands. "Why is that such a stupid statement?"

"Stella and I hooked up because she lives to piss off her dad, has a weird fetish for quarterbacks, and knows she's not going to break my heart when she's done with me"—I open my mouth—"or vice versa," he finishes.

I snap my trap shut. Apparently they have an enemies-with-benefits arrangement. I mean...

"Say it." He sighs and gestures for me to start talking.

"Sorry! But I thought you had real feelings for her. That one night we hit up that new club along the East River last semester, Stella spent the whole night talking to the basketball guy and you went home in a bad mood."

"My mom had called to tell me Rascal was sick, remember?"

Rascal was Ace's dog. He passed away soon after that call.

I nod, but remind him, "You looked more pissed off than grief stricken."

"Can we just drop it? I want to talk about how you and Ives hooked up."

"I didn't hook up with him!" I protest but feel myself turn an alarming shade of red because last night I had a pretty dirty dream.

"Then why are you asking questions about him and defending him?"

I curl my hands into fists so I don't give in to my urge to slap Ace silly. "You're the one who brought it up! I told you I hadn't seen him, and then you decided to tell me some awful story about two of your teammates. What's going on, Ace?"

"I told you it was nothing," he says curtly. At my frown, he mumbles an apology and heaves himself to his feet. "I'm going to shower and get ready." He sniffs his shirt. "I stink. Pick out something for me to wear, will you?"

I guess we're done with Stella and Matt. Tight-lipped, I do as he asks. There's no point in pressing him because he's not going to say anything until he's absolutely ready. I rummage through Ace's things and find a clean pair of jeans and a royal blue long-sleeve T-shirt with a waffle texture. After tossing the clothes inside the bathroom, I unpack my things.

Ace wanders out, dressed in the clothes I picked out, his wet, brown hair looking darker than usual.

He stops by the bed and traces the raised letters on the mock trial packet. "You don't even like football players. You once told me that dating a football player seemed about as exciting as dating a block of cheese."

"Are you still on this?" I rub my temples. I can feel a headache coming on. "I'm not going out with him and you're right. I find most football players to be boring. You all have tendency to talk about only one thing, which gets boring after a while." Except the two nights we talked, Matt didn't say one word about football. *I* was the one who brought it up. God, am I ever going to get him out of my mind? *Stop it,* I order myself and refocus on Ace. "I love you, Ace. And I love all of your friends, but all you guys do when you get together is talk about the game. Different routes. Throwing down the seam. The seam? Really? Who thinks of these names? They're all so sexual."

"Guys think of them. That's why they're sexual. And if you think we're bad, you should watch some wrestling. They have moves like 'going out the back door' and 'rear naked choke hold' and the 'camel clutch.' 'Running up the seam' is innocent compared to all that shit. Besides, guys only have one thing on their mind." He points a finger at me. "Remember that."

I refrain from rolling my eyes. I've gotten this lecture from Ace once a semester since he discovered sex. "What about food? Isn't food important?"

"Only in the context of getting more sex. Proteins to keep it up."

"Ewww. Can we not talk about dicks and hard-ons?" I shudder. I hit him with a pillow, which he wrests easily from my grasp. He might only be the quarterback but he's still damn strong.

"Have you taken your medicine?" He jerks a chin toward his desk where my box of needles, medication, and blood tester rests.

"Not yet, Dad. But thanks for the reminder. I haven't done this for the last ten years by myself or anything."

He shrugs off my testiness. "Just making sure." He abruptly, and wisely, moves on to a different topic. "Are you sure you don't want me to say something to that Heather chick?"

"And say what?"

He pats me on the head. "Dunno. Stop making my best friend's life miserable. I know you aren't a fan of conflict."

I give him a hug and realize he's just looking out for me. "No, it's too late. We've already spent the money on the registration. Is everything in life so expensive?"

Ace doesn't have an answer because there is no answer. We both grew up in modest families. We are in that sweet spot where our parents make too much money for the really good grants, but not enough to pay for our schooling. Ace has a full ride due to his arm and I've got a half-tuition scholarship, but neither of us has a lot of extra spending money.

"I don't think you should have given up your closing position to her," he tells me as he pockets his ID.

No money for Ace. He doesn't need to buy a drink on this campus. Everyone else is happy to buy it for him.

"She's better at it than I am." Or at least that's what I believed after hearing her audition. I'm having second thoughts.

""Meh, you're smarter than her."

"You haven't even seen her in action." And smarter doesn't mean better. The debacle of my freshman year pretty much proves I suck at closing argument. "Besides, it was a condition of her joining the team. Sometimes you have to make sacrifices for the better of the team."

He snorts. "Making selfless sacrifices means you get left behind."

Classic Ace. Always looking out for himself, but maybe I should take a page from his playbook. After all, my mock trial team can't make it out of Regionals and Ace took his team to the National Championship game. "Well, on that depressing note, you should go or my inspirational closing argument that I'm writing for Heather will be full of negativity, and I doubt we'll win any points for that."

Gratefully Ace accepts that. "Are we still up for the movie this Thursday?" he asks.

"What movie is that?"

"*The Expendables 3.*"

I make a face. A bunch of aging action stars running around making jokes I don't get because I never watched the original movies to understand the references? No. "I close the Brew House on Thursday."

"Not to worry. Movie's over at four forty-five. Besides, you promised," he reminds me.

"I'm sure I was drunk."

"Drunk or sober, you said you'd go. I'll see you on Thursday at two p.m. sharp." Hand on the door, Ace calls back. "Stay away from Iverson. He's bad news."

"I don't have any reason to see him," I reassure Ace.

11

MATTY

"SON OF A BITCH!" THE curse words greet me as I open the door to Jack Campbell's pad. Flash, as we like to call him, offered up a half-full bottle of whiskey when we ran out of booze at our place.

We rock, paper, scissored it and I lost, which is why I ran three houses down to fetch the liquor. The pleasant buzz I'd fostered at the Gas Station is wearing off, and that needs to be remedied as quickly as possible.

Jack said the booze is in a cabinet next to the refrigerator and I make a beeline there.

"Honey, I'm home," I yell out just in case someone's having fun in the kitchen. In these houses, you never know. Being an athlete on a team that's expected to compete for the National title every year carries a lot of stress. Most of us forego heavy drinking during the season, which leaves us few options as an outlet for that pent-up stress. Sex is the easiest, and most fun, way to burn off that mental pressure.

I don't find anyone making out in the kitchen. Instead I find something better: Lucy Washington, complete with an apron tied around her waist. Her hair is tied up and with the apron on? She looks like a page from the fables my mom read to me when I was a kid. Goldilocks. Unfortunately, Goldilocks has had an accident and if she actually gets the butter out of the wrapper onto her fingers, it'll only make the burn worse.

My pants get tight as my dick tries to rise up and greet her. Why does she have to have long legs in addition to a nice rack? Why? I tell my traitorous equipment to settle down as I stalk over to the kitchen sink.

She spins around, her lips forming a perfect "O" of surprise. "Matty!—uh, Matt—Matthew," she sputters, and I try not to laugh. The fact that she went with the nickname first says a lot. "What are you doing here?"

"Came to grab booze." I twist the faucet. With the cold water on blast, I beckon for Goldie to come closer.

"I thought you were supposed to put butter on burns," she says warily.

"Old wives' tale." I tug her over to the sink and plunge her fingers under the water.

She flinches at the shock of the cold, and I briskly run my fingers over hers in an effort to warm her up a little. Or at least my intention is to be brisk, but the minute I make contact with her, my touch slows down.

Her fingers are slender, elegant. The middle finger has a slight callus as if her pen or pencil has been pressed there one too many times. I rub the tip of my finger over it once and then again. I have my own calluses from lifting, from slapping the tackling dummy a hundred times on the right, and then a hundred times on the left and repeat. My calluses say my hands are my weapons. Her callus shows her skill is with the pen.

She doesn't make a sound. Not a complaint that the water is too cold or that I'm standing too close to her. Our faces are only inches apart. If I leaned just to my right, I could rub my cheek against hers, like a big cat seeking a scratch behind his ears—among other places.

I try to focus on the water, but I don't see it. All I can focus on is her hand in mine. All I can hear is how her breathing has changed. How it catches and releases faster than is normal.

I rub her fingers again, slower still. My finger traces the curves between each digit. I fall down the tiny valley and climb up to the tip only to take the same exhilarating trip all over again. The cushion of her palm makes me imagine other tender, plump places on her body.

I turn my head and her eyes lock onto mine. Her lips are parted slightly and she stares at me with disbelief. I can't believe it either.

"How do you feel?" My voice comes out hoarse. Jesus, I'm rock hard just from touching her fingers. Under *cold* water.

"Since you're giving my fingers an ice bath, I don't actually have feeling in them," she lies through her teeth and deliberately breaks our connection. Pulling her hand out of mine, she lifts her fingers to inspect the damage.

"Then they aren't burning," I say rather unsympathetically because I'm exasperated at how she keeps denying this thing between us. I push her fingers back under the water. I leave her to stand at the sink while I pick up the now cooled cookie sheet.

"I can do that," she protests as I kneel down and hand sweep the dead cookie remains into a pile.

"I've no doubt that you can, but surprise, so can I." *And this way*

I'm not staring at the way your nipples are poking against the Harry Potter T-shirt you call a nightgown or the fact you have man socks slouched around your ankles. I am, stupidly, bothered by that fact. It looks intimate and wrong—mostly because they aren't my socks. I bet they're Ace's.

"If you're looking for Ace and the guys, they're at the Gas Station tonight," she informs me, as if she can read my mind.

"I know. I was just there. I told you, I came to get some booze." She frowns at the curtness of my voice. And frankly I don't know why I'm pissy. Or, more accurately, I don't want to acknowledge why my buzz has burned off and I'm stomping around like a kid who had a toy taken away from him. What I do know is that I want her. Desperately. I want to kiss her and touch her and fuck her and— "Dust bin?" I force myself to ask.

"I don't think they have one."

"Right." Because the cleaning fairies come once a week. I drag the trashcan closer to the cookies and scoop up the mess as best I can. Behind me, Goldilocks makes a frustrated noise. I check my watch. "You're probably good to go now."

"Thank God. I'm turning into Elsa here." She wipes her hands on a towel. Her voice is unaffected, but her legs are shaky as she strolls over to a cabinet next to the refrigerator and pulls down a half-full bottle of Jack Daniels. At least I'm not the only one affected by this. That would suck. "This what you are looking for?"

I start to take the bottle, but I realize if I do take it, I'm done here. And I'm not ready to be done. Not by a long shot. I'm not sure what her hold up is, but I'm starting to think it might be Ace.

There's a pile of baked cookies on the counter near the fridge. My stomach rumbles at the sight of them. "What do I have to do to get one of those?" I gesture behind her.

She turns to look at the cookies. "Feel free to have one, or ten. But they're sugar free."

My hand pauses over the pile. "What's the point?" I can't help myself from running my eyes over her again. She's nicely rounded all over. Hips, tits, face. I like it all. It's as if I shook a bag with all my preferences and out she fell.

Luce merely shrugs. "I like them that way."

Hell. A cookie is a cookie. "Sounds delicious."

"And you sound dubious," she laughs, completely unoffended. "Go sit down and I'll bring you a plate. Want milk?"

"Does Elmo like to be tickled?" I grab a chair and watch her bustle around making me a plate of cookies and milk.

"I actually don't know if he does. What if he hates being tickled but everyone does it anyway just to hear him laugh?"

"But he does laugh," I point out.

"Sure, but it could be a nervous reaction. Like someone laughing at a funeral when they're actually super sad."

"You're ruining my childhood with your theories," I say with mock sternness.

She presses her lips together to keep from laughing. "I didn't take you for an Elmo lover." The plate of cookies slides into view.

"Are you insulting my manhood now?" I pick up one of the cookies and take a bite. It's…pretty good. I tell her so. "These don't have sugar? I feel like you're just full of lies."

"Entirely sugar free," she declares and takes a seat next to me.

I fake a shocked gasp. "You're sitting down? At the same table as me? The guy who's too risky to go out with?"

She flushes. "I was just..."

"Just what? Being polite?" I arch a brow. "Being a good hostess?" A smile tugs free. "Just admit it—you like me. You like talking to me, and you like being around me."

She sighs.

"I promise I'll keep your secret, don't worry."

I polish off the remainder of the cookies and milk and lean back, shoving the Jack Daniels behind me. I'm in no hurry to go anywhere.

"So why *are* you playing hostess?" I ask curiously. "And how come you're here by yourself?" She opens her mouth, but I hold up a hand. "Wait, let me guess. I'm going to assume that you're here because your roommate is celebrating her six-week anniversary with her new dude. You needed a place to crash and wandered around campus until you found this house. Knowing the guys, the door was unlocked and you thought that with all the empty rooms and beds, this must be a campus-designated safe place for young, temporarily homeless women such as yourself."

She grins, almost in spite of herself. "And why am I not in bed?"

"Because, like Goldilocks, you couldn't find a bed that was comfortable enough. Hint, you're in the wrong house."

"My apartment complex is being exterminated for supposed cockroaches. Ace said I could crash in his room."

Hmmm.

"What's that noise mean?" she nudges my foot with her socked toe.

"So you're Ace's…" I let the answer question hang between us, willing her to fill in the blanks.

"Friend," she finishes.

That doesn't sound right to me. Actually, it sounds perfect to me, but I don't think I trust my judgment. She's here, alone in his house, wearing pajamas, and what I believe to be his socks. I've had girls steal my T-shirts, try on my jerseys, but never my socks. That's real intimacy. My skepticism weights the silence that hangs between us.

She huffs, "Don't tell me you're one of those guys who believes girls and guys can't be friends."

"'Course not," I lie.

One delicate eyebrow arches in disbelief. "We are friends. We met in the nurse's office in the third grade."

"Why haven't you dated him? I mean, I'm a guy but I'm confident enough in my masculinity to say that Ace is attractive. Plus, he's the quarterback, and I understand from girls that the position automatically adds a couple points to his tally."

"So what? I mean, there are dozens of good-looking guys around here, but I'm not interested in dating them. Are you interested in dating every attractive girl you see?"

"No," I answer truthfully. Dating doesn't interest me. Sleeping with them? At least once? I might be down with that. "I asked you out, though. If you turned me down because you're after Ace, I get it."

I don't like it, but then I don't have to like it.

"We're *friends*. I saw him eat a worm once." She shudders. "It was gross. You can't ever date a guy you see eating invertebrates."

"Okay." I pause thoughtfully. "So if Ace isn't in the picture, I guess this brings us back to your unfounded belief that I'm a 'risk.'" I air-quote the word, and her brown eyes flicker with resignation.

"You think I'm nuts," she says. "I get it. I know I can be anal about—"

I snicker. Yeah. I'm thirteen, apparently.

Lucy looks like she's fighting laughter. "Seriously? You can't hear the word *anal* without—"

Another snicker. Goddamn it. I'm usually a lot smoother than this.

"Fine, I give up. I'm not saying it again."

I drag my mind out of the gutter and fix her with a serious gaze. "Anyway, about this risk thing. You know what I think?"

"No, but I bet I'm going to in the next five seconds."

She sounds resigned, but the fact that she's still here, talking to me, feeding me? It all gives me encouragement. "Prepare to be enlightened. I feel like you haven't given me a proper risk analysis. Maybe you weighted things incorrectly or haven't accurately identified all the benefits. If you're going to turn me down in the face of our clear attraction to each other, I deserve to see the assessment."

"Hmm, let me think." She taps her cheek with one finger. "And no."

"I know you've got "football player" in the con column, but do you have increased stamina, ability to hold you up with one arm so my other hand is free to do lots of things like—"

"No." She nudges me warningly with her sock-covered foot to tell me I shouldn't finish my example. I really hate that sock.

I grab her foot and pull it into my lap. "Let's do a risk/reward test."

"Let's not." But her foot doesn't move.

I massage her foot beneath the sock, pressing hard against the ball and then digging into the arch. She releases a tiny moan, and her head falls back in a dick-hardening sexy motion. *Fuuuuck.* If this is how I feel from just touching this girl's hand and foot, what would it be like to be between her legs, to suck on her tits, to feel her pussy pulse around my dick? Light-headed and incredibly aroused, I almost fall off the chair.

I gotta focus here. If I'm ever going to get past the foot and hand, I need to convince her that the reward with me would be off-the-charts amazing.

Clearing my throat, I keep rubbing her foot. "Having your foot in my lap, that's a risk, right? But you're enjoying the rubdown. That's a risk worth the reward."

"Keep rubbing and stop talking," she orders. Her eyes are closed.

Okay, but I'm not touching some other guy's sock, particularly the guy whose bed she's sleeping in. I don't know if I fully buy into her "just friends" explanation for Ace. He has her picture in his locker. She's wearing his socks. For all that, he's at the Gas Station dry-humping a Kappa and Lucy's home alone. I pull off the sock and toss it aside and stare at her toes.

"Your nail polish is blue." Since when did I think toes were sexy?

She wriggles them. "Yes, on both feet. You're very observant. Haven't you ever seen a girl's toes before?"

"I'm sure I have." I just don't remember them. I have this strange feeling I'll remember hers, though.

I run a light caress over the anklebone, down the spine of the Achilles tendon, and around the edge of her instep.

Her breathing hitches, so quiet and so soft, I might have imagined it.

"What're you doing?" Her words are a husky whisper, and my body responds accordingly.

My balls tighten, and my dick's so hard I'm worried it'll snap in half, but I can't reach into my jeans to readjust or I'll scare her away.

"We're testing your risk assessment." And driving myself crazy.

"You should stop."

"I can't." I move my hand up her ankle to cup the slender calf. "Feel good? Worth the risk?"

"I'm not sure."

That's an invitation if I ever heard one.

Is it possible to come from just rubbing a girl's leg? I might test out that theory. "And now?" My fingers find the tender hollow behind her knee. Her pulse beats rapidly against my palm. She's as turned on as I am and I haven't even gotten to the good parts.

"It feels riskier," she croaks.

Yeah, because pretty soon my hand is going to be on your thigh, and I don't know how I'm going to stop there.

Her fingers are turning white as she grips the sides of her chair. Is she holding herself back? Or keeping herself there?

Fuck, I want to kiss her so bad. I want to kiss her lips but I'd settle for her toes or her knee orshit, if all she'll allow is for me to touch the tips of her fingers, I'd be okay with that. I need a taste of her. I'm *dying* for a taste of her.

Desperately, I plead with her, "You sure you don't want to take a chance? I really don't take up that much time. I'm low-key, fairly un-demanding. I'm the bargain purse. I have all the same hardware as the expensive purse, but I'm cheaper. I bring my own booze, remember?"

I don't know who moves first. Later she would say it was me. She could be right. I've been wanting to kiss her since I discovered her here. Since I saw her at the coffee house. Since maybe before we even met.

I dig my fingers into her long blond hair and pull her onto my lap where her soft parts meet my hard, aching parts. Her hands grip my head and our tongues converge in a wet, hot collision.

She tastes as sweet as she looks. Like the most decadent baked good ever.

My poor dick is aching to feel her bare skin against it. I want to peel off her clothes until the heat of her warms my cold skin. I've been itching to mold her tits in my palms, lick the pulse point of her neck.

My mother could come in and ask me my name and I wouldn't have a response. I'm full of Luce. Her sweet taste, the heat of her touch, the vanilla smell from the cookies.

She wriggles, trying to find the hard spot to alleviate the ache between her legs. My hand drops down to find the smooth skin of her thigh, made bare where her pajamas has ridden up. I hitch her leg higher.

She sighs with relief and moans with pleasure when I press my weight against her. I nearly cry. It feels that good.

I want to both kiss her until the sun comes up and throw her down onto the first surface I can find. Fucking hell, man, who needs a flat surface?

I grip both her hips and drag her slowly across my dick. Her head slowly lolls back, exposing her smooth, beautiful throat. Her fingers are tangled in my hair, and the sharp pulls keep me from going over the edge, keep me from tearing off her kiddie pajama top and pulling down her silky shorts until she's completely naked.

I swear she's ready for me, that she's wet between her legs. Her feet hook into the ladder of the chair and she begins to ride me. I place a hand around her neck and pull her closer so that I can ravage that porcelain skin with my teeth and tongue.

I should be gentle. This is my first chance to show her the reward is worth any risk, but it's so damned hard.

She smells like the first burst of spring. The clippings from a genuine grass field. Real, honest...*mine*. I feel like I could just live off the taste of Luce alone. That she's all the sustenance I'll need, which both thrills me and scares the shit out of me at the same time.

It's a crazy, exhilarating feeling, and I seriously cannot get enough. I drag her mouth back to mine so I can drink straight from the fountain. God*damn*, this kiss is better than any sex I've ever had. Her mouth is hot and wet, and she kisses me back as if she's starving and I'm the first food she's seen in days.

She's voracious, and every need in her calls forth an answering desire in me. I want to give her anything, everything. I want to kiss her mouth until we're both too drugged up on each other to do anything but lie on the floor and count our breaths. I want to—

The door slams open. Noises burst into my eardrum. My name is called. Once, twice, a dozen times. I don't hear it but Lucy does.

She shoves me away.

"I...I should go." And then she runs off. With my dick trying to punch his way out of my jeans and what sounds like the entire fucking team out in the hall, I can't really do much about it. I'm awkwardly rearranging myself so I don't look completely obscene when Hammer strolls in.

"What the fuck was that?" Hammer asks. "Isn't that Ace's girl?"

I run a hand over my hair. My world's been tipped upside down with that kiss. "I don't know, Hammer. I just don't know."

12

I COLLAPSE ONTO THE SAFETY of Ace's bed. Lord, Matt Iverson is potent. No, he's *dangerous*. I nearly burst into flames when those big, powerful hands were running over my foot. My legs. My sex. If we hadn't been interrupted…God, I would have had sex with him. Right there in Ace's kitchen, where anyone could've walked in on us. That's how deep of a spell he had me under.

I rub my hot cheeks and try to ignore the even hotter feeling between my legs. I was grinding against him like I was trying out for a spot as a cam girl. I've never felt like that about a guy before. Maybe it's because I haven't had sex since last year. A year is a really long time to go without. I'm just experiencing a…sexual re-awakening. It's like when your limb falls asleep and when you wake it up, you're full of intense pain and buzzing until it wears off.

I just need for it to wear off. The next time I encounter Matt, I'll be prepared.

Next time? Oh, God, am I already anticipating a next time? How about never again? And shit, I promised Ace to stay away from him. But I don't have to sleep with Matt. I could just…what?

Talk! That's what we'll do. We'll talk it out. Eat some food, have a drink—beer for him, Diet Coke for me—and we'll both laugh and realize that we're better off friends.

I try to force myself to sleep, but my mind whirls in circles. I need to stay away. But I can't help myself. But he's no good. But he's funny! He makes me laugh and, fuck me, the size of the monster in his pants— *No! Do you not remember those Instagram photos? Do you really want to be the next member of the panty parade in Matt's bed?* But I'd have to be dead not to appreciate what a perfect specimen of masculinity he is. How I was on fire just from him touching my fricking ankle!

And the circle goes around again. I toss and turn until Ace's door slams open. I bolt up in bed wondering where the fire is only to sag back immediately when I see two shapes wrestle inside, half-laughing, half-trying to discover what the other person had for dinner.

I clear my throat as the two stumble and fall onto the sofa. "Ahem," I say a little louder.

Ace peers over the blonde's shoulder and his eyes flicker in some dim remembrance.

"Oh, Luce. Forgot you were here." He's drunk so the words are slurred together, but I get the gist.

"I am here," I remind him.

"Can you just…" He spins his finger around in quick circle.

I gape. "For real? You just want me to cover my head and pretend you're not here?"

"No. We're going to pretend *you're* not here," the girl shoots back. I don't recognize this one. She's not the blonde from earlier, and she's not Stella.

Ace looks out at me glassy eyes. "You don't mind, do you?" His hand runs up the back of his companion, and she responds by rubbing her chest all over him.

I stare at the two of them in disbelief. He wants me to pretend he's not having sex on the couch? I take too long to respond because my inability to form words is taken as consent by the girl. She proceeds to noisily kiss Ace's neck, sounding for all the world like a fish flopping around on a dock.

He must be so drunk he can't hear her or so horny he doesn't care. Maybe it's both.

"I do mind, actually."

"Don't be a cockblocker," the girl says, her mouth partially muffled against Ace's neck.

"That would be cuntblocker," I correct impatiently. "You don't have a cock."

"Did you just call me a cunt, bitch?"

I turn to Ace. "You know how to pick them."

"I'm not judging her IQ, just the quality of her snatch," he replies crudely.

And the girl? She doesn't even flinch. If anything I think her expression grows victorious.

"Nice, Ace. Real nice."

"Lucy, give us…" He looks down at the girl and back to me. "Twenty minutes."

"Twenty minutes?" His friend squawks. "I want to spend the night here."

"Right, I really don't do sleepovers," Ace tells her and starts to rise.

"You have someone in your bed!" She points to me. Yet my presence, no matter what the reason, doesn't drive her off.

"It's just Lucy. She doesn't matter."

I know he's drunk, but that was rude. And here I was feeling guilty that I'd kissed his teammate. After this, I should have the right to kiss the whole damn team! I climb out of bed, find my socks, and grab my backpack. Ace reaches out to grasp my hand as I leave.

"Don't go. Just wait downstairs. I'll be a half hour. Hour tops."

"No, you won't." The girl takes Ace's face between her hands. "I'm going to rock your world. You don't need her."

Without waiting for any response, she pulls Ace's hand down between her legs and starts rocking. Oh. My. God. Ace is really losing it. I hustle out of there before the contents of my dinner decorate their rapidly discarded clothes.

Outside Ace's room, I slip on my socks and then glance back into the room. The two are going at it on the very sofa he screwed some other girl on just a few hours previously.

I run a hand through my hair. I don't know what's going on with Ace. He's usually not like this. Yes, I know he has sex, and I know he has plenty of girls on campus after him, but I could have sworn he had real interest in Stella last semester. Now he's acting like a manwhore without a conscience, and that's just not him.

Something is wrong with Ace, but short of stalking in there and pulling the girl off of him, I can't really address it with him tonight. Or, I guess, it's morning. I pull out my phone to check the time. It's nearing two in the morning. I have a ten o'clock class. I'll deal with Ace tomorrow but for now? I just want a damn place to sleep.

If my apartment wasn't being fumigated and if breathing pesticides wouldn't kill me, I'd go home. But I'm stuck here. Somewhere in this place has to be a place for me to crash.

I trot downstairs and find the living room empty. It's not my first choice, and half the house is still out partying, which means I could fall asleep only to be woken up several times as Ace's roommates straggle home, but I don't have many more options.

A couple of raised voices coming from the porch catch my attention. I quietly approach the front door to see who's arguing, only to jerk back like a character from a bad spy movie when I see Matt and Jack.

Shit. I'm totally not prepared to deal with Matt so soon. The imprint of his body is fresh in my mind. I might still be a little drunk from his kiss. I need some time and distance to build up an immunity to him so I can see him and not want to tear off my clothes and his.

I peek through the sidelight. Whatever Matt is trying to sell, Jack isn't buying. His arms are crossed and his jaw is set in a hard, unhappy line.

What did Ace say this morning? *Better than former National Championship player demoted in favor of true freshman recruit.*

Surely he wasn't referring to himself? Surely…I yank open the door and the two shut up the moment they see me.

"What are you doing here?" I accuse.

"I live here," Jack says with a grin. It's a fake grin. There are worry lines around his eyes. The suspicious kernel that formed when I first saw the two arguing starts to take shape.

"This is about Ace, isn't it?" When the two don't answer, I reach out and jab my finger into Jack's chest. "Your quarterback is losing it. He's drunk, screwing random girls, and acting like a teenager with her first bout of PMS."

Jack raises his hands. "I'm too drunk to deal with this right now." What a fricking lame-assed excuse. Jack's as sober as a judge on Monday mornings. "Good night, Lucy." He leans down and gives me a kiss on my temple. "Nice jammies."

I look down at my Harry Potter pajama top and matching shorts. "They *are* nice," I yell at his departing back. I turn my irritation on Matt. "What's wrong with my jammies?"

"Nothing's wrong with your pajamas, Goldie, but I'm definitely not a fan of your socks. Where'd you get those?"

"Goldie? What happened to Luce? One nickname's not good enough for you?"

"You looked like a fairy tale tonight with your hair up like that." Matt spins his finger toward my head. "Are you trying to avoid my question about your socks?"

"What is your obsession with my socks?" I lift one foot up. "These are my dad's."

"Then your socks are fine." There's a banked heat in his eyes that makes it hard for me to meet them without blushing.

"Speaking of Ace—"

"I wasn't actually speaking of Ace," Matt interrupts. "I was speaking of us. You and I and how you're really heartbroken that we were interrupted before we could take a few more risks. Me, too." His voice thickens seductively. He steps forward, and I step backward because it's two hundred and fifty pounds of male coming at me, and he keeps coming until the door is closed behind him. "But we can patch our bruised hearts by seeing each other tomorrow night."

"I'm busy." I cross my arms, in part to ward off his charm and in part to keep from grabbing his shirt and whipping it over his head.

"Yes, studying, but you can't study all the time, and you aren't studying now." He pulls gently on my crossed arms, dragging me across the wood floor until there's hardly a breath between us. "How was the reward, Goldie? And don't tell me it didn't exist because you'd be lying. I was there. I felt you. I swallowed your sexy little gasps, and I felt you grind—"

"Okay!" I throw my hand across his mouth. "I felt something. Something good." His eyes gleam in the night. He's like this big cat just waiting to devour me, and worse? I want to be devoured. "But it's late, and my head is muddled. I can't think or sleep."

I know I've just admitted to him that I can't stop thinking about him, that he's actually keeping me up at night, but the words tumble out of me. And once they're out, I have a certain sense of relief. The tension had been building and building, and it had to come out.

His whole face softens beneath my hand. He presses a small kiss into the palm and then pulls it gently away from his mouth.

Still holding my hand, he asks "Why aren't you in bed, Goldie?"

"You know why." It's embarrassing. "Because Ace brought a girl home."

His eyes search my face, looking for hurt, I suppose. I'm not hurt. I'm pissed off and tired.

"I think he forgot he said I could stay."

Matt's lips thin out in disapproval. "You can't sleep down here. Half the offense is still at the Gas Station."

"I know. I wasn't planning on getting much sleep."

His eyes dart to the sofa where I left my backpack. "You're coming with me." He releases me to go over and shoulder my backpack. He stops near the front door and eyes all the random coats hanging on hooks. "Where's your coat?"

"Upstairs. Why?" I ask with growing suspicion.

"I guess you don't need it." He throws out a hand. "Come on. Let's go."

"No." Oh no. I'm not going home with him and *sleeping* in his bed. I wasn't born yesterday.

"Now, Goldie, despite all evidence to the contrary, I believe you're a standup woman. If you pinky swear to keep your hands to yourself and not take advantage of me, I'll believe you." He wiggles his pinky in my direction.

I can't even do the pinky swear because I don't know if I can keep my hands off him. After what happened in the kitchen, he'll be lucky to make it to his house unmolested. Spending a whole night with him by my side? He's going to need a chastity belt.

At my hesitation, he points upstairs. "Or you can go upstairs and enjoy Ace's floor show."

I tell myself that I'm agreeing to go with him because it's the only good choice I have left.

"Fine." I grab one of the coats from the hall and shrug into it. But there's no way we're sharing a bed. Absolutely no way. "You'll be sleeping on the floor."

13

"ARE YOU REALLY MAKING ME sleep on the floor?" Matt lies on four yoga mats taped together while I'm ensconced in his cozy bed. His room is about the same size as Ace's with a small refrigerator, a desk, and a chair situated by the window overlooking the back of the house and into the common area all the houses share. It's why they call this particular set of student housing the Playground. The guys party out there during the warmer weather and throw snowballs during the colder weather, or so Ace tells me.

There's a door situated slightly behind the chair that leads to the bathroom. All the bedrooms have their own bathrooms. How nice for them. How awful for the cleaning crew.

Matt also has a nice large bed, larger than my twin, but instead of the sofa running across the far wall like in Ace's bedroom, there are the yoga mats.

His bed smells nice, like citrus and…well, him. Of course, I like it, as I seem to like everything about him, and surreptitiously take another deep sniff. I'm going to have to buy an orange and rub it on Heather so that the smell starts having a negative connotation. Otherwise, I'm going to get excited at breakfast every morning.

Want any orange juice?

No, ma'am. It makes me orgasm. Can't drink OJ in public now.

"Yes, I'm making you sleep on the floor. Why do you have the mats there anyway? If you had a sofa, you'd be able to sleep on that instead of the mats."

"Because I like to stretch. Good stretching equals fewer injuries. But these mats are meant for stretching, not sleeping."

"I know you don't have practice tomorrow and that you don't have practice for like three weeks, so I don't care." I stare at the ceiling so I can avoid looking toward Matt. He got undressed in his bathroom but came out wearing flannel sleep pants and no shirt. And those sleep pants are somewhere on the floor between us. He'd taken them off under the thin blanket covering him.

I almost swallowed my tongue at the sight of shirtless Matt, so I huddled under the covers, hands clenched together, exerting as much control as I can so I don't launch myself at him. "You're the reason I have to sleep here anyway. If you and the rest of the team hadn't made Ace miserable, he wouldn't have come home with a woman and essentially kicked me out of my room."

"Why were you there again?" he asks.

I can hear the skepticism in his voice. It's so typically male of him to think the opposite sex can't be friends. Ace and I've tried to explain it. Most of my female friends get it. Ace's friends assume we slept together and when Ace moved me into the friend zone, I continued to hang around hoping he'd realize what a prize I truly was.

"Because Ace is my best friend. Has been since third grade. We met in the nurse's office. Ace had childhood asthma, you know."

"No, I didn't know," he admits. "What were you in there for?"

I prevaricate, not willing to get into the whole diabetes thing tonight. "Wasn't feeling well."

He moves again on the mats. It can't be comfortable down there. I can feel myself weakening.

"What if we sleep with the pillows between us like the Puritans did?" he suggests.

I can't help but laugh. He's got a one-track mind. "Did you take that class, too?"

"You bet your ass I did. Who knew the Puritans were so horny?"

"I don't think it was the Puritans who were horny. I think it was Professor Collinsworth." Professor Collinsworth is a tiny woman who looks like a raisin with white hair. Her class, Early American History, is all about sex and violence during the colonial period.

"When did you take that class? Were we in that class together?" There's more rustling, and I can't help myself from glancing in Matt's direction. I find him lying on his side, propped up by an elbow, his golden, perfectly formed chest highlighted by the moon.

"Yes, but not until last semester. I didn't know about it until my roommate Charity told me that it's a great filler class." A class to pad your GPA.

"Ahh, my student advisor signed me up for it second semester sophomore year."

"You have Public Safety with her."

"Describe her for me." His head falls onto his hand as if he's settling in for a nice, long chat. There's something irresistible about a man who wants to listen about nothing and everything. I mentally add that to the reward column, which keeps getting longer each moment I spend with him.

"She's about a foot shorter than you with wavy brown hair. Kind of has a '50s pinup style to her. Wears a lot of silver bracelets on both arms. Jingles like a Christmas tree. Very attractive."

Matt squints as if trying to picture her. "Not seeing it."

Neither of us seems interested in sleep. It's like the first night we were together, when all we wanted to do was talk. "If you slept with her, would you remember her?"

"Yeah, why wouldn't I?" He shrugs. His shoulder roll actually highlights his muscles, lifting the pecs up into the light and then down into the shadows. "I haven't slept with *that* many women."

"So you could name them all?" The seemingly unending list of *winners* that popped up in the hashtag scroll by in my mind's eye. That bit weighs heavily in the risk column.

He sighs deeply. "Probably not. Does it matter, though? The women I've slept with have wanted the same thing. Simple, easy release. There's no shame in the hookup. Not for the girl or the guy as long as everyone's on the same page." He rolls onto his back, taking the peep show with him.

He has me there, and frankly, I don't want to know his list of past conquests. I don't know why I brought it up in the first place other than I need a reason to dislike him. I need to remind myself that he's a risk with a capital "R" because my defenses toward him are so weak right now.

I play my last defense card. "You're really not going to tell me what's going on with Ace? What made you and Jack argue earlier?"

"No."

He shifts again on the mats but doesn't invite himself into the bed, even though I'm pretty sure he wants to. He's not the only one.

Finally, I give in, because I'm weak and he's so damned attractive. "You can sleep on the bed with me, but I swear to you if you try to feel me up tonight, I will cut off your hand."

He's up and at the bed before I finish.

Grinning down at me, he says, "I kind of need my hands. Would you consider cutting off a finger? Or three? Because apparently you can still be a damned good linebacker with only a few fingers."

"Depends on the infraction." I move over to the far side of the bed. Matt climbs in beside me.

"I like you, Goldie. And your insistence on labeling me as risky does not make me like you any less," he says cheerfully and tucks his hands under his pillow. His elbow lands close enough to my head that if I simply turned my cheek, I could kiss it.

I force myself to lie still.

"I don't know what that means," I tell him.

"It means I'm not done with you."

I frown. "You don't get to decide that."

"Nope. You can't stop me from liking you. It's just a *thing*. Like the sun rising and the tides coming in."

"You're bored, aren't you? You're an obsessive sort of guy, and without the object of your obsession—aka football—to distract you, you've latched on to me for some reason. Is that it?"

"If that argument makes you feel safer, go with it." The smile is still on his face. I can hear it in his voice. "The thing is, Goldie, if you don't sleep with me now, it'll be this niggling regret you'll have all your life. You'll be thirty-five and on your wedding day—"

"I'm not getting married until thirty-five?"

"Hush. This is my story. Anyway, you're on your wedding day. The wedding march begins. The double doors open. At the end of the aisle stands some pasty-faced groom you settled on. In the back of your mind, you think, I wonder what Matty Iverson was like in bed. And then you won't be able to walk down that aisle. You're haunted by this lack of knowledge. You turn on your heel and run. Ultimately you ruin this poor sap's life, make enemies out of his entire family, and spend a shitload of money you'll never get back because you didn't take up this opportunity when you had it."

"That's quite a line."

"It's the truth."

I roll over and try to forget I'm lying next to the first guy I've been attracted to in a long time. Matt has no such problem. His gentle snores fill the air minutes later. It's a long, frustrating night for me.

14

LUCY

I DREAM THE DIRTIEST DREAM that night. It consists of Matt's very large hands throwing the covers aside and then running themselves all over my body. I moan so loudly when his fingers delve between my legs, I wake myself up. Only to find him sleeping next to me like a baby.

I place my hand over my galloping heart and breathe a huge sigh of relief that I haven't woken him up and that I haven't done what I warned him against—middle-of-the-night creeping.

Matt's still sleeping and hasn't moved an inch since last night.

I give myself a few moments to gawk at him. He has a hard, hot body that apparently does not need any covers because the sheet and blanket are kicked down around his thighs, revealing an expanse of golden skin stretched over muscled shoulders, chest, and abs. He's an athlete, I remind myself. They're all hardbodies. But as much as I tell myself he's not my type, I can't keep the lie in my head long enough to be convincing.

In my dreams, he was exactly my type. Probably my *only* type. I shudder and try to shake free of the vision of him touching me, kissing me.

His right arm is thrown across his forehead and his left rests across his abdomen. His fingertips are touching the waistband of his underwear and I'm helpless to stop my eyes from drifting downward where an impressive morning erection is barely held inside the stretchy fabric. My fingers itch to reach over and palm that bulge.

Holy hell, I feel lightheaded this morning.

I allow myself ten more seconds of ogling before I push myself upright—only to immediately fall down again. I guess my weakness is due more to low blood sugar than to my inability to control my body's response to Matt. Or maybe it's just my body thoroughly betraying me on all levels.

The thump serves to rouse Matt from his sleep. He blinks, slowly, gradually gaining consciousness. I avert my eyes when his hand drifts lower to cup himself. He halts halfway there, as if suddenly remembering my presence in his bed.

He turns his head lazily toward me. "Hey."

"Good morning." I try to smile but even that seems like too much of an effort. Is it any wonder I'm cautious? Because here I am in a gorgeous guy's bed, and I have to tell him I'm not healthy enough to leave. I battle back my embarrassment.

"Sorry about that." He gestures with his head toward his crotch. "Habit."

"No worries," I reply as if seeing a guy fondle himself is a regular occurrence in my life. "So I have to ask you a favor."

"Sure. What do you need?" He rolls over and props himself on one elbow.

"Can you grab my backpack? There's a black acrylic case, about the length of a pencil. I need that."

He leans forward, concern etched in his strong, sexy face. "You okay?"

"I'm a..." I take a breath because even after all these years, I hate telling people I'm a diabetic, but he's going to open the case and look at the needles and wonder if I'm a drug addict. Besides, what does it matter what Matt Iverson thinks of me? *It matters because you like him more than you should.* I shove that voice aside and say levelly, "My BG feels low but I need to test it."

He doesn't hesitate. One moment he's on the bed and the next moment he has my case in hand. I fumble with the latch. Without a word, he snaps the case open and holds up the glucose meter. "Tell me what to do."

"You sure?"

"Goldie, I deal with this shit all day long. We're always getting injected with something. Cortisone, platelet injections. Can't be a football player and be scared of a needle."

I search his face to see if he's hiding any disgust or dismay, but all I can find is readiness. This is *ordinary* to him, and the risk list I've been adding to—the one with all the pictures of his past liaisons, the one scribbled with the warnings of Ace—starts to look badly imbalanced.

"Prick my finger and press the strip against the blood." I bite my lip. "I don't have any communicable diseases, but you might want to get some gloves."

"Nah, I trust you." He handles the equipment with ease, pulling out a lancet, taking the sample, and then shoving the strip easily into the meter reader. "So what's BG stand for? I'm guessing not 'big guy.'"

"Blood glucose. You're good at this," I observe. "If the football thing doesn't pan out for you, you can go into medicine. Be a nurse."

"What do you mean if this doesn't pan out? I'm a football god." He winks at me. "Small 'g.'"

I believe it. Despite the tiny number of college players moving on to the pros, Western has sent more players to the NFL than any other college in the country. It's why Ace came here even though he knew he wasn't guaranteed a starting position.

"What about after football?"

"Well after my fifteen years of dominating at the inside linebacker position, I'll retire from the pros and focus my time on terrorizing my kid's friends."

The glucose meter beeps and he turns the screen so I can see the readout. I make a face. It's lower than it should be.

"Two boys to follow in your football god—small 'g'—footsteps?"

"Nah. I want to have tea parties and a reason to dress up silly and post pictures on Instagram that will go viral and have everyone saying how awesome a dad I am."

"You've given this a lot of thought." I check the meter again, but the readout hasn't changed. I grimace. "Can I ask you another favor?"

"Yep, and you don't need to ask for permission, either."

"I need a glass of orange juice or skim milk."

"We have OJ for sure. Probably not skim milk though." He pats his firm stomach. "Growing boys and all."

My eyes linger there far too long to be polite. When I finally pull my gaze away from his ripped torso, I find him grinning at me. There's something devilish on the tip of his tongue.

He doesn't disappoint. "I'm pretty to look at, aren't I?"

"Yes, yes you are," I laugh with relief that he doesn't mind I was totally perving on him.

"You lie here and think about how awesome I am while I go and get your juice." He walks out, uncaring that he's still sporting a bit of wood in his shorts. I guess that's what it's really like to live in a house full of guys.

He returns in no time, bringing a plate of eggs, toast, a huge mound of bacon, a glass of orange juice, and a Gatorade.

"You were only gone a couple minutes," I say suspiciously as I struggle into a seated position. He drops the plate on the side of the bed and hauls me upward, slipping a pillow behind my back before taking a seat by my side. He hands me a glass.

"I stole it from Hammer." He sweeps my hair out of my face as I sip on the orange juice. "You okay?"

The first hint of worry bleeds through. He was so nonchalant earlier, as if having a girl in his bed with a medical problem was no big deal, but by the concern in his eyes I can see now that he was trying to put me at ease.

My risk assessment suffers another blow.

"I'll be out of your hair in fifteen minutes."

"There's no hurry." He drapes himself like a giant cat across the lower half of my body, reaches over for the plate and sets it between us. He doesn't try to feed me or treat me like a baby. Instead, he watches me with studied casualness as I eat my eggs, occasionally stealing a slice of bacon while I gobble up the breakfast he stole from his roommate.

I can't remember the last time I've been pampered like this. If this is the kind of treatment women get after a night with Matt, I can see why he's so popular.

"I can see by the sad face you're thinking of something not good, and I have to say that the rule of this bed includes no bad thoughts," he declares as he grabs his Gatorade and proceeds to drink a quarter of it.

"You have rules in bed?" I find myself fascinated with the movement of his Adam's apple. Even the act of him drinking is somehow sexy and strong. I give myself a mental slap. *Get it together, Luce.* Oh Christ. Now I'm referring to myself with *his* nickname.

"Only one: everyone has a good time."

My mind gallops toward all the interesting pictures that a good time entails. His head between my legs. His hands cupping my breasts. His mouth moving everywhere.

"Those eggs must be really good," Matt observes.

"Why do you say that?" I ask as innocently as possible. Surely he couldn't tell what I was thinking about.

He grins. "You just moaned a little."

"I did not." Did I? If I did, I want to die. Really just want to crawl under the blankets and hope the earth swallows me up.

"Okay, maybe you didn't."

I assess him suspiciously but decide the best way forward is denial all the way. I have a feeling that if I reveal I'm in any way receptive to him, he'd have me on my back, clothes off, faster that I can say *hut hut*.

As if that's a bad thing, the evil creature in the back of my mind whines. I push her aside and finish eating my breakfast.

"You thinking about Ace or whatever big thing you were sighing about the other night?" he asks.

Neither. I was thinking about you and your sexy body. Do you mind putting on a shirt? "Both topics violate your rules of the bed."

He heaves a big sigh. "See, I'm trying to ignore that you're nearly nude and that I would love to explore all that creamy skin, but I'm guessing that's off the table, so I'm trying to change the subject."

I try to remember why we aren't actually doing the things he's suggested, but then I remember my stupid risk assessment. "Oh."

"Yeah, oh."

Changing the subject is a superb idea. I clear my throat. "So do you have class today?"

He takes a deep breath and looks past my head out the window. "Yeah, I have Public Safety with your hot friend."

His reference to Charity as hot annoys the heck out of me. Mostly because there's no impediment to the two of them getting it on. And the thought of Matt feeding Charity breakfast in bed, despite Charity being one of my closest friends, makes me want to Hulk Smash this breakfast plate. "You think Charity is hot? I thought you didn't know her."

"You said she was hot. I'm just repeating your description. Although…" …" He pauses to take another sip of his Gatorade. "A girl's definition of hot is different than a guy's definition."

"Well, by all means, educate me." I fold my arms.

"Okay, but I'm going to be crude. Since we're besties now, though, I figure that's okay."

"How are we besties?"

"What? You have sleepovers with people who aren't your besties?" He slaps a theatrical hand over his bare chest, and my eyes unwillingly fall, again, on that beautiful piece of art.

"Matt…" I say warningly.

He grins into his bottle, not at all chastened. It would likely take a gaggle of nuns to get him to behave and maybe not even then.

"Hot is a word used to describe anything that gets our dicks hard. It could be red lips or a sliver of skin between the waistband of a girl's jeans and the top of her shirt. It could be, hell, smell. Hot's not the same as pretty or attractive or interesting or nice. It's just, *fuck that makes me hard*. Girls use it to describe guys they want to bang." He snaps his mouth shut as a thought occurs to him. By the naughty gleam in his eyes, I know exactly where his dirty mind went. "Does that mean you want to bang Charity? Because, Goldie, I would be so down for that."

I roll my eyes. "That's a negative in the risk assessment."

"Ah, I was just kidding." At my raised eyebrow of disbelief, he clarifies, "Okay, I'll admit that seeing you with another girl would be hot. But the truth is seeing you in any kind of sexual situation would turn me on. I was at the Gas Station over the weekend. There are willing women every two inches, but I didn't find any of them hot even though, objectively, I'm sure other people would. It's not the other girl in that threesome fantasy. It's *you*."

And crap. That's a positive in the risk assessment. The way he says *you*—as if he really means it, as if I'm currently the only thing he finds hot right now—is so damn tempting.

I flail like a drowning victim for another lifeline.

"Ace says you're a player and would break my heart."

15

MATTY

"DOES HE?" THAT ASSHOLE. I can't believe he's breaking the locker room code. Maybe it's all friendship to Luce, but Ace hasn't gotten the message. Jack's not this way with his sister, Ellie, and Hammer's been trying to pawn off his little sister to any teammate willing, despite the unwritten locker room rule of no sisters, no girlfriends. None of us has taken him up on this. His little sister is fucking terrifying.

She gives a small, noncommittal shrug as if she's slightly embarrassed she brought it up, but now that it's hanging out there, I want to address it. At least I know what some of the things are in her *con* column.

"I don't know that I like hookups more or less than any other guy," I say diplomatically. But what in the hell am I supposed to say? I've had my share of hookups, but what college guy hasn't?

She makes a humming sound, which doesn't sound like approval or disagreement.

"I mean, I'm not a virgin, and I don't believe in the whole myth that sex saps your energy."

She hums again. Christ, could she say a few words? I'm dying here.

If I had a collar, I'd be tugging on it. "I make sure everyone has a good time. Remember rule number one?" She nods, another wordless gesture. "You can jump in here anytime."

Lucy swallows and smiles a perverse little grin. "No, I was enjoying the show.

"You little shit." I grab her knee and squeeze it through the blankets. She doesn't even flinch.

She takes another baby sip of her orange juice. "Can I ask you another question? I don't want you to be offended."

"Well, we *are* besties…" I gesture for her to continue.

"Why is it so many of you athletes are such…well, players? Ace showed me that Instagram feed. I agree hookups aren't a bad thing. I've had a few of my own, but that *many?*"

My first reaction is to growl at the thought she's had *any* guy but me, but then I realize how frickin' hypocritical that is. It never occurred to me that the multitude of times I've had my picture taken with a pretty girl would slot me into the risk category.

I scratch my head, trying to think of the most non-offensive way to explain this. Because me saying I just take what's offered to me on a nonstop basis isn't going to win points. Not with this girl. Hell, probably not with any girl I wanted to have a relationship with.

And is that what I want? A relationship?

I guess so, because I wouldn't be chasing after Luce this hard if all I wanted was a lay. I knew where to get that, how it feels to have that non-emotional hookup. Somewhere along the line, maybe after I heard her sigh the second time at the coffee house, I thought *I want to be the one to make this girl sigh with happiness, not with frustration.* Then she slayed me with her soft eyes and her smile and her hilarious risk assessment ideas.

I need to find the right words to make her understand that I belong in the reward column.

"Football is hard," I start. "To be a college athlete at this level, football is your number one focus. Sure we say we're student athletes, but we spend six hours a day doing football crap and two hours doing schoolwork. Our job is on the field. That's what we're paid to do. We go to practice, travel to the games, work with the trainers, watch film, and when we're not doing those things, we have to be lifting, so there's not enough time to develop a relationship."

"But they do happen. I mean, Ahmed's been dating someone his whole time here."

"Ahmed's girlfriend is one he had from high school. In fact, most of the girlfriends are pre-college. Or maybe the guy met his girl during his redshirt season where he didn't travel and wasn't playing every weekend."

Her head tilts to the side as she considers my words. "So you're saying it's just easier to sleep with multiple people? Why not the same one over and over?"

"Because you sleep with anyone more than a few times and it gets messy. Feelings start to develop and then everyone ends up unhappy."

Her voice is low, soft when she says the next unexpected statement. "You sound like you're speaking from personal experience."

I swallow and look away from her. Her words stir up a few uncomfortable memories. But somehow I find myself spilling them. My mouth opens, and the words fall out, as if I need her to know that I tried hard to be something other than the prototypical college athlete. "I dated a girl during my redshirt year. You don't do much as a redshirt because you aren't going to see one down of football on the field. The most important task is strength and conditioning and learning the playbook, but it's not the same thing as actually playing. She was a fun chick and the relationship thing seemed doable. Then I started the second game of my redshirt freshman year after Donovan Highsmith got injured. I never gave the position back. Coach noticed me and told me I had a real chance of going pro, but I had to give it my all."

"And your girlfriend didn't understand?"

"She…yeah, that's a nice way of saying it." Megan, my only college girlfriend, had turned from being a sweet, fun girl into an unhappy, demanding one. I could never spend enough time with her.

She wanted to go out and I wanted to go to bed at nine so I could be alert and energized for a 6 a.m. run. The only time I drank was Saturday after a game. Never before. My classes were designed to accommodate my football practice and playing schedule. She wanted me to take classes with her.

In the end, she spent more time screaming at how horrible a boyfriend I was than we did having sex. "I disappointed her a lot. Didn't want to do that again. I was a shitty, shitty boyfriend," I finish. And that wasn't the worst of it, but Luce doesn't need to know the details of my failure.

"I can't believe I'm saying this, but I think your philosophy not only makes sense but is kind of honorable." Her hand creeps across the covers to touch mine.

Her words lift something inside I hadn't realized I'd been carrying for a while now. My breakup with Megan hadn't felt honorable at the time but, looking back, it was the best thing for both of us. I fold my fingers around Luce's, hoping I'm not holding too tight. Hoping she doesn't realize how I'd like to have her hand in mine for the foreseeable future.

"So where's your ex now?"

I shrug. "No clue. She graduated. She was a year older than me and I'm a fourth year junior. I suppose she has a job and is somewhere living an adult, responsible life, dating junior execs and middle managers." At least I hope she is. "How about you? Any guys moping around campus because you broke their hearts?"

"Nope." She pops the last bit of dry, uninteresting toast in her mouth before answering. "My sole boyfriend was in high school and he broke up with me my third week of school. He goes to Cal Poly and decided he didn't want to try out the long-distance relationship thing."

"That sucks," I say, but in reality I'm thrilled.

"You look torn up over it," she says sarcastically.

Have I mentioned how much I enjoy it when she busts my chops? Because I do. I grin unrepentantly. "I'm sorry you got hurt, but not sorry you're single."

"That's honest, at least." She tugs her fingers, and I reluctantly release her. The plate is empty, and it's obvious she's getting fidgety. I guess I can't keep Goldie here if she wants to leave, no matter how much I'd like to. "It doesn't really matter whether you're a player or a monk," she says.

"Are we back to the risk assessment?"

"Partly. Tell me what else you're interested in other than football.

Because Ace? Ahmed? Jack? The only thing they ever talk about is football."

"Hey, it's not my problem the offense is full of guys who are one dimensional. I've got other interests," I protest and get to my feet.

"Like what?"

She doesn't even look at me. Under her disinterest, my near nudity feels awkward and embarrassing. I swipe the flannel sleep pants off the floor and shove my legs into them.

"Like…" Fuck, what *is* the last non-football thing I've done besides drinking and screwing? "I like movies."

"As in you review them? Study them? Write papers on them?"

"I think that shit moves movies from the fun column to the work column." I do a mental inventory of the bathroom. No towels on the floor. No condoms. No random bits of underwear. Deciding it's safe, I offer it to Luce. "You need the bathroom?"

"That'd be great." She pops in and closes the door.

I know she'll hear me talking because the door is as thin as two notebooks pressed together. "I like basketball."

"That's a sport. Falls under the same rubric as football."

Shit. It sort of does. My eyes fall to the chair by the window. "Reading. I like to read."

The rustling inside the bathroom stops. Aha. She likes that. I should have gone there first. Of course she thinks reading is an important skill. Girls like guys who read. There's a whole Instagram feed for that, which I know because Hammer and I were on it and have scored more than one out-of-town lay because of it. Last year, during our championship run, a newspaper did a piece on the secret lives of the Warriors football team.

Hammer and I were in the same Lit class, and we happened to be reading *Moby Dick*. We took that book with us everywhere, not because it was a great read, but because it was so frickin' boring. We had to force ourselves to finish it. Coach caught us one day and dragged the public relations person in.

We were told to wear our football pants and team workout T-shirts for the article so the outside world would believe we were something more than dumb jocks. As if we sit around the locker room with pants on. What a crock!

"What's your favorite book?" she asks.

"I don't have one favorite book." I try to keep the triumph out of my tone. Don't know how successful I am.

"Name one and don't be so smug."

Not very successful.

"It's a series. Harry Potter. I grew up reading that series."

"What's your Patronus?"

"Ah ah ah," I say. "You're not getting that out of me. I'm not near drunk enough." Tell her the spirit animal I picked out at the age of eight? No.

"I work at the Brew House. If you tell me what it is, I'll make your Patronus out of foam."

"That's tempting, but still no." I lean against the door, thinking this is probably the least sexual but most interesting conversation I've ever had in my bedroom before. "Can you really do that? Make pictures out of milk."

The door opens and Lucy appears in skinny jeans and an oversized off-white sweater that hides all the good parts, including her ass. But she still looks sexy as hell. It's like the wrapping on a present. I can't wait to peel it off her.

"Actually, no. The most I can do is a leaf and a heart." She drops her folded pajamas into her bag and picks up her insulin case. "I'm not quizzing you anymore, so you don't have to answer if you don't want to, but favorite character of the series?"

"Snape," I answer immediately.

"Really?"

"You think I was going to say Ron?" I'm slightly offended.

She laughs. "No. I don't think Ron is anyone's favorite character. But don't most guys like Harry or, I guess, Draco?"

"Nah, Snape was the best. He had a big heart and was courageous."

She chews the corner of her lip. "Also a bully, but I can see where you get the other characteristics." Lightly, she tosses her case from one hand to the other. "So no class for you today?"

I shake my head. "Nah. I attended last week. I don't want my professors to keel over in shock by going too often. Besides, this is my break. I don't get a fall break, Thanksgiving break, and only about three days off at Christmas. Even Spring Break is out because we're in the middle of spring ball, so I don't go to class full-time until after Signing Day. All the professors know this and deal with it." It's a perk of being on the championship winning team, and I take full advantage of it. "What do you have?"

"Policy and Prose, which is about writing persuasive legislative works."

"You interested in politics?" I ask in surprise, halting in the middle of clearing away the breakfast shit. She just didn't seem the type—not that I really know what that type would be.

"No, I'm interested in policy. I'd like to get a job at a think tank and just write all day. That'd be my dream job. It's one of the things I like about mock trial. It forces you to look at one problem from both sides. We have to present both defense and plaintiff sides of the case."

"Cool." We need smart people writing our laws. Her black case catches my eye. "Do you need to give yourself a shot? I assume you can do it yourself, but I'm here to help if you need it."

"Yes, but I'd rather not while you're here."

"Gotcha. I'll take this stuff downstairs. You have everything you need before we leave?"

"Before we leave for where?" Her forehead crinkles.

"Before we leave for class."

"I thought you weren't going to class."

"I'm not. I'm walking you to class."

As I exit, she's still sputtering.

16

MATTY

IN THE END, I LET her go by herself. I know full well she doesn't want to be seen with me because of Ace. Isn't that a kicker? I've never had a problem with someone—girl or guy—wanting to be seen with me. Where the hell did he think she was going to sleep? Shit, that he just kicked her out and didn't make sure she had a safe place last night really rustled my jimmies.

Even if I did have a friend like Luce whom I hadn't tried to bone a hundred different ways, I wouldn't have made her sleep in the living room of a house that saw more action than a brothel in Reno.

"You want to tell me what the hell that's about?" Hammer questions when the door closes. "When we gave you all that information, I thought you'd use it to, like, persuade her to help our cause. Not into your bed." He stops and glares at me. "Are you trying to use your dick to convince her that Ace needs to move?"

"I don't know whether to be chuffed or disturbed you think my dick is that powerful." I scratch my chest, debating whether I want to go over to the athletic facility for something to eat or just rustle up a mid-morning snack here. Five pieces of bacon and a piece of toast aren't enough to keep a bird alive.

"Seriously, man. Sleeping with her? That's low, buddy." Hammer follows me into the kitchen.

"I'm not. Or I did sleep with her, but that's all we did. Sleep." The refrigerator is alarmingly empty. During the season, we almost always grab food at the athletic center. Dinners are on campus. But we're in that weird period of no practice and no games. There's only the morning weight training that we're unofficially required to attend daily, and so we're eating more at home. So much so that we only have a half gallon of orange juice, a case of beer, and what looks like a brick of moldy cheese. Hammer must have used the last of our food to make breakfast.

"Brother, you can tell me. I'll only judge you for today."

"I'm not lying to you. Shit, I can't believe I'm trying to convince you I didn't sleep with a chick." I throw up my hands. "Why don't we have any food?"

"Because going to the grocery store is more painful than an enema?" Hammer suggests. "Look, I believe you. But how'd that happen? She just trip and fall into your bed? She pass out on the way to class and you carried her home?"

"How about her apartment was being fumigated, she was supposed to crash in Ace's room, he brought home a jersey chaser, and she was stuck sleeping on a couch in their living room?"

Hammer's mouth drops open. "You're fucking me."

"Nope."

"Duuuude."

"I know." I head for my room and start dressing. We need food and probably some basic supplies. I check the toothpaste in my bathroom.

Yup. Almost gone.

"What is wrong with that guy?" Hammer asks. He has three sisters and ever since his away-game hijinks with his ex, he's turned over a new leaf. He's been pushing his sisters at his teammates because he loves us and knows—despite our occasional propensity to be dogs—that we're decent human beings and would make good partners...eventually. Actually, if there's a guy who should be giving advice in a women's magazine, it probably *is* Hammer. He claims he's a reformed man.

"This stuff is fucking with Ace's head."

"I don't know, man. You don't treat a friend like that," Hammer says dubiously.

"Don't make me defend him anymore. He told me yesterday he's not moving."

"The D guys are already watching the boy on YouTube. The backfield was talking about him over at Bish's place and they were more excited than they would be if a whole busload of prostitutes were dumped off."

Bishop Green is charge of the backfield—the captain over the safeties, corners, and defensive backs.

"Terrific," I say in a tone that conveys it's anything *but* terrific. After shoving my feet into some boots, I grab my keys. "Come on. We need some food. Once we have something to eat, we'll be able to think more clearly."

I think of Luce and her diabetes. I wonder which kind she has. No wonder she made sugar-free cookies. She probably has to watch every bite that enters her mouth. What a drag. "And I need to call my mom."

"What for? You sick?"

"No. I've got a med question for her." I motion for him to go get socks and shoes on. "I'll meet you downstairs in ten."

Hammer gives me a suspicious look but leaves without argument.

Mom answers on the second ring.

"Hello, Matthew," she says in her brisk manner. A stranger might assume she's cold. They'd be wrong. Although she's a pediatrician with a busy practice, she's always made time for me and has come to a surprising number of games. "What can I do for you?"

"What kind of food can I buy for a diabetic?"

"Vegetables," she answers immediately. "Stay away from corn. There's a high sugar content in that. Essentially green things. Fruit is okay but not great because, again, sugar. Apples are good because they are high in fiber. Fish is low in saturated fats. Speaking of fats, fatty foods aren't necessarily bad. You should take her out for sushi," Mom suggests. "This is about a girl, correct?"

It is, although why I'm considering Lucy's dietary needs in my grocery planning, I'm not sure. Or, at least, it's not something I'm ready to examine very closely. The kiss the other night rocked my world in an unexpected way. "A friend of mine has it. I just want to be careful."

"I can send you a list. You could buy her some sugar-free items as a treat. Only in moderation, of course." I roll my eyes, which, if I did that in person, would earn me a slap on the ear. "Sugar alcohols like sorbitol are fine. Does she have type 1 or type 2?"

"I have no idea." Just like I have no idea what sorbitol is. "Is that important?"

"Not for you, dear. I have to go now."

I caught her in between patients, I realize. "Okay, thanks."

"Love you, dear."

She hangs up before I can respond in kind.

Hammer's at the front door, punching something into his phone. He slips the device into his pocket when he sees me. Guilt is all over his face. "Who're you texting?"

"No one," he says innocently. At my steady glare, he caves. "Okay, Bish. It was Bish, all right? He had a good idea."

"What is it?" There's no point in not asking. Hammer will, well, *hammer* away at this idea of theirs until I give it a hearing.

"She's in mock trial, right?" At my nod, he gains enthusiasm. "You need to present this to her as a case."

"I'm not studying to be a lawyer," I remind him. The conversation is put on pause until we both climb into my Rover.

"You're the closest thing we've got. The only other guys that come close are Jay, who's a psych major, and Eggers, who's studying humanities."

Jay's a second-string linebacker and Eggers is a cornerback.

"I've never understood what a humanities major is."

"Fuck if I know." Hammer shrugs. "The point is, you're the captain of the defense now that Masters has declared for the draft, so even if you weren't into the law like you are, you'd still be the person to do it. And she slept in your bed last night."

Goddammit. Since when do I have to be the "leader" of this team? I don't mind calling the plays on the field. That shit is fun. Even going to the center of the field and trying to intimidate the opposing team's quarterback during the coin toss is high on my shits and giggles list. But dictating what's right or wrong for our team? That's the fucking coach's job, not mine.

"Hammer." I shoot him a quick glare. "You did not tell Bishop she stayed overnight."

Hammer looks guiltily down at the phone he's pulled out of his pants pocket. "He saw her coming out of the house, and I might have said something about how you've got an inside track on her."

I take a deep breath and count to ten so I don't give in to the urge to pull over, rip off Hammer's arm, and beat him with it. "What exactly did you say?"

"That you had the inside track."

"I thought you were all incensed that I was using her." I slam the brakes a little harshly at the stoplight. "And now we're telling the entire team Luce and I are fucking."

"No way, brother. I told Bish the whole story about her getting kicked out of her apartment and then Ace dragging some girl home from the Gas Station." He waves a careless hand. "Bish already knew that because apparently Ace had sex with the girl in the storage closet before they left."

"This is why we need to be drinking at the Playground and not out and about," I grind out between my teeth. The boys had convinced me that going to a bar on Tuesday night would be okay because there wouldn't be many people out. But once word leaked that the team was there, everyone showed up. I dragged the defensive guys home with me when the bar started filling up.

"They better not be talking shit about Luce," I warn.

"No. It's all good," he assures me. "So you gonna do it or what? Because if anyone can convince Ace to step aside for Mr. Texas, it's his

BFF."

I hesitate. Hammer's not wrong there. Ace and Luce have some kind of relationship, even if I'd prefer to deny it existed. But it's strong enough to put me in the risk column even after last night. She was still holding back this morning.

But if I could present it someway to her… Hell, it would make my life so much easier. If *she* were to persuade Ace to move to safety, then Coach would be happy, the boys on D would be happy, and the offense would have to accept it.

The major potential downside of this is if I piss her off by even bringing up the subject. Last night, she was steamed when she thought Jack and I were talking about Ace. She clearly knows something, and if she thinks I'm trying to use her? My dick and balls would be cut off and stuffed down my throat before I could blink twice for help.

I'd even put myself in the risk assessment for that. But maybe if I just laid it out for her…like Hammer suggested. As if I was making a case for Ace, and she could decide for herself if it made sense to sway him one way or the other.

"I'll think about it." But the sick feeling in my stomach tells me it's not a good solution. Obviously Ace is whispering Iago-like into her ear that the football team is full of shitty guys. If she takes this wrong, there's no coming back from it.

Plus, I don't like how Ace is so influential with Lucy. On the flip side, maybe she's influential with him. But using her would be crappy.

I swing into the parking lot of the grocery store. Hammer joins me inside the store. I pick up a basket. We exchange a look and both shake our heads. I put the basket back and grab a cart.

"Let's get our shit and get out." Hammer heads toward the snack food aisle while I loiter in the produce section. I throw a few plastic containers of veggies into the cart and then go find some frozen fish.

"What the fuck are you buying?" Hammer asks me as I roll the cart toward the checkout aisle. "Did you get an email from the trainer?" He looks me with concern. "Shit, do we have to start earlier this year?"

"No, I didn't get any email. This is just…" I rub the back of my neck self-consciously because I'm buying food for a woman who I haven't even slept with. I'm fucking wooing her with broccoli heads and apples.

"Just what?" Hammer prompts.

"Just thinking I should eat better. Set a good example," I improvise.

"Then I guess this is all for me." The bastard shakes his bag of Doritos.

I force myself to turn away before I start drooling.

"That'll be sixty-eight fifty," the clerk says. She smiles prettily up at us.

Hammer leans forward. "You're gorgeous, honey. What's your name?"

"She's sixteen," says the kid at the end bagging the groceries.

The girl shoots the boy a dirty look. Someone's not getting laid. He shrugs philosophically. "Didn't want a Warrior to get suspended for some underage tail."

Hammer reaches out and daps the bagger's fist. "My man, you're all right."

"No problem. Want me to carry this out for you?" He lifts the plastic bags.

"We got this," I say before Hammer can adopt the pimply-faced kid and bring him home with us.

"Congrats, by the way," the kid calls after us.

"Close call there." Hammer wipes a hand across his forehead.

"Were you really thinking about picking up the checkout girl?" I ask incredulously. Maybe we do take fucks too casually. Hammer gives a tiny shrug.

"She was cute. No harm in flirting. Maybe getting her number. Townies are good for a little variety, right?"

"Right," I say faintly.

On the way back home, Hammer lays out the plan he and Bishop have cooked up, the checkout girl already a distant memory, so far behind he can't even remember seeing her in the rearview mirror.

Somehow I don't think gathering a list of all the quarterbacks who never made it to the next level is going to be very convincing. On the other hand, I can't come out and say, "Hey, your buddy Ace can't be quarterback anymore. Want to help me convince him moving to safety is the right call? And, oh by the way, I think you're sexy as hell. Can you introduce me to your mattress before we ruin your best friend's life?"

I think I better get used to eating broccoli instead of chips for the next couple of weeks.

17

"SO WHEN YOU WERE KISSING him, did you feel bored and weird, like this guy's tongue feels like an uncooked piece of meat? Or was it more like, holy hell, we should set up a national kissing booth because this guy could retire this country's debt in one day," Sutton asks as we go for our mid-afternoon walk.

I hate exercise, but I need some kind of regular activity daily or my BG levels go haywire like they did this morning. Sometimes, no matter how careful you are, a diabetic can fall into dangerous levels of too high or too low blood sugars. Or sometimes, like me, you drink too much your freshman year and your roommates call campus security because they can't wake you up from your hypoglycemic coma and your dad ends up having to pay a huge ambulance bill he can't afford.

"Definitely the latter. It was so good I'm considering giving up sex for the rest of my life because everything hereafter will be a disappointment."

"Girl, why did you not have sex with him?"

"Honestly, because at first he wasn't my type." Before Sutton can voice her disgusted astonishment, I hold up a hand. "Yes, I know. He's so good looking that he's probably Mother Teresa's type, but every guy I've ever been attracted to in the past has been pretty much the opposite of Matty."

Sutton arches her eyebrows. "Matty? You have a little nickname for him."

"Everyone calls him that," I protest. Although…Ace calls him Ives. I hide my cheeks inside the collar of my coat just in case I'm blushing. I don't need Sutton to see that and use it against me.

"Fine, what are your other reasons, Miss Risk Averse?"

"He's a player. There were so many pictures of him with his arm around a girl on Instagram, I got tired of scrolling. Ace says Matty's dick has seen so much vag it's now writing journal articles for *OB GYN Today*."

"Make him double up." Sutton shrugs. "And what the hell is Ace's problem? He's no angel himself. I can't believe he brought some girl home and expected you to watch him."

"I'm not happy about it, but isn't Ace's warning even more meaningful? Because he clearly knows what he's talking about. Like you're a film major, so I respect your opinion on films. Ace is obviously getting his degree in random hookups."

One of the girls from my PoliProse class runs by. Sutton waits until the girl passes before turning to me. "I know you don't believe me, but I think Ace is really hung up on you." This time it's her turn to hold up a finger and ask me to wait. "Hear me out. Your mock trial thingy is big on hypotheticals right? I always hear you practicing with Randall, 'assume the sky is green and the grass is blue. That would make everything inverse, correct?'"

"You do a nice imitation. Maybe next year, you can be on the trial team."

"I love you, Lucy, but never in a million years. I find it really boring."

"I know. I don't care."

"Which is why we're friends, but going back to Ace, let's do a hypothetical, 'kay?"

"Go ahead." It's not like I can say no. Sutton would hound me until I listened anyway, even if it took climbing into my bed tonight and whispering it in my ear.

"Let's assume Ace is in love with you but he knows you don't love him back. He decides he'll wait you out. Someday you'll wake up and see the amazingness that is him." She ignores my rolling eyes. "Until then he has to ward off any potential suitors. He does this two ways. He first tells the team you're off-limits because he's close to you. He's called 'dibs,' so to speak."

"Because we're property and therefore dibbable."

"Right." Sutton nods, ignoring my sarcasm. "After warning away the team, he prevents any potential slippage by making sure you have a bad opinion of his teammates. These are all prime, datable alpha males. Girls flock to them but some girls, like you and me, base attractiveness on personality. So if we believe they're stupid assholes likely to cheat, it doesn't matter how good looking they are. You, especially, are going to slot these players into the 'no' column."

"Your hypothetical doesn't work because Ace and I have no feelings for each other besides friendship. I've known Ace since he was a snot-nosed eight-year-old. Any potential romance between us died out long ago, buried under a pile of bad-smelling clothes." I tick off a list of reasons why. "Ace didn't learn about deodorant until he was way past puberty. When I think of Ace, I don't think dreamy male, I think of his constant farting in the fifth grade. He thought it *hilarious* to point his gas cannon in my face." Sutton wrinkles her nose. "Exactly, thank you. I had to complain to his *mother* before he stopped. Plus, he has horrible taste in movies. Do you know what he wants me to see this Thursday?"

"No. I'm scared, though." She looks alarmed.

"You should be. *Expendables 3*. Need I say more?"

"Okay, but these are all the reasons you're not in love with Ace, which I believe 100% because I don't get any vibe that you like him, which is why I sorta can buy into your 'Matty isn't my type' thing. But none of those are reasons why Ace isn't in love with you."

"Does a guy who's in love with someone else bring a girl home and try to screw her in front of said love interest?"

Sutton bobs her head back and forth. "Fair enough. But maybe he's one of those tortured, Byronic heroes who can't stop hurting everyone around him because he's in so much pain himself."

"Oh, Lord, Sutton. You definitely think with the creative parts of your brain." I throw up my hands. "You're conjuring up a scenario that doesn't exist."

"How is that different than what you're doing with Matty? All your excuses about not dating him involve things that haven't happened. You don't have any proof he cheated on someone. So he enjoys the ladies. Big whooping deal. In fact, didn't you say he dated someone his freshman year and it broke up because he didn't pay enough attention to her? That's not the same as cheating on her. It's not like you want some guy breathing down your neck. You've got a lot of shit on your plate. It would be a relief to go out with someone who's as busy as you," Sutton argues. "Plus, you spent the night with him and he didn't even make a move. That doesn't say player to me. He's totally respected all your boundaries. I know you like to play it safe, but right now, honey? You're being chicken."

She's right. There is a difference between being cautious and being cowardly. I grab my head. "I keep going around and around in my mind about this. You're right. He doesn't come off like a guy who just wants to get into some girl's pants."

"So why are you holding back? Why are you punishing yourself?"

Sutton's practically echoing Matt's words. *Sounds like your risk assessments keep you from having fun as opposed to keeping you safe.*

"You look stressed, Goldie."

My head whips up and there's Matt standing outside of the small university bookstore at the south end of campus. Sutton and I have walked nearly two miles arguing about Matt and I'm just now realizing it.

"This is a goddamned sign," Sutton hisses in my ear. "You can't escape this, Lucy. A higher power is conspiring to get you two naked. Give in or the apocalypse is coming." She backs away without even introducing herself to Matty. "I'm blaming you if the zombies come," she yells and starts running in the other direction.

He lifts his T-shirt to his nose. "Do I stink?"

"No. Sutton had an emergency." A meddling emergency.

"Your roommate," he identifies. "Not the one I have class with but the other one? Which one is taking up my spot on your lease?"

My lips quirk up. I can hardly believe he remembers what we talked about our first night together. But then it was only a week ago. Still, how many guys remember their flirtations in such detail? "That would be Sutton. Charity and I had a class our freshman year and we met Sutton in the fall. She had problems with her roommate, and an apartment over on Oak came open."

"Good call." He nods approvingly. "I've heard Oak's a nice place."

"Were you getting a study aid?" I tip my head toward the bookstore.

"Nope. Buying some guy porn." He holds up the latest Ludlum thriller. Under the pretense of inspecting the book, I let my eyes drink him in. He looks like a modern day James Dean. Black leather coat unzipped over a dark blue Warriors T-shirt. His eyes are as blue as an untouched robin's egg. Jeans barely contain his powerful legs. Black boots finish off the bad-boy look.

It doesn't help anyone that his long hair is mussed from the beanie that's half hanging out of the right coat pocket.

And I kind of hate that my heart sings and sighs at the sight of him. But I'm done fighting my attraction to him. What's the point? I'm in college. I'm supposed to have fun. He's not the same kind of bad as drinking five shots of tequila at a frat party. He might feel as heady, might make me just as reckless, but I'm not going into any coma after having sex with him.

Besides, the sex would be good exercise. It would actually be healthy for me to sleep with him. It would be good for both my mind and my body. If I did him just once, I'd be taking only a tiny risk. The smallest. The minutest. It's almost not even a risk to be with him once.

Unless you become addicted, whispers my internal risk advisor. I order her to shut the hell up.

"Maybe you don't need that book tonight." I take a bold step forward and pluck it out of his hands.

18

I'M SPEECHLESS. SHE'S LITERALLY RENDERED me completely without speech.

"Just for tonight?" I manage to croak out when her confident look starts to falter under my stupid, stupid silence.

"What else do you want?"

Fuck, so much, Goldie, I think, but so I don't scare her off, I say, "I'd like to date you."

"You told me you were a shitty boyfriend before."

I'm not the wordsmith she is. I want to put my true feelings out there as best I can, but I've never had to say anything like this before. Not even to Megan did I articulate my feelings, but looking back that's probably because I didn't have many beyond, *she's a nice girl and a good lay.*

I've had plenty of sex since then but nothing like the kiss in the kitchen. Nothing like Lucy. Her golden hair shines with its own sort of light, and I can't stop myself from curling a wayward lock around my finger. "Yeah, I freely admit I sucked at the boyfriend thing before, and you have every reason to think I'm going to fail at this, but I'm going into my senior year. I've been doing the practice, school, game thing for three years now. I think I can add in a girlfriend to the mix without throwing everything off."

"I don't know." She hesitates. "A date?"

"Yep. Movie. Dinner. Long walks on the snow-covered sidewalks since we're in the Midwest and not the coast and it's winter."

She's silent too long, and I don't have the first clue what's going on in her head. I'm hopeful she's going to say yes, but the longer I get nothing, the more worried I become.

"Admit it. You're curious. Our kiss was hot the other night," I remind her. So hot that I've been thinking of it nonstop.

"My friend Sutton says players like you only have one night stands because your enormous egos can't handle knowing that you aren't good in bed."

"Your friend Sutton has never slept with me."

"She's one of the few then."

I walked into that one. "Then you owe it to yourself to give me one night and see if I'm worth it. One night to see if we're even compatible. How about that?"

If she won't agree to a date, then I'll have to use tonight to convince her that whatever risk grade she's assigned to me is outweighed by the rewards I can provide.

Dusk settles in, and the newly lit campus lights give her a fairy glow. *Goldilocks, you're sleeping in the right bed tonight.* Her eyes fix on my face, and she studies me for at least two long breaths. She ends her inspection with a firm nod.

Her somber face switches instantly, and she gives me a brilliant smile. "Okay."

"Okay what?"

"Okay, one night."

She takes the lead, marching briskly toward her apartment. "Do you have condoms?" she asks. "Because I don't."

"If I say yes, are you putting a check in the *con* column?" I ask warily.

"No, it'd save us time. Otherwise we'll have to stop somewhere."

"Maybe we should stop anyway," I suggest because I only have the one. I've carried a condom in my wallet since I was twelve. My mom gave me the first one after I had my first embarrassing wet dream, and she found me shoving my sheets into the washing machine.

"Why? Don't you have any?" she asks.

"I only have *one*." I emphasize the number. Her eyes widen.

"You think we're going to need more than one?" She laughs.

Some guys' nuts might have shriveled up. I view this as a challenge. "Goldie, we're going to need at least three."

"No way," she scoffs, but as she realizes I'm not kidding even a little, her laughter turns to skepticism. "Really?"

I resist rubbing my hands together. "You can keep count."

We stop at the store and buy a box of condoms. The clerk smirks and starts to make a dumbass comment but between Lucy's withering look and my warning glare, he wisely rings us up silently and tucks the box into a brown paper bag.

"I forget sometimes that you're a world-class athlete," she mentions as we climb the steps to her apartment. "And sex is an athletic event. You know Paul Brown believed women shouldn't be allowed around his Cleveland team because they sapped the players' energy."

"First, the only athletic event I've been involved in for the last couple of weeks has been seeing how much I can drink in one night and second, please, I want you to sap my energy. I want you to sap me until I'm dry."

"You can stop now," she says repressively. "I get it."

I guess my dirty-talk skills need work. We stop at her door. As she fits her key into the lock, she says, "I have roommates, so you'll need to be quiet."

I run a finger across my lips. "Done."

Lucy doesn't really get it, not yet at least. But I want her bad enough that I'd dress up as a woman if it got her clothes off and us on her bed.

For all her worry, the apartment is dead silent when she opens the door. Her roommates are either hiding in their rooms or they're at dinner. Given the quiet in the apartment, I'm guessing dinner.

I help Lucy out of her coat, then take mine off and drape it over my arm. I'm not sure where she wants me to put my stuff.

"You can hang your jacket up and, um, take your boots off?" It's more question than instruction.

I like that she's unsure what to do with me, that *this* event is foreign enough there's no practiced routine of where the visitor's coat and shoes go. I toe off my boots and drape my jacket over hers.

"Do you want to watch some TV?" I ask, trying to give her an out and desperately hoping she doesn't take it.

"No. I don't want that, do you?"

"No." I lean down and brush my lips across hers because it's been a while since I've kissed her and I need to feel her sweetness against me.

She sways into me, her body telling me all I need to know. "Lead the way," I mouth against her lips.

"First door."

A floor lamp flicks on when she hits a switch. Her room is small and white, and I feel sort of like Gulliver amongst the Lilliputians. "Your bed is really small," I say inanely.

"Maybe you're too big," she suggests.

I give her a cheeky wink. "Said no guy ever."

Fortunately, she laughs. "Do you want something to drink?"

"No." My need for food, water, football? They seem like distant desires in the face of the fierce ache I have for her. I feel like I've wanted to touch her for forever, even though I've only known her a few days. When she starts to pull her sweater over her head, I stop her. I sit down at her desk chair, which feels miniature. I pat my leg. "I would like you to come here."

She walks over and stops in front of me. I position her between my legs and lay my head against her chest, listening to her heartbeat. It flutters, excited and nervous against my ear. My own pounds like a herd of stampeding horses is trying to escape from my chest.

With shaky fingers, I slide her sweater over her head. Underneath she wears a thin silky thing and no bra. Her pert nipples poke against the fabric. I run my hands up under the material, tracing the bumps of her spine, the jut of her shoulder blades. Her eyelids shutter down when I reach the tender base of the back of her neck.

I don't want to rush this. I might not get another chance to touch her again.

The tiny strap of her top slides down her shoulder, the fabric snagging on one erect peak. My mouth waters, and I can't wait another second without laying my mouth against her bare skin. I nudge the fabric down with my chin. She helps me by wriggling her arm out from the strap, first one and then the other.

I take another moment to admire her. "You're beautiful," I say, unable to keep the reverence out of my voice. "So beautiful."

Her fingers find their way to my scalp, scratching and scraping through the strands then lightly pushing me forward.

I blow a stream of hot air against one nipple and then the other. She shudders, and it's like a live electric feed running from her body into mine.

Fucking Christ, but I want her so damn bad.

I take one succulent tip into my mouth and cover the other with my hand. She's smaller than I expected but twice as delicious, and as I swirl my tongue around her nipple, I can't help but think she was made perfectly for me.

Her fingers sink into my scalp, pulling me closer. We both shift. I slide to the edge of the chair; she straddles me. I keep sucking, and she keeps pressing closer and closer.

There's a moan that fills the air, a guttural sound of need and want. I don't know if it's mine or hers. It's probably mine. In my life, I can't remember ever wanting anything as much I want her.

I've hungered for wins on the field, championships, success, but never a person. Not until Luce.

19

THE SUCTION ON MY NIPPLES is making me dizzy. I can't recall if I've ever felt this much *pleasure* from having my nips sucked. I swear I can feel it between my legs with each deep pull.

I never really doubted he'd be good in bed. He knows all too well how to use his body to maximize its athletic ability. And sex is an athletic event. But guys can be selfish, and no matter how well they know their own bodies, it doesn't mean they care to know how to work another's body.

But Matt isn't selfish in any way. He's incredibly giving, and I enjoy being a recipient of that benevolence right now. Any other guy would have me on the bed, my jeans down around my ankles and my panties pulled aside. Which is not to say I don't want to do that with Matt, but his unhurried manner is a welcome surprise.

Him kissing my breasts isn't a step toward a good fuck. It's just pleasurable and wonderful in its own right. Just like our first kiss. Just like sitting on his bed and talking. He savors each moment.

And I can tell by the press of his erection against my stomach that he's enjoying the hell out of this. I rock against him, relishing the pressure of his dick, even through the layers of denim and cotton.

He pulls back, and the cool air against my wet skin is its own kind of erotic sensation.

Reaching over his shoulder, he grabs my insulin case.

"What's going on?" I ask curiously.

"I would feel like a piece of shit if you passed out in the middle of us having sex. That would definitely be a black mark in the risk column. So how about we test your blood sugar?"

That's simultaneously one of the sweetest but also one of the least sexy things that have been said during foreplay. I curl my fingers into my hands so I don't have to take the test. "And if it's too low?"

"Then we get you something to eat if you need it and we sleep."

"And we forget this ever happened?" I'm starting to get angry.

He cocks his head. I don't know if he hears the slight bitterness in my tone. "I hope not." He strokes a hand from my shoulder down over my breast to stop just at the edge of my waistband. My whole body tightens and leans into the caress. "I want one night with you. One full night. If that's all you'll give me."

The unspoken request for more hangs between us. I don't know what I can give him, so I let him take the BG measurement.

"How often do you have to do this?" he asks as I prick my finger and press it against the test strip. I still sit in his lap, straddling him. My hand brushes against his T-shirt-covered chest as I work. The muscles jump and bunch in a gratifying way at my accidental touch. There's something intoxicating about how he responds to me. How easily turned on he is by everything about me.

"Ten to twelve times."

"A week?"

I give him a withering look. "A day."

He swipes the back of his hand across his mouth. "Christ."

"Yeah, so don't tell me about things that dominate your life. I know all about it."

"I suppose you do."

We wait until the measurement flashes on the screen. It says *84*.

"Is that good?" he asks.

"Yes. It should be between 70 and 99 unless I've eaten and then under 140."

I reach past him and place the kit back on the desk. "Anything else you want to test?"

His fingers slide into my waistband, under my panties. "Yes." His eyes darken and it's clear he's not referring to my BG level anymore. "But don't worry. I'm going to do all the work."

"You will, huh?"

"Yeah." He surges to his feet and in two steps drops my ass on the bed. He strips down so fast. His shirt flies off his head and his jeans and underwear fall to the floor in no time. He stands before me like the "small g" god that he jokingly called himself.

His body is perfectly formed, a testament to a careful diet and non-stop workouts. He has hair on his chest, a light dusting over his pectorals and a darker trail that leads right down to his penis. He leans forward, his shaft hanging heavy between us, and plants a hand on either side of my waist.

"I can't wait to get my mouth on you and test out how good you taste."

He lifts me with one hand and somehow drags down my jeans with the other until I'm wearing nothing but my camisole around my waist and a pair of damp lavender lace panties.

"I can't wait to feel you and test out how wet you are."

"Matthew," I warn.

"What? Does the dirty talk embarrass you?" He slips a finger between my legs. "I told you I like to talk during sex. Besides, even if you're turning redder than the Oklahoma uniforms, it turns you on. I'm going to suck on your clit here." He rubs my clit, and I can't deny the flood of excitement that washes through me. "And then tongue-fuck your sweet pussy until you come all over my face."

I grow wetter and redder with each word. "Matt, shut up."

He laughs and strokes me again over my panties. "You know this is the Aussie kiss. Because I'm doing you down under."

"Shut up!" I repeat with a half groan, half laugh.

"I don't know if I can. Maybe you have some idea about what I can do with my mouth." His tone is light but his gaze is hot and hungry. Another finger presses against my aching core, then those two fingers sweep my panties away to touch my bare skin.

But the touch is maddeningly light. He looks at me, waiting.

I give in because I want this so bad. "You should get on your knees and put your mouth on my…pussy." I push the word past my lips.

His eyes light up in mischief. "Yes, ma'am."

He does just as I ordered. He falls to his knees and pulls the rest of my clothes off. And as he did with my breasts, he takes his time.

First he looks, telling me how gorgeous I am. Then he traces the rough pad of his finger over every peak and valley. I think I should be embarrassed at how exposed I am, but he doesn't allow it. I can *hear* the obvious pleasure and delight he takes in just looking at me, and when he finally does place his lips and tongue against me, it's as if he's never done anything so marvelous in his life. It's crazy how good this feels.

I lie back, close my eyes and give myself over to Matt. His hands dig into my butt, simultaneously kneading me and pulling me closer. In his strong grip, I don't need to be careful because he's there to catch me, to carry me, to hold me. And as regressive as that is, it feels wonderful.

The release starts in my toes and winds its way up, twisting and curling until I'm gasping for air. I tug on his head, wanting him to let go, but he shakes me off and delves deeper. His tongue arrows into me, drawing the tension so tight that it's either give in or implode. I come so hard I nearly pass out.

He holds me as I shake, still drinking me down as if he can't get enough. Only when I've calmed enough to open my eyes does he draw back. His mouth is glistening with the evidence of my enjoyment.

A few seconds later and he's on the bed, condom in hand.

"How's the risk/reward assessment going?"

"I'm taking points away if you keep bringing that up," I warn.

"Fair enough. Which one of us is going to put this on the big guy?" He grins, but there's a tension behind that smile, a feral need that he's trying to hide so I won't be scared off.

I raise my hand, and he slaps the condom into my palm. "Of course you call it big."

I place one corner of the foil between my teeth and tear.

"Even if I had a tiny dick, I'd say it was a big one. I'd lie to myself until I believed it. No man can walk around with any confidence if he believes his dick is too small."

"You don't seem to lack confidence, that's for sure." He's entirely comfortable in his nudity.

"Because I'm big." He even reaches down to pat his dick, which is, as he describes, big. And actually sort of beautiful. The mushroom-shaped head is flushed an angry red, and the veins push prominently against the skin. He looks…virile and manly and the opposite of me. And even though I'm not one for male nudity, the sight of him on my bed—unclothed and erect—is mouthwatering.

I position the reservoir over the ruddy head of his penis and begin to roll it down. I don't get much past the head before he puts a hand out to halt me.

"Wait," he says and pulls my hand away. He holds it to the side while he finishes covering himself with the condom.

"What?"

He closes his eyes for a moment, and when he flashes them open, the bare hunger is no longer shielded. "I'm too close to the edge and would like to be inside you for at least a couple of seconds before I blow my lid."

He tries to smile, but there's too much want there to be disguised, and it instills a confidence in me, a surety, that I never really had with a male before. I crook my finger. "I figure you're good for another round. You did buy a whole box."

"I did, didn't I?" He dives for me.

I might be wet, but it's a tight fit. Partly because I haven't had sex in a while and partly because he is big. His dick is proportional to the rest of him. Big hands, big feet, broad shoulders. Poised over me, one hand braced by my shoulder and the other guiding the broad head past my entrance, all I can see is *him*.

He works himself in inch by excruciating inch. The feel of him inside me is headier than I remember. There's something exquisite about the heavy weight of a body above yours. The way a body like Matt's presses you into the mattress. How all your senses are engulfed because you can't see, hear, or feel anything but him.

There's nothing in my head but the roughness of his hair-covered legs against mine and the smell of his citrus-spiced scent that I suck into my lungs. Beneath my fingers, his shoulder muscles clench as he fights for control to give me everything I need.

He lasts longer than a couple of seconds—much longer. He grits his teeth, mumbles numbers under his breath, and stares off into the distance as he pumps his hips in a steady, perfect rhythm against me. I feel each drag of his plump head along my sensitive tissues as he withdraws and the fierce possession as he drives forward. It's more wonderful, more erotic than I could have imagined, than I can even put words to.

And the way he's trying so hard to keep it together long enough for me to enjoy this part as much as when he was kneeling at my feet, his mouth sucking and licking until I came undone, makes my heart squeeze. In this moment, with every part of his body and mind, he's making the case that he's worth *every* risk.

His hard planes rub against my tender parts. And it isn't just my body that responds to him. My heart opens.

And I know I shouldn't be feeling these things with him, not for one night. I know I should wrap my emotions up in a tight ball and simply enjoy the physical aspect of it. But between the really amazing sex and the tender, almost loving touch Matt lays against me, I can't seem to keep it in, keep it together.

I let his warmth seep into every pore.

He dips down, his strong arms holding his body at the perfect angle above mine, and takes my mouth. His tongue makes love to me with the same patient pacing as his body. We suck on each other's tongues. I hang on his shoulders, wrapping myself around him, arms and legs, until we are one measured, beating being moving in perfect synchronicity.

Why would I want to keep it together? Why not just let go?

He reaches between us, one hand finding my clit. "Here?" he asks.

"Yes, there," I tell him.

He smiles against my mouth and presses and pinches and pulls the second orgasm out of me.

I'm barely conscious of him tensing and muffling a shout against my shoulder. And when his heavy weight pushes me deeper into the mattress, I only have enough energy to wrap my arms around his torso. I don't even care that I can barely breathe.

He rests in my embrace for the count of ten breaths, maybe more, before heaving himself to the side.

I mewl my disappointment, and it wrenches a weak chuckle from him. "Woman, let me recover."

"I'd slap you if I wasn't so weak."

He wedges a hand underneath me and, in one move, flips me onto my side. "Have I mentioned how small your bed is?"

"You might have complained a time or three."

He grunts and hauls me back against his chest. His knees fit into the back of my knees. One strong arm is under my head and the other is banded around my waist. His thumb idly strokes a path from between my breasts down to my navel. It's simultaneously soothing and arousing. The duality of the touch sums up Matt himself. He's both a guy who has had a countless number of partners in the past but somehow still manages to make the girl he's with feel special.

I don't, in any way, feel like I'm one of the nameless crowds. I should be worried about that, about how I'm already erasing the image Ace had sketched out and am filling in my own image, but it's too late. It's a done thing. Matt has become my Matty—an unselfish guy who seems to only want to make me happy, both in bed and out of it.

"Take a nap. We have to prepare for round three." His breath ghosts against the back of my neck.

I've told him one night, and it appears he wants to get in as much action as possible.

"No. There's no round three. I'm not an athlete. I'm a delicate flower."

He leans forward and presses his mouth against my neck, right below my earlobe. Shit, that's a sensitive spot. "What did I tell you? I'm going to do all the work."

As I fall asleep in the cocoon of Matty's body, I wonder how I'm ever going to be satisfied with one night.

20

"I'M NOT TRYING TO BE annoying, but I have to ask. How was it?" Sutton blurts as the door of our apartment building closes behind us.

"He's the unicorn," I admit glumly.

"Damn." Sutton jams her hands into her pockets, and we trudge along.

I give her full marks for waiting this long. After Matty left this morning, Sutton and Charity banged on my door and yelled for me to get my ass out into the living room where I would be subject to a full debriefing.

I feigned sleep and hid, not because I was embarrassed, but because I wasn't sure what it all meant.

Sutton was dressed in her coat, hat, gloves, and boots when I got home from class. No more escaping her. I did make her wait while I tested my glucose. It was disgustingly normal, so I shrugged on my sleeping bag of a coat and now we're going for our walk, or interrogation.

The snow is bunched up on the sides of the sidewalk where the snowplow pushed it a few days ago. The sun's out and there's no wind,

- 203 -

which means there are plenty of people out getting a little fresh air. Sutton waits until we're relatively alone to pepper me with more questions.

"When are you seeing him again?"

"I don't know."

"Did he say he would call you?"

"I can't remember."

She stops. "What's that mean?"

"It means…" God, how do I put this delicately? "I was too worn out this morning to remember my own name. He whispered something in my ear, but I just wanted to go back to sleep." We'd made real inroads into that box of condoms.

Her mouth drops open. "Damn," she says finally. "Please tell me that you're going to see him again. Or that if you're done with him, I can get a shot."

Every hair on my body bristles in protest. Matty with Sutton? My stomach flips over. Matty bracing himself one-armed over Sutton's sexy body? I fist my hands. Matty whispering in her ear that he wants her to come all over his dick until there's not an ounce left in her body? I nearly bare my teeth at her. Sutton knows immediately, without me saying even a word, how much I don't like the thought of Matty with anyone *but me*, and bends over to howl with laughter.

"Shut up," I say, but there's no fierceness in my command. It's more of a lament.

I wait until she's done gasping for air to start walking again.

"So what's your hang-up?" she says when she catches up a few minutes later—tears from her laughter still clinging to her eyes. "Because if I felt that possessive about a guy, I wouldn't be letting him go the next morning without a second date chiseled in the sidewalk in front of the student union."

"Why stop there?" I say sarcastically. "How about I brand him? Put my initials on his ass."

"No," Sutton disagrees. "If you're going to brand him, it's got to be a place where everyone can see it. Like his wrist. Maybe his knuckles."

"Are you serious?"

"A little bit." She spreads her index and thumb in a mock measurement of sorts.

"See, that's why I'm worried. He's gone a lot, and when he's around and I'm busy, he's going to get bored and wander away." But when I hear myself criticize Matty, I know immediately it's unfair. He told me himself that he hadn't wanted a repeat of his failed freshman romance. I shouldn't insult him by doubting him when he's given me no cause for concern.

"He's not your mom," Sutton chides me gently.

"You mean I'm not my mom." I'd hope not. I've spent my whole life trying to *not* be her.

"No. I meant what I said. You're afraid every hot, attractive guy is your mom, who will end up dumping you and leaving you with your pants around your ankles and a little girl to raise."

I really have to stop talking to Sutton so much about my past.

"I…" I don't know what to say, but I don't have to because Sutton isn't finished.

"You aren't your mom. You never were. You're just not made up that way. What you fear is falling for someone like your mom—flighty, irresponsible. So you date people who you perceive are just like you. If you were afraid of being your mom, you'd stay away from people who feel like mirrors."

I tug my zipper down to let some cold air into my suddenly too-warm coat, but I don't dismiss Sutton's theory out of hand. I've always chosen guys who were careful and cautious. Low angst sort of males. Ones who I figured were too dull or lazy to get tired of me and move on when, in fact, the relationships never got off the ground because of the overwhelming dullness of them.

Not one had been flighty or silly. Matt's not either, but he's bold and that's shocking to my careful, plodding existence. Slowly, I start to put words to my jumbled thoughts. "Assume everything you say is true—"

"It is. Always. Forever," she says smugly.

I ignore her. "Assume what you say is true. That still means Matt and I are opposites, and while the saying is that opposites attract, what happens after they've collided?" I slap my hands together. "My parents were opposites. My dad's a hard worker, my mom is flighty. They don't have anything in common, and it led to a lot of heartbreak for them." For me, too, for that matter. "It's hard for me to envision two people who are opposites sticking together."

Sutton chews on that for a moment. "I don't see you and Matt as opposites. You're more alike than you think. You both love being part of a team. You both want to excel at what you do. Really the only difference is that you tend to take a more cautious approach to things, and Matt seems to be a feet-first kind of guy."

"Isn't that a really big difference, though?" Isn't it? Or am I making a bunch of mountains where there doesn't even need to be a hill?

"Only if you want it to be."

* * *

MATTY

"Eat shit, asshole." My thumb presses the controller to the right while I trigger the kick mechanism.

"Too late, dickweed. I've got this." And fuck if Hammer doesn't block my shot.

"Fuck." I toss the controller down. I can't concentrate for shit tonight.

"Are you thinking about that chick?" Hammer guesses immediately that I'm preoccupied with Luce but can't believe it. He asks in astonishment, "How can you miss her? Didn't you spend all night hauling her ashes?"

"Hauling her ashes?" I shake my head. Hammer's getting stranger and stranger.

"No bueno?" He pulls out his phone.

I shake my head. "It sounds like she's dirty inside."

"Hmm. I don't want that."

"Why are you even asking? Aren't *fuck*, *sex*, *laid*, and *tapping it* good enough?"

"I'm writing my next article about obscure sexual euphemisms." He makes a few notes in his phone.

"How the hell did you decide to write that?"

He grins. "Apparently the magazine gets a lot of searches for that topic, so we're beefing up our search engine optimization by writing on topics people are interested in. What do you think of *doodling the alphabet*?"

"Only if it's oral, but are you really doodling? I mean, if you're doing it right, you should be applying some serious pressure down there."

"Fuck, man, since when are you requiring dirty sex terms to be so damn precise?" He presses the delete key on his phone a little harder than necessary.

"I don't know." I reach for my beer. This conversation requires me to be a lot drunker than I am. "You asked for my opinion and I'm giving it to you."

"Yeah. Yeah. How about *sheathing the sword*?"

"Doesn't sound very obscure. That's been around since the Middle Ages." I drink half the bottle. If I get drunk enough, I can drown out Hammer and forget Lucy. Actually no, if I get too drunk, I'll probably end up outside Lucy's apartment.

I did agree to only one night.

Or did I?

I mean, she said one night, but I don't remember making any explicit promises that I'd stay away.

"What about *caulking the tub*?"

I raise my hand. "Caulk the tub?"

He grins. "It's white. Sticky. You're spreading it all over her."

I want to give him shit, but he's kind of right. "Is this a list for construction workers or women?"

He makes a face. "Good point. Was it any good?"

Normally I didn't have a problem sharing details with Hammer. Hell, we'd even double-teamed a girl or girls from time to time. So why did the thought of him knowing anything about Lucy's body, her thready moans, her propensity to fuck with her lips slightly parted and her eyes squeezed shut make me want to put a fist through his face?

"What? Not telling me?" He sits back with a smirk. "Are you in *love*? Should I shake my tux out of storage? I barely hung the thing up after Masters's wedding."

"I like her. Deal with it." I scowl and pick up the controller again. How'd this off-season become so damned complicated? One minute I was bathing in champagne and the next I'm stressing about the team and now a girl.

"You're not messing with her, are you?" Hammer's concern for Lucy should piss me off, but it's *Hammer*.

"How come Masters didn't get this lecture?"

"Because he was a virgin. It was obvious he was in love with Ellie or he wouldn't have given it up."

"You think I'm an amoral dog? You wanted me to date your sister, for Christ's sake." Okay, now it's starting to piss me off. Hammer's done his share of the dirty deeds when it comes to girls. "Do I need to bring up suitcase girl?"

"Nah, man." He flushes under his dark skin, and I feel a tiny bit guilty bringing it up. Hammer always says his lowest moment was that night. "Look, you're a good dude and an awesome teammate, but the whole 'girl hiding in a suitcase' is exactly why I'm worried. We've done some shit neither of us are particularly proud of."

Casual sex had been our modus operandi since I broke it off with Megan at the beginning of my sophomore year. Hammer had never been able to stick with one girl, no matter how hard he tried, so we figured the next best thing was one-night or two-night stands with girls who wanted the same thing—no-strings-attached fun in the sack. Or the bathroom. Or the nook by the ice machine in a hotel. The out-of-town girls were the absolute best. They knew you were coming in for the night and didn't expect anything but a good time.

I delivered on every occasion. Lucy wanted the same thing, so why didn't it sit right?

Hammer does write for a women's magazine. He's got sisters. Of all my friends, he's the most qualified to give advice...I think. Fuck it. What do I have to lose by getting another point of view here?

"Lucy was the one who wanted one night. Think she means it?"

"Dunno. Why not text her and find out?"

Why don't I just text her? She did, at least, give me her phone number last night before kicking me out. I want to slap myself on the forehead. And I told Luce to stop overthinking things.

I pull out my phone and start typing.

"How about *surfing the curve*?" Hammer says.

My fingers pause over the screen as my mind takes a minute to figure out exactly what the hell Hammer is talking about. "I think I read that on the Black Twitter hashtag."

"Fuck. I think I did, too." He presses the backspace on his phone.

Shaking my head, I text Lucy.

Me: *What're you doing?*

Luce: *End of mock trial practice. May not make it home. Was so horrible may commit hara-kari.*

Me: *Can that wait until tomorrow? I'd like to see you again.*

Luce: *I plan to watch a psychological drama with my roommates. U?*

Me: *Losing badly at FIFA Soccer to Hammer.*

"What about *laying the lumber*?"

I look up from my phone and share a smirk with Hammer. One

particular college football commentator constantly uses some variation of "laying the lumber" or "laying the wood" when referencing a hard hit. Why? None of us can figure it out, but we laugh like we're in middle school every time he says it. He says it a lot.

"Absolutely, you need to include that one," I inform Hammer before returning to my texts.

Luce: *Sounds thrilling.*

Me: *How hard and fast was that one-night rule?*

There's a long pause, and the stupid animated ellipsis cycles repeatedly from one end of the tiny gray balloon to the other while I stare at the screen like Moses waiting for the ten commandments to be inscribed in the stone tablets. Whoever thought of that texting feature should be shot.

Finally, the text comes through.

Luce: *I don't know. Suppose you can come over.*

I get up the second I'm done reading the text. Hammer grabs my sweats. "What the hell? We're in the middle of a game."

"I forfeit."

"You going to Lucy's place? Have you talked to her about Ace yet?"

"I'm handling it." I scowl. Way to be a buzzkill, Hammer.

"Handling it how? Because I was talking to Bish the other night and he said Ace hasn't indicated that he's interested in joining Bish's backfield. Plus, he said that some of the O-line guys are pissed off about it and are looking for a little off-season throwdown. Situation is going to get out of control if you don't do something."

"Great. Why don't you tell Bish to worry about getting the secondary in shape with the guys he has? I'll worry about Ace."

"This Lucy girl has to have some influence on Ace. I mean, look at Masters and Ellie. She's got him wrapped around her finger. If she asked him to move to safety, he'd be doing drills with Bish tomorrow," Hammer insists.

"I'm getting sick and tired of people lumping Ace and Lucy together. They aren't a fucking couple."

"Hey, man. Maybe not in Lucy's mind, but he's got her picture in his *locker*."

"So fucking what?" Jesus, I'm reduced to being jealous of a girl's friend. I don't like that about me, but I can't deny the truth of it. Every time I think of Ace and Lucy together, it makes me want to crush objects into tiny, dusty particles.

Hammer backs away. "Why don't you put your guns away. We don't have to talk about it right now. We can table it." I look down and see my hands curled into fists. "I do have some advice about Lucy, though. First, you should admit your feelings to her. Girls love feelings. They love talking about their feelings. So tell her that she makes you think of birds and flowers."

"Birds and flowers?" I gape at him. The last thing I think of when it comes to Lucy is birds and flowers. Big words, long blond hair, yes. Delicate, fluttery things? No.

"Second," he continues as if I'm not even here. In fact, is he dictating into his phone? "Don't ever mention that you had sex in the past. It's good to be experienced but not too experienced. You want to be the gentleman in the streets, but the guy who can get his freak on—because you read it in a book—in the sheets. Third—"

I hold up my hand before Hammer can go on. "No, sorry. I don't listen to your advice anymore."

He looks hurt. "Why not? I'm a professional."

"Your articles consist of *how to recognize when your type is the ass-hole and what to do next* and *how to enjoy yourself when your partner is selfish*, which have zero to do with dating."

"They have everything to do with dating," Hammer protests.

"If you have a vagina, which I don't. I'm asking Masters."

"Wait a second. Masters? Dude was a virgin six months ago."

"And now he's married."

I run upstairs to the third-floor apartment and pound on the door. It swings open a minute later, and Ellie steps out, flushed. "Bye, babe."

Masters is right behind her sporting sleepy eyes and a smug-as-shit smile. They just had sex.

"Ellie, just the person I want to talk to. I'm going over to a girl's place. Should I bring something?"

"I don't know. What's the context?"

"We're just hanging out." Hopefully having sex later so I can wear the same smug-as-shit smile.

"Yeah, I'd definitely bring something. Maybe something to drink. A snack even. If you're hungry, bring something for yourself."

I know exactly what I'll bring. "Thanks."

Hammer's at the base of the stairs looking offended. "I could have given you that advice."

"Dude, fine. Next time I need some advice on obscure phrases for sex, I'll come to you. Now get out of the way. I need to throw some clothes on and get to the Brew House."

* * *

"Hey, ladies."

Two girls, one with purple hair who I saw walking with Luce the other day and a brunette, stand just inside the entrance to Luce's apartment. Both faces hold a certain amount of skepticism, as if opening the door wider might let in a host of demons, not just one dude.

"I'm Sutton, this is Charity." The purple-haired girl tips her head toward the brunette.

"Nice to meet you. I brought coffee." I hold up the cardboard beverage container. "I wasn't sure what you all wanted but the Brew House said Lucy usually drinks a sugar-free peppermint mocha. I got the fully leaded for you guys."

"You went to the Brew House and asked what she likes to drink?" Sutton's eyebrows shoot high onto her forehead.

Shit, have I made a mistake here? Should I have played it cooler? "Too stalkerish?"

"Too awesome." Sutton drags me inside and slams the door shut.

"What else did you bring?" the girl with enough rings on her fingers to start a jewelry store asks. She takes the beverage holder from my hand, and Sutton reaches for the bag under my arm.

"He brought sugar-free ice cream," announces Sutton.

The two stare at me like I've got two heads.

"What? Why are you looking at me like that?" I ask with slight alarm. I look down to check whether my zipper is shut. Yup, the barn door is closed.

"Did you really bring over a container of sugar-free ice cream and a skinny latte with sugar-free flavoring?

I take a sip. "It tastes okay." Fuck, coffee is disgusting but this is for

Luce, so I'm suffering through it.

"What are you?"

"Are you real?"

Their skepticism is disconcerting. "I think the real question is what kind of guys are you dating that this is a phenomenon rather than an ordinary occurrence."

Fortunately, Luce blows in before the two can dissect me any further. "Here." I shove the drink into her hands. "For you."

"Thanks." She takes a deep sip and hands the drink back to me along with her backpack.

"How was mock trial?" Sutton asks.

"Terrible. Heather seems to have forgotten everything. I was off my game and kept missing objections. Emily was completely rattled and Randall had to leave the room four times to keep from yelling at us. I don't get Heather. She's like two different people. One day she performs flawlessly and two days later it's like she doesn't even remember that she's on the team."

"Maybe she's a twin. My former teammate Masters has an identical twin. They used to do twin switches on us all the time." I take Lucy's coat and hang it on the hook, placing mine on top of it. There. It's my jacket covering hers. Not Ace's. Not the Ken doll's from the coffee store. Mine.

Mine. Mine. Mine. Mine.

I'm an only child. I don't like to share. Won't share. Don't believe in sharing.

Lucy shudders. "A twin? The world does not deserve two Heathers. But you know? I don't want to talk about it. Let's turn the television on."

"You sure you want to watch that show?" Sutton asks in a stage whisper.

"Why wouldn't we?" Luce responds with annoyance.

Sutton jerks her head toward me. "Because *he's* here."

"Don't change your plans on my account." I raise both hands.

Their version of a psychological drama is a show about wedding dresses. During the opening credits, my phone rings. I ignore it. Lucy is sitting only a half cushion away from me and I'm plotting how to eliminate the distance. With her two roommates watching my every move, I don't make much progress.

Against my will, I'm drawn into the sad story about two women who can't stand up to their moms and how they're desperate for just a smile from the older women. I guess it *is* a psychological drama, but hell, I'd watch a dozen weepy chick flicks if it meant Lucy was within touching distance. Halfway through the second one, she's pushed her bare feet under my thigh. For warmth, she informed me. *Whatever excuse you want to give, Goldie. I'm here to warm everything from your toes to your pussy to your delicious-looking mouth.* My phone beeps again.

"You can get that," Lucy says.

"You're sure? I don't want to be rude." I don't really know the details of dating anymore. I know answering my cellphone when I was dating Megan was a huge pet peeve of hers.

"Yeah, I mean, the show's pretty repetitive. Charity's on her phone and Sutton's doing homework."

I slip out my phone. "It's Hammer." I turn the screen to her so she can read the *'sup?*

Me: *Watching TV.*

Hammer: *What do you think of spa day?*

Me: *I guess?*

Hammer: *Ask your panel of experts.*

Me: *Panel of what?*

Hammer: *Lucy and her friends. Ask them.*

Oh, for fuck's sake. I turn to Lucy. "My roommate Hammer writes a man's advice column for a women's magazine. He wants me to consult you on whether his list of euphemisms for sex is any good. Feel free to say no."

Charity slaps her hands against her face. "Oh my God. Is Harry Wright Jr., your roommate?" At my nod, she turns to Sutton and Lucy. "Harry writes 'From My Three Eyes' column in *Monologue*."

"'Three Eyes'? For real?" I had no idea what Hammer's column was named.

"It's cheeky. We know what it means." She rolls her eyes at my shock.

Cheeky? Sounds vulgar. I realize my assumptions of women are all wrong, but that's my own damn fault for not spending more time with them when they have their clothes on.

"I love 'Three Eyes,'" Sutton exclaims. "I had no idea he was a football player or that he went to Western!"

"He wants to know if he can come over to hang." I turn the phone again so Lucy can read his message, knowing she'll appreciate it. *I'm available to meet with my new fan club. Tell me when and where.*

"Sure, why not?"

"Tell him to bring us something," Sutton declares. "What do we want?"

"We're out of microwave popcorn,"

"On it," I tell them.

Me: *Price of admission is popcorn. There are five of us.*

Hammer: *Make that six. Masters is bored now that Ellie is at work.*

"Okay if my buddy Masters comes over? His wife is working."

"Sure. The more the merrier, but someone will have to sit on the floor."

"Hammer can. He's used to it. He has three sisters."

I don't know if he's used to sitting on the floor, but he'll do it and he'll like it because I'm not moving my ass from Lucy's sofa until she physically hoists me out of here.

I'm part of her life now. She's not getting rid of me.

21

LUCY

MATTY IS TOO DAMN CHARMING for his own good, I decide the following morning.

And it isn't his size or body or face that turns me on. It's *him*. His easygoing nature, his willingness to answer anything put in front of him, the way he makes fun of himself. It's so easy to be around him. He brought me sugar-free treats last night, watched four episodes of *Say Yes to the Dress,* and we laughed ourselves silly over Hammer's list.

He left with his friends but not before giving me a long hug—one that left me in no doubt whether he'd have liked to stay the night. Both Charity and Sutton gave me a hard time, saying I was a fool not to take what was being offered to me on a silver platter.

I open my can of soup and consider the whole risk assessment thing. Sutton's right. He doesn't appear to be much of a risk at all, or no greater risk than any other guy I've gone out with before. And the rewards? Holy hell, the rewards are like having a million dollars at the bottom of a bungee jump. My stomach's in my throat, but it's totally worth it.

As I dump the can into the bowl, the wall phone rings. I pick it up, hoping it's Matty. If it is, I know what I'm having right after lunch. I grin to myself.

My happiness fades when I hear the voice.

"It's me. Let me up," Ace says impatiently.

He texted a few times since the Tuesday night debacle, but I haven't completely forgiven him. It was an asshole thing to do, and none of his texts have been apologies. I suppose he thinks I'm going to that movie with him tonight. I'm not. I scheduled a practice with Heather and Randall.

I feel a twinge of guilt that I broke my pact with Ace: he'd stay away from my roommates and I'd stay away from the football team.

It was easy up until I met Matty. After all, I lasted nearly three years unimpressed and unmoved by the entire team. And it's not like there weren't opportunities, but none of them interested me. If I'm going to date Matt, I'll need to tell Ace. He deserves it.

However, Ace acting like an asshole doesn't really mean we aren't friends anymore. At some point, we're going to have to hammer this issue out so we can go on being friends. I press '9' on the phone for a few seconds to release the lobby door and let him in. "Hey, Sutton. Ace is here and I think he wants to talk about something."

"Want me to disappear into the bedroom?" she asks from the couch where she's been vegging out the past forty-five minutes.

"Do you mind?"

"Nah, I can work on my Roman history paper. Should I pop out and save you in say, twenty minutes?" She flicks the television off and pushes up off the sofa.

"Hopefully not."

A knock on the door signals his arrival. Sutton mouths that I should yell if I need her.

I pull the door open to find Ace bracing himself with one hand against the wall. He looks worn and tired.

"Are you still drunk from last week?"

"I wish." He raises his sunglasses so I get a good look at his bloodshot eyes. "Sorry about the other night."

Finally, an apology. I forgive him immediately. No point in holding grudges, but hopefully he'll tell me what's wrong. Still, I tell him exactly what I thought of his behavior. "It was a shitty thing to do, but you're forgiven."

After all, I got to spend the night with Matt, no matter how chaste it was. And since then I've had my "spa day" with him. No, spa day does not work. The night spent with Matty was not full of zen moments and tinkling wind chimes but of hot, needy, sweaty excitement. I'll need to report to Hammer that spa day as a euphemism for sex has to go. "Come on in."

Ace sort of slumps in, walking heavily as if his joints hurt. He drops into a kitchen chair with a thud and leans back on two legs.

The kitchen set is my favorite piece of furniture in the whole apartment. Charity, Sutton, and I had driven to Chicago over Spring Break because that's all Sutton and I could afford. Halfway there we stopped for lunch at a small-town diner and discovered they were renovating the place, getting rid of their old metal-rimmed tables and vinyl-covered chairs—the ones with the sparkly fabric underneath the plastic coating. We fell in love with them immediately and Charity's parents paid to ship them back to our apartment.

The set will be Charity's when we graduate, and I don't want Ace breaking a chair leg before then. I hit him on the back of his head on my way to the microwave.

"Ouch! What the hell was that for?" he yelps. The chair, however, is safely back on all four legs.

"You were leaning back on the chair." I stick my bowl of soup in the microwave and punch in the time. Turning around, I rest my butt against the counter and wait for Ace to tell me why he's here. Other than to apologize.

He heaves a sigh. "I guess I deserve that."

"You want to tell me what's going on? First, you're a total ass on Tuesday. If you didn't want me to stay at your place, you should have told me." I count off his sins on each finger. "Second, you send me lame 'what's up' texts when you know you should be apologizing. If you don't start talking, I'm calling your mom."

"You got any more soup?" he asks, ignoring my question.

"Third, you're ignoring me even though you're about to eat my food, which is so rude there's probably a picture of you next to the word in the dictionary right this minute."

He waves his hands in surrender. "Yes. Fine, I'll answer whatever you want, just...I need some food."

The microwave beeps, and I carry the soup over to him. "Start talking."

He stirs the beef stew around a few times, as if he can find the answer to his problem when the potatoes and carrots are positioned exactly right.

"Is it that your coach wants to replace you with a new player?"

His head jerks up. "Christ, is it already out?"

My heart squeezes at the pain in his voice "No. No, it isn't. I guessed based on what you said the other night." He gulps, and the look on his face reminds me of the time he showed up on my doorstep when we were ten to tell me his daddy was moving out. I say as gently as possible, "Eat your soup, Ace."

I turn and busy myself with the routine of lunch. All the noises of meal prep—opening the can of soup, dumping it into the bowl, opening the microwave—sound overloud when there's complete silence behind me.

When Ace does speak, his voice is tight and hard. "The Warriors are signing a five-star recruit, ranked number three in the country. He's a quarterback."

"So?" I carry my heated soup over to the table. "You won the National Championship. He can start after you graduate."

"Coach says that I can either move to safety or play backup." His mouth twists into a bitter line. He shuts his eyes, likely wanting this to be a bad dream he wakes from.

I reach over and squeeze his hand. "What do you want to do?"

His eyelids flip open. "I'm the quarterback. I want to stay the quarterback."

"But if you don't move, then you'll be benched, is that right?"

He releases a harsh laugh. "You know what's so ironic? In football, the bench is for starters. You have to earn that place on the bench. No backup, no clipboard Jesus, dares to sit there. Don't know why they call it *benched* in football."

I let him vent. If he's come here for advice, I don't know what to tell him, what to say. The only thing I can offer is a sympathetic ear. "What's the rest of your team say?"

"Like Iverson?" he asks snidely.

I carefully set my spoon by my bowl and remind myself that Ace is like a wolf with his foot in a trap—hurt and angry. "Like Iverson. Like Jack. Like Ahmed. Like all of them, Ace. You're a team. It's not golf. You can't go off on your own, score a bunch of points, and then be hailed as a winner. You have to play with twenty-one other people in order to prevail."

"Whose side are you on?" His hands fist on the table. He's not hearing anything I'm saying.

"Yours, of course."

"Really?" He stares at me as if he somehow can divine all the dirty thoughts I have about Matty in my head. He leans forward, and there's a look, an expression, that I don't like.

"Ace—" I say warningly.

He ignores me. The angry part of the wounded animal is taking over. "I'm sure that you think you're qualified to give me advice about sacrifice and the greater good because you're too piss-ass scared to step outside your careful little box you've constructed for yourself, but I want something bigger for myself."

I strive for calm. Ace is lashing out, saying something he'll regret and apologize for tomorrow. This is nothing.

"I know you're hurting, JR, but—"

"Fuck." He rises from the table so fast the chair tips over and soup splashes over the rims of the bowls. "I don't know why I came here. You don't understand. You'll never understand."

He slams the door so hard my jacket falls off the hook.

Sutton pokes her head out as soon as the apartment door slams shut.

"What was that all about?"

"Ace is having a difficult time," I hedge. At the sink, I grab a sponge and start mopping up the mess. "He and the coach are having a disagreement."

"Didn't Ace just win them a championship?" Sutton pitches in without asking. I throw her a grateful look as she holds up the bowls so I can clean underneath them.

"That's what I said, but I guess the coach is thinking about a new direction. Already. And Ace isn't taking it well."

"I bet he's mad about the Matty Iverson thing, too."

"I didn't even get into that," I admit. "Ace was too angry, and he stomped out of here before I could even bring it up."

"I don't know why you put up with him," Sutton mutters.

"Right now? I don't either." My friendship with Ace started so long ago I can barely remember a time that he wasn't part of my life, but even childhood bonds can get so strained that they break.

"At least tell me that you're still thinking about Matty."

I raise rueful eyes to hers. "I can't stop."

22

MATTY

TWO DAYS LATER, I'VE ADDED a second workout to my routine in order to sweat off some of the tension that not fucking is creating. Jerking it at home while I fantasize about Lucy isn't working for me. I know what it's like to be inside her, and my dick is treating my hand like I'm betraying it. I remind myself to be patient. She'll come around.

After watching a wedding show one night, I got invited back for a second round of shows—this time a cooking competition. It didn't matter what was on television. We could have been watching *Sesame Street* and I would've been happy.

Lucy's eyes hardly ever stray far from me. I sense she's on the verge of making a decision, and based on the number of times she's invited me over, my guess is that fortune will fall on my side of the scale. Until then, I plan to tire my body out as much as I can.

Judging by the crowded room, it appears quite a few members of the team are feeling a little anxious about the upcoming Signing Day. There are twelve scholarships being offered, and the quality of recruits we're getting at Western is better every year. This year? After we just won the National Championship? After Masters was on the cover of

Sports Illustrated? The national media is watching us, and for a guy who wants to play at the next level, that is influential shit. Everyone wants to be a Warrior.

"Goddammit, Fozzy, watch where you're going," Hammer chides when Fozworth Royce, our three-hundred-pound carrot-topped center, brushes by him as Hammer's setting down his weight bar.

"Why don't you get out of the fucking aisle," Fozzy mutters.

"I'm standing in the middle of the pad, Foz." Hammer points to his feet, which are, to his credit, planted in the center of one of the large mats lining the floor in front of the wall of mirrors.

"You are now," Fozzy replies sullenly as he walks away.

The sound of Jeezy's "Seen It All" rocks in the background, punctuated by the grunts of about forty guys. We've got a week until Signing Day and then our asses have to be back in practice.

I spot Ace and Jack over in the corner, throwing a weighted medicine ball at each other. Bishop and a couple of his boys are doing box jumps. I turn back to Hammer, who's still glaring at Fozzy's back.

"Taylor Swift it, man," I order.

"What the hell does that mean?"

I shake both my hands. "Shake it off."

"You're spending too much time with the girl squad." Hammer leans over to start another rep of squats.

I lie back on the bench and continue my fly exercises. "Gee, sit around in the stench of passed gas and sour beer or watch television with three babes who smell like a candy store and look better than a Vicky's Secret runway show. Can't imagine why I'm hanging out with Luce and her roommates. Admit it, bro. You're sour because they haven't invited you back."

"I think you're being selfish, keeping them to yourself," he whines. "I've got another list I want to run by them. This time I'm working on the top ten foods that look like dildos."

"No. Not happening."

"Okay. How about a list about the euphemisms for a girl's cooch? I'm guessing sausage casing would be out. I can already see the brunette screwing up her little nose at me. Say, she dating anyone?"

"Charity? Nah, I don't think so."

"You oughta hook me up."

"Who's hooking who up?" Darryl asks.

"Matty's girlfriend has two hot roommates. I think one of them should be doing me." Hammer takes a break and swallows a half gallon of water.

"Matty, bruh, I didn't know you were dating anyone," Darryl says. He leans against the bar above the bench while I glare at Hammer. He's going to jinx the whole deal.

"It's early stages yet."

"Is Masters contagious or something?" Darryl asks warily. "I never thought I'd see the day that you'd be dating someone. I guess that means more at the Gas Station for me."

Stung, I bark back, "I'm not a poon hound. I haven't dated anyone lately because I hadn't met anyone worth dating."

"Then introduce us."

"No way." I wipe my forehead with a towel. I'm trying to convince Lucy that I'm a decent guy worth risking her time and energy on. I bring these yahoos to the party and even though they mean it out of love, I'm already cringing at the types of embarrassing and unsavory stories they'll trot out in an effort to impress her with their not-so-great wit.

"What the fuck, Foz? I have water up my fucking nose," Hammer yelps. When I look up, the rest of Hammer's water jug has been emptied over his face and chest. "Watch where you're fucking going!"

I deduce by the water and the position of Foz at Hammer's elbow that Fozzy must have bumped Hammer while he was drinking and the water splashed everywhere.

I wait for Fozzy to apologize but he doesn't. Instead he takes the nearly empty jug, walks calmly over to me and dumps the rest of the contents over my head. I rip the plastic jug out of his hand and wipe myself off, counting silently to ten, before snapping. "What is your problem today? Your jock a little tight after one too many of momma's cookies at Christmas?"

"You fucking defensive players. You think you're so hot. That you won the Championship last year." Fozzy leans closer, so close I can smell the meat he had for lunch and it's not good. I shift away. He follows like a dank stalker. "That game that we lost last year. That was you guys fucking up. The offense scored thirty-five points. All you guys had to do was make one stop but instead, you allowed the team to score. A team that we embarrassed the year before. If anyone needs replacing on this team, it ain't Ace."

I look past him to Ace, who's standing over in his corner looking smug as fuck. Doesn't he get that this is bad for the team? No matter what happens, we can't be fighting like this.

"Fozzy, we're one team. We're not offense or defense. We're one team, and we win and lose based on the team effort." I reach for patience, wondering how in the hell we've come to this point. Not once during last year, even during games the offense managed only a couple scores, did our D grumble about the offense. We all worked hard and that's what mattered. What happened to measuring that? I wave toward Jack. "Hell, Jack's almost part of the defense what with his sister and Masters getting married. One team, Foz." I stand up and punch him in the shoulder. Not as hard as I want, but hard enough for him to know I didn't appreciate my surprise bath. "Save the water for your gut next time."

"If we're really one team, why aren't you standing up for our boy Ace?" He jerks a thumb over his shoulder. Ace is now leaning against the wall, arms crossed, staring back at me.

The whole room is staring back at me. Fuck me. This is exactly what I didn't want to happen. Can't this team just carry on like it did last year? What difference did it make who was sticking his hands under Fozzy's ass? It *is* the damned defense that carries this fucking team. I take a deep breath before I spew all my shit out onto the weight room floor. Voicing these sentiments might win me favor with the defense, but the stuff I told Foz was true. We rise and fall as one.

"I'm standing for the team," I tell Foz. I tell them all. "The Warriors stand together. They fight together. Or we lose…together. It's not about one player. It's about all of us."

"Then you don't stand for Ace. Well, fuck you then." Foz spits at my shoes.

Hammer has had enough. He lunges for Foz. I can't get up from the bench fast enough to stop the clash. Foz swings at Hammer. Hammer goes low and knocks him backward. Darryl throws himself into the mix and soon, it's defense against offense. There's pushing and shoving and fists are flying.

Bishop runs from across the room and launches himself, Iron Man-style, onto Fozzy's back. Fozzy starts swinging the smaller man around like a cape. Visions of weight benches and racks tipping over causing serious injury flash before my eyes like some kind of nightmare on Elm Street, gym version.

I wade in and start throwing guys to the side.

I finally make some headway through the mass of bodies when someone's fist glances off my chin, and I have to take an extra moment to prevent myself from introducing *my* fist into someone else's face. In the space of that moment, it all goes to hell again until Coach walks in.

He blows the whistle long and hard, and like the trained animals we are, we snap to attention.

"*What in tarnation is going on in here?*"

I heave Roberson off my chest and stagger to my feet.

No one answers the coach. He eyes Ace, whose hair is mussed but other than that looks like he wasn't touched. I don't know whether to be impressed that the O-line did its job protecting him even in the weight room or pissed off that his pretty-boy face doesn't have a scratch on it.

"Anderson, care to tell me why in the blue hell half your line is on the floor looking like they're about to host a goddamned Greek orgy?"

Ace folds his arms across his chest.

Coach turns to me. "How about you, Iverson? Got anything to say for yourself?"

Nothing you'd like to hear. I swipe a hand across my mouth. It comes away bloody.

He spits on the floor in disgust. "You two are clowns." He swings around and eyes every player in the room. "Maybe I should replace the whole lot of you. None of you have guaranteed scholarships. You boys better whip yourself into shape real quick or you'll be paying for the rest of your college career instead of enjoying the free ride that Western so kindly provides."

What bullshit. Western gets millions of dollars from us. Our bowl games fund academic scholarships and music shit and art shit that is totally unrelated to football. And Coach? He wouldn't enjoy his three million a year if it weren't for us and our backbreaking efforts. My throat aches from swallowing all those thoughts down.

Still no one stands up to him because he's Coach.

"Ace, you're the hotshot quarterback. Rein in your boys. And Iverson." He turns back to me.

"Yeah?" I know whatever he's going to say I'm not going to like.

"You got a lot to prove this year, and so far you look like your pants are around your ankles. Maybe the defense was good because Knox Masters was the leader in the locker room. I guess we'll see this year, won't we?"

I haven't been embarrassed in a long time. Not like this. Now my cheeks burn with the way he's dressed me down, implying I was only good because of Masters. What about my average of thirteen tackles per year? Or the sixteen in the championship game along with the sack at the end? Those count for shit, huh?

I'm going to need to see a dentist from all the grinding of my teeth that I'm doing right now.

Coach isn't even done. "It's fucking embarrassing to walk in on this shit. What if I had a recruit with me? You two start working together or you'll both be holding clipboards come this fall. And that goes for the rest of you yahoos. Get lifting. This isn't some retreat, motherfuckers. This is the home of the goddamned Western State Warriors. You start acting like the repeat champions or get the fuck out."

He storms out, slamming the door behind him. The room is dead silent. I hadn't even noticed before but someone turned the music off halfway through Coach's rant.

It takes a moment to shove his boot out of our collective asses, but one by one we go back to our tasks. I sneak a glance at Ace who's glowering in my direction as if I'm to blame for all this.

Hammer nudges me. "Dude, you gotta fix this. You're the only one who can."

And by me, he means Lucy.

Fuck me, but I think he's right.

23

LUCY

AFTER YEARS OF NEVER SEEING him, Matty has been everywhere. He hung out at the apartment, watching our shows without complaint. He sat in the Brew House, drinking hot cider and studying. Sometimes, his friend Hammer came with, but more often than not, Matty was alone. He said the smell of coffee was growing on him. Hammer whispered loudly that coffee wasn't the only thing growing on Matty.

I presume he meant me and not some terrible fungal infection.

Matty often waited until I was done with my shift and left at the same time. He held the door for me and asked how my day was, whether I've eaten, and how I was feeling.

I mumbled some kind of response under my breath, but hurried away like the coward I professed I wasn't. But I'm afraid to talk to him, afraid that if I look into his blue eyes, I'll lose all my self-control. Because every time I close my eyes, I see him.

Every night I feel him moving inside of me, over me, under me. The imprint of his hands on my skin, his mouth against my lips, haunts me. One night? I don't know how any woman can be okay with having a single night with Matthew Iverson.

For the last three days, I've brooded. But I'm done with that. I'm going to jump off the cliff and hope he catches me because he's in my blood now. It may be foolish and reckless, but I know exactly what kind of reward is at the bottom of the canyon.

"Lucinda!"

My head snaps up to see the faces of half my mock trial team frowning at me. It takes me a moment to collect myself because I've spent the last ten minutes staring out the window daydreaming about Matty.

"I didn't catch that." I pretend like I was paying attention the whole time.

"I'd like to reserve any remaining time for rebuttal. Is that right?" Heather asks.

"Yeah, that's the right language.

Randall, acting as judge again, nods his head regally. Heather turns to the chairs we've set up as our mock jury. Tonight our practice group consists of just Heather, Randall, and me—we're practicing cross-examinations and arguments. Randall already gave a really amazing opening statement, but Heather's been struggling.

This is the third time she's run through it and each successive attempt is more boring and more pedantic than the last. When she's done after only using five minutes of her allotted eight, Randall's head is lying on the desk and he's mock snoring. No wonder I drifted off. I shift anxiously in my chair. I can't wait to get out of here to tell Matt that I'm ready. Hopefully, the offer is still open.

"What's wrong now?" Heather exclaims. "You told me the closing has to include me listing off all the evidence."

"We don't have time for you to list all the evidence, just the important points. But more importantly, this is *argument*," I stress, trying to hurry Heather along. "You need to be convincing and persuasive."

"Why don't you do you do it if it's so easy!" Heather stomps past the counsel table and throws herself into a desk chair.

"Heather, come back. I'm sorry if I was too critical." *How about you grow a thicker skin?* I want to say, but I bite my tongue. She appears on the verge of tears, and the last thing I want to do is destroy her confidence.

"Why don't you show her?" Randall suggests. "Just do a quick closing."

"I don't do closings," I remind him.

"But you're okay with criticizing the hell out of mine," Heather shouts.

I shut my eyes and count to ten so I don't leap out of my chair and throttle her. I can do a closing if that's what she needs. I do them in my sleep. I just can't do them in a competition.

"Come on," Randall cajoles.

"Fine." I stand up and take Heather's abandoned spot in front of the chairs. If I do this, we can all leave.

"May it please the Court." I gesture toward Randall. "Opposing counsel." I pretend Heather is the attorney for the other side, which is easy because I feel we're oceans apart on the concept of an effective closing. "Members of the jury." I face the chairs. "We have asked you to sacrifice a day out of your life, and your sacrifice does not go unappreciated. One of the greatest strengths of our legal system is that we are allowed to bring our disputes before a jury of our peers. No matter how thin our wallets are, no matter our position in society, under the eyes of Lady Justice, we are all the same. We thank you for what you have done today and what you will do on behalf of our client, Emily Hartog."

"Do I really have to go through all of that?" Heather interrupts. "Because I could thank everyone in one sentence. Yo, peeps, thanks for your attention. Here's why you should find in our favor."

I grit my teeth. "No, Heather. You do not have to go through all of that. Do it your own way. Make it your own, but sell the jury on the fact that you are truly grateful for their presence here. We don't want them pissed off."

"Fine." She imperiously waves her wand. "Go ahead."

Randall bangs his pencil against the desk. "Proceed, counsel."

"Thanks." I scowl at both of them. I take a deep breath, gather my thoughts and pick up where I left off. "In the Old Testament, the Jewish people were required to sacrifice a lamb for their sins on a yearly basis. But the lamb that was chosen was special. It had to be a lamb with the nicest wool, the best-looking hooves, the clearest eyes, and the strongest gait. It was, after all, a stand-in for the Lord and therefore must be as perfect as a human-raised lamb could be."

Randall and Heather are watching my every move now, hanging on every word. I hide a smile of confidence. This story gets people every time.

"The leaders were charged with picking out the lamb, and once chosen, the tribe would cast their sins upon the back of that lamb, that perfect creature. They would confess their cheating, their envy, their blasphemies, and then the leaders would drive that blameless lamb out into the wilderness. It is from that practice we derive the word 'scapegoat.'"

Heather sucks in a breath, and I give her a nod of acknowledgment. *This is how you do it.* A movement in the back of the room catches my attention. My eyes widen at the sight of Matty. With a tip of his head, he silently asks if it's okay that he's here. *Is it?* I ask myself. Why not? It's not like he's judging me.

I turn back to the fake jury, but my attention is still on the back of the room. I can feel his eyes on me as I spread my hands and once again argue for my client. "Ms. Hartog is the scapegoat for IMC. They designed, produced, and assembled a faulty ice resurfacing machine. Instead of accepting responsibility for this, they want to place the blame on Ms. Hartog, citing operator failure, but the evidence clearly shows that even if Ms. Hartog operated the machine perfectly, the brakes still would have malfunctioned, she still would have been injured, and we would still be here today asking for the same thing—for IMC to be brought to justice. At the beginning of the trial, my co-counsel told you we would prove these three things." I lift the demonstrative aid identifying the elements of our charge. "And we did. Allow me to revisit a few of the highlights."

I tick off each element, reminding the fake jury of the key bits of testimony and documentary evidence such as the co-worker who described the previous problems with the machine, the company paperwork that revealed internal concerns about the braking mechanism. Randall starts giving me the wind-up motion. Shoot, eight minutes goes by so fast when you're having fun.

"Emily Hartog came to you in pieces. She broke her leg, lost her job, her house. Her car was repossessed. You can't make her completely well again. She'll always have that limp. But by finding in her favor, you can give her new wings. Thank you."

Loud, slow clapping booms from the rear of the room. I duck my head in slight embarrassment, but I am proud of what I did. It felt good too.

I stop by my table and address Heather. "So, something like that. Start with a catchy opening, recite the elements of the law. Hit the key points of our case and close with an emotional appeal."

"Gotcha," Heather replies with wide eyes.

I busy myself with the papers on the table to hide how pleased I am that she's finally looking at me as if I'm not the weakest link in this group, that I can actually contribute.

"I think we're done." Randall's voice is gentle, but filled with affection. He knows how much this means to me.

Gratefully, I gather up my stuff and fly to Matty.

"The jury finds the defendant not guilty," he says instantly.

I grin stupidly. "It's not that kind of trial, but thank you."

He hugs me and leans down to give me a soft kiss on the lips. "How about we celebrate the verdict with some food?"

How about we celebrate with some *you*? I swallow back the naughty words. Instead I say, "That sounds wonderful."

24

AFTER WATCHING LUCY MAKE THE closing argument, I'm convinced of two things. First, there's no one better than her to convince Ace to move to safety. And second, why in the hell is she pawning this task off on Heather? The other guy had it right. That Heather girl's good at curing insomnia but not much else.

"Jesus, that was good. I think you could sell baseballs to a football equipment manager. Here, these round balls are much faster than those oblong pigskins you're using." I hold out my hand, pretending to present a ball.

"Plus, no pesky deflation problems," Luce grins.

I snort. "Why aren't you doing this for your team? I mean, if that was practice, just off-the-cuff argument, you must be mind-blowing in competition."

Her grin immediately falls off, and her shoulders hunch up. "It's actually the reverse. I'm good in practice, good when it doesn't matter, but during competition? When something is actually on the line? I suck hard."

"I can't see it. After watching you back there"—I jerk my head behind us to the practice room—"I just can't envision you being anything but awesome."

Hammer's right. Luce is my best option.

"Thanks, but it's true." She takes a deep breath. "The summer before I came to college, I prepped for weeks for the mock trial tryouts. I wanted to be a lawyer. I'd spent four years in high school mock trial. Had a pre-law track all set out in front of me. I killed my tryout."

"I'm guessing the story doesn't end happily?" I take her hand and tuck it into my jacket pocket as we walk out of the room.

"Not once in the fifteen-year history of mock trial club here at Western had it fielded a winning team. We've never made it out of Regionals, let alone to a national tournament. After my tryout, everyone was convinced that I was the closer they'd been looking for. So we were at Regionals and we were slaying it. Randall delivered an awesome opening, and I nailed their expert on cross. Caught him making up facts that weren't in the packet. I was so excited for the closing. So excited."

Her eyes are gleaming in remembrance, but I know it's not going to end well, so I brace myself. From what she's revealed before, it's not hard to guess what happens next.

"When I stand up to give the closing, I can't remember a thing. I open my mouth and nothing comes out. It's eight minutes of total silence. Do you know what that sounds like? What it feels like? It sounds like death and feels worse." She looks pale, as if her mind—and her confidence—are back in that mock courtroom, suffocating under the weight of silence. "Closings aren't for me," she says in a shaky voice.

And neither are risks. I get it now, better than I ever did before. Being with Luce these past couple of weeks has showed me how rigidly she has to monitor herself. What she eats, what she drinks. I don't blame her for being cautious. The one time she took a step outside her comfort zone, she was humiliated. It's burned into her psyche.

Success in sports is almost entirely mental. The best quarterbacks have terrible short-term memory. You have to forget your mistakes or be paralyzed by them. Luce hasn't moved on from that. Still…it says a lot about her that she didn't quit on the team entirely.

"You're tough. Anyone else would have quit and run away."

"I love it too much," she admits. "Like you love football."

"I do." I hesitate, gulping hard.

"What's wrong?"

I grip her hand tightly. I'm afraid of how she's going to react and I feel, foolishly maybe, that if I'm still holding her at the end of this, we'll be okay.

"I hate coming to you like this. I really do, but you're my last resort."

Is she really? my conscience chides me. *You haven't really done anything to smooth this over with the team.* But Luce is clearly made for persuading people. It's in her blood. She might not be able to do it in competition but one-on-one? She'd be able to persuade someone to willingly walk the plank. And hell, maybe she'd even want to do this. After all, Ace is her friend. She wants him to succeed, right?

"I really think you're the only one who can do this."

"What is it?" she asks warily.

We've reached her apartment. I draw her to the side, away from the center sidewalk and down toward the empty parking lot.

"There was a fight in practice today."

"Oh no. Is that where you hurt your lip?" Her fingers come up to touch the corner of my mouth. "Ace wasn't an ass to you, was he? He's going through something right now."

I nod grimly. "I'm fine. Ace is fine. Physically, that is."

Her face falls. "Physically? Did the coach talk to him again?"

"You know then? He told you about the QB thing?"

"Yeah."

"We weren't supposed to tell anyone outside the team," I answer, but even though Ace was supposed to keep his mouth shut, I'm relieved she already knows the general gist of the situation.

She shrugs. "Ace doesn't really think the rules apply to him, and besides, it wasn't like I was going to ESPN with this or anything."

"Right." I exhale heavily. "The situation is grim. I need to say something, ask you something really important."

Her face pales under the harsh glare of the apartment's floodlights. "I'm not going to like this, am I?"

I try to think of the most positive spin on this that I can. "I'm only bringing this to you because I think it's right." Although I don't know what's right other than if our team keeps fighting like we did this afternoon, we'll be a basket case this fall, and we'll be lucky to win half our games, let alone make another run at the title. "You can say no, and I understand if you don't want to hear this, but…I'd like you to make the case for Ace as a safety."

"No," she says immediately and turns away, but not before I see the hurt in her eyes.

My stomach falls somewhere around my boots, but I've started down this path and I might as well see it to the end.

"What if I told you that I want Ace to succeed?" I ask.

"So?"

"So this isn't just about me wanting to win another title. I want that, but I'll admit I'm not as hungry as I was before. A repeat is great, but my aims and goals are different now, and I bet that's true for Ace. Only he's not seeing it clearly because all he sees is embarrassment from losing his position."

"I don't really care." She pulls away again. Hard, and I finally feel compelled to let her go.

I don't like that she's so far away from me, but I'm afraid if I step toward her, she'll run inside and that will be the end of it. I grab the back of my neck but my anxiety doesn't subside. "You know what the Heisman is, right?"

She nods. "The trophy given to the best college football player each year."

"Do you know how many Heisman-winning quarterbacks fail in the NFL or don't even get drafted? There have been seventy-seven winners and a third have been quarterbacks. Combined, they don't have a winning record in the NFL. College success doesn't translate to pro success for most quarterbacks. Ace won with us, but it was a team effort. In the pros, he'll be exposed. If I were told that I was too small, too slow for my position but that I could have a shot in the pros if I played a different position, I'd move in a heartbeat. What do you think Ace wants?"

Ace wants to play in the pros, no question.

"You know what he wants."

Yeah, she knows him.

"Right. I do. Have you heard of Scott Frost?"

"No, doesn't ring a bell."

I take a step toward her. Just a small one. I'm not trying to intimidate her; I want to convince her that this is the right thing for everyone. "He led his Nebraska team to a National title over Peyton Manning and the Tennessee Volunteers. He had a record of twenty-four and two when he graduated. Despite his extremely successful college career as a quarterback, he was drafted in the third round and played safety in the NFL. You've heard of Tim Tebow, right?"

"Who hasn't?"

Her responses are terse, but she's still here, so I barrel forward. "Lots of folks have said Tebow would be playing in the NFL if he'd only move to tight end. He's big and athletic but has a shit arm and shit throwing mechanics."

Not unlike someone else we know. I don't say Ace's name explicitly, but we both know who I'm talking about. "But Tebow wouldn't move. He was too damn stubborn. It was QB or bust. And for him? It's bust. He'll never play in the NFL again. Julian Edelman with the Patriots was a college QB. Eric Crouch won the Heisman in 2001 as a quarterback for Nebraska. He played safety and wide receiver in the NFL, but because he wanted to play quarterback, he ended up in the Canadian Football League. Never came back to the NFL."

"You're saying that Ace has a better chance of being a pro if he moves," she sums up flatly.

"That's what I'm saying." I nod with relief, feeling as if I've made a breakthrough.

"It's still no."

My relief fades. "You won't even consider it?"

Lucy's brown eyes flicker with annoyance. "No, I won't. Because it doesn't matter how solid your case is, or how well researched your facts are. Let me ask you this—if you were defending a murder suspect and needed to put a character witness on the stand, would you call up the sister of the guy your client is accused of killing?"

I see where she's going with this, but she doesn't even give me a chance to answer.

"Of course you wouldn't! Because you know the witness's loyalty lies elsewhere." Lucy takes a breath. "Ace can be an asshole. He drives me crazy sometimes. But he's like a brother to me, and I'll always have his back. If he wants to keep being quarterback, then I wouldn't be a good friend if I didn't support that decision, even if it's not the right one."

"Luce—"

"I told you, Matty. It's. A. No." She turns away.

Okay. It's a no. I knew it would be a no. I always knew it, which is why I'd been putting it off, but after today I had to try. What else could I do?

"Where are you going?" I ask, hurrying to match my strides with hers.

She halts abruptly. "I won't do it."

"I heard you." I place a tentative hand at the low of her back. Through her puffy coat, I swear I can feel the heat of her body. "And honestly, I respect it. It's rare to come across that kind of loyalty these days."

"Is this a trick?" she asks suspiciously.

"No."

"You're just going to accept my no?"

"I have to, don't I?"

She ponders that for a moment, her brows scrunched together in confusion. "Then why do you have your hand on my coat?"

I look down at her in disbelief. Is she really that clueless? Under the heat of my stare, she blushes.

"I had to get the Ace thing out of the way. It would have bothered you like a pebble in your shoe if I hadn't." I don't know that for sure, but their connection sure as hell bothers me.

Luce wrinkles her nose. "Not really. I think I could have gone a long time without hearing your litany of failed quarterbacks."

"Doubtful. As a bonus, next time you play a trivia game in the bar, you'll have a few obscure answers."

I can barely see any of her body wrapped up in that silver, puffy monstrosity, but I still want her.

"Because that's what I do with my time at the bar—play sports trivia games."

"What do you do at a bar?"

She shrugs. "Drink, talk, dance."

"Ask me what my second reason was for coming to your practice tonight."

Her eyes meet mine, and this time there's not a hint of confusion or embarrassment or shyness. Warmth heats my blood. "Why'd you come to practice tonight?"

"Because I can't stop thinking about you. I keep tasting you on my tongue. I keep feeling you under my hands. I look at you next to me on the sofa when we're watching TV and I can barely keep myself from attacking you."

"Do you think I'm a pushover?" she asks unexpectedly.

"Hell no." I huff a small laugh. The woman has a steel-trap memory and doesn't mind throwing things back in my face. Does she really think she's a pushover? She's so far from it, I'm surprised the word is even in her vocabulary. "Or you'd be at Ace's place talking him into the switch."

"Right." She sounds surprised at herself. "I did say no, didn't I?"

"You did."

"Don't bring up the Ace thing again," she tells me. "Or I can't do this between us."

"I swear it." I make an X across my chest.

"Then come upstairs."

I nearly fall to my knees in relief. Then I take my own risk because I want to wrap myself around her all night. "How about my place? Your bed can't fit the two of us. I'd like you to spend the night."

It's a risk that pays off because she says yes.

We talk about nothing on the walk to my house. The weather. I think it's unseasonably warm. She's wrapped up in her sleeping bag she swears is a coat. Underneath our meaningless chatter, the tension is ratcheting up.

I'm hard from the casual brush of her arm against mine. I start breathing heavily when she combs her fingers through her hair. I clench my fingers inside my pockets so I don't drag her into the nearest corner and do her right there.

"Want something to eat? Drink? Your BGs okay?" I ask when we get to the house.

"I'm good. You hungry? Feeling faint?" she says with a slight tone of mockery.

Okay, I get it. Leave her diabetes alone. But I can't help it. I care for this girl. I worry, but I'll try to keep my concern to myself.

"I'm hungry all right. Ravenous even." I know what I want to be eating and it's not in the kitchen.

"Me, too."

I close my eyes and thank God. Lucy gives a small laugh, and at that happy sound, I kind of lose it. I haul her into my arms and run up to my bedroom. Good thing no one comes out of their rooms, because I would have mowed them down.

Once inside my room, I let her feet drop to the floor, but I don't let her go. We tackle our own clothes, too anxious to be skin to skin. Her coat falls to the ground. I whip my T-shirt over my head. She tugs her jeans down; I tear at my own pants. In between garments, we grab each other for a hungry kiss until finally, nothing's between us. It's just her smooth, perfect skin against my hard, rough body.

"Christ, I need you." I nip at her mouth, kiss her cheek, lick the delicate shell of her ear all the while palming every curve I can get my hands on—her shoulders, her tits, her round, delicious ass. That ass.

I spin her around and drop to my knees. "Bend over." The command comes out harsher than I intend, but Luce doesn't hesitate. She turns and bends at the waist, resting her arms on the surface of my desk.

"Tell me your favorite part of what we've done so far. Is it the fucking? Or do you like it when I'm going down on you?"

She moans a little, half in embarrassment, half in desire. "Why do you have to talk so much?"

I smile to myself and rub both hands over the plump cheeks, holding them up so I can sink my teeth into one and then the other. This time the sound she makes is definitely a lusty one.

"Because I like it, and I think you do, too. Let me tell you how this is going to work. I'm going to eat you out, then I'm going to slap on a rubber and fuck you until you're coming so hard you can't stand up. You let me know if there's any part of this plan you don't like."

She mumbles something and squirms a small amount but doesn't utter one word of disagreement. I spread her legs farther apart and dive in because I wasn't lying when I told her I was ravenous. For days now, I've been thinking about having this pussy against my mouth again.

She squeaks in surprise and then rises slightly on her tiptoes, as if trying to escape. I clamp an arm around her waist and hold her tight against my onslaught. She trembles like a leaf in an autumn storm, held in place by my arm and tongue.

My cock is hard as a spike, angry at being left out of the party, but the rest of me is enjoying eating her out too much to stop. There's something addicting about her. Above me, Luce is making a dozen different moans and gasps, pleas to God and for me to *stop, no don't stop, there, right there, Right. There.*

I slip my hand around to the front so I can get a thumb on her sensitive clit, making her stiffen and then lose control over her limbs. I catch her before she falls, surging forward to drive into her in one swift, demanding gesture.

The throb of her orgasm feels wild against my dick, her honey coating every inch of my shaft. The soft grip of her pussy is otherworldly. I'd give up everything for this, for her. Football, fame, glory, money. None of it can compare.

Her head falls back, those long, beautiful strands of blond hair sticking to the side of her face, falling over my shoulder. I grip her jaw until we're kissing. The angle's awkward, my legs are shaky as fuck, but I want this joining, too.

She wraps an arm around my neck and hangs on, clinging to me as if I'm the only safe thing in a wild and dangerous world. I clutch her just as tight, driving forward with all the power in my legs to make sure she feels it, not just today but for hours, days afterward. When she's sitting in class or standing in the Brew House serving up coffee, the vibrations will still echo between her legs. She'll remember my tongue ravaging her mouth, my hands on her boobs, my broad body covering her back.

"This feels good, doesn't it, Goldie? You shuddering around me. I'm so hard right now. It's difficult for me not to come. I want to, but I'm not gonna. Not until I feel you cream all over my dick like you came on my tongue."

She shudders but doesn't tell me to shut up as she usually does. I sweep my hand up to her neck. She's delicate under my rough hands, callused from the hours spent lifting, slapping at the tackling dummy, bashing against the offensive line. Delicate, tender, soft. All those things I'm not, and it makes me feel powerful, like the small "g" god I joke to her that I am.

But she's not weak. She grinds down on me, reminding me how effortlessly she's captured me and made me hers. No matter that I'm bigger and stronger, I'm putty in her hands. Malleable clay for her to shape in whatever way she desires because I'd do anything for her.

Her body tightens, and the telltale flutters of her pussy signal the arrival of her orgasm. This feels different. Hotter, deeper, more erotic.

I'm five strokes in before I realize why I can feel every tiny flutter and twitch of her pussy. I'm barebacking her. Shit, I haven't had sex without a condom—ever. I've never lost it so much that I've forgotten to put one on, no matter how horny or drunk I've been in the past.

I freeze and start to pull out, but she moans her unhappiness.

"Goldie, I'm not wearing a rubber."

She doesn't push me away, not my cautious sweet girl. Instead she pushes back against me, her plush ass cheeks slamming against my thighs and groin. "Just...just pull out."

I'm safe, she told me when I was testing her blood sugars.

"I'm taking care of you. No risk on my end either," I growl into her ear. She nods faintly and that's all the permission I need.

I push her forward and cover her, plunging so deep and so hard she has to put out a hand to prevent being driven into the wall. The heavy wood desk scrapes against the floor as I power into her, stroke after stroke. She sobs into the desktop, and when my own release threatens to swamp me, I reach around to find her clit, squeezing and rolling that nub between my fingers until she tightens and then explodes around me.

I almost lose it then, almost bust it inside her, but I manage to pull out and spray my come all over her trembling, gorgeous ass. I've marked her and now she's mine. With regret and the exertion of the last bit of energy I have left, I grab my shirt off the floor and wipe her off. She jerks when I dab between her legs, and I may have rubbed some of my spunk into her skin rather than cleaning her entirely.

Tossing the shirt to the side, I gather her into my arms and stumble to the bed.

"What are we doing?" she asks.

I pull a blanket up over our bodies. "We're enjoying each other."

"For how long?"

Forever is a good start in my book, but this is my careful girl, and she needs a careful answer. "However long you want it."

Her answer is a contented sigh that fills me with an inexplicable amount of satisfaction. It occurs to me that I don't remember being this happy even when I hoisted the championship trophy, and that doesn't bother me one bit.

25

LUCY

"YOU DON'T WORK TODAY, RIGHT?"

"It's Friday, right?" It's hard to concentrate these days.

"All day, Goldie."

I shiver when he uses the nickname. "Then no. Not until tomorrow."

"And your last class is over at…"

"One," I fill in.

"I'll meet you outside your apartment at one-thirty then."

"For what?"

"It's a surprise. Wear layers. I have a black Land Rover. See you then."

He disconnects before I can muster a response. I pull the phone away from my ear. "Sure, I'd love to go to your little surprise. Thanks for asking," I tell the phone. But was I going to refuse? No, and Matty knew that.

I text Sutton to let her know our walk is off.

Me: *No walk today.*

Sutton: *??*

Me: *Am going somewhere with Matty.*

Sutton: *!!*

I can see her high-fiving herself.

Sutton: *Charity and I were on the verge of sending you to 1C for shock therapy.*

Me: *Thanks for nothing.*

Sutton: *You're welcome. We're the best roommates ever.*

Me: *You're my only roommates.*

Sutton: *Also best ever.*

Me: *If you say so.*

But I'm smiling when I pocket my phone because she's right. I do have the best roommates ever.

Wear layers, he'd said. Given that it's still winter, my guess is we're doing something outside. I find a tight-fitting pair of yoga pants, a long-sleeved thermal shirt and top that with a sweater. My long coat will keep my legs warm, and when I run out of my apartment at 1:30 p.m. Matty's already there, leaning against his big black SUV, legs and arms crossed, looking delectable. I'm not the only one who thinks so. The girls from 1C are walking home from class and can't seem to take their eyes off of him.

But Matty doesn't spare them a glance. When he spots me, he pushes away from the truck and strides over to embrace me. Not just embrace me, but cup my head and plant a deep, hungry kiss against my lips that leaves me breathless and needy.

"Let's go upstairs and count how many condoms are left," I tell him when he lets me go.

He grins but shakes his head. "Nope. We're going sledding. We'll do the condom thing later."

"Sledding?"

"Yeah, snow, hill, plastic rectangle." He makes a downward gesture with his hand that I suppose simulates sledding. "Come on." He tugs me forward excitedly.

"I haven't been sledding since I was a kid," I admit after we're buckled in. Matty points the SUV toward the east side of town.

"Then this will be fun. I'll even spring for hot cocoa."

"You big spender, you."

He winks. "You know it."

"Why sledding?"

"It's less risk—" His voice catches on the word. Our eyes meet, mine filled with humor and his with surprise. He clears his throat. "Less risky than skiing. I don't want to break a leg and screw up my season."

I smirk. "So weighing the risks. That's a sound thing to do. I guess I'm not so weird, after all."

Matty shakes his head but can't keep his own smile from breaking through. "Never thought you were weird, Goldie." He reaches over and grabs my hand and settles it on his thigh.

It takes twenty minutes to arrive at the amusement park.

"I thought this place closed during the winter." I peer out of the window where I see a hill lit up and a bunch of people who must be riding sleds down a very, very large incline.

"All the rides are, but they've got a big hill that's not high enough for skiing but makes for killer sledding."

He neatly swings into a parking space near the edge of the lot and hops out. He takes my hand again, and we walk up to the rental booth to pay for admission and our sled.

"Just one," he tells the attendant. "It'll be more fun going down together." The attendant turns to get our sled. "Less risky," Matty whispers in my ear.

I'm not convinced it's less risky. Matty's extra weight in the front makes the sled go faster—something about momentum and acceleration that he swears he learned about in Scouts building soapbox racing vehicles. Plus, he serves as a natural windbreak. Later, we switch up with me positioned between his legs with his arms bracketing my sides. I'm in a Matty-style nest.

And he carries the sled up every time.

We spend two hours on the slope until dusk falls and our stomachs start rumbling. Finally, we decide to call it an afternoon.

"Come on, let's get something hot inside of you, Goldie," he says after returning the sled.

At the small concession stand, he buys us hot dogs and hot chocolate. There aren't any tables, so we wander down toward a wooded area and settle in out of the wind that's picking up. I watch him gulp down the hotdog in three bites before asking, "What's with the nicknames?"

"Nicknames are important. Feel free to pick one out for me. I can provide a list of suggestions. Big Guy. God. Master. Awesome Master."

He finishes the hotdog and goes to pay for another, so he doesn't see me roll my eyes.

"How about overweening ego?" I offer when he returns.

"Not my favorite. All kidding aside, names reveal a lot. Your first name says something about your parents. How'd they come up with Lucinda?" He squirts ketchup on his hotdog. I take a bite of mine before answering.

"It's a family name. It was either that or Maude."

"Same. Matthew's my grandad's name."

You're more alike than you think, Sutton had told me.

"Who started calling you Matty?"

"I can't remember. Probably my mom. Some of the guys on the team call me Ives, but my closest friends call me Matty."

I want to ask him how he introduces himself to girls he's just met, but I guess I know. He called himself Matthew. And now...now he's Matty to me.

"So what else do names reveal?"

"Professors want us to use their last names to create distance and authority. Nicknames imply a certain closeness or familiarity. You can use a person's first name as a weapon, too, to imply that you're in a position of power."

I can feel my mouth open slightly in surprise. "This is pretty interesting stuff. Was this in a class?"

He looks down at his boot and even in the dimming light, I can see a faint hint of pink on the tops of his cheeks that's not because of the wind.

"I learned it in a book."

"A Ludlum book?"

He kicks the heel of his boot against the ground as if trying to shake off the snow but I can see he's faintly embarrassed. "Nah, I read stuff about profiling. When I'm done in the NFL, I'd like to join the Feds."

"FBI?"

He nods.

"That's very cool."

He's really blushing now, and it's beyond cute. I don't know why. Having plans for after football seems smart to me, but maybe this dream is one that he's uncomfortable talking about. I'm rather touched he's sharing it with me. "When do you think you'll be done with football?"

"Ten? Fifteen years if I'm really lucky. I kind of view my life in two stages. Football is stage one. I've got to be careful" —we share a smile when he uses that word one of mine—"and watch what I eat, work out a ton, and spend time on the road. Take a lot of physical abuse. Stage two is where I don't necessarily watch what I eat, work out less, take only a little physical abuse, and use my brain more."

Oh, Sutton, you were so right. Matt and I aren't that different, after all. He does his own risk assessments. He's careful in his own way. He's nothing like my mother. He's his own person. A wonderful, genuine, smart, and sexy as hell person. I smile at him, the edges of that curve so high the corners of my lips feel like they are up to my eyeballs. I like him so much.

"You're sure you'll be drafted?"

"Yes." No false modesty here, only genuine confidence. "Not as high as my friend Masters, but by the second round I think. And once I'm on the team, I'm not giving up my position to anyone."

"I believe you."

"Yeah?" He reaches over and grabs my hand.

I squeeze him back. "Yeah."

"And what about you?"

"Post college?" My hand's still in his as we sip our drinks. Neither of us is in a hurry to let go.

"I figured you were in pre-law or something and that you wanted to be a lawyer, but you're doing this public policy thing?"

A little pang plucks at my heart, but I push it aside. What's done is done. "I thought I wanted to be one, too, but I'm kind of bad at something lawyers need to excel at."

"What's that?" He looks confused as if he can't imagine me being bad at anything.

"I'm not good at thinking on my feet. I tend to freeze up, and that pretty much moves me outside the lawyer framework."

"You seemed pretty awesome the other night."

"It's because all of that was prepared. I have a pretty good memory. I heard it once and I can regurgitate it, but in a competition? No." Again, the dark cloud creeps in, threatening my good mood. "Anyway, I changed my focus with the help of my advisor. I can still do a lot of reviewing of facts and then rearranging them into consumable bits of information."

"So you can't go to law school anymore?"

"Oh no, I could. Pre-law is just a track. You could have any major— even sociology."

"Law school doesn't interest me, and if it doesn't interest you anymore, that's cool. But for the record, I think you're pretty damned amazing in your mock trial thingy."

My cheeks heat up under his praise.

He scoots closer, until one long leg is pressed against mine. I can't feel the cold anymore. "It occurs to me that I used your risk assessments more often than I realized in the past."

"How so?"

"I used to think dating was a risk. That it'd either take away from football or I'd end up treating someone badly."

"What made you change your mind?"

"You. I think the reward of you is worth the risk."

My heart flips over and then cheers as his mouth descends on mine. We kiss leisurely, as if it's summer and we're on the beach and the sun is baking us into the sand. It's a hot and lazy kiss and heats us better than any summer sun. When we finally part, I'm surprised to see that the snow hasn't utterly melted around us.

"I'm ready to count the condoms in that box now," he says huskily.

"Me, too." Then I jump up and run for the Rover with Matty hot on my heels.

He starts the engine, and then we have to sit for a minute for the car to warm up. His cheeks are flushed, and his hair looks wild and messy—not dissimilar to how he looks when he first wakes up in the morning.

I unbuckle my seatbelt and lean across the center console. "Why are you so goddamned attractive?"

"I'm sorry?" He smiles, clearly not one bit apologetic.

"Shut up and kiss me."

He's still smiling when he cups his hand around my skull and pulls me against him. I can feel of the curve of his lips as they soften, part, and then open for me.

This time I'm the one devouring him. He tastes fresh and clean, like freshly fallen snow. His hand drops to my ass and drags me onto his seat so we can get a better, deeper angle for kissing. His tongue and lips force me to open wider for him. He kisses me deep and hard until I feel it everywhere. His kiss is in the throb between my legs, in the tingle on my fingertips, in the tightness of my skin.

I rip at his T-shirt, pulling it up out of his jeans. His skin is warm against the cold of my palms. His little nipples tighten up when I pass over them. I give them a little tweak like he does to me. He chuckles and then his hands glide under my sweater and tank to release my bra strap and grip my aching breasts in his hands.

Straddling him, I grind down to find the right pressure to alleviate the ache between my legs, but it's difficult because we have so many layers between us. It doesn't stop me from trying to find relief against his body.

I whimper because my need is so strong.

Matty shushes me. "It's okay, Goldie, I've got you."

With the hand at my back, he slips under my leggings, my thermals. His callused palm sweeps over the curve of my butt, and his long fingers pierce my aching sex in one driving, satisfying motion. The cold is a shock to my system. I can't help from crying out.

Matty dips his head and latches on to a nipple. I clutch his head to my chest and ride his fingers. Thank God he has big hands because those thick fingers inside of me are almost as good as his big hot cock.

And if it isn't enough, this illicit car sex in the darkened corner of the amusement parking lot, he starts talking.

"You are so wet and juicy." His fingers stab at me. My toes curl. It's a toss up whether I want to ride them or just sit and enjoy the fullness of it. "I love being inside of you. It's so good, Goldie. You feel so good." He moves to the other nipple, leaving the abandoned one wet and sensitive. "One of these days, we're fucking in front of mirror because you need to see how gorgeous you look right now."

He tugs on one lock of my hair. "Lean down and give me your mouth. I need to taste you."

I drop forward and claim his mouth, sucking in his tongue as if it were his shaft.

He ravages me. There's no other word for it. His mouth lays waste to mine. I can't breathe. I can't think. I forget where I am. There's only Matty and the feel of his fingers working my sex, his hand gripping my waist too tight, his big body surrounding me and keeping me safe.

"I want you to come so hard you're shaking. That you can't even breathe." he tells me, pushing me back again. "I love the feel of you gripping my fingers. Your pussy is so tight. Do you know that? Do you have any idea of how good that feels?"

"It's good," I pant. "So good."

"I wish we had class together. We'd sit in the back, and I'd pull up your skirt and play around a little until your panties were soaked. I'd take my index finger and slowly rub your lips until they were nice and plump." He pulls out and demonstrates. "I wouldn't hurry it along." *God, why not*, I think. I can't be any more on edge than I am now.

"Back inside." I gasp out the order. "I need your fingers back inside of me."

"Like this?" He shoves them in hard, this time it's three of them. I shriek at the pure pleasure.

He adds a thumb down the front of my pants, and I come like a rocket. When I float back out of the clouds, down to earth, I find that I've two chunks of Matty's hair in either hand, and I'm suffocating him against my chest. I slowly force myself to release him, gently brushing his hair back into place and rearranging the mess I've made of his clothes. He grins the whole time.

"You like that?"

I nod. "Best sledding trip ever." I reach down between us to cup his gigantic hard-on. "Let's get home so I can take care of you."

He licks his lower lip. "Best after-sledding trip coming up."

26

LUCY

THE FOLLOWING FRIDAY, I WAKE up to the sound of the shower. Matty is gone, but the bed is still warm. The sheets are an utter disaster, and I don't know how I fell asleep on them because that kind of messiness drives me nuts.

Oh right, Matty fucked me into unconsciousness.

I stretch a bit and revel in the soreness of rarely used muscles. I wouldn't have to do my daily walk today because I've had enough exercise to last three days, at least.

Sutton and Charity have declared that Matty's good for me, and I won't deny that I've never been happier. These past couple of weeks have been a revelation. I thought dating Matty would be hard, but it isn't. Despite school, work, and mock trial, there's always time for each other. And it's a relief that he's as busy as I am.

In fact, starting next Tuesday, he'll be even busier because spring practice starts. When he said he'd do all the work and I just had to enjoy the rewards, he wasn't kidding.

The only thorn is Ace. He finally apologized, but he did it via text. I'm sorry for him, but I'm not going to be his punching bag. When he's ready to be an adult, I'll talk to him. Until then, he'll have to stew in his own juices.

I should get up and test my blood sugars, but I don't want to. I want to stay here in bed, wrapped up in the warmth of Matty's body and the scent of us together. In fact, if I close my eyes tight enough, I can even conjure up a slow-motion replay of my favorite part of last night. I think it might have been at his desk where he bent me over and took me from behind, all the while whispering dirty things in my ear.

Lord, that boy has a mouth on him.

"That's a smug sex smile if I've ever seen one."

I flick my eyes part way open to see Matty strolling out of the bathroom using his towel to dry his hair. His dick hangs free between his legs looking quite delectable.

I give him a lazy smile as he pulls on a pair of sleep pants. "Don't worry, babe. You're playing a starring role in my fantasies."

"I'd be worried if I wasn't, cuz that would mean I'm not doing a very good job of rule number one, which is to make sure you have a damn good time."

"If I had a better time, I might not be conscious."

Concern immediately falls over his face. "You feeling okay?"

"I'm feeling pretty awesome, thanks."

"Good." He presses a knee into the side of the bed. "I'm going downstairs to get something to eat." I make a motion to get up, but he presses me back. "I've got this."

I allow him to leave, then heave myself out of bed. My monitoring kit is in my backpack, which got flung onto Matty's desk. There's a folder, a notebook, and some papers lying on the floor. We must have knocked them off in our haste to undress.

I stoop down and gather everything up. The notebook's partly open and I take a quick peek. In it is a list of plays. Various offensive schemes. I chuckle a bit. Matty's a serious student but his number one topic is football. Which makes sense. We're all studying so we can get a job out in the real world, and Matty's working toward a potential multimillion-dollar-a-year job after college. It shouldn't surprise me his primary focus is football.

I stack the loose papers on top of the notebook and grab the folder. I pick it up by the wrong end and the contents flutter out.

"Crap." I'm making a bigger mess than what I started with. As I'm gathering the stuff, I spot my name on one of the papers. An awful sensation starts churning in my stomach. With trembling fingers, I pick the paper up. Two notebook sheets with precise printing—the kind you see on architectural drawings—are headed with my name in big block letters. I scan it. It lists my major, where I work. That I have two roommates.

I'm only bringing this to you because I think it's right.

My work schedule at the Brew House is printed out. Wednesdays, Thursdays, five to close. Saturdays, open to noon. All of my classes are listed as well.

Lucy Washington, junior.
Major: Public Policy
Job: Brew House
Extracurricular: Mock Trial

I rip open the folder, but the only thing in it is a sticky note with seven scrawled names. I nearly vomit when I make out the first one. It's a guy from the Sigma Chi frat that I hooked up with in my freshman year. Four other names are either of boyfriends I had or hookups. Two I don't know.

I look down at my body with horror. I'm wearing Matty's shirt. The shirt of some guy who has spent weeks romancing me for no apparent reason. Just out of the blue, a guy who hates coffee, shows up at the coffee house. Flirts with *me*. Follows *me*.

I tear the shirt off, my tears wetting the fabric as I struggle to get it off me. I can't stop crying. The water drips out of my eyes and splashes onto the paper, smearing the ink but the words are all embedded into my brain.

In all the different risk scenarios I had played out in my mind, not one of them had ever, ever included a betrayal like this. That he might cheat on me? Yes. That he might forget me? Also yes.

But those were normal. Those were things anyone could overcome. But this? The pain slices through me. I wrap my arms around my waist and bend over to hold it in, to keep myself together.

How could he do this to me? How could he be so sweet? Should I have somehow guessed? Wasn't it really odd how he'd sit through those wedding shows without complaint? Ace wouldn't do that and we've been friends for over a decade. And how he was so patient with me? How he didn't make fun of my cautiousness?

I pull my backpack from the desk and onto the floor because I don't yet have the strength to get up. My hands are shaking so much it's hard to open the zipper, and it takes a couple of tries. I shove my *dossier* into it. Matty doesn't get to keep this. He doesn't get to keep any of these.

I look around for my clothes. My panties are lying obscenely in the middle of the floor, mocking me. I snatch them up and stuff them inside my backpack too. God, I have to get dressed and get out of here. *Come on*! I shout to myself. *Stop sniveling and get out of this hellhole!*

Dimly, I can hear myself making awful sounds. I hold a hand up to my mouth to silence the moans before anyone can hear me. I've got to get out of here. I've got to go.

Matty breaks into the room and rushes over to me. "What's wrong, Goldie? Did you fall and hurt yourself?"

Fall and hurt myself? Yeah, I guess I did. I flinch when he lays an arm around my shoulders. I can't stand his touch. It makes me sick.

"Are you injured?" he says in concern, trying to turn me around so he can inspect me.

And suddenly I'm enraged. He's concerned I'm not going to do his dirty work.

"You're just going to accept my no?"

"I have to, don't I?"

Right. He's just going to accept a no. I knew that sounded like a trick when he'd said it, but I wanted it to be true, so I accepted it. I didn't listen to my internal warning system. I threw away all my careful assessments and what happened? I let Matty eviscerate me. He couldn't have done a better job of tearing me apart if he'd put my heart through a wood chipper.

"Don't touch me," I snarl and scuttle backward. My feet hit my jeans. I drape them over my lap. Behind me is a blanket, and I wrap that around me, too. If I had to rip down a curtain, I'd do that as well.

Anything to cover myself up.

"What's wrong, Luce?"

Matty is wearing a completely bewildered expression, as if he doesn't have the first clue what's going on. As if he and his little team didn't completely research every facet of my life. I was just another challenge for them to conquer.

"How'd you get picked?" I ask. "Draw the short straw? Was it hard to abstain from fucking a different girl every night, or did you do that anyway while lying through your teeth about being only turned on by *me?*"

God, all the lines, all the things I fell for. I couldn't be more humiliated if I had to walk through campus nude. That eight minutes of silence I experienced my freshman year? Even *that* didn't make me feel as low and dirty and awful as I do now.

"What are you talking about?" he barks out and then, as if realizing he's supposed to be nice to me, he gives me a strained smile. "I'm sorry, but I'm working blind right now. I know you're angry, but I don't know why. Is it about the Ace thing? Because you seemed to be okay with it."

"Seemed to be?" I say. To my disgust, my words come out shrill and quavery. "Before today I didn't know how long you've been plotting this out. How you and whoever went around and compiled a more thorough background check than the FBI. When did you figure out that Ace and I were friends? Was it that first night you came to the Brew House? Was it before then? After? When?" I'm screaming at the end. Literally screaming. I stand up and start dressing. It doesn't matter what he answers. I'm not going to believe him.

I can't believe I slept with him. I can't believe I let down all my defenses. I can't believe I didn't listen to myself. I knew he was a risk. *I knew it. I knew it. I knew it.*

But I let him talk me into bed. Hell, I jumped into bed with him. I told *him* it was for one night and then went back for seconds and thirds. We've been carrying on this charade for nearly three weeks! He was so damn clever.

"I don't know what in the hell you're talking about!" Matty yells back. "If you'd tell me, I'd give you an explanation. Hell, I'd apologize, but I don't know what the fuck is going on!" His hand goes to the back of his neck. A classic Matty sign of frustration.

I struggle into my T-shirt and then stomp over to my backpack and pull out the folder. I thrust it into his hands.

"This. This is what I'm talking about. You knew my class schedule, where I worked. That I was in mock trial. You even have a list of my fucks! I'm surprised you don't have my goddamned medical records in there. Or did you know all along I was diabetic and were planning on using that against me, too?"

Matty's face pales. He flips open the folder that is empty except for the note stuck to the back flap. He reaches in and crumples it up. Then the whole manila folder folds in on itself as he fists his hand. "God-dammit, no. I didn't use any of this shit. I didn't even know you and Ace—" He breaks off. "Fuck, I hate saying your names together in one sentence. I'm so fucking lost on you that I get irrationally jealous when your names are linked together because you don't belong to Ace. You belong to me."

"I don't belong to anyone. Least of all you!" I jab him in the chest.

That was a mistake. He grabs my hand and pulls me into his arms, banding his muscle, bones and tissue around me like strong rope. I struggle, but he doesn't release me. We look ridiculous. Like some black-and-white silent film villain and weak maiden.

"When did you know?" I choke on the words. "When did you know? Did you intentionally seek me out? Did you sleep with me to persuade me to talk to Ace? Did you?" I pound my fists on his chest, and he stands there and takes it. I pound and pound and pound and scream and cry until I'm too exhausted to say or do anything else but collapse in his arms.

He picks me up and carries me to his chair by the window.

"I didn't know," he says in a strained voice. His arms are loose around me, but he's tense everywhere else. Ready, I suppose, to capture me if I try to flee again. Right now I'm drained. "I didn't know until a day or two before you came to stay at Ace's place."

"Before we had sex," I mumble into his chest. When I gain my second wind, I'm going to get up and leave.

"Yeah, before we had sex."

"So you used me," I say dully.

"No, goddammit. No. I fucking…no."

"What were you going to say?" I feel like I've heard everything at this point and believe nothing. Nothing that I don't see with my own eyes, at least.

He's quiet for a long time. His chest rises and falls as he takes these giant gulps of breath, as if he's preparing for something big. He better tell me the truth. I hope that's what he's gathering his courage to do.

"I think I'm falling in love with you. So, no—I did none of those things you say I did. But I don't blame you for thinking them. I didn't ask for that stuff to be done, and I'm sorry it was. But I'm not sorry I met you. I'm not sorry we made love."

"Love?" My head's spinning now. It's a good thing I'm sitting down, even if it is on Matty's lap, because I'm seriously confused.

"Yeah. I mean, do I know what love is? Probably not, but I can't stop thinking about you. I grin at odd times during the day like a goddamn fool when I come across something you said or did. Sex with you is off-the-charts amazing. Kissing you. Just kissing you make me horny as hell. Other women walk by and I know in the past, pre-Lucy, I'd be attracted to them, but now they are like oatmeal to me. Bland and un-interesting. You're the sugar in my life. So yeah, I'm falling in love with you."

I have no response to that. We haven't known each other for that long. Only a few weeks. It doesn't make sense to me.

"I know it's crazy, right?" he whispers into my hair. "For Masters, he said it was immediate. First time he saw Ellie, his wife, he told me the earth moved. I didn't realize the earth was moving when I saw you the first time. I didn't realize everything in my life was changing because it happened slowly. One meal, one conversation, one kiss at a time."

My cheeks are wet again. I've never had anyone say these words to me before. I don't know if they're false. They don't feel false. But can I even trust my instincts anymore?

He sighs again, and the breath ruffles my hair. I dig my face into his chest because I don't want to talk. I don't have the words for what I'm feeling right now. Happy, angry, sad, confused, elated. They are all inside of me, fighting for domination. The cocktail of strong emotions is making me dizzy and weak.

Matty rubs my arms slowly. "I swear to you on a stack of Holy Bibles, my grandmother Betty's grave, and the Outland Trophy I won for last year's season that I did not know who you were when we met at the Brew House or when I ate with you at Crowerly's. I knew who you were when I found you baking cookies that night at Ace's place, but I slept with you because I wanted you, not because of Ace. I hate that you have a relationship with Ace. It makes me jealous as fuck. And I'm not thrilled I'm in this position with Ace, but Coach laid it on me."

For some reason, this sets off my bullshit meter. I push away from him so I can see his face.

"Coach told you?" I ask with some skepticism. "And you just do it?"

Matty raises his eyebrows. "I'm guessing your mock trial is set up a little differently but in football, your coach is your daddy, the Holy Trinity and the President of the United States all wrapped up into one foul-mouthed body. If he asks you to murder someone, you respond with 'Should I use a knife or a gun?'"

"That sounds healthy," I say sarcastically.

"It's just the way it is," he admits. "But he has us for four years, or in my case five since I redshirted, but for the time that we're here, he owns us. We're his chess pieces on the big green board." Matty leans back against the cushion and stares at the ceiling. "I think that's why college coaches suck as pro coaches. Here we do everything he says, but once you're out and making money, he doesn't have as much control."

Matty tips his head and points his startlingly blue eyes directly at me. "I'm not going to lie to you. I sat in the back of that room when you delivered that closing thinking how you were the perfect person to deliver the message to Ace because you're so amazing. If you came to me, with a passionate and reasoned argument like you delivered, I'd do just about anything. So yes, in all honesty, I did use you but not in the way you're accusing me."

I suck my lips into my mouth and mash them between my teeth. "I'm so confused. I don't know what to think or do right now."

"You don't have to make any decisions, but I'd like a chance to prove myself to you." His gaze doesn't waver, and I can't see anything but sincerity in his eyes.

"How?"

"I won't bring up Ace again." He shakes his head slowly. "I'll be honest. I feel like I'm outkicking my coverage. Not only would I want you to be my lawyer, but I'm not sure I'm worthy of being your boyfriend."

"Is that what you are?" I ask. My heart is telling me to believe. I've lived my whole life being careful. Do I want to be careful again? I think back to the agony I felt when I thought he'd betrayed me. *Thought*? As in past tense? Had I forgiven him? Was there anything to forgive? "My boyfriend?"

"Damn straight I am." He squeezes me. "I'm buying a letterman's jacket and you're wearing it."

I laugh against my will. Matty's too good at finding the cracks in my armor—as if I even have armor against him. "They don't have letterman jackets at Western."

"It's the internet age. I'm sure I can find some seller somewhere to whip me up one. We'll have matching jackets. Mine can say 'property of Lucy Washington' and yours can say 'property of Matty Iverson.'" He leans back again and looks off into the distance as if envisioning us in some weird *Grease* production wearing his version of promise rings.

"I like that. You think you'd be open to getting a tattoo of my name on your ass?"

"No. No. And also no," I reply firmly.

"Yeah, I thought that was a bridge too far. But I'm getting you that jacket and you're wearing it and you're going to like it."

"I am, am I?"

"Yeah." He looks down at me pensively, his grin fading away. "I'm really sorry for hurting you. This thing between you and..." He won't say Ace's name, and somehow his jealousy, no matter how wrong it is, soothes my battered pride. "It's a tangle, but it doesn't mean I don't have genuine feelings for you or that we can't be together."

"When I saw my name and all of that stuff, I felt violated. I don't want to feel that way again."

"It was shitty. No excuses."

"Don't hurt me. Don't make a fool of me."

"I won't. I'm not playing here. You're not a game to me."

I draw a shaky breath. I didn't realize how much I needed to hear that until those words came out of his mouth.

He draws my stiff body against his and holds me there for a long time until I relax. He doesn't make any move to take off my clothes or kiss me or try to use my attraction for him against me, and that goes further in soothing my hurt than even his words do.

"The Outland Trophy? Why not the National Championship?"

"Because the Outland Trophy's an individual award. I can't swear on a team achievement, Luce."

Well, duh. I chuckle. He laughs, and it seems like we've weathered the storm.

27

LUCY

MATTY CONVINCES ME TO SKIP classes, which I rarely do, but I only have two today, and I'm über responsible every other day of the year. I'm wrecked emotionally from this morning and wouldn't be able to pay attention anyway.

There are a few guys on defense I haven't met before, and Matty introduces me around. Hammer tries out some web lists he's working on after I tell him that "spa day" as a euphemism for sex doesn't work.

"I'm working on an article about the top ten foods that look like dildos," he says as he works the controller to launch a shot on goal. I block him easily. I played a lot of this with Ace when we were in middle school and junior high. I haven't forgotten my skills.

"Ew, no. I'm not sticking a cucumber up my lady passage." I dribble past him, break a few of his players' ankles, and score.

"Sausage casing?"

"Gross."

"Shit. How are you so good at this?" He looks over at Matty. "This isn't fair. You bring a ringer into our house to stomp me?"

Matty shrugs and shoves a carrot into his mouth. His refrigerator is surprisingly full of things I can eat without much worry. Lots of non-sugary vegetables. Some vegan dip. It's really impressive. I don't have a lot of extra money to keep my fridge stocked with fresh goodies like this. Matty even shoved me out of the kitchen and told me to go play with Hammer while he prepared everything.

I'm enjoying being pampered. Maybe this *is* a spa day.

"Let's switch gears," Hammer suggest. "How about 'perfumed palace'"?

"Better." I pop a cucumber slice into my mouth.

"Scented cavern?"

"Cavern borders on rude." I flick my thumb over the toggle and steal the ball.

"What do you think of 'secret garden'"?

"Way to ruin my favorite childhood book." The ball goes sailing into the corner. Hammer and I race to get it.

"Och, lassie, you needn't worry naught for nothing," Matty intones.

I set down my controller. "What was that?"

"Yorkshire accent," he says with mock offense.

"Sounded like a southern accent with a touch of Canadian. In others words, not Yorkshire."

"So no dirty talk with an accent?"

"No."

"Ohh, you guys do the dirty talk?" Hammer crows. "That'd be a great article. Say a few lines for me," he orders.

"No!" I give Matty a stern look that says if he opens his mouth right now, I'm shoving the entire vegetable tray in it.

He snaps his mouth shut. "Sorry, Hammer. No can do."

"Man, bros before hoes," Hammer mutters.

Later we watch a movie. During a particularly hot love scene, Matty gets up abruptly and hauls me into the bedroom. I might have been rubbing his dick under the blanket.

"You are going to pay for all that teasing." He bends me over the bed and kicks my feet apart. Like I imagine it would be like if I got arrested. Suddenly, the image of hot Matty in a police uniform appearing at my apartment door pops into my head. I get a little excited. Okay, a lot excited.

Matty notices. "What's got you all turned on?"

He rubs a hand over my ass.

"Don't worry," I tease. "I'm fantasizing about you."

"Yeah? Well, tell me about it so I can make it good for you."

And I realize one of the reasons I'm so willing to forgive him is because he does take all of the risk. There's no shame in telling him what I want, because he wants it, too.

He is *really* in tome. Into *us*.

"I was thinking how this position makes me imagine Hot Cop Matty. Didn't you say you wanted to be in the FBI?" He told me that after we went sledding, when we were talking about after the NFL and what else he'd do besides his Instagrammable tea parties.

He chuckles low and I feel it in my tummy. "What am I investigating?"

"Um, theft of state secrets." I pluck something random out of the air.

"Alright, Miss Washington, I'm going to have to search you now. Don't move."

I wiggle my butt. "Shouldn't a lady agent be doing this?"

He smacks me lightly. "You want to go to prison? Or do you want to make this problem go away?"

"Go away," I say with a forced tremble in my voice.

He slides down to his knees. "Then you're going to do exactly what I say, when I say it, aren't you?"

This time when I speak, the quaver is entirely real. "Yes."

He pushes my legs even wider apart. "Then you have to stay real still and real quiet while I eat your pussy. Otherwise, my partner's going to hear you." He leans forward and rubs his tongue along my entire sex. "And if he hears you, he's going to come into this room and then I'm going to have to share you. I don't want that, do you?"

I gulp. "No."

"And if you're not quiet and you're not still, I'm going to come in my pants. We both know you want me in your mouth, don't you?" He licks me again and again and again. I shove my face into the comforter and pant. Yes, God, yes, I want him in my mouth again. The heavy weight of him on my tongue, the way he looks at me like I'm the only light in a dark place, the way he moans and groans and jacks helplessly as I drive him completely and utterly out of his mind.

"Yes."

"Then take your punishment like a good little girl."

I'll do the best that I can, Officer. I swear it.

* * *

"I need to go." Reluctantly, I untangle myself from Matty's embrace. The clock says the sun will be rising soon and I should get home. I've spent too much time with Matty this past week. This is going to be a tough day for Ace. As soon as Remington Barr announces his intentions to come to Western, Ace will be inundated with questions, and even though we haven't talked much lately, I don't want to rub any more salt on his wounds.

Matt's unhappy I'm leaving. I see it in the straight line of his lips and the tenseness in his large frame. He doesn't say anything while he throws back the covers and swings out of bed. My breath catches in the back of my throat at the lithe movement of his body. For a large man he's very graceful.

He throws on a pair of sweatpants and then digs around in a dresser for socks.

I pause in zipping my jeans. "You don't have to walk me home."

He looks at me like I'm nuts. "Yeah, that's not happening."

"It's fine. It's almost dawn." I peer through the slats of his vertical blinds.

He bends down to tie his boots. "You could stay but you won't, right? Because you don't want Ace to know you're sleeping with me?"

I let the blinds fall back into place. "I stayed a few nights," I point out, but, yes, I can't deny part of my decision relates to Ace. "He's hurting right now. I don't want to twist the knife in any further."

Matt's jaw clenches, but he's skating on thin ice since I found my *dossier*, so whatever jealous thoughts he has he keeps to himself. Instead, he steps toward me, halting close enough that I have to tip my head back to look at him. "Want me to talk to him?"

"No offense, but I don't think he'd listen to you." Although, if this situation on the team is going to get resolved, Ace and Matt and the entire team are going to have to talk *and* listen to each other.

"You're probably right." He pulls me against him and I breathe deep, enjoying the smell of warm, sexy Matt for a moment longer.

"I can't stay tonight. Tomorrow—today," I correct myself. "Today is going to be hard for him, and I need to be there. He'd be there for me."

A flicker of unhappiness flits through his eyes at the reminder of my closeness with Ace, but then his easygoing nature breaks through and he gives me a rueful smile. "I can't believe I'm trying to talk a woman into spending the night with me."

It's my turn to glance down to hide the sting of his comment. He means it as a compliment, but it's a reminder of how many girls have shuffled in and out of this bedroom.

"Hey, you." He tips my chin up. "No one else is spending time in here just because you aren't around. I hope you know that."

I push the doubt away and cling to those words.

* * *

Ace sits in front of the television, his bloodless hands gripped between his legs, looking as angry as I've ever seen him. I immediately text Sutton and Charity and tell them to take a long time at dinner.

My thoughts flit to Matty. I never thought to ask him if he was worried. He probably isn't in any danger of being replaced, but I never asked, either—too caught up in my own drama. I tell Ace I need to use the bathroom and slip away to shoot off a quick text.

Me: *Day going okay for you?*

Matty: *It's all good. Thanks for asking. You?*

I'm doing okay. Worried about, I don't want to bring up Ace again, so I just type, *friends.*

Matty: *Got it. Call me if you want to talk or meet up. I'll be up late.*

Me: *I'll probably be busy.*

Matty: *Practice starts tomorrow. We'll work it out.*

When I get out, Ace is pacing.

"Have you decided what you're going to do?"

"I'm the quarterback, Lucy, or did loverboy convince you otherwise?"

"Ace, I'm behind you. It doesn't matter who I'm dating."

He snorts out an ugly laugh. "Does it feel good to be Ives's current slam piece?"

I grind my teeth together to keep from lashing out. "If you're going to be an asshole, you can leave."

Ace runs a hand through his closely cropped hair. "What is that you see in him?"

"He's kind." I think back to how he made me breakfast, his thoughtfulness in taking my glucose measurements.

"He's working to turn the team against me. The entire defensive squad follows his lead. If he stood up and supported me, the team would support me. If I don't have him, I'm as good as gone."

I rub my lips together. I don't like where this is going. I didn't like it when Matt presented his side of the argument to me and I definitely don't like Ace trying to leverage our friendship. "I have no influence over him, just like I have no influence over you."

Ace's jaw works furiously as he holds in whatever horrible invective he'd like to spit out at me. Finally, he fixes his attention on the television and we watch the show in silence. For two excruciating hours. I'm so stressed out I end up checking my glucose levels five times. I open my mouth to ask him to leave just as the show flips from the studio to the camera at Remington Barr's home.

If I thought Ace was angry before, it's nothing like the rage consuming him now. He squeezes the remote so tight, the plastic cover over the battery cracks in his hands.

I get up and move to the kitchen because the tension in the living room is suffocating. The phone rings, startling me. I glance at my phone, but I realize it's not mine ringing. It's Ace's. It rings and rings until the voicemail cuts in.

Then there's a series of pings that signal an influx of text messages or emails arriving. Ace sits there like a statute. I feel stupid and useless. Should I answer the inquiries for him? Say no comment? Block them? Or hell, just turn the stupid thing off.

"Ace, honey, can I help you?"

He doesn't answer.

I fumble with my phone and text Matty.

Ace is frozen and his phone is blowing up. What should I do?

The phone rings immediately. Ace's head tips slightly to the side, as if registering it's at least not *his* phone.

"Hello?"

My heart leaps and my stomach drops at the same time.

"You okay?" Matty asks.

"Hey," I answer vaguely not wanting to pour fuel on Ace's already triggered temper.

"He's sitting next to you?"

"Close."

"Fuck."

The animosity between the two is growing, and I can't help but feel like it's my fault. I turn away from Ace and whisper into the phone. "He's in a bad place right now."

Matty sighs. "Do you want me to come over?"

I clench the phone in my hand. "No. It'd make it worse."

There's a long pause at the other end of the line. I know he doesn't like this, but Ace *is* my friend and I can't abandon him now, no matter how rotten he's been to me lately. Matty finally sighs, "Call me if you need anything. Anytime, okay?"

"Okay," I say with relief.

He starts to say something but decides against it, and after we exchange goodbyes, we hang up.

"Was that him on the phone?" Ace asks immediately. Apparently, he's not dead on my sofa.

I almost lie, but then I decide Ace deserves the truth about as much as I deserve to see Matty if I want.

"Yes."

Ace breathes through his nose. "Are you *dating* him?"

The disbelief in his voice grates hard. I snap out, "Yes."

"What makes you think you're relationship material to him?"

"I...I..." The question is so surprising, so insulting, I barely know how to answer. "Am I not? Do you know something about me that prevents me from being, um, relationship material?"

"Yeah, because you're too fucking nice. College is a cesspool of people who are fucked up, Lucy. You think you know them one minute, but you don't. I don't know what Masters was thinking marrying some chick he knew for the span of a semester, but we all know he's going to be divorced before he gets his signing bonus." Ace pauses. "No, after, because the chick will take his money and run off with it, after she's fucked all of his teammates."

"Ace, what are you talking about?"

"I'm talking about the fact that you're making a huge fucking mistake. You want to survive with your soft little heart intact, then smarten up. I've told you time and again that guys here only want one thing. You think somehow your pussy is the golden one that suddenly turns Ives away from all the free pussy he has access to?"

I flinch.

"No, you're a novelty. He thinks the chase is great, but once you stop running, he'll be bored and move on to the next tasty treat on the menu. How long did your dad spend staring at the bottom of the bottle waiting for your mom to stop fucking my dad?"

I jerk back, feeling his words like a physical blow.

He swipes a shaky hand across his face. "Guys like us. Like my old man. Like Matty. Women are just a convenience. There for the taking. There all of the time. The only thing we can do to minimize the damage we inflict is to pair up with women who want the same thing we want. They don't want love or romance. They don't require devotion. They give their bodies. They take from you, and you're both fine. But that's not how you're built, Lucy."

I hardly know what to say in response because he's right. I tried the hookup route after my high school boyfriend dumped me. Those weren't satisfying, so I tried dating my safe, solid boyfriends. Those weren't successful either. I tried one night with Matty but couldn't stick with it because he was too charming, too fun, too wonderful in bed and out of it. But I do require loyalty, faithfulness, and a certain amount of devotion. Matty's already admitted he's been a shitty boyfriend to one girl.

"Maybe I've changed," I manage to choke out. The lie tastes bitter on my tongue.

"When did you start fucking him? Have you known all along? Have you been laughing about this shit behind my back?" The veins in Ace's neck are bulging against his skin. He's red-faced, and some of his words are wet, laced with spittle and venom.

I can feel a spike of stress messing with my system. "I slept at Matthew Iverson's place the night my apartment was fumigated," I say as evenly as possible.

"You slept with Iverson four weeks ago?" Ace yells like some outraged virgin.

My own temper fires up. He's not the injured party in this scenario. I slam my spoon down again. "Yeah, because you were fucking some jersey chaser on the sofa, and I didn't want to watch the porn show, okay? Matt offered me a place to stay."

"Oh, I bet he did."

I stare at him in confusion. "Yes, he did. And he was a perfect gentleman. He didn't try anything. He made me breakfast and sent me on my way. We got together later and had sex."

He screws up his face. "You know what? Take your little walk in the gutter with Iverson. But don't come to my house weeping that he's broken your heart and given you an STD."

I rear back as if he's slapped me. "That's not fair."

"Welcome to life, Lucy. Nothing is fuckin' fair," he spits out.

"Ace." I try to soften my tone, but it's difficult. His hurtful words are branded in my mind, making my hands tremble. "This has nothing to do with you. I promise you. I'm on your side. What position you want to play, what Matty wants, it doesn't matter."

Nothing I say penetrates Ace's rage. He snatches his sunglasses off the table and is at the door in four long strides. Hand on the doorknob, he turns back. "You're going to regret this. When he moves on, and he will, and you end up being humiliated after dozens of pictures are plastered on the web with him and some jersey chaser, you're really going to feel good, aren't you?"

"Please go." My throat is tight. I can't believe he's saying these things to me.

"I'm telling you this because you're too soft for Matty Iverson. If you have any doubts about what I'm saying, Google his fucking name. There are a helluva lot more pictures out there than what I showed you."

I try swallowing, but there's a huge lump in my throat. "What Matty did before me makes no difference."

Ace looks at me like I'm the dumbest fucking girl on the planet.

"Have fun fucking him tonight." And with that, he's gone.

At the computer, I hesitate. I slam the laptop lid shut and then pace. I pace back to my desk and open it again.

I type in his name. Most of the pictures are of him in uniform, him on the field. There's one link on the second page of him bending over, his broad shoulders between another girl's legs. She's wearing jeans but her shirt is off. His shirt is off. I don't know what he's doing there.

There are other pictures of him and another girl. Him and Hammer and two girls. They were all taken the same night.

My heart twists as I look them over. The dates of the pictures inform me that they were taken the night after the championship game. Just a few weeks before he came to the Brew House. Just a few weeks before I had my own personal, up-close picture of Matty between my legs.

I knew exactly how it felt for him to be there, licking and sucking and fingering me in ways that made my sex clench just to think about it. It kills me to know there are other women out there who have experienced that same pleasure.

Not a rational feeling, but it's there and I can't make it go away.

Can he change? Ace says no.

But then Ace has his own issues, his own demons that Matty doesn't struggle with. I shut my laptop firmly and push it away.

So Matty had sex in the past. Big whooping deal. I repeat that to myself a hundred times, but Ace has stirred up the fear I thought I'd put behind me.

28

I TUCK MY PHONE AWAY and try to curb my impatience. Wishing Ace and Luce weren't friends is a fruitless exercise. They are, and I'm going to have to deal with it. I still think Ace is the snake in my garden because there's no way he hangs Luce's picture in his locker without having stronger feelings than *friendship* for her. But…there's no point in bringing that up with Luce.

She thinks they're friends, treats him like a friend. They've had plenty of time to knock boots in the past and haven't done it. So I just have to trust that whatever feelings are involved, they aren't on Lucy's end.

"Where's everyone else?" I ask Hammer as I wander into the living room. Earlier in the day we had half the defense in here watching ESPN's Signing Day special, and now it's just Hammer.

"Most of the guys went to the Gas Station. A few went to work out."

Probably the guys who play the same positions as the blue chip recruits announcing today.

"You think about the guys you were replacing on Signing Day?" I ask. I know I hadn't. I was too jacked up to get here and show everyone

I was the man.

"Fuck no. I was thinking how I couldn't wait until the fall was here and how I could strut my stuff on national television. I was practicing my hammer move." He brings his arm down in an abrupt chop.

"Yeah, me, too. I wanted to replace those guys. Fuck, I was a terrible shit. I didn't even care that they hazed me. I felt invincible, even when I was running around the stadium with just my jock on."

"Good times." Hammer reaches his fist out and I knock mine against it. "You talk to Lucy about Ace?"

"Yeah, last week. It didn't go well. She's not going to talk to him."

"Ah hell," Hammer sighs. "What're you going to do now? Maybe if you bring it up with her later? After sex maybe, when you've softened her up."

And maybe someone will knife me in the gut because that's how I felt when I went up there and saw her, nude, crouched over on the floor weeping like she'd just seen her dad killed in front of her.

"No."

He rears back in the harshness in my voice. "Bro, it's not like I asked you to fuck her in the quad."

"Hammer, man, I love you, but Luce is my girlfriend, and I'd like you to start treating her with respect." I stare at him. Hard.

He blinks a couple times and nods in acknowledgment. "That's cool. What about Ace, though?"

I grind my teeth together at hearing his name.

"What about him?"

"If Lucy isn't going to talk to him, then are you going to him again?"

I run an agitated hand through my hair. "It'll straighten out by itself. Coach will work the two guys out during summer camp. Let the chips fall where they may. On the field, like how it's always supposed to happen."

Hammer snorts.

"What?" I ask with exasperation.

"We both know that if Coach don't like you, all the talent in the world isn't going to keep you on the field. And if you aren't on the field, there's nowhere to prove yourself. Your skills atrophy and die."

My answer? To pick up the remote and turn the volume up. It's juvenile, but I'm fucking done with this conversation. Mostly because Hammer's right and I don't have a good goddamned response.

A little while later, my phone beeps but it's not Lucy. She's still dealing with the drama queen. It's Stella Lowe, telling me that Coach wants me in his office in the next ten minutes.

"Coach wants to see me."

"Sorry, son." Hammer gives me a thumbs-up sign and a sympathetic smile.

He can smile because it's not his ass going to the coach's office. Again.

* * *

Coach Lowe's behind his desk. The television is on and ESPN is handing out preseason grades based on our recruiting class.

"They're saying Western's going to be dominant for another four years," Coach informs me as I settle into a chair.

"Congrats." I try to keep the sarcasm out of my voice.

"What kind of progress are you making with Ace?"

I launch into the argument I devised on my way over. "He doesn't want to give up the quarterback position. And you know that he's a smart player. He took us where Wilson Rogers didn't, and we all know Rogers is going to be our next black president." I smile, but Coach simply stares at me like I'm a moron. Still, Rogers, the quarterback who graduated last spring and almost led us to a National title my sophomore year, knew every player on the eighty-man roster and could probably tell you their moms' names as well as their girlfriends'. That man was going places, although not in the NFL. He's in graduate school now and is going to run the world someday. I power on. "I know Ace doesn't have the most accurate arm, but he makes good decisions for the most part. This new guy coming in will be raw. He's never played at the college level—"

"You become coach when I wasn't looking?"

I wince and fight the urge to shrink in the chair. "No, sir."

"Then you can keep your amateur scouting reports to yourself. You're here to play the game as I tell you to play it, on and off the field. Remington Barr is going to be our starting quarterback next year. Whether we field a cohesive team is going to be on you. And, son, if you can't convince a bunch of raggedy-ass boys to follow you on this field, there's no way you're going to play at the next level."

What'd I tell Luce? That the Coach is the lord of your universe? I guess I didn't tell her that you could hate the one in charge even as you played hard to win. Because you weren't playing for him. You were playing for each other.

"Ace will either be holding the clipboard on the sidelines all season or he'll be on the field as a safety. Your job is to make sure everyone gets behind our new quarterback."

"Yes, sir." I say the words even though it's worse than swallowing a bunch of razors. If there's a Mount Rushmore for crappy coaches, Coach Lowe is getting my first nomination. I sit there fuming in silence as Coach pretends I'm not sitting in the chair five feet away from him. Finally, when the ESPN college crew breaks for commercial, he swivels toward me.

"You're still here?"

Yeah, meathead, I'm still sitting here like a good little soldier waiting to be dismissed. When Masters said he was declaring early, I didn't envy him a bit. I was having too much fun. The real world could wait another year. I didn't know that Coach was going to spend the year shitting down my throat while ordering me to smile as he did it.

"You're dismissed." He waves a hand, shooing me off like I'm a pesky, bothersome gnat.

One more year, I remind myself as I stiffly rise from the chair and walk out.

Ten minutes later, Stella finds me in the weight room punching my way past a tackling dummy.

"Matty, I need to talk to you."

God, I do not need this. I'm too busy pretending Coach Lowe is standing in front of me. I've gotten three good hits in, but I'm still sore from the proverbial fist Coach slammed into my face while I was in his office. That said, I can't very well walk away and pretend I can't hear her, can I?

"What's up?" I say abruptly.

"No matter what you say or do, Ace is going to be either benched or moved."

Wariness rises. "What do you know?"

"My dad…he found out about us," she admits. "He caught me coming out of Ace's room last year. The night that we ended up staying over in Wisconsin because of bad weather?"

"I remember." I fucked a local chick and Masters walked in. I invited him to stay. I can't remember the woman's face or even if the sex was good. Only that I invited Masters to join us and he barely even noticed what was going on. At the time, I remember thinking, *Poor Masters. Still hanging on to his V-card.* He was wooing Ellie. I didn't get at the time how one person could transform your life.

"He's had it in for Ace ever since. He sought out Barr. He wasn't even recruiting him hard. He had his eye on another quarterback from Utah. Thought they would try to sneak some reps in during this upcoming year. Anyway, when he learned about me and Ace, he told me to enjoy Ace this year because it would be his last."

"Stella," I say with a mixture of disappointment and dismay.

She hangs her head and I feel like a piece of shit. It's not her fault that her dad's a Grade-A prick. She should be able to sleep with whoever the hell she wants to. "I know. I argued and pleaded and told him I'd break it off with Ace. He told me to go ahead. So I did. I told Ace we were done and he laughed. He said he didn't care what Coach made me say. So I told him I slept with Dayton Carter."

Dayton Carter, power forward for the Western State Warriors's basketball team. Now I'm feeling even worse. For her. For Ace. For all of us. "Oh, fuck, Stella."

She nods sadly. "Ace…he told me that I was a convenient hole and he didn't care who I slept with, only that he figured he should go get checked out since I was such a slut." Her mouth twists in pain.

I furtively look to the door, wishing for all the world that someone would come and save me, but it's no use.

It's just Stella and me and her uncomfortable confession.

"Ace was probably…" Shit, I have no idea what Ace was feeling but for Stella's sake, I make something up. "Torn up and…" What would I do if Luce told me she slept with someone else? I'd go beat his ass and then ask her what the fuck. And then, I guess, maybe I'd go sleep with a dozen chicks to make me feel better? Because that's apparently how Ace dealt with his heartbreak. "He didn't take it well."

She snorts. At least she's not crying. "I think he took it just fine." She swallows a couple of times. "Coach…he wants to stay here with the Warriors. He's spooked by the firing of the Chattanooga coach. Ten winning seasons but only one title, so the guy gets shown the door."

Last year was a blood bath for college coaches. Down in the trenches, I don't pay much attention to that. Who's coaching which team only matters when you're making your college commitment to a school.

"So Remington Barr is a two for one. He gets back at Ace for violating his precious daughter and hopefully secures his future."

"That's right. Coach is never going to allow Ace behind center again so long as Barr is healthy, and even then…" She shrugs. "I think even then the third string would probably be given the nod. Ace is done, and someone has to convince him of it. Anyway, I just wanted you to know that you can't do anything to change Dad's mind. It was made up months ago." She walks to the door.

"You should tell Ace," I call after her.

"I've tried. Many times." Then she's gone.

I spend another hour working the tackling dummies, the sleds, and then finally I give up and just pound away at the punching block, but the cloud of dread never escapes me. It hangs over me, like Damocles' sword. I'm just waiting for it to fall and stab me through the skull.

* * *

"Stay away from Lucy."

No hello. No preamble. Ace just storms into my room before dinner, his eyes livid and his cheeks flushed red.

I almost wish he'd saved this confrontation for later. At least until I was able to put some kind of plan together. All I have at the moment is the vague idea of persuading Ace using the same case I presented to Luce. It'd be good for his future. So few quarterbacks make the transition. More safeties, d-backs and corners out there than quarterbacks. I'd ease into it, though, nice and slow.

"Sure, come on in, Ace. Good to see you. Nice that you could knock," I say sarcastically, tossing my phone on the bed. "Beer?" I offer because that's all I have in my room and from the wild, tense look in his eyes, he needs about five of them with a chaser of whiskey.

"Sisters and girlfriends are off-limits." Ace ignores my offer, preferring to stand and glare at me. I've had enough of people spitting on my head in anger today. I get to my feet, fold my arms across my chest, and glare right back.

"And Lucy Washington is neither sister nor girlfriend as far as I know." Ace had been hooking up with Stella all last semester, banging everything in a skirt, and now he's trying to jockblock me? I'm going to need to lance this boil.

Ace's lips thin into an unhappy line. "Lucy is my friend."

"Like I said—neither girlfriend nor sister. So the locker room rule" —stupid as it is and one that nobody really observes—"doesn't apply."

"It does if it's invoked, and I'm invoking it right now."

I scratch my temple and reach for some patience even though that character trait isn't even on my top twenty list of strengths. It lives somewhere down around my feet along with impulse control and re- straint. "We're not in grade school anymore. We can't call out new rules on the field."

"Lucy is not a jersey chaser," he grinds out. "She's not the type who's interested in one-night stands and hookups, which is probably hard for you to understand given that's all you do."

Jesus. If this guy wasn't taking it on the chin in the football arena already, he'd be kissing my knuckles.

"Okay, man, you need to take a step back." I might have gotten around in the past, but I'm twenty-two. I was single, and there were women throwing themselves at me. That I accepted a few—or sever- al—of those invitations doesn't make me an asshole. "Seems to me that we're two pumpkins in the same patch, brother. It wasn't Stella Lowe who was sucking your dick at the after party in Phoenix after the Na- tional Championship game two weeks ago. Unless Stella suddenly grew red hair and has a twin that we don't know about. And I could've sworn that you were screwing a Kappa in the bathroom at the Gas Station on Monday night."

"My point exactly," he huffs. "We both know that we're here to play football, first and foremost. Everything else, including women, come a distant second, so stop screwing around with Lucy. You're only trying to use her to get to me, and it's not going to work."

That pisses me off on Luce's behalf. "Take your head out of your ass for just a moment and stop thinking about Ace Anderson, buddy. I like Lucy because she's hot and interesting. She likes me because I'm…well, I'm awesome. It has nothing to do with you."

"So you're just going to fuck her to make a point."

"Not that it's any of your business, but I'm not *fucking* her. She's my girlfriend, and while that might get your jock in a twist because you've been holding a torch for her for a long time, that's just too damn bad. She's not your girlfriend. She's not your sister. You can't go around tagging all the single ladies on campus you might want *someday* saying that they're off-limits. Doesn't work that way."

"So what? You want to take away my position on the team and take away my best friend too?" he hurls bitterly.

Clenched jaw, I look at him in frustration. "I don't want to do either."

"But you will do both if you want, is that what you're saying?" He sneers. "Stay away from her, Iverson. She's too good for you." He stalks to the door. When he gets there he turns around, "And I'm not moving from quarterback. I earned that goddamned position, and Coach Lowe will have to pry me out of there with a backhoe. You can spread that around the defense along with all your other messages."

He slams the door behind him, his exit something out of a fricking soap opera. Quarterbacks and their fucking prima donna attitudes.

I drop my head into my hands. So much for taking an easy and nice route with Ace.

I could do a better job screwing up my life, but not by much. At least I have Luce. I cling to that.

29

LUCY

"DO YOU HAVE TIME TO go to the mall with me?" Matty asks when he picks up the phone. He texted and asked if I'd call him when I had a chance, and the first opportunity I've had all day is my mid-evening break during my shift at the Brew House.

"Sure, you run out of Under Armour shirts and sweatpants?"

"Har har. Never heard you complain."

"I'm more interested in what you've got under your clothes," I tease.

"Tell me more."

I lean my head against brick exterior of the Brew House and conjure up a vision of Matty sitting in his desk chair with his feet up, wearing his sweatpants and a tight workout shirt that clings to all of his muscles. "No. I'm taking a break and I don't want to get excited."

"Mmm. This is like a challenge. Do you think I could get you off, just talking to you? Like telling you how if I was there I'd be on my knees, kissing your pussy until you cream all over me."

"Matthew Justin Iverson, you need to be quiet right now." I turn hot enough to melt the snow.

He chuckles. "You're bringing out the big guns."

"Matthew…"

He swallows his next laugh and tries to soothe me. "I swear no more talk about your sweet pussy and my hard dick."

"I'm hanging up now." My panties are becoming uncomfortably damp.

"Seriously. Shutting up. My mom's birthday is coming up in a week and I need to buy her a gift. You in?"

"Yes." I find that's the only response I ever seem to give him these days.

"Great. I'll pick you up at your apartment around five and we can have dinner out by the mall. There's a vegan restaurant not too far away."

Now my heart's melting. "I'll be off in two hours."

"Cool." He pauses.

"What?"

"Love you, Goldie."

He hangs up before I can respond. He's such a devil. And I love it. And him.

He picks me up right on the mark. I bring him a spiced cider from the Brew House and give him a long, thorough kiss.

"So are you telling me that you don't want to go to the mall?" he jokes after I let him go.

"No, that's my 'I love you, too' kiss."

His eyes gleam with warmth. "I like those kisses."

"There's more where that came from."

"Yeah? How many condoms we got left?"

"We're perilously low," I tell him. "We should make a detour tonight."

"Detour? Hell, it will be our first stop."

"Before we leave, here's this." I present the gift I've been working on for the past week.

"What's this?" He leans against the door panel and hefts the gold-wrapped package for inspection.

"It's for you. Someone told me it was your birthday." I sidle in beside him to look at the present.

Matty flips the package around with both hands while sliding me an amused glance. "Last October."

I shrug. "I missed Valentine's Day."

"Hmm," he muses. "That was last week, wasn't it? Hammer was going off about how he was writing about how to give the best Valentine's Day blow job, but I figured he was writing ahead."

I hurry to assure him that I'm not upset because I'm totally not. I didn't expect any Valentine's Day present. "I hate that made-up holiday. I'm so glad we didn't do anything."

"You sure?"

Is he kidding? I couldn't have a more attentive boyfriend. Yes, we don't do a million things together because we're both busy, but he's there when I need him. He listens to me vent about mock trial, about the stress of midterms, about my mother. He holds my hand when I confess I'm scared of the upcoming competition and doesn't deride me for being overly cautious.

And, most importantly, even though he goes out with his boys now and then, I haven't seen any pictures of him with his arms around another girl, which makes me feel a little foolish for having any concerns about him in the first place.

I rise on my tiptoes to give him a kiss on his cheek. "Completely. Now open this up so we can eat. I'm starving."

That gets him moving. These days he's more careful about what I eat than I am. He's always looking for vegan places, even though I've assured him a million times that I eat meat. That always leads to him giggling like a schoolboy. Maybe he just drags me to those places to hear me say the words *I eat meat.*

He rips off the paper. Just takes his hand and tears the wrapping right down the middle and then stares. Looks at me. Then back to the frame to stare some more.

It's a square frame and inside is his jersey from the Championship game he played and won that second weekend in January right before we met. Hammer found it stuffed in the bottom drawer of Matty's dresser. In a cutout inset in the bottom, which took me three tries and five ruined mats before I got right, his stats for the game are listed along with the Outland Trophy he was so proud of.

"This is some present," he murmurs, almost to himself. He admires every part of the gift, from the dark stained wood frame, to the matte glass covering, and the white mat surrounding the blue and gold jersey, the patch of the bowl game turned outward on full display. We stand outside in the rapidly dimming light. I should be getting cold, but there's something about the way that he's smiling that heats me up inside.

Finally, after several moments pass along with students who cast curious gazes our way, Matty's done inspecting the gift and hits the key fob to raise the back gate. Carefully, he stows the framed jersey under a netting strapped to the floor of the trunk and then pushes the hatch closed.

He helps me into the passenger side and then rounds the front. Inside the car it's toasty warm. On the way to the mall, he swings into a drugstore parking lot.

"I thought you forgot," I say amused.

He arches an eyebrow. "Are you kidding? After that thing back there, I'm thinking about skipping the mall and hauling you back to the house so I can thank you properly. Stay here while I run inside."

It's the third box we've needed since we started dating a month ago.

Matty's full of endless amounts of energy. Even though practice is in full swing, there's not a day that goes by without a phone call, personal visit or text. Usually they all include some kind of sexual innuendo and the days we don't see each other are just one long period of foreplay that makes it all the more exciting when we finally do get our hands on each other.

He pops back in and throws the box into my lap. I toss it between my hands, thinking about the one time Matty forgot the condom and how hot that was. I throw it back at him. "Want to stop using these?"

He jerks, his hand skittering off the gearshift to collide with the dash. He takes a deep breath and then another before swiveling his head toward me, his black hair nearly obscuring his face. I reach over and tuck the strands behind his ear.

The heat in his eyes nearly singes my fingers.

"If you didn't want to shop, you should have just told me," he finally says. "Because right now, there's no way I'll be able to get out of this vehicle without being arrested for public indecency."

"I'll take that as a yes."

He straightens and then cups my skull, pulling me close to his lips. "It's a yes."

After kissing me senseless, he returns to his seat and starts the Rover. I put myself to rights, pulling down my bra he had shoved up along with my sweater and buttoning my jeans I hadn't even realized he'd loosened.

"Talk to me," he orders as he stares into the rearview mirror and then navigates around the other cars before entering the stream of traffic.

"About what?" I'm still a little dazed from the kiss.

"The unsexiest thing you can think of."

"How's Ace?"

Matty shoots me a dark look. "That'll do it." He sighs, leans his head back and relaxes against the seat. "He's okay. Coach hasn't moved him yet."

"When do you think that'll happen?"

"When Barr gets here in the summer." He sneaks another glance at me. "You guys still hanging out?"

"Not really. He's texted, but we…I don't think he's happy." Ace hasn't really said anything since he stomped out of my apartment on Signing Day. Absent a few texts, our communication has been brief. He hasn't come over to the house, and I haven't encouraged it. It's sad, like the last part of my childhood is being severed from me, but I can't give up Matty just to appease Ace's petulance.

"About us?"

"About everything."

"Let's talk about something else? Mock trial?" He looks over as I make a face and an unhappy sound. "Okay, striking mock trial off the list."

"What are you thinking about for your mom?"

"I dunno. That's why you're here. It was either you or Hammer, and I didn't want to listen to another of his lists."

I smother a grin. "What are some of her hobbies?"

"Hmm. She likes to read but she already just buys everything she wants, so I've got to be creative."

Matty and I decide to shop first. We stop in at a jewelry store. "How much do you want to spend?"

He shrugs. "Under five?"

I point out a couple of necklaces, lingering over one that has a circle with a small pearl in the middle. It's delicate and lovely.

"Let's see that one," Matty says.

"This is a beautiful piece." The sales lady flips open a black velvet pad and drapes the gold necklace across it.

"I think I need to see it on." He picks it up and gestures for me to turn around.

"Your mom is four inches taller than me," I protest, worried that if I see it around my neck, I'll want to keep it.

"So? You both have necks right?"

I can't argue with that. I lift my hair and Matty hooks it in the back. The gold sparkles in the brightly lit store.

"We'll take it." He hands over the card to the store clerk. I start to take it off, but Matty grabs my arm. "I heard you had a birthday." His smile is bright, his words an echo of mine.

"In May."

He tugs my hand away from my neck and curls his fingers around my own so I can't remove the necklace. He gives a chin nod to the clerk who scuttles off to run Matty's credit card before we can change our minds.

"What about your mom?" I ask, my hand still under his.

"I bought her a Fitbit already. I know I forgot Valentine's Day."

"Matthew…"

He laughs and catches me up in a hard embrace. He dips his head and kisses my neck, catching both chain and flesh under his lips. "I've missed all your previous birthdays, Christmases and Valentine's Day, so this is something small. Don't tell me you don't want it because you'll hurt my feelings."

"I highly doubt that, but thank you. It is too much." I saw the price tag, and this is definitely the most expensive piece of anything I've ever owned besides the laptop my dad surprised me with when I graduated.

"I wanted to." He kisses me again, this time on the lips.

Had I ever thought Matty was a risk? I was such a foolish girl.

30

MATTY

"WE'VE GOT A RECRUIT COMING," Coach announces. March has rolled around and we're halfway through spring practice. I'm antsy for it to be over because it means I'll have more time to spend with Luce. I'm looking forward to this summer, particularly grateful that she's a townie and will be here with me because I'm getting tired of Coach's shit. It's eroding my love for the game. "You and Ace are going to show him a good time."

I've spent more time in Coach's office since the National Championship game than I had in all four years prior. I'm getting sick of the leather chairs, the nice carpet, and frankly, his goddamn face.

"Isn't this guy a linebacker?" Ace asks sarcastically. "Mr. Texas isn't here yet."

Ace's attitude toward Coach borders on insubordination. It's definitely insolent, but what the hell? It's not like Ace has a lot to lose. I feel sorry for him. I really do, but then I think about the shit he vomited all over me a couple weeks ago. I still can't convince Luce to spend the night with me. She doesn't want to hurt little Ace's feelings, even though I sense a serious amount of distance between the two of them.

I'm guessing Ace had a throw down with her, much like he had with me. Like me, she didn't take it well. Unlike me, she kinda cares.

There's something highly ironic about the fact I'm pretty much begging her to stay with me but she keeps turning me down. If I want to sleep with her, I have to do it in her apartment, in her tiny-ass bed that's about as comfortable as sleeping on my yoga mats. Which is to say, not fucking comfortable. We only do it when I'm desperate. So like three, four times a week.

"You two need to start working together. Your team is falling apart and I want you to fix it. Starting with this new recruit."

I half believe Ace will tell Coach that the new recruit can go suck a goat, but he doesn't.

Instead, we take Lucious Deakins—for serious, that's the fucker's name—the new recruit, out for dinner. He's big bodied, and needs to lose about thirty pounds of fat and trade that in for fifty pounds of muscle. Worse? He's got a loud fucking mouth and I'm not talking volume. The kid has a Twitter account, a Facebook account, an Instagram account, and a fucking Pinterest board where he pins pictures of food.

I hate that I'm even using the word *pin*. I could feel the testosterone draining out of me each second I had that site up on my computer.

His Twitter account is the worst. He's been documenting every single thing associated with his recruiting trips from the snacks he received on the airplane to the sidewalk cracks outside each stadium.

Oh, yeah, and he doesn't shut up.

"What are we doing later tonight?" he asks.

Two seconds later. "You guys bringing me strippers?"

Before I can draw my next breath. "Are they jumping out of a cake?

I've always wanted a stripper cake."

Jesus, does he think we're putting on some Mardi Gras parade for him?

"No," I say shortly.

"How about the booze. I can do a two-story beer bong." *Call me Lucious cuz that's my name* rubs his hands together.

I share another long-suffering glance with Ace, who smiles back at me. He's enjoying this. "You're eighteen. We can't serve you booze," I tell him.

"But...why are you taking me around then?"

"So you can get a feel for the campus. You want us to violate some NCAA rules and make it impossible for you to get a D-1 scholarship here?"

"Uh, no," he stutters, showing a modicum of sense for the first time during the whole trip. Truth is, if we liked him, if we thought he wasn't a total washout, then we would treat him to a few Warrior perks. But this guy isn't worth the effort. This is our punishment.

"Good, then follow me, don't drink, and don't touch anyone."

"What if they touch me?"

I close my eyes. "That's fine. If they touch you first, feel free to touch them back, but for God's sake, don't offer to pay them anything. These are students, not hookers."

Ace muffles a laugh behind his hand. I give explicit instructions to the bartenders at the Gas Station that this is an underage, loud-mouth recruit. They nod and serve him a Coke when he asks. I take a shot of whiskey because the only way I'm making it through the night is with really, really dulled senses. Numb, in fact.

There're plenty of women in the Gas Station to make up for the lack of alcohol. I tell one of the girls to pretend like she's spiking his drink while she pours club soda in it. A couple of other players show up and take him off my hands for an hour to play pool.

Ace leans back in the booth across from me and looks at me with assessing eyes.

I give a tired gesture. "Whatever you've got to say, spit it out."

"Why aren't you taking my back in this?" Ace asks. "You really think I'm that shitty of a quarterback?"

I sigh. I don't know if I've ever really hated anyone, but I'm getting close with Coach. "No. You're a good quarterback and I'm proud to wear the same colors."

"But I'm not great."

"We don't need you to be great." I squeeze the back of my neck. "Look, it doesn't matter what I think. Coach has made up his mind. The kid's coming here and he's going to start him. He...he doesn't like you, man."

"Because of Stella."

"Yeah." I breathe out a sigh of relief. We're finally getting somewhere. "Because of Stella."

Ace shakes his head. "We stopped fucking a long time ago. Barely into the season. What was it? Week four?"

"How long had you been going at it?"

"Since summer. It was just a fling. The shelf life was getting stale at that point anyway. I guess I'll just continue being the thorn in his side."

"Why? You're real athletic. You have great hands. Why not try for safety?" I launch into my spiel about how there's so much more opportunity for him in the NFL beyond the stupid quarterback position. Who even gives a crap about that position anyway?

"I don't want to play that position. I've got one year left to prove that I'm worth a draft pick or at least a tryout or two."

"But if you're not on the field, you can't prove anything other than you look good holding a clipboard."

"You know that the favorite player in the stadium is the backup quarterback," Ace replies confidently. "That freshman comes in and he gets his first hit, he's going to come crawling over to the sideline and I'll be there to step in and save the day."

I down another shot because that's the only way I'm going to make it through the night between the raw-ass recruit who's determined to get drunk and screw as many college chicks as he can, and the grand delusions of Ace.

"You don't believe I can do it, do you?"

"I don't know what's going to happen this fall," I tell him frankly. "I want to win again. I want to enjoy our senior year. I want to know that we did everything we could to repeat. But I don't know what's going to happen. Maybe it goes just like you say. Or maybe Mr. Texas comes in and plays just well enough to keep his starting job and you don't see squat and become a footnote in Warrior football. And I don't want that for you, man. You're too good of an athlete. Too good of a football player."

Ace considers my words for a minute and then leans forward, folding his hands on the top of the table. "I tell you what, you stop seeing Lucy. You tell her that you're done with her and I'll move to safety."

I choke on the vodka shot. Ace rises up and slaps me on the back, too hard to be termed friendly, but at this point I need it.

"What'd you just say?" I demand.

"You heard me."

"I heard some words, but I don't think I understood them."

"No, you heard me clearly. I'll make it easy for you, for the team. For Coach. For everyone. But, in exchange, you give Lucy back to me."

I narrow my eyes. Something isn't right here. "You and Lucy are friends."

"No, not really. She thinks we're friends but we've always been meant to be together."

I've only had three shots, but I feel dazed. He's been denying they've been anything but friends and now he's willing to trade his precious QB position for her? As if she's a piece of property I've got control over?

"Ace, brother. For the four years we've been teammates, you've screwed your share of blondes, but not one of them has been Lucy. And you've insisted that you and Luce are just friends. I'm getting whiplash here."

"Know how many guys Lucy has slept with?"

I can't really say I don't know because I have the list from Ahmed, but I don't think I should admit that. Ace doesn't care.

"I do. It's six. You and her loser high school boyfriend and a few randoms in between. Know how old she was when she lost her last baby tooth?"

So Ahmed was wrong. Good thing I didn't hunt them all down and gouge out their eyes for having seen Luce naked. "No."

"Thirteen. She had to have braces after that. Know what she wore to her senior prom?"

"A dress?" I'm tiring of this game real fast.

"No again. She wore pants. One of our friends came out as a lesbian and didn't want to wear a dress and so Lucy wore a tux in solidarity."

That sounds very Luce-like. "Okay."

"My point is that you don't know shit about Lucy, and you haven't spent the time to find this stuff out."

"When she lost her baby tooth is pertinent how?" I drum my fingers on the table impatiently. Ace is getting to me a tiny bit. I don't know all this stuff, but I can learn. Doesn't mean we aren't right for each other. Doesn't mean Ace gets to claim her. That sentiment is ridiculous, and if Luce were here, she'd shove that right in his face.

"I know her. She knows me. We're meant to be together. So step back and let her find her way back to me."

"No."

Ace's fingers curl into fists, and he looks like he's ready to launch himself over the table. But something changes his mind. Maybe the fact that we're in the fucking Gas Station, a public place, penetrates his tiny brain. Whatever the reason, he sits back, rolls his shoulders and pretends to relax. "Fine."

"That it?" I ask flatly.

"Not really. Since you're determined to fuck up my life, the least you can do is drink a few shots with me."

Is this an olive branch? I grab at it. "Sounds good."

* * *

"No shmore."

"You can do one more," Ace cajoles.

Jen Frederick

"No. I can't." I can barely sit up. "Where's our recruit?"

"Sarah and Lara volunteered to take him home."

I blink at the two blondes. One's wearing a red dress and the other is in blue, and the garments are so short you'd think we were in the tropics and not knee deep in snow. They're from a sorority, but I can't remember the name of it. "That's solid of you two. Real solid." I shake my head and it keeps shaking, like a bobblehead. I place a hand on the top of my head to stop it.

"Let's take some pictures so the boy has some memories he can go home and brag about it to his friends."

That's fair. We both know he won't be back here. Lucious jumps up enthusiastically and grabs both blondes by the waist. Ace snaps a few pictures while I pull out my own phone and text Hammer and Masters.

Me: *Dudes. I'm waisted. waisted. fck. waisted. fck. u kno wht I mean. Got a recruit. Make sure he gets home. Gas station.*

I tuck the phone away.

"Come on and get your picture taken."

"Nah."

"Lucious wants it," Ace says.

Turing my head toward Lucious is about as easy as steering a crane but I manage it.

"Okay. Okay." Anything to get the girls to stop squealing. I heave my drunk ass up to their side and lean in.

"Closer," Ace gestures. "I can't fit you into the frame."

"Dude, I can barely stand up."

"Hold him up, Sarah," Ace orders.

Sarah slides her arm around my waist. I drape my hand behind her back and rest my hand on Lucious's shoulder. Nothing about this feels right but I can't pinpoint exactly what bothers me. The blonde rests her cheek against my shoulder.

"Matty," she breathes softly. "I heard you were dating someone. Is that true?"

I look down at her, thinking of how much I'd like Luce to be here, holding me up and looking at me with her big brown eyes. I can feel my own face soften. "Yeah, true. I really dig this chick. She's smart and interesting." And hot as hell. I can feel my jeans getting tight thinking about her.

"Ahh, that's sweet." The girl rises on her tiptoes and kisses me. Right on the lips. *Motherfucker!*

"Uh huh. No kisses from anyone else." I let her go and shake my finger at her. "Not cool, Sarah."

"Don't be such a stick in the mud, Matty. It was just a kiss." The girl flounces away.

"We better get the recruit home," I tell Ace.

"The girls will take him home," he protests.

"Nah, he's our responsibility. Come on." I peel Lucious away from the lips of Blue Dress.

There's a chorus of disappointed sounds, but somehow I manage to muscle Lucious outside and start pushing him toward the Playground.

"We don't want to disappoint Coach Lowe," I tell him.

"Yeah, I hear ya." The cold air must be blowing some sense into him.

Hammer and Masters meets us halfway home and Ace peels off to his own place.

"How's it going?" Masters asks, his wary gaze fixed on Ace's retreating figure.

"With Ace?" I slur. "About as good as you can expect."

And then I stumble home, type out a few incoherent messages to Luce, and pass out.

31

WHEN I GET UP I see Matt has sent me a text. It's garbled and the time stamp says two am.

Matty: *Im drnk mss u.*

Matty: *Plc Matty wtns u.*

Matty: *Lv u*

Plc? Police Matty? Please Matty? Lv u? I think that's Love you. I can't figure the other one out. Apparently drunk Matt doesn't know where the vowels are. I text him back.

Me: *It's tomorrow. Do you need a shot of my insulin?*

I'm surprised when a response comes right away.

Matty: *No, but I do miss you. I'm still in bed.*

Me: *On a scale of one to ten, how drunk are you right now?*

Matty: *Two. I'm still burping up the shots from last night.*

Me: *That's super gross. Thanks for sharing.*

Matty: *np*

Me: *Need me to come over and rub your back?*

I figure he'll be all over this since he was texting me last night, drunkenly asking me to join him at the Gas Station where he was entertaining a recruit with Ace.

Matty: *No. I stink and my head aches. I could get you drunk on my leftover fumes. U never told me Ace could drink entire gallons of booze wo damage.*

Me: *He's always had a hard head.*

Ace could drink an entire team under the table.

Matty: *I need to sleep now. I'll call you later.*

In fact, the next text I get is from Ace. *I want to apologize to you. In person. Can I come over?*

Does Ace deserve a chance to say I'm sorry? I suppose he does. But I feel like it's a last time sort of thing. He doesn't get to keep doing this over and over, no matter how long we've been friends.

Sure, I text back. *But your apology better be good.*

Ace: *Buzz me up.*

I make a face. His demand is presumptuous, but whatever. Might as well get this over with. He needs to acknowledge that Matty and I are dating and that we can all get along.

I swing the door open at his knock. He straightens from the doorframe, looking out at me through surprisingly clear eyes.

"I'm amazed you're still upright. Matty texted me this morning and said he was too drunk to move."

"Yeah, I want to talk to you about Ives, but before we go into that I want to apologize," he says as he brushes by me. He takes a seat on the kitchen and re-arranges the other chair so that it's uncomfortably close to him. Like right between his legs, close to him.

I take the chair and move it back about a foot and sit down. "You think?"

He has the grace to look a little ashamed. "I don't know what came over me. I care about you a lot, and I guess I just don't want to see you get hurt."

"I don't want to get hurt either. You know how careful I am in my life and I realize that dating Matty is a risk. But…I can't live my life as if I can't take a blow. You're the one who accused me of sitting in my safe little box, not taking chances."

He winces. "Please don't tell me that my comments pushed you into Ives's bed."

"No, but you're right. I do have a tendency to be too careful. To some extent, I have to because otherwise it could be dangerous to my health, but I'm almost twenty-two. I'm graduating in a year. There's going to be failure in my future and heartbreak, whether it's from a job lost or a person lost. Part of being an adult is learning how to deal with that." I reach over and take a sip of the tea I brewed for breakfast. "Matty makes me feel really wonderful."

Ace's expression grows sickly. I wave my hand downward. "Oh, stop with the disgusted expression. I'm not talking about physical stuff."

Although, privately, I grin to myself, because Matty has made me feel physically more wonderful than I thought was possible. "I'm talking about the fact that he makes me laugh, that he makes me feel good inside. He's interesting to talk to. He reads. Taking a risk on Matty makes me think I can take other risks."

Ace's eyes run over my face. "You're changing."

"Maybe I am."

"Not for the better," he says.

My hackles rise. "I thought you came over to apologize, not to say shitty things to me."

"The truth isn't a shitty thing to say to you, Luce."

The nickname Matty uses sounds weird and strange coming out of Ace's mouth, as if he's trying to claim a connection that doesn't belong to him.

"Yes, it kind of is."

He presses his lips together. "All these years you said you wouldn't go out with a jock. That the type didn't interest you."

"They didn't," I insist. "Matty's different. We talk about a lot of different stuff. Books he's read, movies, stuff that's going on in the world."

"We talk about stuff like that." Ace directs those words to the floor where he's currently staring a hole into the tile.

An uncomfortable feeling sets in.

Ace has feelings for you, I can hear Sutton's voice in the background.

Slowly, Ace raises his eyes off the floor, and there is so much anguish, all the moisture in my mouth dries up. My hand flies to my lips. "Oh, Ace," I say through my fingers. *Oh Ace, don't open your mouth. Please don't say what I think you're going to say, please*, I beg silently. Our relationship will change irrevocably.

But he doesn't heed the warning in my eyes.

"Lucy, I've always thought it was going to be you and me. Always," he says hoarsely, his eyes penny-bright.

His statement makes me angry. Angry because he's changing the dynamic of our relationship into a form I'm not prepared to deal with. I want to clap my hands over my ears and say I can't hear him, but I just told him I was growing up. So I have to act like the adult I claim to be.

"You've never acted like that. You've had so many girlfriends. And when you don't have girlfriends, you're constantly sleeping with someone else." Not to mention the times where there's considerable overlap. "You practically screwed girls right in front of me. Those aren't the actions of a guy who thinks I'm his one and only."

"I know." He thrusts a hand into his short hair. "I wanted to enjoy being young and playing the field while I could. Kind of get all that shit out of my system so when I settled down, I wouldn't have the urge. But I always knew you and I would end up together."

He says it again, as if by mere repetition it will become true. It's the most insane thing I've ever heard, and I tell him that. "That's crazypants. You can't do that and expect me to look at you in anything but a friendship light. In fact, you're lucky I've known you so long. I overlook a lot of really crappy things that you've done because we've been friends since third grade, but I...I could never love you." It hurts me to say those words to him, but he's forcing them out of me.

Ace rears back as if I've slapped him. He looks at me with wounded eyes that flood me with guilt. "But, Lucy, we *have* been friends forever. I know everything there is to know about you."

"I'm sorry, Ace, but you don't." This is so hard. I wish I wasn't an adult. I wish I could run from this room and stick my head under my pillow and pretend this was not happening. But I force myself to gut it out, knowing it'll be over. I'll mourn this relationship but, in the back of my mind, I must've known it was coming because I'm not surprised. Frustrated, resigned, angry. But not surprised. I've just never wanted to acknowledge it.

"If you truly knew everything there was to know about me, you wouldn't have treated me this way. If you truly loved me, you wouldn't treat me this way. Or if this is how you treat people you love, well," I swallow before delivering another painful truth, "that's not going to be good enough for any girl."

I rub my dry lips together. He sits there like a stone. I don't know what he's thinking. Re-evaluating his definition of love? Wishing he'd never shown up here? If I'm honest, Ace and I have been growing apart for a long time before Matty ever appeared in my life. I told myself that he was busy with football and my path took me in an opposite direction, but the reality is we had less and less in common as we grew older.

I don't know if telling Ace this would help him, but I give it a shot. "We aren't the same people we were in third grade. There's no way we could be. If destiny meant for us to be together, we would have been together a long time ago, but I've never felt that way about you, and if you search your heart, you would know that the same is true for you. You don't love me, Ace. I'm not the one for you. I'm your…safe option." That felt right when I said it. It's even there in his words. I'm his fallback option. Maybe he uses this so-called love for me to stay emotionally distant with the girls he's with. But he's never *loved* me. "I swear to you, you would not act like this with a girl you loved."

His eyes turn from pained to flinty, and I try to brace myself for whatever horrible thing that's going to come out of his mouth next. I'm learning Ace has a nasty mouth on him.

"And you think Matty loves you?" Ace laughs harshly. "That he would never cheat on you. That he would never look at another girl with…lust in his eyes."

And that uncomfortable feeling I had before? It seizes me by the throat. I watch in horror as Ace pulls out his phone. I don't want to see it. I want to close my eyes and pretend whatever he's going to show me doesn't exist. Whatever happened last night doesn't exist. If I don't see it, I can go on in my own little world believing Matty was worth the risk.

Ace lays his phone on the table and the picture is so clear and so big I can't *not* see it. I bite my lips together as Ace flicks his finger. It's a slideshow of my worst fears.

"All these years you've friend-zoned me." His voice is quiet. Ominous even.

"I never friend-zoned you. We were friends. Are friends," I correct when his eyes narrow at my Freudian slip of the past tense. "True ones," I mumble almost absently as I stare at the pictures.

Ace's voice falls to a whisper. "You fell for Matty Iverson. A blockhead. His best friend is a guy named Hammer. Their favorite thing to do is get loaded and bang jock chasers. Their hobbies include liking Instagram posts of chicks at out of town games. He's an *idiot*."

"He reads *Harry Potter*," I defend, almost by rote.

"So he read one fucking book a year until he graduated."

Matty has women on either side of him. In another photo one of them is kissing his cheek. Ace flicks his finger again. Matty's looking down adoringly into the blonde one's eyes. *Flick.* The blonde is kissing him on his lips. *Flick.* Matty's hand is outstretched trying to prevent the picture from being taken, but there's a lopsided smile on his face and he's *still* looking at the blonde.

Ace's finger stabs at the table. "No matter what he promises you, this is what he does. I don't know what happened last night. I don't know if she's still there this morning."

I swallow again, but there's nothing in my throat. It's dry, and every time I gulp it's like swallowing sand. The tiny bits and pieces scrape and tear fissures into my tissues that grow and grow and grow like the cracks in the desert's crust—until every part of me is torn asunder, only held together by a slender film of skin.

Ace is relentless. "How come you're not over there right now? I know when I'm drunk, I'm horny as fuck. Do you know if he's alone?"

I stand up, hand Ace the phone, and pray my tears don't fall. Not until Ace leaves. "I don't know," I say in a small voice. "But whatever happens between Matty and me isn't your business. You need to go now."

I stretch out my arm and point to the door. It doesn't shake and, for that, I'm thankful. I'll take whatever victories I can at this moment.

Ace rises, too, but he doesn't leave. "What are you talking about?" He protests. "I just showed you what a dog Matty is." As if the pictures would magically transform Matty into the frog and Ace into a prince? In addition to being mean, I hadn't realized how delusional he was becoming.

"Get out." My arm is getting so heavy.

"I'm saving you heartbreak here."

"Get out!" I scream. "*Get out. Get out. Get out. Get out!*"

I push at him until he starts moving, and I keep pushing and slapping and repeating my high-pitched demands until he's on the other side of the threshold.

"Don't call me. Don't text. We're done." I slam the door shut.

"You're shooting the messenger," he shouts through the closed door.

Ignoring him, I pick up my phone with shaking hands.

I'm coming over, I manage to type out, but I don't press send. No. That would give him time to put her in some suitcase.

32

LUCY

I GET DRESSED IN A hurry. Ace has thankfully taken off. I swear if I saw him, I would kick him in the balls. Twice.

And then in the face. Despite the distance between Matty's house and my apartment building, the time flies. Or rather, I do as I sprint toward the Playground. The snow crunches under my boots. I almost lose it around the quad because someone forgot to salt a small patch of ice. But I make it to his house in one piece.

Panting, I don't even pause to knock on the door. Oh no. I fling it open because these assholes never lock their doors.

Hammer's sitting on the sofa.

"Hey, Lucy." He gives me a wave.

"Better give your boy a ten-second warning, because I'm going in," I yell as I race upstairs.

The last thing I see before reaching Matty's door is Hammer's shocked and confused face. I wrench on the knob and throw the door aside. It bangs against the wall. The lump on the mattress barely moves.

I storm over to the bed and rip the covers back...to reveal a hungover Matty wearing clothes from the night before. I can tell it's the same clothes because it's so clearly obvious he slept in them.

The T-shirt is practically twisted around his neck. His jeans are pulled down far enough that I can see at least half of his underwear-covered ass. His left foot is bare but the right one still has a sock hanging off it. It looks like he managed to toe one of them off and got halfway done with the other before giving up.

I stumble backwards, nearly dizzy with relief.

He lifts his head and there are creases on his cheek from the sheets.

"Goldie." He smiles happily and pats the bed beside his body. "I was just dreaming about you."

I ignore his invitation and walk over to his desk, collapsing in the rolling chair situated in front of it. My heart is beating so rapidly I'm afraid it's going to jump out and flop onto the floor like a dying fish.

"It's too much for me. You're too much for me," I gasp out.

Matty struggles into a sitting position and gives me a lopsided smile. "Too much what? Greatness?"

For once his teasing doesn't come off as funny, but irritatingly arrogant.

"I can't do this anymore." I bend over and place my head on my knees, trying to catch my breath. I can't remember the last time I took a glucose measurement. I feel weak and sickly. Hot and sweaty. It's either I'm crashing or I'm experiencing physical side effects of my heartbreak. Maybe it's some dangerous combination of them both.

"Do what?" he asks in bewilderment.

"I can't take this risk with you anymore. My heart can't take it." I rub my palm across my chest as if I can eradicate the pain with enough friction.

I don't know whether the pain is forming because I'm breaking up with Matty or because I dated him in the first place. I always knew this day was going to come. *He's going to hurt you* was number one on the risk assessment. But stupidly, foolishly, I'd kept decreasing the weight I'd afforded that particular item on the list.

The truth is you can't really prepare yourself for what it feels like because you never know how much anything hurts until the wound is inflicted. Until the knife is in your belly.

If I stay with him, he'll only hurt me more. Just like my mom hurt my dad over and over.

I sit up and stare at him, into his precious blue eyes that I know I'm going to be seeing for years when I'm dreaming. When I'm just sitting and drinking coffee, I'll see them. In that cloudy space right before I fall and asleep and right before I wake up, I'll see him. It's going to take a long time to get over him. A long time.

What did I expect, though? This is how I knew it would all play out. Oh, I didn't have the exact scenario right, but it all ended the same. Safe may be boring, but it sure as hell isn't as painful.

"You and me, Matty. We're done."

"What…what happened? I told you," he stutters. His brain isn't firing on all cylinders, and it's taking him a moment, or five, to catch up. "I told you I wasn't going to talk to you about Ace anymore."

Still not with me. I lay it out as plain as can be. "Ace took some pictures of you kissing a girl last night."

His face moves from confusion to comprehension to anger. "Goldie, I was drunk off my ass last night."

The careless statement, the accusation that lurks behind his words that *I'm* the unreasonable one here, only fuels my rage. I feel myself shaking and this time I know it's not because my blood sugars are out of whack. It's because of *him*. Because I took a chance on *him* and he was supposed to understand this. He was supposed to act like he cared.

"I don't care that you were drunk! If I was drunk, I would not be out kissing someone and getting my picture taken. That has never happened to me in all my years here at Western, in all my years of drinking." I fling my arm out. "Even the night I drank so much my freshman year that Sutton had to call 911 because I went into a coma, that didn't happen. I danced. I drank. I passed out. I didn't press my lips against some random person!"

"I didn't ask for her to kiss me. I didn't want her to kiss me," he insists. He swings his long, powerful legs over the side of the mattress and for a moment I'm distracted. His shirt is still askew, framing his defined abs like a half-drawn curtain. My eyes are drawn to the light dusting of hair that arrows from his belly button into his groin.

My mouth becomes dry for another reason.

He's so damned sexy, and for a moment, my resolve wavers. I cover my eyes so I can't be tempted anymore. A spot of self-loathing gets mixed into the cocktail of churning emotions, and suddenly, I'm just so tired. I want to be done here. I push to my feet and force my explanation out.

"I know you didn't, but the point of the matter, Matt, is that your lifestyle is only going to get worse when you go to the NFL. There's only going to be more women, more road games, more time for me to worry. Every sports blog, every forum, every newspaper is full of stories of pro athletes screwing around on their wives and their girlfriends. I don't want that to be my life, and, really, you deserve someone who's stronger than me—who isn't as afraid of risks as I am," I finish drearily. I'm disgusted at myself. At Matty. At Ace. It's an ugly reality that I'm facing. I don't like myself much right now, but at some point, I've got to protect myself.

"So you're doing this for my own good is what you're saying?" Matty's own anger is beginning to fire.

I've burned through anger and now I'm swimming in regret.

"You can take it whatever way you want."

"How big of you," he growls. "This stuff you're spewing is some of the worst bullshit I've ever heard. If you don't want to be with me, then have the balls to say it outright. Don't be mealy-mouthed about it."

I can barely get the words out, but I say them. "I don't want to be with you."

Matty stands up then—a giant in his room towering over me. Angry is too soft of a word for what's on his face. I've never seen him like this.

His words come out sharp, like a knife, and ice cold. "Get the hell out of my room."

Unlike Ace, I don't have to be told twice. I race out of there so fast that I'm sprinting by the time I hit the main floor. Hammer's standing at the base of the stairs, but I can't muster up even a polite goodbye.

33

IT FEELS LIKE MY INSIDES have been scooped out by a melon baller and filled with acid. I go home and cry my head off.

"This calls for real ice cream," Sutton says darkly.

Charity holds my head against her chest as I give myself two shots of insulin. That's bad, I know, but I'm a mess.

Neither of them judge me. Neither of them tell me I'm a fool for breaking up with Matty, no matter that I cry so hard I become dehydrated. Sutton even runs to the store and buys some water they give babies because it has extra electrolytes.

Two weeks pass, but my phone remains silent. I have no idea if Ace is still calling or texting because I've blocked his number. I don't block Matty's because I still want him to call me and convince me I was wrong in my risk assessment, but he never does.

It's hard to believe that in two short months, Matty made such an impact on my life. He was like a meteor, a hot flash of delight followed by a huge crater of destruction.

I throw myself into mock trial, but it doesn't consume me the way it has in the past. Every time I enter the practice room, I can still feel

Matty in the back, his eyes glowing with pride.

Heather's reverted to sucking, but I can't summon the energy to correct her even though we have only two practices before regionals.

When she stands for the third time and approaches Emily on the witness stand without permission, I fear Randall's head will come off.

I try to prevent the impending explosion.

"This is like a game of Randall Says but instead of 'Captain, may I,' you say, 'May it please the court.'" I stand up and demonstrate. "May it please the court."

Randall nods smugly from his position on the makeshift bench.

Heather rolls her eyes. "May it please the court," she repeats.

"You may proceed, Ms. Bell," Randall intones. He's enjoying this far too much. I flick a glance to Heather, who's rolling her eyes. That's better than her itching to hit Randall, so I lean back.

"May it please the court, may I approach the witness?" Heather says.

I wince at the awkward phrasing.

"No," Randall interrupts loudly. "Say 'May I approach the witness, your honor.'"

Heather slams her hand on the side of the table. "You just told me to say 'May it please the court' every time," she hisses through clenched teeth.

"No, we told you to ask for permission," Randall glares back. "It's redundant when you say 'May it please the court, may I approach.'"

"This is fucking stupid as hell!" Heather yells and storms out.

I drop my head to the desk and wonder if I can go to sleep now and wake up sometime after I've graduated.

"Can we take a break?" Emily asks.

"Yes. Take a break," I mumble against the table.

"We shouldn't even go to Regionals," Randall remarks as he slides into the seat next to me. It's a week away. I don't bother to lift my head, which Randall takes as permission to keep complaining. "I don't know why you asked her to join us," he snipes.

I finally do raise my head to glare at him. "You were there. Don't try to pretend you weren't. She had the best closing of everyone who tried out. She was fucking *moving*. I think you were near tears."

He averts his face. "I was not."

"Liar."

He sighs and swivels back to face me. "You could have done it. You could do the closing just as well as anyone."

"Not really." This time it's my turn to look away. I stack my already neat pile of papers and tap them so their edges are all perfect.

"You know what your problem is?"

"Gosh, Randall, that question is such a fun one to hear and to answer. I've got so many faults, though, we'd be here all night listing them all." I curl up the edges of the papers and fantasize about smacking Randall in the face with them.

"Your problem is you don't take enough chances."

My stomach clenches at his accusation. "I took a chance on Heather."

He scoffs. "That's not taking a chance. That's you hiding again."

The team files in before I can respond, but his criticism burns as hot as if he held a flame under my chair. As I watch everyone take their places—Emily on the witness stand, Randall back behind the two desks we set up to be the judge's bench, Heather at the table opposite me—I wonder if Randall's right.

Is that what I'm doing? Hiding behind Heather? Behind Ace? Do I use all these excuses so I don't get hurt? So I won't fail? Do I take the easiest path? And pretend that makes me happy?

"Ahem," Heather clears her throat next to me. "Are we going to do this thing?" She gestures toward Emily.

"Yes." I try to shake off Randall's hurtful words. "Yes, we're doing this thing."

The rest of the team springs to action, and we make it all the way through the trial without stopping. None of us corrects Heather's errors, or our own for that matter. We let it all slide. I'm too tired, still stinging from Randall's rebuke, and too heartsore to really care.

"We'll take a ten-minute break and do closings," I say after finishing with the last examination. Beside me, Heather looks fresh and invigorated as if the last two hours weren't completely draining. "Heather, I have some notes I typed up—"

"No, thanks," she interrupts me. "I've got this. In fact, we can start now if you want."

Randall wiggles his eyebrows at me, but I'm still angry at him to join in any of his games.

"Sure." I slump against my chair. Anything for this practice to be over.

She stands and strides confidently toward the open space in front of the fake jury box. She extends one hand toward Randall. "May it please the court? Opposing counsel?" The other hand floats toward me. "Women and men of the jury. On behalf of my client and co-counsel, we thank you for your time. The right to trial by jury is as fundamental to this country as owning a gun or the right to vote or the right to practice one's religion. It's in both the 6th and 7th Amendments to the Constitution. By sitting here today, you are upholding the very document that created this country."

Her reference to the Constitution is smart. I jot a note to make sure she includes it every time. Heather proceeds to tell the room full of weary students exactly why her client was victimized by a callous corporation seeking profits over safety.

Her rich voice, unhurried, weaves a tale of a hard worker, taken advantage of by a shoddily designed product that was inevitably going to hurt someone. In this case, that someone was our client.

By the end, we're sitting there with our mouths hanging open, and I, pretending to be the counsel for the manufacturer, want to throw myself at her feet and beg for forgiveness.

After her last thank you, the entire room is silent until Randall releases an awe-filled, "Damn."

And he keeps repeating it as our teammates jump out of their seats and rush Heather. They clap and smile and hug her. Every mistake she's made, every insulting word she's said, it's all forgotten.

And seeing my whole team embrace her makes me feel even shittier than when I thought we were going to send another losing team to Regionals.

Maybe I've been too hard on Ace.

"What?" Heather demands. "Why are you looking at me like that? Did I fuck up again?"

"No. Everything was perfect." And it was. Everyone performed flawlessly. Heather remembered to ask the court for permission. I didn't screw up any questions on direct. All the witnesses looked either smart or vulnerable or, in the case of Emily, both.

"She's just in shock," Randall jokes. "Want to run through it again?"

"No." There are thirty minutes left in our practice time, but I want to leave on a high note. "We're ending early."

The team whoops with joy. Even Randall, who ordinarily wants to stay longer, is excited. He leans down to give me a quick hug goodbye and gives Heather a kiss on the cheek. She shoos him away and soon it's just her and me.

"Need something?" I ask as I gather the materials together. Evidently she wants to talk and if there was ever a time that I didn't want to deal with Heather's shit, it would be now.

I'm emotionally tapped out. I kind of just want to go back to my apartment, cover my head with a pillow and cry for a few hours—as I've done nearly every night since I broke up with Matt.

"Yes. I want to know what I did wrong tonight. You haven't said more than two words to me. I want to know if I'm fucking up." She juts out her chin pugnaciously, as if physically preparing herself for me to bust a fist across her chin.

"You aren't fucking up."

"I know I didn't set that cross-examination up right. That I didn't get her to admit she was under oath before asking her to read from the deposition."

"Yeah, it's okay, though. That's a small error. Do you want to run through it right now?" I pull out the deposition.

Heather pulls it out of my hand and sets it behind her. "No, I want to know why you didn't call me on that bullshit during the practice. You would have any other night."

"You were in the groove, and it didn't make sense to interrupt you." I decide Heather can keep that copy. I can print out a new one. I shove everything else in my backpack, but before I can close it, Heather's hand reaches out and rips the bag out of my hand.

"Something's wrong." If it were anyone else, I'd say there was concern in her voice. But this is *Heather*. Despite some evidence to the contrary, Heather is focused on herself alone. In some ways, I really admire that. She's a sophomore, a year younger than me, but has the drive, determination and direction that people ten years older lack.

I reach for the bag, but she shoves the bag under the desk and plants her ass on the seat. I'll have to crawl underneath her to get it, which sounds as appealing as running nude in front of the Playground.

I lose my temper. "For the past ten weeks, you've treated me like a nuisance at best and a demon who hates you at worst. Every time I've given a suggestion on how to improve, you've snapped my head off. Now you want me to confide in you?"

Heather waves her hand dismissively, as if the past few weeks of contentiousness haven't happened. "I don't want to be your friend, but I want to win this competition, and I know that if you're not on top of your game, we aren't going to win, so if talking it out is going to help you get your head out of your ass, then I'm all ears."

"Gosh, Heather, with that kind of invitation, I don't know why I'm not barfing out all my emotional drama to you," I say sarcastically.

"Aha! So something *is* wrong," she says as if she's won something. But hasn't she? I denied something was wrong. She kept pressing until

I lost my cool.

I can't keep in my surprised laughter. "Aha? Yes, Ms. Perry Mason, that was a pretty perfect cross-examination."

Heather flushes. "I *am* getting the hang of things, aren't I?"

"Yes. Yes, you are," I agree. "Which is why I didn't correct you even though you didn't ask Emily if she was under oath at the time of her deposition just as she was under oath now."

"Ahh, that's the phrase." Heather snaps her fingers. "I ask to approach the witness, wait for permission, and then ask the witness when she testified previously if she was under oath."

"Right. That way you get her to subtly acknowledge she was either lying then or lying now."

"And how many points do I get for impeaching the witness?" she asks.

"At least one full point, and they'll lose points, so it's a win/win for us."

"Does that happen often?"

"Rarely."

"Bummer." She pushes her bottom lip out.

"On the plus side, you know how to do it now." I hold out my hand. "Can I have my bag back?"

"No. Not until you've told me what is wrong."

"I can fight you for it."

"But you won't because you believe in being patient and kind." She taps the backpack with the heel of her foot.

"I don't like you very much right now." I stare at her in frustration. Heather's completely unaffected by my growing irritation.

"As if that's different from any other time."

Oh hell, why not. I throw my coat down and take a seat across from her. "You remember Matty, right?" He'd come to a few practices.

"Did I suffer amnesia? Of course, I remember fuckboy."

I stand up. "We're done now."

"No, come on, sit down," Heather pleads. "I know I suck at this. Give me another shot." I don't move. "Please," she says.

"What's wrong with you?"

Heather shrugs. "I don't know. I have no filter. My dad is a no-bullshit kind of guy, and he doesn't tolerate any filter at home, so I'm a bitch." She laughs, but it's a bitter one. "But the ironic thing is that he dates these...babies who talk like babies and act like babies and every-thing that comes out of their mouths is fake and childish, but it's me that he hates. I'm doing this whole thing to show him that I'm exactly what he made me."

Jesus, that sounded awful. I sit down.

"So it's guy trouble," she muses.

I nod slowly. "Yes. It's guy trouble." She makes a winding motion with her hand. I heave a sigh. "I have a guy friend, and he was angry I'd been seeing Matty."

She interrupts. "Can we have names or identifying marks?"

"Identifying marks?" I query.

"Yeah, like this one guy I slept with had a mole on his neck so I'd call him Spot and this other guy I slept with had a square head so I'd call him Frank."

"Short for Frankenstein?" I guess.

"Exactly. So you have Matt and who?"

"JR. Or Ace. Everyone calls him Ace. Ace and I have been friends for a long time. He just busts out with the friend-zone accusation when he finds out I've been sleeping with Matty. But Matty apparently can't keep his hands to himself. Ace took pictures of Matty being drunk and handsy with another girl."

The latter accusation is a bit unfair to Matty, but there's a ring of truth to it. I don't trust him. I never really did, looking back. When he said he was falling for me, I was too afraid to give him the same reply in return, even though I knew I was under his spell from the minute he tossed me the aspirin packet.

Still, I know he didn't exactly cheat on me, and even though he's not here, I'm impelled to clarify things. "Okay, that's not fair. He didn't cheat on me. He was drunk and another girl kissed him. Pictures were taken and I felt like a fool when I saw them."

She tips her head to one side and then the other, as if assessing the quality of my reasoning. "Are you saying he didn't respect you?"

I think about it. "No. It's really his life. He's super attractive. He's literally one of those guys that every man wants to be and every woman wants to be with. When he goes out to a bar, women are all over him. And even if he tells them he's taken, they still push themselves on him, hoping to convince him otherwise."

"How is that his problem? I mean, other than he can do a better job of projecting his 'taken' status."

I shake my head. "It's not his problem," I admit. "It's mine. I told him it was my problem."

"So you didn't break up with him because of anything he did. You broke up with him because you're weaksauce." Heather chops me down to my knees with a few matter-of-fact words.

But she's not wrong. "Yes."

She shrugs fatalistically. "So you're weak. At least you admit it."

It's the ugliest description I've ever had applied to me, but I can't dismiss it. It's the truth. I didn't believe in myself more than I didn't believe in Matty.

"Your lack of confidence is why you can't do a closing. You know that, right?" she prods.

"Yes, I know that." I can't do a closing because my throat shuts down. "It's a version of stage fright."

"Which you could overcome if you actually believed a little bit in yourself. Take it from me. If you don't believe in yourself, no one will. Think I'm standing here because my dad's a big supporter? Hell no. He wanted me to marry one of his junior partners." My mouth drops open in shock. "Yeah, your hero, Paul Bell, is a real asshole misogynist. So if I did what my dad always wanted, I'd be married, with two kids, no education, wondering which strand of pearls I should choke myself with before my husband comes home smelling like his secretary. I believe I'm better than that. Better than most people, frankly."

She reaches under the chair and pulls out my backpack. "You'd be a lot better in everything if you said, 'Fuck what anyone else thinks of me,' and just do whatever the hell you want."

"I don't operate that way." The words sound like sanctimonious bullshit the minute they leave my mouth. "Fuck, okay." I scrub two hands down my face, but the scorn on Heather's expression doesn't change. "I know I lack confidence and that's why I don't do closings. I stick to the stuff I am good at. That's not being a coward."

"So knowing you're chickenshit is a good excuse? I'd rather suck at something and keep trying than just quit."

I lose it. I jump to my feet and point an accusing finger at her. "I am not a quitter. I stuck with this team even after I crashed and burned. I have never quit on anyone."

"Oh really? I bet Matty would disagree." She throws the backpack into my chest.

34

MATTY

I'M NOT REAL PROUD OF how I handled myself with Luce, but what's a guy supposed to do after he lays bare his heart and the girl stomps all over it with her sharp, pointy heels? She told me she didn't want me, and I was tired of trying to convince her otherwise.

I'm not a masochist. I don't do pain without reward—Christ, I'm starting to think like her.

In the past, whenever I've had stress in my life, I've coped with booze, weed, and chicks. During the season, it's almost solely chicks because of the random drug testing, and because unlike Hammer and Ace, I can't drink like a fool and still get up the next day and do fifty burpees without puking halfway through the set.

Learned that lesson freshman year.

So that's what I do again. It seems like the perfect antidote after being told I'm not worth some neurotic girl's time.

Hammer and I cruise the local town bars, staying away from the Gas Station, on the shaky premise that I'm tired of Western coeds. Hammer wisely says nothing as I pick out and discard woman after woman after woman.

I've ridden this amusement park attraction for three years and the thrill is entirely gone. It's not just that my dick is dead in my pants but that I can't even summon a smile for these pretty women.

"If you keep growling at these ladies, I can't go out with you anymore," Hammer declares. "You're a shit wingman and your conversational skills are lacking. I'd have a better time with a potato."

"Yeah, yeah," I mutter and throw back another shot.

Hammer eyes me with caution. "You may want to slow down there, brother. That's the fourth shot you've had in less than two minutes."

I roll the empty shot glass in my hand, wondering how my perfect life went to shit in under two months. "Worried I'm going to ralph all over your new shoes? Promise I'll save it for the entire O-line tomorrow."

"No, I'm worried for your liver. You've drank enough this past week to move past pickled and into mummification." He gestures for the bartender, who hops right to. He's a fan. So many fans in here. The one person I want to be a fan? Isn't, of course. Because that's how life apparently works for me now.

The team that I love is in shambles. We can't work out at the same time now because half of us hates the other half.

The girl I thought I loved threw my declaration—something I've never said to any female other than my mom before—back in my face.

My streak of Academic All-American semesters might be in jeopardy because I can't concentrate for shit. And because I'm too hungover to haul myself to class. In January, the profs were lenient. We had just won the National title. In March? Apparently they care if you show up thirty minutes late to a fifty-minute lecture.

These past couple months have shown me one thing. Success is fleeting. Enjoy it while you can.

A glass of water appears like magic in front of me. I look up with a scowl. "This is not booze."

Hammer claps me on the back hard enough that my chest bumps into the edge of the mahogany bar. "Fucker, that hurt." I massage my chest, wishing the pain inside could be so easily rubbed away.

"Good. I was worried you were too numb for this." He reaches out and slaps his open hand across my face. It's not a hard blow. My head barely moves when he makes impact, but the shock of it? The sound of flesh striking flesh? I jump up, forgetting momentarily where I am and who just hit me. My fists come up because my fight or flight instinct? Definitely, one hundred percent fight.

I swing, and then sense or God or something sets in and I check myself inches away from Hammer's unapologetic face.

I drop my arm to my side. "What the motherfucking hell?"

"You need to wake up," he says simply.

"I have no fucking clue what you're talking about." I slide back onto the bar stool and clench the glass of water between my hands so I have something to do other than punch Hammer's lights out. One of my best friends. I hang my head. What is wrong with me?

"Haven't you had enough?" Hammer reaches past me and taps the rims of all my empty shot glasses. All eleven of them. I swallowed two within seconds of ordering them—the third by the time Hammer ordered his drink and then four more in quick succession. I wasn't paying for them. They kept appearing in front of me like a cartoon version of shots where there's no bottom to the booze and the glasses multiply magically. So I drank them.

"Don't know. Why don't you hand me the one at the end that's full and we'll see if I'm still upright?" I gesture toward the end of the row.

"Is drinking really making you feel better? Because we've drunk every night this week and I'm beginning to feel overstuffed. Kinda like how your pants are too tight right around the time that the second NFL game starts on turkey day."

"Because I have a dick, I'm not allowed to be sad about something?" I snap. Someone starts playing Buckley's "Hallelujah," the saddest dirge about how cold and broken love can leave you. Nice. I grab the last shot glass and down the contents. My throat's so numb I can't even feel the burn as the liquor slides down my throat. I'm going to have to switch to whiskey.

"You ain't sad. You're feeling sorry for yourself. You're moping around like someone took your football away. On the field, you're awesome, Matty, but off of it? You're letting everything fall apart. I don't know exactly what went down between you two but I can guess. And she might be a stone-cold bitch and you're better off shot of her. But at some point, you gotta stand up and work for something off the field."

He rubs a hand down his face. "I don't know why I'm trying to have a conversation with you."

It's the disappointment in his voice that finally penetrates my thick, dumb skull. "Football gives back what you put into it. The rest of it, like Buckley's saying." I wave my hand in the general direction of what I think might be the jukebox although it might also just be a bunch of boxes of empty beer bottles awash in neon. "Love just ruins you."

"Bullshit."

"What?"

This is Hammer. Who loves football. Whose entire wardrobe consists of Warrior T-shirts, shorts, and workout gear. He bleeds blue and gold. I knock my hand against my ear. Did he just call bullshit on the only true and reliable facts of our lives—football is *it*.

"We both know I'm not going pro. Most of the guys that play at Western won't ever even get to sniff the turf at a pro stadium unless they're paying to be there. That's why I took this job writing articles for a woman's magazine. You think it's funny as hell, but this is going to get me a good paying job when I graduate."

Hammer grabs my shoulder and forces me to look at him. "This thing with Ace? It's not even about winning anymore. It's whether we're going to enjoy playing together. Matty, fuck, this is our last year. I don't want to go out wondering *what if*, and regretting the time I spent. Even if we don't win another title, I still want to know that I gave it all I had because I was playing with the best motherfuckers in the world. I don't like saying this, but you kinda need a wakeup call. Is it possible she had a good reason for kicking your ass to the curb?

You aren't a good risk.

She'd known it all along, and I'd laughed it off. Because on the field, I'm reliable as they come. Off of it, I duck anything close to responsibility. It's not that I mind a challenge. Challenges are fun. But conquering a challenge isn't the same as shoving on a pair of shitkickers and getting down in the trenches into messy, dirty, uncomfortable things.

The night we took Lucious out, I got drunk rather than stick to my own rules of no booze, no chicks.

I wasn't thinking of Luce that night. I was thinking of myself.

I was a good lover because it reflected well on me.

I pursued Luce because it was fun—for me.

It's always been about me. Even when she broke up with me, I didn't see things from her point of view.

We were even in this random joint twenty miles from campus because *I* didn't want to be around Luce.

I feel sick, and it's not because of the liquor. The acid of self-disgust is mixing with all that booze, and I can feel it climbing upward.

"I need the john. Where is it?"

Hammer sizes up the situation immediately and starts pulling me through the crowd. People scatter in the wake of his two-hundred-and-eighty-pound form until my drunk ass is in the bathroom. I barf up the shots I'd been pounding since I arrived like I was participating in some cheap Spring Break contest. Guy who drinks the most shots in two minutes gets a free chaser of beer and a card with the local ambulance number on it.

I wipe my face with toilet paper. Flush three times and then dunk my head in the sink. After I wash away any residue and hopefully some of my dumbassery, I grab a handful of paper towels and run them through my hair.

"What do you want to do?"

"Me?" Hammer points to himself.

"Yeah, we've been doing my crap all week. What do *you* want?"

He ponders this. "There's a redhead out there who's been eyefucking me. I wouldn't mind doing her."

Okay. "Here or back home?"

"Here. Definitely here."

Which is how I find myself sitting on the dingy barroom floor, directing people away from the men's room for thirty minutes while Hammer and the redhead enjoy an energetic and sometimes noisy interlude.

* * *

The next morning, we're greeted with some unwelcome news. Because of our inability to get along, according to Coach Lowe, we're shipping off for a "retreat." We're sent home to pack our bags, which means I can't go over to Luce's place like I need to. Like I want to.

I debate texting her, but that's a low-class move and one that doesn't have much chance of success anyway. Over the phone, via text, it's easy for her to ignore me.

If I'm going to apologize, I need to do it in person.

Tensions in the locker room are high as we gather our shit. Players are chirping at each other and not in a fun, friendly, busting your balls way. Fozzy tells Darryl that he's slower than molasses off the block and snidely wonders whether Carter Hunt, the incoming freshman center, is going to replace him. The two get into a shoving match right in front of Ace, who leans back and watches the interaction as if it's a goddamned sitcom.

The team is falling apart.

Yeah, it is. And Ace isn't going to save it. Masters isn't here anymore. So it's me or nobody. Hammer gives me a *whatchu doing about this mess* look. I make a face because once I stand up, that pretty much means I can't pummel Ace into the small ball of dust he should be reduced to.

Responsibility kind of sucks donkey balls, which is why I probably avoided it for so long.

Shooting one last annoyed glare in Hammer's direction—who gives me an irritating two thumbs up—I rise to my feet and stride over to where Fuzzy and Darryl have their arms interlocked like two combatants in a WWE match. We just need Bish to come flying in with a chair.

"You two think this is a dance class?" I bark out. Darryl's head jerks around because he's not used to this from me. Fozzy tries to take advantage of Darryl's inattention but I'm able to shove them apart.

"I'm sick and tired of you all fighting about this. We are a goddamned team. Let's act like it." I turn to Ace. "Bro, I'm sorry. What's going on with you sucks balls. But you're wrong. I have never once said to Coach that I think you should be anything but our QB. But it doesn't matter. It doesn't matter what I say. What I do." I wonder how many people know I'm talking about more than football.

"Coach has moved on. We can either fight with each other or fight for each other. The first option means we lay eggs on the field. We lose and we lose and we lose. I'm not going to like that much, and I don't think any of you will either.

"The second means putting aside our feelings about what's going on with Ace and moving forward. We don't have any idea what Remington Barr's going to be like. Maybe he sucks. We all know of high school stars who wash out in college because everyone they meet on the field was a high school star. Maybe he's awesome. I don't know.

"For about twenty of us, next season is our last. We can look back at it as a lost season, embarrassed by how we went out, or we can look back on it with…" I search for the right word.

"Joy," Hammer offers.

"Yeah, joy. Thanks, man." We bump fists.

He winks and gives me a thumbs-up.

I walk over to Ace. None of these guys know how he wronged me, but there's a strange kinship between us, created by the fact that Luce broke both our hearts.

"I forgive you, brother." Ace's eyes grow wide with shock as he stares at my outstretched hand. I extend it even further. "For the sake of this team, I forgive you."

Ace's hand rises slowly, as if he doesn't really want to shake my hand but something deep and decent within him—whatever it was that called Luce "friend" for all those years—pulls it up, inch by mother-fucking inch, until his palm is against mine. Our handshake is brief. We will never be friends, but the sad truth is that Luce was right.

No one forced all those shots down my throat. I didn't have to get so messy drunk. I didn't have to stand so close I could feel the line of the girl's underwear press against my jeans-clad leg.

If I'd seen Luce kissing some guy, her eyes glassy with booze, and his arms around her body, I'd have been enraged. And maybe if I'd had the same past as hers, the same fears, I would've been done, too.

So I forgive Ace for burning the cord tying Luce and me together because I lit the match.

I leave Ace then and turn to Fozzy and present my hand to him. He knocks it away and lifts me in his arms.

"I love you, brother," he shouts. My ears ring for hours. There's a round of handshakes and bone-breaking backslaps and even a few more hugs before we get back to the basics of football—strength and conditioning.

On the ride up to the hotel in some Podunk town in Illinois, about an hour west of Chicago, Hammer peppers me with questions about Luce. He says it's because he's concerned. Privately, I think he's doing research on another article.

"How're you going to approach this? Like, are you going to say sorry first or are you going to make her say it?"

"What do you think I should do?" I parry because I have no fucking clue what to do. I've never been in this situation before—chasing after a girl who's rejected me more times than she's said yes.

"What does she want?"

"Fuck if I know."

"Then you're not winning her back."

Thanks for nothing Hammer. "I told her that I loved her."

"There's your problem."

"What's my problem?"

"Your belt's gotta match the shoes," Hammer says.

"What the fuck does that mean?" I grind to a halt and put my hands on my hips.

"Means your actions gotta line up with your words. You gotta do the love stuff if you mean it."

"Did you read that in your women's magazine?" I ask suspiciously.

"No," he perks up, "Do you think that's an article I should suggest? Top ten ways to show her you love her?"

My lips quirk up in a half smile. "Yeah, that's probably a pretty good article."

"Shit, I should have written it for Valentine's Day instead of the

'Best Ways to Give a V-Day Blowjob.'" Hammer slaps me hard on the back. "Don't worry. I know you're going to win her back."

And Hammer's belief in me actually fills me with relief. I am going to make this right with her. I did it with the team, and I can do it with her as well.

Failure is no option here.

35

LUCY

"I HAVE A COLD COMING on," Heather says ominously as she pulls into the hotel parking lot after dinner. Even though she hates her old man, she doesn't mind the things he buys her. The Mercedes coupe is so luxurious, I nearly cried when I took a seat the first time.

"Tell the cold to stay away. Believe it away, Heather."

"You mock, but deep down you know I'm right. We rocked today."

We did rock. We've rocked all weekend and now we have only one match left before we can crown ourselves Midwest Regional champs and claim our spot in the national tournament next month.

"We were pretty awesome," I admit. I roll my neck from one shoulder to the other. Despite our wins, I'm still tense. You would have thought I'd be euphoric by now, but I'm not.

Heather puts the car in park and then pulls down the mirror to inspect her face. "Do I look pale to you?" She turns to me.

"No, but if you don't feel well, you should lie down."

"I feel sick."

"It's called nerves," I explain wryly. It's somewhat heartening that Heather has some. For a time there, I felt like she was impervious, a hardened shell built up as a defense against her dad's careless neglect. "Tomorrow's the Championship round, and you're feeling what commoners call anxiety."

"Could be." She looks doubtful. "I think we should do something to really psych ourselves up for the big match."

"You just said you felt a cold coming on? Shouldn't a good night's rest suffice?" I sounded like a fifty-year-old mother already. I should've bought a pair of orthotic insoles at the drugstore along with some menopause medication.

"No, because we're in Chicago, duh. Or—" She snaps her fingers and smiles brilliantly—evilly almost. I narrow my eyes in suspicion. "We could go on a road trip."

I know immediately what she's talking about. "No."

"I heard a certain football team is having a retreat an hour away."

"No." Except this time my *no* isn't as firm because I miss Matty so much. I want to see him, but I figured I'd get the tourney out of the way and then throw myself at his feet and beg for him to take me back.

I'm not sure of my reception, and I didn't want to suffer a crushing "no" blow right before competition started. If I'm lacking confidence, that wouldn't be the way to go about gaining more.

But, as Heather knows because Hammer waited for me outside of our last practice—does everyone know my effing schedule?—Hammer thinks Matt would forgive me in a heartbeat. Since then Hammer's been texting me.

Hammer: *Matty's a good guy.*

Hammer: *I was there. He didn't touch those girls.*

And

Hammer: *Luuuucy. Not saying he misses you, but if you don't come soon, he's gonna turn into a pickle.*

Pickle? I assume that's due to heavy drinking. But regardless of his preserved status, Matt has not texted me once. Or called. Or showed up anywhere he's showed up before. Even Keith noticed it at the Brew House, asking where the jock crew was. I pretended I was too busy making foam angels to respond.

"Come on, Luce," she cajoles. "You know you want to. Plus, you getting back together with Matty would make you soar tomorrow."

"Soaring isn't a thing. Soaring is what happens to your brain on some quality molly, not from confronting your ex."

"Hammer's his best friend. He wouldn't be texting you if he didn't think you had a chance."

"Maybe Hammer's playing the long game and this is Matt's revenge. They get me to show up and then I'm confronted by a full-on orgy in the living room. Hammer jumps up, 'Surprise, bitch! No one here really misses you, but if you want a piece of Matty, you can stand in line behind ho number two.'"

Heather smothers a laugh. "Do you always skip to the worst-case scenarios?"

Probably. That's what you do when your entire life is one risk assessment after another. "Even if I did want to go, I'm sure it's a closed, players-only thing. They only do these retreats when there's real problems and they want to get everyone on the same track."

"I wonder if you have anyone in your contact list who might be able to help you. Let's think, hmmm." She taps the corner of her mouth in mock thoughtfulness.

"I'm not calling Ace."

"Hmmm."

"Or Matty."

"Mmmmhmmm."

"This is totally irresponsible," I say as I pull out my phone.

"Mmmm."

Me: *Hammer, it's Lucy Washington. I'm an hour away. Would Matty see me?*

Hammer replies before Heather can hum again. *Thank Fucking God. I was Googling 'how to hold an intervention,' and that shit don't sound fun at all. Zero fun, Lucy.*

Me: *What about your coaches?*

Hammer: *Get your ass here. I'll worry about the coaches.*

I stare at the phone for a minute while Heather drums out the beat to The Replacements' "Can't Hardly Wait."

"So we going or we spending tonight wishing we were somewhere else?" she asks impatiently.

I put the phone face down. "We're going."

She starts the engine and backs out of the parking lot.

"Don't you wish it was summer and we had a convertible?" Heather says as she speeds toward Matty.

"And we'd wear scarves and Brad Pitt would be shirtless in the back and then we'd drive over the cliff and die?" I add sarcastically.

"I was with you until the cliff thing."

* * *

"Lucy?" Matty's expression is one of surprise and not the joyful *you've made my ever-loving week* surprise, but more of the *what the fuck are you doing here* version.

"I'm..." *Here to apologize, to admit that I totally overreacted and that I'm trying to start taking all those risks that I keep saying I'm going to take but never do,* but I already feel so vulnerable and stupid hiding in his closet, I can't bring myself to blurt any of that emotional stuff out. I settle for, "I'm here to see you."

"It's a closed practice," he says. Practice isn't the only thing that's closed. His face is a solid wall of nothing. I can't read if he's pleased to see me, pissed off, or annoyed, but I'm tired of ducking under the hangers in the closet.

I gesture behind him. "Do you mind letting me out?"

He steps aside but doesn't change his expression. I stumble out of the closet with as much dignity as possible. The small hotel room doesn't offer me many options but I'm too uncertain of my welcome to sit on his bed and afraid of what he'll think if I sit on Ace's bed. I can't believe the two are being forced to room together.

I opt for the small, uncomfortable desk chair. "Mind if I sit?"

He exhales slowly, and my heart flips over unhappily as he ponders my request. He's not sure if he wants me to be here long enough for me to sit down. I plant my ass anyway.

"In my head, this went a lot smoother," I offer.

"How so?"

"Um, I guess I throw up my arms and say 'surprise,' and you say, 'Goldie, you're a sight for sore eyes,' and then I respond with, 'you, too.' After we get those awkward, trite greetings out of the way, you haul me into your arms and give me a movie star kiss. We pretend it's raining and that we're at the end of a Nicholas Sparks movie and you swear your undying devotion."

"According to my mom, everyone dies at the end of a Sparks movie, so my devotion appears to be short-lived."

"True, but the promised love is undying, so even after your ticker gives out, the devotion lives on."

I swear I see his lips twitch, but he sobers up quickly to reply, "I think you've got plenty of undying devotion in your general vicinity."

"Is this about Ace?" I ask.

He doesn't directly answer the question. "Where is my wonderful roommate and does he know you're here?"

Ace's face was frozen when Jack and Hammer laid out the deal to him. He slapped the key into Jack's hand and stalked off. Uncomfortable is an understatement, but if I want Matty—and I do—then facing down Ace's icy stares is just going to be something I'm going to have to deal with. "He's with Jack and yes, how do you think I got in here?"

Matty raises his eyebrows and all the other times he's come back to a hotel room with a naked girl rushes through my head. "Don't answer that." I rush forward and place my fingers against his lips.

I've heard these stories from Ace, and they don't paint a pretty picture of my gender. Or him, frankly.

For a second I can feel his lips press against my fingers, but he backs away.

"I think before we go any further, we need to talk."

You know it's bad when the guy says those words.

"Can I go first?"

"All right." He tilts his head and waits.

This shouldn't be so hard. Wasn't the hard thing coming here? I take a deep breath and let it out slow. Matty's gaze is steady, not welcoming but not frosty either. "I never told you why I'm so risk averse."

He arches a brow. "Thought it was your diabetes."

"It is and it isn't. I don't think I ever told you, but I live here in town. Not in this town but where Western is."

"I know."

God, he's not making this easy on me. "Oh?"

"Yeah." He finally decides he's done standing and leans a shoulder against the wall. "Ace is a local, and you and him were friends as kids."

"Nice deductive reasoning."

"You're stalling." His words are terse, his frame is tight. I need to get on with my story.

I rub my sweaty palms together. When giving an opening or closing, the most persuasive part of your argument is the facts. Plainly stated, no frills. I go that route.

"My dad, Ron, works on the line at a tire manufacturing plant. When I go home, I go to my dad's house even though my mom lives only twenty minutes away. I talk to her once a year, at the most. Dad makes me go to her house on Christmas. Her parents died when I was a baby and her only relative, my uncle, lives in Washington State. So unless I visit, she's alone." I grab the water bottle that has a tag that says it costs $2. I rip off the cap anyway. It's worth it. I feel like I'm dying here under his impassive stare.

"It's always awkward as hell. We make small talk. She almost always has a new guy by her side. Most of the time I don't even bother learning their names because they're temporary. She told me once she sees herself as a butterfly. I'm sure she meant me to interpret that as her being beautiful, but I kept thinking about how she can't stick with one guy." I swallow. "It kind of ruined my dad for a while. She tends to ruin a lot of things—like Ace's family."

Something like comprehension starts flickering behind his eyes. "Do I need to sit down for the rest of this story?"

"I don't know. Watch a lot of soaps? You might be able to guess it." I try to smile, but talking about this is always so painful. Most of the time I try to forget it.

He pushes off from the wall and comes to sit down on the mattress closest to me. His long hands dangle between his thighs. I wish I could crawl into his lap, but I inject some steel into my spine and fast forward to the pertinent parts.

"After Ace and I met in the nurse's office, our families got to know each other. My mom and his dad, in particular. When Ace's mom confronted the two, his dad just kind of shrugged. Fidelity is for suckers, I think, are the exact words he told Ace. My parents didn't get a divorce, but they separated. Mom's lived in a different house than me since I was ten. Her home is a revolving door of unhappiness." I exhale deeply. "Screwed up by mommy is a tired excuse, but I guess it's why I was scared."

"Christ," he says after a long silence. "That's fucked up."

"Yeah, really, really fucked up." The distance is too much for me. I screw up my courage and walk to him. Once there, I drop to the floor between his knees, place a hand on either side of his thighs and look up with regret in my eyes and my heart in my throat. "I'm sorry I told you

I didn't care. I do care. So much, and it terrifies me, but if you give me another chance, I'll prove to you that *I'm* worth the risk."

His eyes flutter shut. A gasp escapes me as the pain of rejection starts spiraling out from my center. But before I can take another breath, he sweeps me into his arms.

"Oh Christ, Luce. I thought you'd never get here."

"You knew I was coming?" My voice is muffled by his chest, but he hears me.

"Hammer hinted. I tried not to get my hopes up."

"You jerk." I wrench back and slap at him, my fingers hurting when they land on rock hard pecs. "I can't believe you left me hanging there."

"I needed it," he admitted. "I'm not proud of that, but I needed to hear from you that you wanted me as much as I want you. But honestly, if you hadn't acted, I would have pursued you."

"Why the hardass act?"

"I was nervous. You really mad that I didn't chase after you?"

"No." I shake my head with relief. "I did the breaking up. I was the one who had to do the patching back together."

"To be fair, in my head, when you pop out and surprise me, you're wearing a lot less and there's a fake cake around you."

I crack a smile. "Really? A cake and a birthday suit?"

"I'm a simple man, Goldie." His smile fades a bit. "My turn."

My brow crinkles in confusion. "Your turn what?" If he's forgiven me, I'm ready for make-up sex.

"My turn to apologize. You were absolutely right that I shouldn't have gotten so shitfaced that I put myself in these situations. You're right that I would have been livid if I'd seen you drunk off your ass and some guy feeling up these curves." His hands run roughly up my sides, as if he's imagining the scene and not liking it very much. "I wish you hadn't broken up with me. The past few weeks have been zero fun."

"For me, too."

His hand comes up to cradle the back of my head. "But you weren't wrong to do it, so there's nothing for you to ask forgiveness for. Having said that, I'm willing to play the hurt party who needs all his wounds kissed and licked."

"Alright." I don't need to be asked twice.

He reaches down to grasp the hem of my shirt and tugs it up over my head. I lift my arms so he can remove it completely. He scoots back until he's leaning against the headboard. "Climb up here." He pats his lap.

I place a knee on the edge of the bed, but he holds out his hand. "Wait, take the pants off first."

As I ease down my jeans pulling my panties with them, his eyes grow slumberous. He reaches out until his hand curves around my butt. His warm fingertips dig slightly into the padding while his thumb runs down the hipbone to the crease where trunk and leg meet.

"You are a sight for sore eyes," he says huskily.

I let the jeans fall to the floor and kick them away. Then, with confidence born of his undisguised lust, I straddle him. I flip my hair off my shoulders with both hands and cup myself.

"Is this going to make up for the lack of a cake?"

His blue eyes gleam. "You bet your ass it will."

"What do you have in store for me?"

"How much time do we have?" His big, rough hands draw circles around my back, pulling me closer to him with every pass.

I struggle to remember the details. "The competition starts at one tomorrow. I should be out of here by nine."

He leans forward and bites the ball of my shoulder before saying, "You're going to need a little sleep. I want you to kick ass tomorrow, so I'll go easy on you. But the minute you step back onto campus, I want you in my bed for a solid twenty-four hours."

"No," I beg, "please be very hard."

We both laugh at my juvenile joke until I reach between us to cup his hard shaft. The sound of him sucking in his breath as I stroke him through his sweatpants puts an evil smile on my face.

His eyes are mere lust-filled slits. "You're going to need to do the hard work because my ribs are sore from practice."

"Too sore? I could just give you a hand job?"

He rolls his eyes. "That's about the most ridiculous thing that's ever come out of your mouth."

I know what the man wants, and I want to give it to him. I want to totally rock his world.

* * *

MATTY

She pushes out of my clasp, but before I can protest, she's on her knees, pulling my cock out of my pants. I tip my head back and close my eyes because the sight of her down there is making me want to come before her mouth is even on my shaft.

Then her mouth surrounds me, and with my eyes closed, the sensation of hot and wet is the only thing in my head. My balls tighten, and I pinch my nose in frustration. I do not want to come right now. I want to enjoy this for just a second longer. Please, for the love of God, where is my self-control?

Her warm, wet mouth pulls away.

"Is something wrong?" she asks. "Am I doing it wrong?"

"Oh, Goldie, no." I groan. "It's so fucking good, I'm scared I'm going to come in the next ten seconds and I want it to last. Not like hours, but even a couple minutes longer would be amazing."

My incoherent ramblings make her laugh. "Maybe you should lie back." She takes my cock in one hand and cups my balls with the other. "Because this is going to be the best blow job you've ever had.

"And miss the show?" I sweep her hair back. "No fucking way."

"You have a beautiful dick," she murmurs and rubs her face along the side of my shaft. I practice deep breathing exercises.

"You have a large frame of reference?" I choke out.

"Naah. I just like the look of it and generally I think penises are gross, but yours is…" She pauses to pet it, one hand on the bottom holding it while the other hand strokes lightly along the top. This is some new kind of torture, I think, but I love it. "It's strong and interesting. So hard and so soft at the same time." Her fingertip runs along the edge of the hood, and my eyes roll back into my head.

But that's nothing to the sensation that roils through my body when her mouth is back on me. She rubs my shaft along the roof of her mouth, cradling my cock with her tongue as it slides toward the back of her tight throat. Her soft hand cups my balls, rolling them gently, perfectly in her palm.

I grip the side of the chair, and my toes curl into the carpeted floor. Each pass of her mouth is more erotic than the last. She hums, and the vibrations make my entire body shiver. I'm harder than the concrete steps of the stadium. Between the suction of her mouth, her wicked, wicked tongue, and her deft fingers, I have no defense. A eunuch would have erupted in her mouth a minute ago.

Sweating and shaking, I push her away. She moans in protest but I shake my head. I tug awkwardly at her bra, while one-handing my aching erection. Her eyes widen, but she understands what I want and whips off her shirt. Her creamy breasts are bound together in a sweet-looking lace number.

I send her a silent word of apology, and with three swift jerks paint my come all over her chest. The milky white seed spurts onto her delicate collarbone and pools in the valley between her tits. The sight of it makes me hard again.

"I would have swallowed," she says in a slightly piqued tone.

"I know, Goldie." I sigh. I pull off my own T-shirt and regretfully wipe off the come. "But I don't know what the carb content of my stuff is, and I didn't want to fuck up your glucose measurements."

A sharp, surprised laugh sparks out of her. "Seriously? That's why you pulled out?"

I nod in confusion. "Why else?"

"I don't know." She giggles again. "I've never even thought about it."

I pull her off the ground and onto my lap. "Well, it was also hot as hell coming all over you, so there's that."

"I think your sperm would have been fine. It's full of protein, right?"

I shrug. I have no idea about the nutritional content of sperm. "Anyway, I think that might have been the sweetest thing anyone's ever done for me."

If I was a blushing man, I'd probably be red-faced at this but as it is, I'm too horny to concentrate on anything but getting Lucy out of her clothes and onto my bed.

"Speaking of good nutrition," I tell her, "I'm going to waste away if I don't get my mouth on you."

She blushes. "Is that right?"

"Never a truer word have I spoken," I declare.

I take her on the desk. I sit her pretty ass on the edge of the shitty hotel room structure, spread her legs and devour that delicious pussy until her nail marks score against my skull.

"You are way too good at this," she whimpers, and I suck on her clit like the sweet candy it is, enjoying the breathy moan that escapes her lips until her whimpers turn to pleas and then escalate into sharp, staccato cries as she creams all over my tongue.

I surge to my feet and then I'm inside her, sliding between her quivering thighs, into the hot clutch of her sex until I'm fully seated. I grab an ass cheek in each hand and hold her, suspended above the desk, while I hammer into her, steady, long, hard strokes.

She places a hand on the wall behind her and plants the other on the desk and meets every thrust with one of her own.

"I lov—"

"Don't say it," I order through gritted teeth. "You say it and I'm not going to last long enough for you to come, and you know I love it when you come. Do you know how good it feels when you come around my dick? I can feel every ripple, every flutter. It's the sexiest goddamn hug a man can get."

Her eyes glitter, and I see her mouth form those words again. The ones I didn't think I'd get to hear again. And because they're what I need and she's so beautiful and irresistible, I lean closer to hear them, even though I know they're going to set me off.

"I love you, Matthew Justin Iverson." Her smile is wide and joyous when she says it, as she pushes me over the cliff.

"Fuck me. I love you, too." Even as the orgasm shoots down my dick and fireworks detonate in my brain, I keep pumping and miraculously, she comes, too, gasping, clutching, and loving me all the way over the same, wonderful edge.

36

MATTY

"FINALLY." I RUB THE BACK of my neck as the last straggler out of the hotel throws his bag into the back of the car and climbs into the back seat.

It took Ace and me forty minutes to round everyone up. It was worse than herding cats. Twelve guys forgot something in their rooms. Thank God for Lucy, because she helped run around, count heads, and generally get everyone's ass in gear.

We couldn't find Getty, who had been sitting on the shitter in one of the bathrooms down by the conference rooms where our team meetings were held that I didn't even know existed. By the stench coming from the toilet, it was easy to figure out why it wasn't ever used by anyone but Getty.

Eight guys left their playbooks in their rooms and three had forgotten equipment on the field. Stoltzy had some chick in his room. He couldn't remember her name and she took about ten minutes to find her phone and dress.

She probably thought she was being cute as she crawled around with her thong and Stoltzy's T-shirt draped like a scarf around her neck, but Ace and I just wanted her ass gone. By the time we were done chewing out Stoltz for breaking yet another rule, he was tired of her act, too.

But here we are—all thirty of us shoved into eight cars, SUVs, and vans—and ready to go.

I slide into the driver's seat and put the Rover in gear. Is this what the captaincy is all about? Riding herd on a bunch of college football players who think they're above the rules? I sigh when I realize that I used to be one of those guys. Back when Masters was in charge, I screwed around as much as anyone.

I had chicks in my room when I wasn't supposed to just like Stoltzy. I was always forgetting something whether it was my jock, my shoes, or my phone. I thought by showing up to practice and then playing my heart out on Saturday, I had faithfully discharged all that was expected of me.

What an asshole I was to assume that I could lead on the field without worrying about stuff off the field. There's a hella big difference between being a teammate and being a leader.

"Uh, Matty, we've got a problem," Hammer says worriedly from the backseat.

"What's that?" I glance up in the rearview mirror.

He holds up a black case. "I think I took your Luce's insulin kit by mistake."

My head jerks back so fast I nearly break my neck.

"What? How did you get that?" Our eyes clash in shock and dismay.

"I don't know. This morning I came in to get my playbook and must've swept it into my backpack."

"Holy shit."

"Let me see." Ace reaches behind and rips the case from Hammer's hands. Ace opens it up and sure enough, her digital glucose monitor and several dosages of insulin lie nestled against the padding of her insulated case. He curses and slams his hand against the dash. "Goddammit, Hammer!"

"I know." He sounds miserable and in the rearview mirror I can see him cradling his head in his hands.

"Holy shit," I repeat. "What time is it?"

"Ten," Jack supplies. He's the only calm one in the entire vehicle. The two guys in the back—Darryl and Jesse—are wisely keeping quiet.

I do some quick calculations in my head. We left at eight. Chicago is three hours in the opposite direction and we have five hours left to get to Western. Curfew is at ten tonight. If I drive to Chicago from here, it's three hours there and then eleven hours back home. I'll never make it back in time for curfew, not even if I flew. I reach into the console and throw the phone at Hammer. "You search out the closest car rental place." I point to Ace. "You text Luce right now and find out if she has any extras."

"She doesn't," Ace says. "She has one kit. This is it."

"Text her anyway." Because we need to know.

Ace pulls out his phone and punches something in.

"Hammer, what's the word?" I call back. My foot eases off the gas and I switch to the right-hand lane so my sudden snail's pace doesn't piss anyone off.

"Man, the closest rental place is two hours away." We exchange sick looks in the mirror. Every mile I advance is a mile farther away from

Luce.

She drove out of her way to come to me when I needed her and because of it, she's going to suffer? No way. Not on my watch. "Call them. Book a car."

"Would it be faster to fly?" Jack questions.

"No, closest airport is four hours north. He'll be back at Western by the time he'd get on a plane." This comes from Darryl in the back. They must all have their phones out now.

"She says she feels fine. That she won't need an insulin shot until after the competition."

"How will she know? Can she buy another blood monitoring thingy? She has to do it every hour!" The miles pass and each one puts more distance between Luce and her wellbeing.

Ace and I exchange a grim look. We both know Luce does not have an excess amount of funds.

"Heather's got a call in to her dad to wire cash to them," Ace reads. So the monitoring kit must be too expensive. I bet Luce is writhing with embarrassment.

"Thought that girl was made of money," Jack asks.

"Her dad cut off her credit cards a few weeks ago," I tell him. "She got a B on her midterm in Calculus."

"She got cut off because of a B?" Jack's mouth falls open. "What kind of shit is that?"

"The kind that turns you into a girl like Heather," Ace replies. He holds up his phone. "Luce is going to drink some OJ and lie down."

"That team has less money than my change cup," I growl. There's only one way to solve this for Luce and that is to get the kit to her. I can be there in three hours. "Hammer, how are you doing on getting me that rental?"

"You'll never make it. Luce's first match is at one. It's already fifteen minutes past the hour. By the time you get the car rented and on the road, it'll be like two or three. You won't have the time."

"I will if I speed."

"You got to be back by curfew tonight." We have a 10 p.m. curfew because of the spring ball game tomorrow. It's a televised event. A shit ton of boosters will be there, and it could make a difference in what our pregame ranking will be in the fall.

"And I'll make it. I'll go and drop off the kit and turn around and come back."

"That'll give you zero hours of sleep and you'll play like shit," Ace notes.

"So I play like shit. Do you have a better solution?"

Hammer pauses and I look up in the mirror. All of the guys look back at me. "If you turn around right now, you'll get to Luce before her match."

"And what? You guys will hitchhike back to Western?" I scoff.

"No. We all go with you." Hammer stretches his long arm past my seat and out the windshield. Ahead of me, the caravan of vehicles carrying all the starters and number two players on the depth chart are signaling left to take the off ramp.

"What the hell, Hammer?" I flick my eyes up to the rear view mirror again.

He holds up his phone to indicate he texted the other cars. "You need to get to Luce. She ran around this morning, knocking on doors, getting everyone up. When Stoltzy forgot his playbook, she went back and retrieved it from the hotel. Plus, you're our captain. Our ship floats or sinks with you."

I look at Ace, who's staring out the window. We don't move without him. He's still pissed at Luce. He hasn't gotten over the fact that Luce chose me. That it wasn't that athletes weren't her type, but that Ace wasn't. He might have been able to have her if he hadn't treated all the women in his life like dirt.

But he had. She saw it. While she loved him like a friend, she couldn't ever love him like he wanted, like she loves me.

Part of him wants her to twist in the wind. I can see it his face.

"Do I drive on or get off at this exit?" I ask grimly.

Hammer doesn't give him a chance to answer. "Turn at the exit. Ace and Jack can go back to Western," he says with utter disgust.

"No way. I'm coming with the team," Jack protests.

"And you, Ace? You with the team?" I ask softly.

He waits a heartbeat longer and then sighs. "Yeah, I'm with the team."

* * *

LUCY

"Fuck, my throat is raw." Heather flexes her jaw. The hoarseness in her voice makes me wince.

"We shouldn't have gone last night." Now that the drug that is Matty Iverson has worn off, I see the foolishness of my decision.

"Stop stressing out about it," Heather scolds me. "The drive didn't make me sick. It's been coming on all week."

"You should've rested up."

She rolls her eyes. "I did rest up. I was sleeping while you were screwing Matty. If we hadn't gone, you'd have been worthless. At least now you can concentrate on the case."

"Right." I pace nervously. Despite my morning insulin, I'm sluggish and weak. I pull out the orange juice I bought from the vending machine and take a small sip. I have no idea about my sugar levels because I haven't taken a measurement in nearly three hours.

My sweaty palms, racing heart, and lightheadedness could be because I'm nervous. It could be because my BG levels are wildly unstable at this point. Dry-mouthed, I take another sip of the juice.

"I have to use the bathroom."

"Jesus, it's like the third time this hour," Heather complains. Even though she's lost her voice, she still manages to eke out a bitchy comment. Classic Heather. I flip her off and walk slowly toward the girl's room.

Nothing comes out of me when I sit down. I flush, stand up and nearly fall backward into the bowl. I'm going to have to tell Randall and Heather and the rest of the team.

Would Randall be able to carry on? Would we have to forfeit? God, that alone makes me want to puke and cry. We're so close.

But there's no time to drive to the drugstore to pick up insulin. I Googled it and the closest one is twenty-five minutes away. The clerk at the gas station I spoke to across the street didn't even know you could buy insulin over the counter. He insisted I would need to go to a pharmacy. Even if we could make it, I didn't have the money. I had to go to Heather and ask for help. She called her dad immediately but neither believed the wire would get here in time.

I push my way out of the stall, ignoring the shakiness of my hand. I wash, dry, take another sip of my juice and go find Randall and Heather.

"I don't know if I'm going make it," I admit when I find them.

"You took one this morning, though, right?" Randall asks. His normally dark skin is looking alarmingly pale.

"Before breakfast," as is my custom, although I've slipped now and again. Like the time I stayed over with Matty.

"Then you're probably feeling like a piece of shit because of your nerves."

Heather agrees with Randall. "You need to do this."

"I can't."

"You have to." She grabs my clammy hand. "You know this case better than anyone. You wrote all our examinations. No one is better suited to this than you. Just stand up there and own the courtroom. Believe you're better and what happened to you freshman year won't happen again."

"Is this some Tinker Bell shit? Believe?" I scoff.

"Hey, that bitch is earning billions in royalties what, a hundred years after her creation? You should dial back on your critiques of her. She might be basic, but she knows what's what."

Randall and I stare at each for a moment and then burst into laughter. Only Heather would call a fairy who can make people *fly* basic. We laugh until we can't stand, leaning against each other until we end up on the floor on our asses.

And that's where Matty and what looks like the entire football team finds us—on the dusty floor of the high school that is hosting the competition—laughing like a couple of loons while Heather stands over us, tapping her expensively shod toe near our heads.

"Matty, what are you doing here?" Wordlessly, he hands me my insulin case. "Did you drive out of your way to bring me this?"

"Of course he did," Heather interjects with exasperation. "How else would he get here?"

"That basic bitch Tinker Bell?" Randall suggests and I start cracking up again because this situation seems utterly absurd.

Matty reaches down and hauls me to my feet. Over his shoulder, he says, "I think she's loopy."

Hammer nods. "Better test her."

Matty takes the case out of my lax hands and efficiently runs the test before I can issue a protest. The monitor beeps and the read out says I'm perfectly normal.

"What's the verdict," Randall asks slowly, as if dreading the response but I'm the one who's filled with dread.

"It's normal."

Heather smirks. "The show must go on."

"Good thing you're sick or I might have to punch you in the face."

Heather flaps her wings and Matty drags me away as if he thinks I'm serious.

"I think I need to retake the test," I whine when he sets me down a short distance from the crowd.

"Sure," he says far too agreeably. We both know the second test will show the same results.

I'm feeling awful because my nerves are about to overtake me, the same ones I suggested that Heather suffered from yesterday. Oh, the hubris.

"You're going to do fine," he says, rubbing my arms.

"Do not give me a half-time inspirational speech," I order. The last thing I need is some rah-rah-rah about being my best.

"Sure. We can go to the bathroom and fuck away your nervousness."

I mock punch him, but I can't say the idea doesn't have appeal. Maybe we'd spend too much time in there and then Heather will be forced to go on with Randall. The judges will feel sorry for us because Heather's so obviously impaired and—

"I was actually just kidding." Matty brings my runaway-train thought process to a halt.

"What if I open my mouth and I can't remember anything? Again."

He shrugs. "So what? You already went through that. You survived. If it happens again, then you know you're not cut out for this sort of thing. But if you don't try, then you'll always wonder. That sort of wistful regret isn't something you want hanging around."

The matter-of-fact delivery of his risk assessment helps calm my nerves. And frankly, it's not like I have a choice because Randall can't do this on his own, and Heather's clearly too ill to go forward. I can either try or sit out here in the hall and hate myself forever for being a coward.

Yesterday, when I was hiding in the closet, there were a dozen different outcomes that kept cycling through my head, from Matty literally tossing me out into the hall to him joining me in that small space.

The last one is ridiculous because not only is he too big to fit in that closet, but because why would we have sex in a closet when the bed was five feet away? But being stuck in a closed space for a half hour gives one plenty of time to come up with silly scenarios.

Despite the harrowing moment in the beginning when he wouldn't smile at me, the rest of the night was one blissful reward. I grab onto that for courage.

Matty bends his knees until he's eye-to-eye with me. "What are you thinking?"

"That last night's risk was worth the reward."

"That's my girl." He dips toward me and gives me another reward—a long, hot wet one.

* * *

MATTY

"How's this work?" Hammer whispers in my ear.

"I don't really know." I've only picked up bits and pieces from watching Luce. "There's lawyers and there's witnesses and something called oral arguments."

"Oral." Hammer snickers into his hand. Darryl nudges him and wants to know what's so danged funny. Hammer whispers something behind his hand and pretty soon the entire side is sniggering.

Luce turns around from the table and glares at me. I hold up my hands to show her I'm innocent but Christ, we're a bunch of guys. The word *oral* kind of sets us off. I slice my hand in front of my throat, and the guys try to compose themselves.

"All rise, the honorable Cristal Cain is presiding."

Three people stream in from a side door and take a seat at the front of the room behind a barricade. Like the mock trial team is going to rush them or something? I guess it looks official. Like a smaller, lower rent version of Judge Judy's courtroom.

Fortunately for all of us, we're told we can be seated. I take a moment to ogle Luce's ass as she brushes her hands down the back of her skirt when she takes a seat.

Then I notice Hammer staring at it, too. I give him a hard elbow to his side.

He returns a helpless look that says *she's hot and it's there.*

My return look says *keep eyeing her ass and my fist will be the next thing you see.*

He merely shrugs.

"Quite the audience we have today," Judge Cain mentions.

"You think she's a real judge?"

"Nah," I whisper back. "She's not wearing the black robes."

"But would they for a competition?"

Good question. "No idea."

A paper drops at my feet. I lean down to pick it up. I unfold it. *SHUT UP!*

I show it to Hammer. He hands it to Darryl and the note makes a trip around the back of the room.

Judge Cain runs down how the competition plays out. The plaintiff, that's Luce's side, goes first with their three witnesses. There'll be a short break and then the defendants, archrivals from Central, a college with a shit football team, goes next. The two parties will then have closing arguments.

"I thought you said it was oral argument," Hammer whispers.

"I guess I mixed it up," I whisper out of the side of my mouth. I swear she used that word once or twice.

"Will the team from Western introduce yourselves?"

Randall, the dark-haired dude, rises and says, "Yes, your Honor. I'm Randall James." He holds his hand toward Luce, who's sitting in the middle between him and the girl Luce can't stand—Heather. Even though she can't speak, she's going to sit at the table and take notes and some shit like that. "And I along with my co-counsel Lucy Washington and Heather—"

We all start cheering and whistling. In the back of the room, someone starts chanting. Lucy. Lucy. Lucy. Must be Ahmed? Jack, maybe?

Judge Cain bangs her gavel on the desk. "Order! Order!"

"Order!" Hammer crows. "Shit, this is just like television." He shifts in his chair to get more comfortable. And like on television, it looks like we're getting a talking to.

The judge leans forward, and not entirely unkindly, but definitely with a certain amount of sternness, says, "This is not a sporting event and we don't allow cheering. At least not until the event is over. If anyone believes they will have difficulty abiding by that, please feel free to use the exit doors at the back."

There's a few random coughs along with some murmurs. I stand up and find myself staring at Ace, who is on his feet, too. He looks at the offense and I stare down the defense until there's utter silence.

Then we both sit down.

"All right. Thank you, gentlemen. You may proceed."

Randall introduces Heather again and then his client and sits down. The other team does the same.

Afterwards, Randall is instructed to come forward and give opening argument. Hammer opens his mouth again, but I shake my head real slow until he shuts it.

The case Randy presents is fairly simple. Their client, Emily, manages a local ice rink. They have an ice resurfacer or Zamboni, although theirs was manufactured by ICE and not the Zamboni company. Who knew Zamboni was a brand name? I learned something and I'm not even in class.

Emily was working, and one of her underlings—Randy calls him an employee—was driving the resurfacer when it stalled. Emily came over to check things out and the resurfacer took off on her. She tried to stop it by hanging on to the machine. She was able to steer it into a barricade but ended up breaking her leg. ICE had documents that showed the machine's clutch had a tendency to slip from neutral into drive and the machine would move even when the brake was on.

An "ooooh" rose up from the football team at the mention of these documents. A wave of the gavel had us all zipping our mouths closed.

Randall tells the room how Emily's life went to shit and she wants some money so she can replace all that she lost.

Which sucks. Hard. What if she'd been an athlete working a part-time job? I want ICE to write out a check by the time Randall sits down.

The other side gets up and explains that the broken leg was sad and unfortunate but that jurors are supposed to decide things on facts and not emotion. Good luck on that. People are driven by emotion. It's why we have locker room quotes up on the wall. To motivate us into crushing weak opponents.

The attorneys for ICE tell us that Emily caused her own accident by using the machine that she knew was faulty. Plus, she was irresponsible with her money, buying a house, a new car, and not saving anything. That's a good point.

By the time ICE's attorney is done speaking, I'm not sure how I feel. And by the way Hammer and the rest of the guys are leaning forward, they're just as conflicted.

Both sides put on evidence. Both sides are pretty damned good. As we near the end, I can see Luce letting the tension get to her. She's gripping her pen so tightly her knuckles are turning white and I'm starting to worry she's actually going to snap her spine if she stiffens any more.

The last piece of evidence gets offered and the defense "rests," which I guess means they're done because the judge starts telling everyone there will be a five-minute recess before closing arguments start.

Many of the guys take this opportunity to piss. I sit behind Luce as she remains at her table, head bent, absorbing the words she's going to get up and say.

I wish I could help her. She reminds me of a kicker lining up to make a last second field goal kick from the fifty-yard-line to win the game. No one talks to the kickers before these stress-filled moments, and I won't bug her now.

I do the same thing, though, as I do with those kickers. I send her all the waves of positivity I can. Hammer nudges me and makes a tiny kicking motion with his finger. Yeah, we're all on the same page here.

"You may proceed, counsel," Judge Cain orders when we're all situated in our places.

Luce takes a deep breath and then rises. She walks calmly to the middle of the room, thanks everyone and then turns to the jury. There's a long moment of silence. A long one. An uncomfortable one. One that makes me wonder if I should jump the railing, pick her up, and carry her away from here.

You can do it, Goldie. I know you can.

She takes a deep breath. And then another. And then, "There's an old Jewish tradition…"

A collective whoosh fills the room as all of us in the back and maybe some at the counsel table release their breaths. Luce's voice, quiet at first, grows in volume with each word. We're all spellbound and after she's done, I can't help but release a whistle.

Which was stupid because everyone starts cheering then. Luce ducks her head into her chin and scurries to her chair. Judge Cain bangs her gavel several times until we stop rioting in the back.

"Your honor, we need a sidebar," says one of the guys clad in blue suits on the other team.

A sidebar is apparently when the lawyers gather by the judge and whisper things. The acoustics in the room are such that we can hear them pretty well.

"That display is completely inappropriate, Judge Cain," hisses the suit. "Western should be penalized."

Luce objects immediately. "I have no control over that. It would be completely unfair to penalize us for something the audience did."

I share a shamefaced look with Hammer. Shit, it never occurred to me that *cheering* would result in Luce losing this match. I feel kinda sick.

"I'm not penalizing Western for the crowd's antics because the jury doesn't decide who wins this case, we do." Judge Cain points to the two people sitting beside her. "And I'm sure you don't believe we'll be influenced by any clapping, do you?" Disdain drips from her voice. She's unimpressed by the dude's complaining.

"No, ma'am." Blue Suit looks at his shoes.

"Then let's finish closing arguments, shall we?"

I hold out my hand and Hammer slaps it as we celebrate our girl not getting penalized. Our happiness is short-lived when Judge Cain addresses the room. "As I stated before, there is no clapping or cheering that is permitted during the match. Another outburst will result in a two-minute penalty to Western."

Luce walks back to the counsel table, glaring at us.

I don't even dare make the zipped-lip gesture. Pissy Blue Suit stands up and makes a very passionate argument about personal responsibility that seems to have the judges' attention. They're nodding. Hell, even the jury is nodding. I think he sounds like a cat in heat, with his high-pitched demands for the jury to make Luce's client accept responsibility for her own poor decisions. At the end, he pounds on the railing separating the jury and him, telling them he knows they'll make the right decision.

One of the jurors makes a few clapping noises until she catches wind of Judge Cain's frown. Heather and Randall exchange a worried glance while Luce is scribbling something furiously on her notepad.

"Do you have rebuttal, counsel," Judge Cain intones.

This time there's no hesitation. Luce jumps up. "Yes, your honor."

She strides confidently up to the middle of the room, turns to face the jury and says in a chilly tone, "When you have the facts on your side, you pound on the facts. When you have the law on your side, you pound on the law. When you have neither…." She pauses dramatically. Everyone looks at the opposing side, who's glaring so hard at Luce right now it makes me want to laugh. Everyone but Luce looks at him, that is. She's still staring at the jury. Softly, because she doesn't need volume when every person in the room is hanging on her words, she repeats, "And when you have neither, you pound on the bench."

Luce dips her head, turns around, then walks right back to the table and sits down.

It kills not being able to clap at that. Fucking kills.

* * *

Judge Cain let us clap after they announced Luce's team the winner.

"You were amazing," I crow when she finally breaks free from everyone who wants to hug and congratulate her. Even Ace came forward. They gave each other an awkward hug, and I didn't even feel like bashing Ace's teeth in for touching her. I feel so evolved.

"Thank you!" She hugs me tight, her face pressed into the side of my chest. "I was pretty good, wasn't I?"

Her uncharacteristic boasting pulls a startled laugh out of me. That's my girl. "Best ever," I agree.

"Come on." She lets go of my waist but grabs my hand.

I follow willingly. While we both know I'd follow her anywhere, I ask, "Where we going?"

"I need a victory kiss."

My steps quicken. So do hers. "Oh, yeah? Any particular place you want that kiss?"

"We have to be quick, so on the lips, but I expect my other parts to get action from your other parts."

Now I'm pretty much running. There was a bathroom down here that I spotted when I arrived. From the direction of Luce's feet, we're headed to the same place.

I slam the door open with the flat of my hand and spin her around so her back is against the door. It's the best way to keep anyone from barging in on us.

I'm on her before she can take another breath. I don't know how long we have, but as I hold her jaw in place with my hand, I fuck her mouth as savagely as she'll allow. She greets me with a furious, wild kiss in return. Sucking and tonguing me like the champion she is.

Soon, it's not enough to kiss her. My entire body is shaking with the need to be in her, part of her. I wrench up her skinny business-like skirt and jam a big thigh between her legs.

"Tell me that we're doing more than kissing," I whisper hoarsely as I scatter kisses along her delicate cheek, her strong jaw, and the tender skin of her neck.

"We're doing more than kissing," she confirms. Her busy hands unfasten my jeans. Another second later, my pants are down around my thighs and my heavy, aching dick is in her hands.

"Fuck, yeah." I push her skirt farther up and pull her panties down, shoving them to the floor with the toe of my boot. Neither of us pause, even as we hear those panties rip or the shuffling of feet outside the door.

We're too eager for each other, too hungry to care about torn panties, undressing, or outsiders.

I hitch her legs up so she can straddle my waist and take my dick in hand. Her eyes flutter shut as I slide the broad head between the wet folds from her pussy to her clit but we can't spend too much time playing, and from the way her nails are digging into my shoulders, I don't think she wants to wait.

"Now," she orders. Yup. No waiting for her.

I guide the blunt tip to her opening and slide in, slow and gentle so I don't hurt her. Her bare walls grip me tight, eroding my control. The impulse to jackhammer inside her until the back of my head explodes takes over. My hips start thrusting as I work my way into her hot passage.

"Sorry. Fuck." I mutter incomplete phrases, hoping she understands that she's just so fucking hot, I can't stop myself.

She laughs, a breathy sort of chuckle, and grips my face in both hands. Her brown eyes are full of happiness and love. She bares her teeth and squeezes her cunt so hard I nearly pass out. "I want you. I want you to fuck me as hard and fast as you can, Matty. "

Oh, God. Her permission makes me wild. I palm an ass cheek in either hand and do exactly what she told me to because, as she is my girl, I am totally, completely, irrevocably *hers*.

* * *

Our victory fucking doesn't last near long enough. As soon as we exit the bathroom—disheveled but blissed out—Hammer jumps me.

"We got to jet, brother."

Reluctantly, I nod. We were hours past curfew and all of us were going to be toast for tomorrow's spring game.

"I'll see you back at Western, Goldie. Love you."

"Love you, too." She rises on her tiptoes to give me another kiss but Hammer drags me away before it lands.

"You kiss her again and you'll be back in that bathroom stall for another fifteen minutes," he grouses with his big hand on my shoulder, pointing me in the opposite direction of Luce.

He's not wrong.

As it turns out, we don't even play because when we pull into the Playground, the entire staff of coaches is lined up on the sidewalk waiting for us.

Coach Lowe wastes no time delivering his pronouncement.

"You're all seven hours late for curfew. None of you will play in the game tomorrow. You are all benched. You and you," he points to Ace and I, "are suspended for the first game of the season. This is my team." He paces in front of us. "Not yours. Mine." He stops in front of Ace. "Have you made a decision yet?"

The implication is that Ace better have made a decision and it better be the right one.

Ace has no sense of self-preservation. "I'll know at the start of summer camp."

Coach swings narrowed eyes in my direction. "And you—where do you stand on this?"

I step up next to Ace and put my hand on his shoulder. "With my QB. We play, sir, for each other. You call the plays. You help us train. You keep us in top athletic form. Our minds sharp. But we do all this because of our brothers. When we're on the field, the only people next to us are those wearing helmets and pads. Ace is our teammate. Barr, he has yet to earn the gold and blue. Maybe he will. We'll definitely give him a chance, but for now, Ace is our QB."

It's dead silent as Coach Lowe absorbs the loss of his team. We may have been his team at the end of the season, but he lost us in his pursuit of revenge or job security. I don't know what's going to happen this fall, but when we hit the field, it won't be with Lowe on our minds. We'll be doing it for each other.

That feels right, no matter how many games he decides to suspend me for.

37

JUNE

MATTY

"COMING, MATTY?"

"Nah, I think I'll hang here."

"Fuck that. She has your balls in your purse now?" Sophomore linebacker Hank Coleman mocks.

I cup myself. "Nope. Still here. You can get on your knees and check it out for yourself if you're unsure."

Hammer smacks Coleman on the back of the head. "Go get the cab for us, rook."

"I'm not a rookie," Coleman protests.

"First year starter? Sounds like a rookie to me." He shoves Coleman toward the door. Bishop comes up behind me.

"We'll watch out for you," Bish says in low tones. "No pictures. No random jockeys."

It wasn't pictures that got me into trouble before, but it's hard to explain to Bish or even Hammer because they're still in nail-anything-that-moves mode, which is fine. I totally respect that. I enjoyed that time in my life, but I don't miss it. Not one bit.

"Nah, I'm good." Tonight is the first night of summer camp. We're holed up in some monastery five hours north of the Western campus. The town is small, but there are a few bars. I have zero interest in going out.

Bish tilts his head. "Between you and Masters, I'm wondering if I'm missing something."

"What can I say?" I spread my hands. "It's good."

It's been better than good. Classes finished up and Luce and I spent a month just hanging around before I had to come back for summer school. She worked, and I met her dad. He likes to play golf in his downtime, which is cool. I'm not much of a golfer, but he was a patient tutor and didn't give me a hard time for being Luce's boyfriend.

I even met her mom, who came off as sad more than anything. She asked about Ace's dad, and Luce and I left shortly after. I took her home to Colorado Springs to meet my parents. We hiked on Pike's Peak where I gave Luce my second present.

It wasn't a piece of jewelry this time. It was a twenty-four-hour glucose monitor. The thing was more expensive than a diamond, but the features are amazing. Through a little needle pack stuck to her stomach or arm, it constantly monitors her blood sugar level and feeds the information to an app on her phone. If the numbers are off, she'll get an alert.

Okay, so maybe the gift was just as much for me as it was for her, but her eyes glowed so bright, I thought she might explode. Safe to say she loved it. Better than a piece of jewelry, in my opinion, although I like seeing my necklace around her collar. Every time I look at it, I think *I bought that. She's mine.*

The guys go off in search of town strange, and I wander back into the hotel.

"Come on." Ahmed pulls me toward a conference room.

"What the fuck is this?" Inside the double doors are a few couches arranged around eight televisions and several game consoles. I see a number of guys there…Jesse shoves me onto one of the cushions and hands me a controller.

"Who do you want to be?"

I check out my options. "Princess Daisy."

"Alright." He picks Bowser.

"What is this?" I ask him.

"*Mario Kart.*" He gives me a *you're an idiot* look.

"I know what the game is, but what is this?" I wave the controller around the room. "And how did I not know about it before?"

"You didn't want to know about it before."

And it occurs to me that this is why the guys who have serious partners are not out getting photographed with a bunch of girls hanging off of them. I shrug and settle in for a hardcore game of *Mario Kart*, and I have as much fun at summer camp as I can remember.

* * *

LUCY

"Hey, Ace." I only open the door a crack when I see him standing on the front porch. Matt's out back grilling, and I don't really want my

Fourth of July to be ruined by a fight between them. Dad's working today to get the double-time pay but will be home tonight for fireworks.

"Can we talk?" He reminds me so much of that sad little boy I found on my steps crying because his dad left. All I knew at the time was that my mom made him sad, and I wasn't going to hurt him like my mom had.

But so much time and so many things have gone on since then, I'm not sure what kind of friendship I can have with him anymore. Still, I can't close the door in his face.

"Sure." I step out onto the porch.

"I…I want to apologize for what happened between us."

A little tension seeps away. "Thank you."

"I'm not going to be seeing you much."

"Oh?"

"You heard of Southern U?"

I shake my head. "No, can't say that I have."

"It's a football school in Kentucky. Knox Masters's brother goes there. Plays Defensive End." There goes Ace again, getting into the weeds of football talk. I try not to let my eyes glaze over. "Anyway, their quarterback got hurt last season. Tore his ACL and he announced he wasn't coming back. Guess he's a med student and decided that he'd had enough. They've contacted me and offered me the scholarship. No guarantee at starting, but I can compete for the job."

"Oh, Ace. I'm happy for you." I reach out and grab his hand.

"I know it might be a stupid decision. That I might be throwing away a chance at the pros by not going to safety, but I'd always regret not trying to follow my dream, particularly when one of them closed here."

I don't know if he's talking about me or the team, but I don't ask. It's a question that doesn't need to be asked. But after this past semester, I fully believe in the *try it, what's the worst thing that can happen* philosophy because oh, Lord, the rewards are so good.

"I'm going to miss you, but if this is your dream, I fully support it."

"Thanks."

"Hug?"

"Yeah."

I wrap my arms around his solid waist and squeeze him tight. He holds me in return. I love this boy as the brother I never had and I try to convey that in my embrace. He gives me a kiss on my forehead and then releases me to walk down my sidewalk and out of my life.

A few tears fall as I re-enter my house. Matt's just inside the door.

"He tell you?"

"Yeah." I give him a watery smile.

"You doing okay?" He draws me into his arms and places his lips on the same spot Ace kissed.

"I am. I'm going to miss him. He's been a big part of my life."

"Yeah?"

There's a little defensiveness in that word. I lean back and stroke Matt's cheek, which is tenser than usual. "Yeah, but my heart's not going with him. It's here with you."

He loosens up. "I knew that."

"'Course you did."

Matty wraps his arm around my shoulder. "He'll come back to you in a better place."

"I hope so."

"What's this?" Matty leans over the table and fingers the LSAT application.

"I'm applying for law school."

"You can still do that?" he asks excitedly.

My eyes shine with glee. "I can."

"That's fucking awesome, Lucy."

"I know."

He wraps both arms around me. "Where are you going to go?"

"I dunno. Part of it depends on where my boyfriend gets drafted. I'd like to attend near him."

If it's possible, Matty's smile grows even bigger. "You have the best plans for the future, Goldie."

"I have a good one for the present, too."

"Please tell me it involves nudity and possibly a bit of whipped cream."

"I was thinking more chocolate sauce and rope, but I can add in the whipped cream. The nudity's a given."

Matty's already peeling off his T-shirt by the time I get my last words out. He looks over his bare shoulder, the action making his muscles bunch in the back. Had I at one time really said I wasn't into muscles? I must have been doped up on some too-serious-sauce. "You coming?"

"I hope so. I really, really hope so."

Then I race forward and jump on his back, and we tumble into my room, ripping off each other's clothes and kissing each other like we haven't touched each other in weeks.

Matty might have been my biggest risk, but he is sure as hell the best reward a girl could ever have.

CPSIA information can be obtained
at www.ICGtesting.com
Printed in the USA
LVHW092039161218
600691LV00001B/192/P